BITTER BITE

"Estep's street-smart characters, lively narrative, and ever-evolving stories keep this series alive and kicking."

—*Library Journal*

"The fourteenth title in the Elemental Assassin series is a fast, furious, and entertaining romp."

—*Kirkus Reviews*

SPIDER'S TRAP

"The continued evolution of not only Gin but all the rest of the core characters as well is what keeps this series fresh and immensely entertaining. These relationships give such rich depth and emotional heft to the otherwise nonstop action."

—*RT Book Reviews* (Top Pick!)

"Nonstop action, great characters, humor, and even some moments where your heart is in your throat."

—*Dark Faerie Tales*

BLACK WIDOW

"Everything that I adore about this series is right here and more so in *Black Widow*. There's expertly crafted fights, banter, and suspense that continued to keep me on the edge of my seat. I can't recommend this book enough and love being on the rollercoaster ride that is Gin Blanco's life."

—*All Things Urban Fantasy*

"*Black Widow* is crazy good and Gin Blanco is still one of the best-written heroines in urban fantasy. I was riveted from beginning to end."

—*Fiction Vixen*

POISON PROMISE

"A knockout. . . . Lots of vividly depicted battles, a high body-count, and high-octane escapes worthy of a James Bond movie keep the pages turning."

—*Booklist*

"A quick-moving plot and characters that jump off the page. . . . Estep finely balances a confident, tough-edged personality with an inner life filled with doubts and emotions, making Gin a surprisingly down-to-earth heroine whom readers will root for."

—*Publishers Weekly*

THE SPIDER

"By virtue of her enormous skill, Estep keeps this amazing series fresh and unputdownable!"

—*RT Book Reviews* (Top Pick!)

"Made me fall in love with Gin all over again."

—*All Things Urban Fantasy*

HEART OF VENOM

"Amazing . . . Estep is one of those rare authors who excels at both action set pieces and layered character development."

—*RT Book Reviews* (Top Pick!)

"Action-packed with tons of character growth. . . . One of the best books in the series, which says a lot because Estep's writing rarely, if ever, disappoints."

—*Fall Into Books*

DEADLY STING

"Classic Estep with breathtaking thrills, coolly executed fights, and a punch of humor, which all add up to unbeatable entertainment!"

—*RT Book Reviews* (Top Pick!)

"I've been hooked on this series from the first word of the first book. I can't get enough."

—*Fiction Vixen*

WIDOW'S WEB

"Estep has found the perfect recipe for combining kick-butt action and high-stakes danger with emotional resonance."

—*RT Book Reviews* (Top Pick!)

"Filled with such emotional and physical intensity that it leaves you happily exhausted by the end."

—*All Things Urban Fantasy*

SPIDER'S REVENGE

"Explosive. . . . Hang on, this is one smackdown you won't want to miss!"

—*RT Book Reviews* (Top Pick!)

"A whirlwind of tension, intrigue, and mind-blowing action that leaves your heart pounding."

—*Smexy Books*

VENOM

"Estep has really hit her stride with this gritty and compelling series. . . . Brisk pacing and knife-edged danger make this an exciting page-turner."

—*RT Book Reviews* (Top Pick!)

"Gin is a compelling and complicated character whose story is only made better by the lovable band of merry misfits she calls her family."

—*Fresh Fiction*

SPIDER'S BITE

"The series [has] plenty of bite. . . . Kudos to Estep for the knife-edged suspense!"

—*RT Book Reviews*

"Fast pace, clever dialogue, and an intriguing heroine."

—*Library Journal*

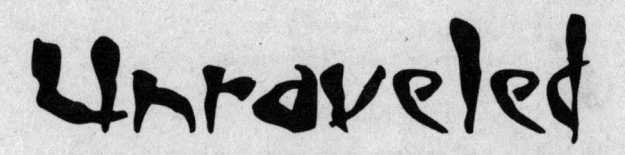

Unraveled

AN ELEMENTAL ASSASSIN BOOK

JENNIFER ESTEP

POCKET BOOKS

New York   London   Toronto   Sydney   New Delhi

Pocket Books
An Imprint of Simon & Schuster, Inc.
1230 Avenue of the Americas
New York, NY 10020

This book is a work of fiction. Any references to historical events, real people, or real places are used fictitiously. Other names, characters, places, and events are products of the author's imagination, and any resemblance to actual events or places or persons, living or dead, is entirely coincidental.

First Pocket Books paperback edition September 2016

POCKET and colophon are registered trademarks of Simon & Schuster, Inc.

For information about special discounts for bulk purchases, please contact Simon & Schuster Special Sales at 1-866-506-1949 or business@simonandschuster.com.

The Simon & Schuster Speakers Bureau can bring authors to your live event. For more information or to book an event, contact the Simon & Schuster Speakers Bureau at 1-866-248-3049 or visit our website at www.simonspeakers.com.

Manufactured in the United States of America

10 9 8 7 6 5 4 3 2 1

ISBN 978-1-5011-4221-5
ISBN 978-1-5011-4226-0 (ebook)

To my mom, my grandma, and Andre—
for your love, patience, and everything else
that you've given me over the years

Acknowledgments

Once again, my heartfelt thanks go out to all the folks who help turn my words into a book.

Thanks go to my agent, Annelise Robey, and my editor, Adam Wilson, for all their helpful advice, support, and encouragement. Thanks also to Melissa Bendixen.

Thanks to Tony Mauro for designing another terrific cover, and thanks to Louise Burke, Lisa Litwack, and everyone else at Pocket and Simon & Schuster for their work on the cover, the book, and the series.

And finally, a big thanks to all the readers. Knowing that folks read and enjoy my books is truly humbling, and I'm glad that you are all enjoying Gin and her adventures.

I appreciate you all more than you will ever know.

Happy reading!

❄ 1 ❄

It was the perfect night to kill someone.

Thick, heavy clouds obscured the moon and stars, deepening the shadows of the cold December evening, and an icy drizzle spattered down from the sky, slowly covering everything in a slick, glossy, treacherous sheen. Icicles had already formed on many of the trees that lined the street, looking like gnarled, glittering fingers that were crawling all over the bare, skeletal branches. No animals moved or stirred, not so much as an owl sailing into one of the treetops searching for shelter.

Down the block, red, green, and white holiday lights flashed on the doors and windows of one of the sprawling mansions set back from the street, and the faint trill of Christmas carols filled the air. A steady stream of people hurried from the mistletoe-festooned front door, down the snowmen-lined driveway, and out to their cars, scrambling into the vehicles and cranking the engines. Someone's dinner party was rapidly winding down, although it was only nine o'clock. Everyone wanted to get home and be all safe, warm, and snug in their own beds, dreaming of sugarplums, before the weather got any worse. In ten minutes, they'd all be gone, and the street would be quiet and deserted again.

Yes, it was the perfect night to kill someone.

Too bad my mission was recon only.

I slouched down in my seat, staying as much out of view of the passing headlights as possible. But none of the drivers gave my battered old white van a second look, and I doubted that any of them even bothered to glance at the blue lettering on the side that read *Cloudburst Falls Catering*. Caterers, florists, musicians. Such service vehicles were all too common in Northtown, the part of Ashland where the rich, social, and magical elite lived. If not for the lousy weather, this entire street probably would have been lit up with holiday cheer as people hosted various parties, each one trying to outdo their neighbors with garish light displays.

Once the last of the cars cruised by and the final pair of headlights faded away, I straightened up in my seat, picked up my binoculars from my lap, and peered through them at another nearby mansion.

A stone wall cordoned this mansion off from the street, featuring a wide iron gate that was closed and locked. Unlike its neighbor, no holiday lights decorated this house, and only a single room on the front was illuminated—an office with glass doors that led out to a stone patio. Thin white curtains covered the doors, and every few seconds, the murky shape of a man would appear, moving back and forth, as though he were continuously pacing from one side of his office to the other.

I just bet he was pacing. From all the reports I'd heard, he'd been holed up in his mansion for months now, preparing for his murder trial, which was set to begin after the first of the year. That would be enough to drive anyone stir-crazy.

Beside me, a soft creak rang out, followed by a long, loud sigh. Two sounds that I'd heard over and over in the last hour I'd been parked here.

The man in the mansion wasn't the only one going nuts.

"Tell me again. How did *I* get stuck hanging out with *you* tonight?" a low voice muttered.

I lowered my binoculars and looked over at Phillip Kincaid, who had his arms crossed over his muscled chest and a mulish expression on his handsome face. A long black trench coat covered his body, while a black toboggan was pulled down low on his forehead, hiding his golden hair from sight, except for the low ponytail that stuck out the back. I was dressed in all black as well, from my boots to my jeans to my turtleneck, silverstone vest, and fleece jacket. A black toboggan also topped my head, although I'd stuffed all my dark brown hair up underneath the knit hat.

"What's wrong, Philly?" I said. "Don't like being my babysitter tonight?"

He shrugged, not even bothering to deny it. "You're Gin Blanco, the famed assassin turned underworld queen. You don't need babysitting." He shifted in his seat, making it creak again, and shook his head. "But Owen insisted on it. . . . The things I do for that man."

Phillip was right. As the Spider, I could handle myself in just about any situation. I certainly didn't need him here, but Owen Grayson, Phillip's best friend and my significant other, had wanted it this way. But I hadn't protested too much when Phillip had shown up at the Pork Pit and told me that he wanted to tag along tonight.

With the mysterious members of the Circle out there, a little backup might come in handy. Even if said backup was whinier than one would hope.

"Why couldn't Lane sit out here with you?" Phillip asked. "Or Jo-Jo or even Sophia for that matter? Why did *I* get elected to freeze my balls off tonight?"

Finnegan Lane, my foster brother, was often my partner in crime in all things Spider-related, while Jo-Jo and Sophia Deveraux respectively healed me and cleaned up the blood and bodies I left in my wake.

"Because Finn is still dealing with the mess that Deirdre Shaw left behind at First Trust bank, and Jo-Jo and Sophia had tickets to *The Nutcracker*," I said, ticking our friends off on my fingers. "And of course, you know that Owen promised Eva that he'd help out with that holiday toy drive she's leading over at the community college."

"I would have been *happy* to help Eva with her toy drive," Phillip grumbled. "Thrilled. Ecstatic even."

Despite their roughly ten-year age difference, Phillip was crazy about Eva Grayson, Owen's younger sister, although he was waiting for her to finish college and grow up a bit before pursuing a real relationship with her.

"Anything would have been better—*warmer*—than this." He popped up the collar of his trench coat so that it would cover more of his neck, then slouched down even farther in his seat.

"Aw, poor baby. Stuck out here in the cold and dark with me tonight." I clucked my tongue in mock sympathy. "And to think that I was just about to offer you some hot chocolate."

His blue eyes narrowed with interest. "You have hot chocolate? Homemade hot chocolate?"

I reached down and pulled a large metal thermos out of the black duffel bag sitting between our seats on the van floor. "Of course I do. You can't have a stakeout on a cold winter's night without it."

I grabbed two plastic cups out of the bag and handed them over to Phillip, who held them steady while I poured. The rich, heady aroma of the decadent drink filled the van, cutting through the icy chill that had crept inside the vehicle. I breathed in the fumes as I capped the thermos and put it away. Phillip passed over my cup, and I drew in a couple more deep, steamy breaths before taking a sip. The dark brew coated my tongue with its bittersweet flavor, softened by the vanilla extract and raspberry puree that I'd added to the mixture.

Phillip cradled his cup like a bum huddled over a trash-can fire. He took a long slurp and sighed again, this time with happiness. "Now *that's* more like it."

We both settled back in our seats, watching the mansion and sipping our hot chocolate.

The folks who'd been hosting the dinner party must have decided to go to bed, since the recorded carols abruptly cut off, and the holiday lights winked out one door, window, and plastic snowman at a time, further blackening the landscape. The icy drizzle picked up as well, turning into more of a steady rain, each drop *tink*-ing against the van windshield. It truly was a night fit for neither man nor beast, but these were my favorite kinds of environments as an assassin. The cold, the rain, and the darkness always made it that much easier to get close to your target and then get away after you'd put him down. If I'd wanted someone dead, I would have waited for a night just like this one to strike.

And I was willing to bet that someone might have the same idea about the man in the mansion.

Phillip tipped his cup at the shadow still pacing back and forth behind the patio doors. "You really think that he knows something about the Circle?"

I shrugged. "He's the best lead I have right now—and the only person still alive who might know anything about them."

Two weeks ago, I'd been kidnapped and held hostage by Hugh Tucker, a vampire who claimed that he was part of a secret group that supposedly pulled the strings on the underworld and everything else in Ashland. That had certainly come as news to me, since *I* was supposedly the head of the underworld these days. But Tucker had claimed that the Circle was an organization of criminals so high-and-mighty that no one could touch them, es-pecially not a lowly assassin like me. The vamp had also said that the Circle monitored everything from behind the scenes—and that they could kill me and my friends anytime they wanted to.

But the most shocking thing he'd revealed was that my mother, Eira Snow, had supposedly been one of *them*.

My mother had been murdered when I was thirteen, a deep loss that I still felt to this day. But I'd viewed her like any other kid. She was my mom—nothing more, nothing less. I'd never really thought about who *she* was, much less what kind of person. The good things she did, the bad ones, how she felt about all of them. I didn't know any of that. But Tucker had turned my world upside down with his accusations, and I wanted to know if they were true: I *had* to know if my mother had been the good person I'd always assumed she was, or just as rotten, heartless, and depraved as the rest of this shadowy Circle.

"You know, we could just go knock on his door and ask him about all this," Phillip said.

I snorted. "He wouldn't tell me anything. Nothing I could trust anyway. He hates me too much for that."

Phillip shifted in his seat again. "Well, at least we could get this over with and go home. That would certainly keep my balls from turning into ice cubes—"

A pair of headlights popped up in the van's rearview mirror. I gestured at Phillip, and we both slouched back down in our seats.

A black SUV cruised down the street, passing our van. The vehicle stopped at the end of the block and made a right, disappearing from sight. Phillip started to sit back up, but I held out my hand, stopping him.

"Wait," I said. "Let's see if they come back."

He rolled his eyes, but he stayed still. "Why would they come back? It's probably just somebody who lives in the neighborhood—"

Headlights popped up in the van's rearview mirror

again, and that same SUV cruised by our position. This time the vehicle turned left at the end of the block.

"Maybe they're lost," he said. "All these cookie-cutter Northtown streets and mansions look alike, especially in the dark."

I shook my head. "They're not lost. They're seeing how quiet and deserted the area is for whatever they have in mind. They'll be back. You'll see."

We sat in the van, watching our mirrors. Sure enough, a minute later, that same SUV cruised by us again. Only this time, the vehicle didn't have its headlights on, or even its parking lights. It whipped a U-turn in the middle of the street, pulled over to the curb, and stopped—right in front of the mansion we were watching.

"Hello," I murmured. "What do we have here?"

The doors opened, and two people got out of the front of the SUV, both wearing long black trench coats akin to Phillip's. They were giants, each one roughly seven feet tall with thick shoulders and broad chests; most likely they were the muscle and bodyguards for whoever was in the back of the vehicle.

Sure enough, one of the giants opened a rear door, and a shorter, thinner figure emerged, also sporting a black trench coat, along with a black fedora and a matching scarf wrapped around their neck. I peered through my binoculars, but the person's back was to me, so I couldn't see their face, although from the size and gait, I did get the impression that it was a woman.

"Some late-night visitors here for a hush-hush meeting with our old friend?" Phillip mused.

"Maybe."

One of the giants squatted down. At first, I wondered what he was doing, but then the woman in the fedora and scarf ran over to the giant, who hoisted her high up into the air. Ms. Fedora grabbed hold of the top of the iron gate and swung her legs up and over it with all the grace of an Olympic gymnast. Landing deftly on her feet in the driveway on the other side, she straightened up and started striding toward the mansion with deadly purpose.

I cursed, realizing that I was about to lose my one and only lead on the Circle. I'd considered the possibility that someone might come here to silence him, but part of me hadn't thought that it would actually *happen* since everything else I'd tried to track down the members of the Circle had been a dead end.

"Not a meeting," I growled. "They're here to kill him."

Since Fedora was already past the gate, I didn't have time to ease out of the van, sneak through the shadows, and stab the giants in the back the way I normally would have. So I dropped my binoculars, kicked my door open, barreled out of the vehicle, and ran down the street toward the SUV.

"Gin! Wait!" Phillip shouted, scrambling to get out and follow me.

But I needed to get to the man in the mansion before Fedora did, so I tuned him out. The giants whirled around at the sound of Phillip's voice and spotted me racing toward them. They cursed, pulled guns from inside their trench coats, and snapped up the weapons.

Pfft! Pfft! Pfft!

I zigzagged, and the first round of bullets went wide. But when the giants paused to take more careful aim, I reached for my Stone magic and hardened my skin into an impenetrable shell.

Pfft! Pfft! Pfft!

The second round of bullets also went wide. The giants had come prepared, and the silencers on the ends of their weapons muffled the sounds of the shots. No lights snapped on inside the neighboring mansions. They wanted to keep this quiet? Well, so did I.

Pfft! Pfft! Pfft!

Two of the shots went wide again, but the third punched into my right shoulder, spinning me around. Still, thanks to my magic, it didn't blast through me the way it otherwise would have. I skidded on the ice coating the street, but I managed to regain my balance and charge forward again.

Instead of heading toward the giants, I ran straight at the SUV. When I was in range, I leaped up onto the bumper, then the hood, then scrambled up onto the roof. Before the giants realized what I was doing, I raced forward and leaped off the vehicle's roof, pushing off hard and trying to get as high in the air as possible. Lucky for me, they'd parked close to the curb and the narrow sidewalk. A second later, my hands hit the top of the wall that fronted the mansion, and I dug my boots into the slick stones so that I could pull myself up onto the ledge. Fedora wasn't the only one who could do gymnastics.

I rolled off the top of the wall and dropped ten feet down to the other side, landing in a crouch. I palmed one of the silverstone knives tucked up my sleeves, surged to my feet, and darted forward across the lawn. The ice-crusted grass crunched like brittle bones under my boots.

The light spilling out from the office perfectly illuminated Fedora, who was fifty feet ahead of me and moving fast, her breath streaming out behind her in a trail of frosty vapor. She must have heard the disturbance out on the street because she picked up her pace, pulled a gun out of her trench coat, and shot through the lock on the patio doors with one smooth motion. A second later, she was inside the mansion.

"Hey!" a man's voice shouted from inside the office. "Who are you? What do you think you're doing?"

I didn't hear her reply, if there even was one.

Pfft! Pfft! Pfft!

Pfft! Pfft! Pfft!

More and more shots sounded on the street behind me, but the giants weren't aiming at me anymore. Phillip must have gotten into the fight. He could take care of himself, so I focused all my energy on sprinting across the lawn, trying to get to the mansion, even though it was already too late.

Pfft! Pfft! Pfft!

Sure enough, gunfire flashed inside the office, as bright as the holiday lights had been earlier. Someone had just been shot.

A second later, Fedora stepped through the doors and out onto the stone patio. I squinted, but the office lights were behind her, and all I could see in the darkness was the pale glitter of her eyes above the black scarf wrapped around her face. She gave me a mocking salute with her gun before ducking back inside the mansion. Now that her mission was accomplished, no doubt she'd leave through one of the back doors and disappear into the woods. All without my even getting a good look at her face.

I cursed. Even though I wanted to rush inside the mansion, I forced myself to slow down and approach the patio doors with caution, just in case she might be lying in wait to try to kill me too. I also grabbed hold of even more of my Stone power, hardening my skin as much as possible, on the off chance that she decided to blast me with bullets *and* elemental magic. As a final precaution, I reached out with my power, listening to all the emotional vibrations that had sunk into the stone walls of the mansion.

Harsh, shocked mutters echoed back to me, from the shots the woman had just fired. Alongside that was a high, whiny chorus of worry, fear, and paranoia. But there were no sly whispers or dark murmurs of evil intent that would have signaled that she was hiding in the office, ready to put a bullet in my head the second I stepped inside. Whoever the woman was, she was long gone.

Still, I was careful as I eased into the office, my knife still in my hand, my other hand up and lightly glowing with my Ice magic, ready to blast whoever might attack me.

But only one person was in the office: the man I'd been watching.

Jonah McAllister, my old nemesis, lay sprawled across the floor.

✸ 2 ✸

I stared down at Jonah, who remained absolutely motionless, his arms flung out to his sides, his legs twisted awkwardly beneath his body. Frustration filled me that Fedora had gotten to him, that she'd infiltrated his house as quickly and easily as, well, I could.

My plan had been to stake out McAllister's mansion and capture anyone the Circle might send to kill him, since he was the most obvious—and so far only—loose end that might lead back to them. Then I would have taken my sweet, bloody time questioning that person about her bosses. But Fedora had been faster and far more clever than I'd expected, and I was once again left with nothing. Just another in my growing string of failures when it came to the shadowy group.

I was sick and tired of losing to those bastards, whoever they really were.

I started to move past McAllister and leave the office to

search the rest of the mansion for Fedora, even though I knew that she was already gone. But then I noticed that no blood had pooled under his body. In fact, I didn't see any blood anywhere—not oozing across the floor, not spattered on the chairs, not even sprayed on top of the papers that had slipped off his desk and fallen around him like oversize snowflakes. So I stopped and took a closer look at him.

Jonah McAllister was much thinner than the last time I'd seen and confronted him in this office. Black circles ringed his eyes, and his cheekbones poked out like arrows trying to punch through his face, as though he'd lost thirty pounds overnight. Even his skin, which he took such pride in and kept young, tight, and baby-smooth with a strict regimen of expensive Air elemental facials, seemed old, loose, and wrinkled, like wet paper that was barely clinging to the rest of his skull.

His silver mane of hair was as glorious as ever, though, artfully styled and as bright and burnished as holiday tinsel even when the rest of him was littering the floor like a broken toy. I wondered how much product he'd used to keep his hair so firmly, perfectly anchored in place even as he'd been shot. Even Finn would have been impressed with his do.

But the thing that caught my eye was the Christmas sweater that covered his chest—bright green with a grinning brown reindeer stretching across the front, complete with a red-sequined nose. Not McAllister's usual slick suited style at all. In fact, the sweater looked handmade, although I couldn't imagine who would take the time and trouble to knit Jonah a sweater—*any* sweater, much less one this hideous.

Given how skeletal the rest of him was, the sweater seemed suspiciously thick and bulky, and I realized exactly what was underneath it. Of course. McAllister might be a weasel, but he was a smart weasel. He knew exactly how angry folks still were with him over the Briartop robbery, and he would have taken precautions against being murdered in his own mansion.

So I crouched down, drew back my hand, and slapped him across the face. McAllister winced at the sharp, stinging blow, but he didn't open his eyes.

So I slapped him again, harder this time.

McAllister let out a little squeak of pain, but he still didn't open his eyes, determined to play possum as long as possible.

"Wakey, wakey, Jonah," I drawled. "You can either open your eyes, or I can keep slapping you. I'm okay with that. I still need to get my cardio in for the day."

McAllister's brown eyes popped open at my threat, then narrowed to slits as he recognized me. "Blanco?" he said. "What are *you* doing here?"

"Well, I was hoping to capture your would-be assassin, but she managed to escape. I can't decide if I'm happy or disappointed that you're still alive." I nodded at his ugly Christmas sweater. "I didn't realize that Rudolph came equipped with a bulletproof silverstone vest these days."

"It seemed like a wise precaution." He wet his lips and glanced around the office, as if he was worried that Fedora was going to come back and finish what she'd started.

I almost wished that she would. Even now, despite how useful McAllister might be, part of me wanted to raise my knife and just end him for all the times he'd tried to have me killed. That would have been the smart move. But I'd been anything but smart these past few weeks. Why start now?

"Gin! Gin!" Phillip called out, his voice growing louder and louder. "Are you okay?"

"I'm fine!" I yelled back. "I'm here! In the office!"

I got to my feet and went over to the patio doors. Phillip ran up to me, a gun clutched in his hand. His breath steamed in the air, and his cheeks were tomato red from the cold. I looked past him at the iron gate, which was standing wide-open now, but the black SUV that had been parked outside McAllister's mansion was gone.

"The giants banged off a few shots at me, then got in their car and left before I could get close to them. I tried to shoot out their tires, but . . ." Phillip shrugged.

I nodded, disappointed but not surprised. Given the way she'd so easily infiltrated the mansion, Fedora had proven that she was clever. Of course she would have told her men to skedaddle at the first sign of trouble, especially if that trouble was me. She wouldn't have wanted to risk the giants getting captured and questioned about her and the Circle. But frustration surged through me all the same. Once again, all I'd accomplished was a big fat lot of nothing, but I forced myself to focus on what was important right now.

"Don't worry about it," I said. "Are you okay?"

Phillip nodded. "Yeah. Just a little winded from trying to catch up." His gaze flicked over to McAllister, who was slowly getting to his feet. "I see that he managed to survive after all."

"Seems our good friend Jonah likes to pad out his

holiday sweaters by wearing a silverstone vest underneath them."

"How practical," Phillip said, "given how many people want to kill him."

"Indeed."

McAllister looked down and pulled his sweater away from his chest. The reindeer's left eye, right over McAllister's heart, had been obliterated, and I could see the glint of the three bullets caught in the black vest underneath. Fedora hadn't been messing around. All of those were kill shots, and the tight grouping was especially impressive. So she could shoot too, in addition to her acrobatics. She'd definitely wanted him dead, which only made me more curious as to what, if anything, he might know about the Circle.

Jonah McAllister had been the personal lawyer for Mab Monroe, the Fire elemental who'd run the Ashland underworld for years before I'd killed her. Mab had also been the bitch who'd murdered my mother, Eira, and my older sister, Annabella.

For years, I'd thought that Mab had killed my family because of a long-standing feud between the Snows and Monroes, as well as her worries about my Ice and Stone magic potentially overtaking her Fire power someday. But Hugh Tucker had claimed that Eira had been making trouble within the Circle, so he and the other members had given Mab the go-ahead to murder her. Something else that had come as a stunning, horrifying revelation, and something else that had made me even more determined to get answers about my mother, the Circle, everything.

Starting right now.

McAllister grimaced and let his sweater drop back down into place, even though the one-eyed reindeer looked anything but cheerful now. He glanced back and forth between me and Phillip, his mouth pinching in thought. I could almost see the wheels turning in his brain as he wondered what we were doing here—and how he could best twist the situation to his advantage.

I was still holding my knife, so I stabbed it at the couch along the wall. "Sit."

McAllister swallowed, but he moved over and plopped down on the couch. I grabbed a chair that was beside the desk and moved it into the open space in front of the couch. Then I turned it around, sat down, and leaned my elbows across the back of it. Phillip stayed by the patio doors, glancing outside and keeping watch, just in case Fedora and her giants decided to double back and take another shot at us.

I looked at McAllister, and he stared back at me, wetting his lips over and over, as well as repeatedly dry-washing his hands. If he knew how desperate I was for information—*any* information—about the Circle, he wouldn't tell me a damn thing, just like I'd told Phillip earlier in the van. So I kept staring at McAllister, my face calm and blank, waiting for him to crack and start talking to fill the tense silence.

It didn't take long.

"What do you want, Blanco?" McAllister snapped.

"Well," I said, still keeping my easy tone and casual posture, "in case you haven't heard, locked up here in your ivory tower, I am officially the queen bee of the underworld these days."

He scowled, but he didn't say anything.

"It has come to my attention that there are some folks who want you dead, Jonah. Well, more so than usual, anyway. Given my new position, you would think that these people would check in and get my permission for the hit, especially when it's so well-known how very much I want you to stand trial for your crimes at the Briartop art museum back during the summer. But these folks didn't get that okay from me, so I decided to come by and spoil their little assassination party."

It was complete bullshit. The only reason I wanted McAllister to keep on breathing was so I could pump him for information, but he didn't need to know that.

"Now, I'll admit that these folks actually surprised me, actually got the better of me. I didn't think that they would be quite so smart, quick, and determined. But that only makes me more curious about who's decided to stir things up in my sandbox."

"Your sandbox?" McAllister sneered. "It's not *your* sandbox, and it never will be. Not the way that it was Mab's. The other underworld bosses were too afraid of her to make much trouble. At least, not so openly. You, my dear, are a completely different story. Queen or not, you've killed enough of their friends that they all want you dead."

I snorted. "Please. My body count isn't nearly as impressive as Mab's. She fried people just for looking at her the wrong way."

"Certainly," McAllister agreed. "But Mab never pretended to be anything other than the stone-cold, ruthless bitch she truly was. Everyone's sick and tired of your little moral code and annoying self-righteousness. Sooner or later, one of the other bosses is going to succeed in taking you out. I just hope that I'm still alive to see that day when it comes."

"Going to dance on my grave, Jonah? That's a bit cliché."

He scowled at me, anger staining his cheeks and making them almost as red as the reindeer nose on his garish sweater.

I shrugged. "You're probably right. I never wanted the job, but now that it's mine, I'm going to make the best of a bad situation and all the bad, bad folks who come along with it." I leaned forward. "Now, tell me what you know about the Circle."

He frowned. For once, his forehead actually wrinkled the way a normal person's would, despite all his years of Air elemental facials. "The Circle? What Circle?"

McAllister was a good lawyer and more than capable of all sorts of theatrics, including lying to my face. I studied him, but for once he seemed genuinely confused.

"The Circle," I repeated, trying to keep my voice smooth and even and not let him know how important this was to me. "They're the ones who sent that assassin after you tonight."

He shook his head. "Never heard of them."

I glanced at Phillip, who shrugged back at me. He thought that McAllister was telling the truth too.

"The Circle," I said for a third time, a bit of annoyance creeping into my tone. "Some secret group that Mab was involved with. I want to know everything you know about them."

McAllister shook his head again. "Sorry, but I've never

heard of any Circle. What kind of idiotic nickname is that anyway? Sounds like a yoga group."

I had to grind my teeth to keep from leaping up out of the chair, shoving my knife up against his throat, and screaming at him to give me some answers. It took me a moment to unclench my jaw.

"Okay, say that I actually believe that you've never heard of the Circle. What about Hugh Tucker?" I asked, trying a different avenue. "Vampire, black hair, goatee, really fast. Tends to blend into the background most of the time."

McAllister chewed on his lower lip. "Hugh Tucker, Hugh Tucker. Why do I know that name . . ." He snapped his fingers. "Tucker. I remember him. Mab used to go out with him from time to time. Smug, smarmy bastard. I never did understand what she saw in him."

That was Tucker all right. My eyes narrowed. "What do you mean *go out with him*? Were the two of them . . . involved?"

He shrugged. "As involved as Mab ever got with any of her one-night stands. Tucker was the only one that she ever had back for seconds and thirds, though. She told me once that the two of them were old friends, that she'd known him ever since she was a kid, and that they'd grown up together. That was one of the reasons why he stuck out to me."

"And why is that?"

McAllister gave me a look like the answer should have been obvious. "Because most of the people that Mab knew for any length of time wound up dead, usually by her hand."

Well, that was certainly true. Mab had never been shy

about roasting people with her Fire magic for the slightest infraction. Still, I kept quiet, waiting for him to continue, but the lawyer stared back at me with a puzzled expression, obviously not understanding my sudden interest in one of Mab's old lovers.

"That's it?" Phillip growled. "That's all you know about the Circle?"

"I told you already. I don't know anything about any stupid Circle—" McAllister stopped and tilted his head to the side, studying me with new interest. "This is really important to you, isn't it, Blanco? This Circle . . . they've really pissed you off."

"You might say that."

I kept my face blank, but McAllister smelled blood in the water, and like any shark he went straight to it.

He smiled, the sinister expression creating deep lines at the corners of his eyes. For the first time, well, *ever*, he seemed genuinely happy to be in my presence. "Now that I think about it, I might know more about Hugh Tucker after all, along with this Circle that he belongs to."

"But?"

"But, as you know, I've been under a lot of stress these past several months, preparing for my upcoming murder trial. My memory's not what it used to be."

Liar. His memory was probably better than mine, but I recognized the negotiating tactic for what it was. I sighed. "What do you want, Jonah?"

"I want out."

"Out of what?"

"Out of Ashland, out of my trial, out of this damn prison you've stuffed me in," he growled. "I want to start over somewhere that no one knows me. I don't even care where at this point. I just want out of *here*." His gaze darted around the office, and his mouth twisted with disgust before he focused on me again. "You make that happen, and I'll tell you everything I know about Hugh Tucker and the Circle."

He sat back against the couch and crossed his arms over his chest, giving me a smug, toothy smile, absolutely sure that I would give in to his demands.

For a moment, I was tempted—so damn *tempted*. Because the Circle already knew every single thing about me, and I was scrambling to play catch-up. I didn't even know who any of them were, besides Tucker, and my friends and I hadn't been able to find a trace of the vampire since the night that Deirdre Shaw had died. If I could at least identify the members of the Circle, then I could study them—kill them—before they lashed out at me again or, worse, my friends.

And I could finally get the answers to all my questions about my mother.

I opened my mouth, ready to give in to McAllister's ridiculous demands, but then I glanced over at Phillip, who was still standing by the patio doors, his gun clutched in his hand, keeping watch. And I remembered how pale he'd looked, lying on the marble floor at the Briartop museum, slowly bleeding out after being shot by one of the giants that McAllister had hired to rob the museum and steal Mab's will from the vault. I remembered how much pain Phillip had been in. I remembered how Eva had cried over him and how worried Owen had been about his best friend.

And just like that, I shut my mouth. Nobody fucked with my friends and got a free pass, not even to satisfy my burning curiosity about my mother and the Circle. I might be an assassin, but there were some lines that I wouldn't cross.

Besides, Jonah McAllister was not the least bit trustworthy. As badly as I'd screwed him over by revealing his involvement in the Briartop heist to all of Ashland, I had no doubt that he would be more than happy to feed me a passel of lies and scamper out of town, secretly laughing at me the whole time. Even if I threatened him, even if I tortured him, even if I cut him to ribbons with my knives, he was stubborn enough and hated me enough to hold out and not tell me a damn thing.

No, I couldn't risk him lying, spinning some story, and sending me on some wild-goose chase. I *wouldn't* risk it. And I especially wouldn't insult Phillip and his suffering like that.

"Well, Blanco?" McAllister crowed, still so confident that I was going to give in to his demands. "What do you say?"

I shook my head. "Never going to happen, Jonah. Never going to happen." I got to my feet and headed toward the patio doors. "Come on, Phillip. Let's go. We've wasted enough time here."

Phillip followed me, although we hadn't taken three steps out onto the lawn before McAllister hurried after us.

"Wait! Wait!" he called out, scrambling to catch up to us.

I whipped around and snapped up my knife, and McAllister had to pull up short to keep from ramming reindeer-first into the blade.

"No, Jonah," I growled. "I don't have time to wait, and I especially don't have the time, patience, or energy for you to try to work your weaselly wiles on me. You might know some dirty little details about Tucker from seeing him with Mab, but you drew a complete blank when I first mentioned the Circle, which means that you don't know anything about them at all."

He opened his mouth to protest, but I cut him off before he could get started.

"I'll admit that torturing you for what little information you might have would be fun, a nice diversion after the shitty couple of weeks that I've had, but I couldn't trust anything you would scream out. And frankly, I have better things to do than getting your blood on my clothes tonight."

He wet his lips again, his eyes darting left and right, as if he expected more assassins to suddenly appear out of the icy drizzle. "And what about me? What do I do now?"

"For all I care, you can stay right here in your mansion, stewing in your own juices just like you have been for months now. Although it won't be long before Fedora realizes that you're not nearly as dead as she wants you to be." I stared him down. "What do you think will happen then?"

I slashed my knife through the air right in front of his throat, just in case he didn't get the point.

He gasped and staggered back. "She'll come back."

I nodded. "That she will, and I imagine that next time, she'll make sure that you're good and dead before she leaves."

His face paled, making him look even more skeletal

than before, as that horrifying fact slowly sank in. Dead man walking in more ways than one.

"Enjoy your life, Jonah," I snarled. "What little is left of it, anyway."

I gave him a mock salute with my knife, then turned and stalked off into the night.

Once again, Phillip followed me, although we hadn't taken five steps before McAllister started hissing at me.

"Blanco!" he said, his sharp voice dissolving into a bitter wail. "You can't do this! You can't leave me here! Not again! I can't take it! Not again!"

I kept right on walking.

Phillip glanced over his shoulder. "You should be happy," he murmured. "McAllister is leaning against the doorframe and clutching his chest like he's about to have a heart attack."

I snorted. "He'd have to have a heart first."

Phillip grinned, but he kept looking at me out of the corner of his eye. "I know why you told him no," he said. "But don't make this about me. McAllister's not the one who shot me."

"No, but he set up the whole art heist, and you got hurt as a result of his plan. Not to mention the innocent people who died just because he wanted to hide the fact that he was embezzling from Mab's estate and didn't want Madeline to find out about it. That makes him responsible for the whole shebang. And now he wants a get-out-of-Ashland-free card for all of that? For some tenuous information about Tucker that probably won't tell me anything that I don't already know about the vampire? No—no way."

Phillip didn't say anything else as we crossed the lawn, and the only sound was the crunching of the ice-coated grass under our boots. After the warmth and light of Mc-Allister's office, the night seemed colder and blacker than before. The drizzle picked up again, turning into more of a steady, icy rain, and our breaths hovered around us in chilly clouds. Or maybe it was just my own sense of failure that made everything feel dark, dreary, and desolate.

Phillip had shot through the lock on the iron gate and shoved it open on his way into the mansion, so we stopped at the entrance and looked up and down the street. But there was no sign of Fedora, the giants, or the SUV, and all the neighboring houses were still dark. No one had heard the gunshots or seen us skulking around. Good. One less headache to deal with tonight.

Phillip and I hurried down the street and slid inside my van. I cranked the engine, turning the heat up as hot as it would go, but the warm air did little to dispel the frigid despair and weariness that filled my body.

"So now what?" Phillip asked. "You're not really going to leave McAllister out here all by himself, are you?"

I looked over at Phillip.

He held up his gloved hands. "Don't get me wrong. Being murdered in his own home couldn't happen to a nicer guy. Frankly, I'd like to strangle him to death with my bare hands for what he put Eva, Owen, and everyone else through that night at Briartop."

"But?"

"But I know how important finding out about this Circle is to you, and especially learning the truth about what your mom was involved in. I would feel the same way, if it were me." Phillip drew in a breath and slowly let it out. "I've always felt the same way about my own parents. I looked for them for years, but never got anywhere. It took me a long time to accept the fact that they were probably dead. Or just didn't care enough to try to find me themselves."

He growled out the last few words, but I could still hear the hurt in his voice. His shoulders slumped, and his body seemed to deflate, like air slowly leaking out of a balloon. He stared out the windshield instead of looking at me, but a muscle in his jaw ticked, as if he were grinding his teeth to keep from showing any more emotion. Something that I had more than a little experience with, especially these past few weeks.

Phillip had been abandoned as a toddler and had grown up in some bad foster-care situations before finally running away and living on the streets. That's where he'd met Owen and Eva, and the three of them had formed their own family, along with Cooper Stills, Owen's blacksmith mentor. Phillip didn't know anything about his parents, although he thought that one of them must have been a giant and the other a dwarf, given his own enormous strength.

I reached over and squeezed his gloved hand with my own, telling him that I understood his pain, anger, and frustration. He looked at me out of the corner of his eye, squeezed my hand back, and slipped his fingers out of mine.

"Enough of that," he said, his voice a little lighter than before. "Wouldn't want Owen to get jealous."

"Someone has a rather high opinion of himself."

"Always." Phillip grinned at my teasing, then jerked his head at the mansion again. "But what *are* you going to do about McAllister? If Tucker and the rest of the Circle want him dead, then he has to know something about them, right? Maybe he just doesn't realize that he does."

The thought of what the slimy lawyer might or might not know sent little spikes of pain shooting through my temples. I rubbed my aching head. "I don't know. I just don't know anymore. Maybe McAllister knows something, maybe he doesn't. Maybe Tucker just wants McAllister dead to prove a point. To prove that he can reach out and kill me and anyone else he likes anytime he wants to."

"But?" This time, Phillip asked the question.

"But you're right. I have to do *something* about him, as much as it pains me."

I sighed, pulled my phone out of my jacket pocket, and hit a number in the speed dial. He answered on the first ring, as though he'd been sitting by his own phone, waiting for my call. He probably had been. He was annoyingly efficient that way.

"Yes, Gin?" the smooth voice of Silvio Sanchez, my personal assistant, filled my ear. "I take it that something happened with Jonah McAllister."

I glanced over at the mansion. McAllister had disappeared back inside, shut the patio doors behind him, and cut off all the lights, as if that would keep him safe.

"You might say that. Someone tried to kill him."

Through the phone, I could hear Silvio pounding away on his keyboard. Even though it was after nine o'clock, he was still busy working, although I had no idea what or why he was typing right now. Most sane people would have been sprawled across the couch, watching TV or reading a good book, but the vamp was always available and always on his computer, no matter how late I called.

"Hmm," Silvio murmured. "Well, that's not an entirely unexpected development. You thought that the Circle might come after him to keep him quiet."

"I don't think that he actually knows anything about them," I said. "That's the real problem."

I filled the vampire in on everything that had happened, including Fedora's assassination attempt on the lawyer.

When I finished, Silvio kept typing for several more seconds before finally stopping. "I've made a note to see if Bria and Xavier can get me the traffic-camera footage from the area in the morning. Perhaps we can at least get a license plate on the SUV they were driving."

"I applaud your efforts, but I'm not holding my breath."

Detective Bria Coolidge, my baby sister, and Xavier, her partner on the force, had been helping me with my search for the Circle, especially Bria, who wanted answers about our mother just as badly as I did. Over the past few weeks, Bria and Xavier had scoured all sorts of police databases, trying to find info on Tucker and anyone he might be associated with. But so far, the two cops had come up empty, just like me, Silvio, and the rest of our friends.

"So what do you want to do about McAllister, Gin?" Silvio asked. "There are any number of options available to you."

He was right. Since I was the head of the underworld,

I could do anything I wanted to with Jonah McAllister, from going back inside his mansion and killing him myself, to having any number of underworld flunkies do it for me, to simply leaving the lawyer to simmer in his own fear, paranoia, and misery the way I had been for the last several months now.

That was the real kicker, the brutal, bitter irony of this whole situation. Everyone thought that *I* was the big boss, that *I* was the head honcho, that *I* was the one in charge, but I knew the dark, dirty truth. That I was just a front man, just a puppet, just a convenient prop for the Circle to hide behind while they merrily continued on with their own machinations behind the scenes. I'd told Tucker that I would never, ever work for the group the way that Mab had, but the Circle was still using me all the same. The thought further soured my mood.

"Gin?" Silvio asked again. "What do you want to do about McAllister?"

I looked back at the mansion, which was as dark and silent as all the others on the street now. No doubt Jonah was still wide-awake, though, hiding in a closet somewhere and clutching a gun. The lawyer was probably still wearing his garish Christmas sweater and silverstone vest, desperately hoping that Fedora wouldn't come back and finish him off.

I doubted that she'd be back tonight since she thought that she'd already killed him, but she *would* come back, and I had to prepare for that. If McAllister did know something about the Circle, something he might not even realize that he knew, then I wanted another chance to pry it out of him.

Oh, I didn't think that I could stop Fedora from killing McAllister if she was truly determined to do it. I couldn't watch or protect him 24-7, not even if I dragged him kicking and screaming to a safe house somewhere. But even if Fedora did succeed in offing the lawyer, then maybe I could at least learn more about her, which might lead me back to Tucker and the rest of the Circle. At this point, I'd take whatever bread crumbs I could get.

"Gin?" Silvio asked for a third time.

"Call Jade Jamison and ask if she can spare a couple of folks who work out in this neighborhood to keep an eye on McAllister. She probably already has some cooking, cleaning, and other people in the mansions out here, especially this time of year."

Jade Jamison was an underworld figure who ran a variety of cleaning and other service businesses throughout Ashland. In this neighborhood, cooks, housekeepers, gardeners, and even security guards would be as invisible as holiday snowmen, and no one would give them a second look. Not McAllister and hopefully not Fedora, when or if she came back to try to kill him again.

"But tell Jade that I only want her folks to *watch* McAllister," I added. "I don't want any of them trying to save him if he gets attacked again by Fedora or someone else. He's not worth their lives, and neither is any information that he might or might not have."

"Roger that." Silvio started typing again. "Anything else?"

"Nah. Although this can all wait until morning. You should go to bed. Get some rest."

"Mmm-hmm." The vampire started typing even faster than before, completely ignoring my suggestion.

I sighed, knowing that I couldn't stop him from calling Jade the second we hung up. Silvio didn't like to procrastinate about anything, not even for a few hours. It was one of the things that made him such a great assistant, even if it sometimes annoyed me.

"I'll see you at the restaurant in the morning," I said, giving in to the inevitable.

"Of course. And I'll have an update for you first thing. See you then."

We both hung up, and I looked over at Phillip.

He frowned at me. "Eyes only on Jonah? That's not your usual style. I'm surprised that you're not storming back in there right now and asking him some more pointed questions with your knife at his throat."

Maybe that's what I should have done, but I just didn't have the energy to be intimidating tonight. Not when the Circle had already outsmarted me again. Besides, I wouldn't trust a word that McAllister said right now, and there was no way to be sure how much he would try to play me just to keep on breathing.

"What can I say?" I drawled. "It's a Christmas miracle."

Phillip laughed as I put the van in gear and drove away into the cold, icy night.

❋ 3 ❋

I dropped Phillip off at the dock to the *Delta Queen*, his home and riverboat casino, then drove along the river until I reached a paved lot that fronted a small park and a wooded area. I pulled in there and stopped, peering out the windows.

I was only a few miles away from the *Delta Queen*, but I might as well have driven to the moon, given the startling differences. Instead of a gleaming white riverboat, high-end shops, and gourmet restaurants, abandoned buildings, cracked sidewalks, and busted-out streetlights dotted the landscape. I was squarely in Southtown now, the part of Ashland that was home to gangs, hustlers, and other violent, dangerous folks.

Normally, I would have expected to see a couple of homeless guys huddled over the trash cans at either end of the parking lot, burning the garbage inside to stay warm. But it was too wet and cold for that tonight, so the area was completely deserted. Good. I didn't want anyone to see me or especially to realize where I was going.

Silvio could—and did—track my phone, so I turned it off and left it in my car, which the vamp could also track, thanks to the GPS locator he'd hooked to the undercarriage. He might be home working, but I had no doubt that Silvio was checking his phone every so often, just to see where I was. I admired the vampire's efficiency and dedication, but knowing that he could keep tabs on me so easily creeped me out a little. Besides, a girl had to keep some secrets to herself.

Especially when it came to the Circle.

I got out of my car. It had finally stopped raining, but the ice accumulations made the air even colder than before, so I pulled up my jacket collar, yanked down my toboggan, and stuck my gloved hands into my coat pockets, trying to seal in all my body heat. That worked for about five seconds, then the first gust of wind slapped me across the face and sliced through all my many layers of clothes. I shivered, put my head down, and started walking.

I left the parking lot behind and headed over to a winding path that ran along the river. During the warmer months, the wooded area was popular with walkers, joggers, and cyclists, but no one in their right mind would be out here tonight, given the weather. Then again, I was rarely in my right mind, according to Phillip, Silvio, and the rest of my friends.

The path was covered with ice, so I walked through the grass to the side, judging that to be safer. I kept an eye out, but everyone had taken what shelter they could find for the night, and I was the only person hurrying through the dark.

It took me about thirty minutes to reach the end of the path, which fed into another small, wooded park. I stood in the shadows of a weeping willow, scanning this area as well, but it was also deserted. So I trudged through the piles of wet, slick leaves and over to the ten-foot chain-link fence that cordoned off the park from the industrial area next door.

Despite the ice that crusted the metal, I easily scaled the fence, swinging my legs up and over the top, and dropping down to the other side. I crouched in the shadows, just in case anyone was on this side of the fence, but I was as alone as before, so I straightened up and darted forward.

I sprinted across a hundred feet of open space until I reached a large metal container, the first of many housed in this sprawling shipping yard. I plastered myself up against the side of the container, looking in all directions, but no one appeared, and no shouts broke the cold quiet. No one had seen my initial trespassing, so I felt safe enough to keep going.

I rounded the far end of that container only to be greeted by hundreds more, all stacked on top of each other in neat rows. During the day, the metal boxes would have shown their true colors of dull, rusty reds, yellows, and oranges, but they were all a washed-out gray in the semidarkness. Lights had been rigged up throughout the shipping yard to deter trespassers like me, but they cast more shadows than they banished, and I was easily able to move from one pool of darkness to the next. In the distance, I could hear the steady rush of the Aneirin River, but that was the only sound that echoed through the night.

I moved through the area until I reached the end of the container maze, then stopped. More open space stretched out in front of me, leading to a large warehouse in the center of the shipping yard. Lights blazed in the warehouse, and I spotted a giant guard sitting in a small wooden shack by one of the loading-dock doors. He was as bundled up as I was and seemed to be watching something on his phone, although he did glance around every minute or so, checking on things.

I looked around, but I didn't see any more guards, so I slipped back into the container maze, moving through the rows until I came to a lone container set off by itself underneath a large maple tree. This container was battered and dented in several places, as though it had been dropped on its sides more than once, and looked to be abandoned, a discarded piece of junk that the workers hadn't yet gotten around to taking to the scrap yard.

I sidled up to the container, crouched down, and reached for my Stone magic, examining and listening to all the rocks that I'd strategically placed around the container. The rocks were in the same places as before, and they only whispered back to me about the cold, along with faint, steady rumbles from all the cranes, forklifts, and other heavy machinery that moved through the area daily. No dark mutters of malice or murder rippled back to me, which meant that no one had been near the container since the last time I'd been here a few days ago. Good. I got to my feet, pulled a key out of my jacket pocket, opened the padlock, and slipped into the container, pulling the door shut behind me.

The inside of the container was pitch-black, but I moved along the wall until I came to a small table. I pulled off my gloves, reached down, and flipped the switch on the battery-powered lantern that I'd brought in here several days ago, along with some other supplies.

Light flooded the inside of the container, and I blinked several times, trying to get my eyes to adjust to the sudden, harsh glare. Instead of being barren, the inside of the container featured a couple of tables, several chairs, and a metal rack with a bottle of gin and some plastic cups perched on the shelves. All put together, it looked as though some homeless person had wandered in here and made this place his new home.

In a way, that's exactly what I'd done.

According to Hugh Tucker, the Circle knew all about me, which meant that they knew about the Pork Pit, Fletcher's house, and where the rest of my friends lived and worked. They might even know about the various safe houses that I used around Ashland from time to time. So I'd wanted some place that they couldn't possibly know about, some place new, some place secure, some place where I could sit, think, and compile all the information that I had on them. I'd stumbled across this container several days ago. Since I'd killed Dimitri Barkov, the previous owner of the shipping yard, this had seemed like a perfect spot to make my supersecret Circle headquarters.

It wasn't any warmer in here than it was outside, and my breath frosted in the air, but at least the thick metal walls blocked the wind. I could have turned on the small heater that was sitting next to one of the tables, but I decided not to. Maybe being cold and uncomfortable would motivate me to figure out the answers to all my questions. Worth a shot, anyway.

I switched on a few more lanterns, then turned my attention to the large dry-erase board that was pushed up against one of the walls. I'd gotten the idea from Bria, who'd had something similar in her house back when she'd first returned to Ashland and had been trying to find me, as well as take down Mab Monroe. She'd had photos, papers, and more tacked up to her board, a visual display of all the leads she was running down.

But my board was depressingly empty.

Oh, it had a photo of Hugh Tucker, and underneath that I'd written the few facts I knew about the vampire. But that was all the concrete information I had. The rest of the board was covered with questions.

Oh, the questions.

Who belongs to the Circle? Number of members? Are they only in Ashland? Who's the leader? What's the power structure? What illegal activities are they involved in?

The questions went on and on, all scribbled in my horrible handwriting. According to Tucker, the Circle had let Mab be the head of the underworld so that all the other criminals would focus solely on her. So I was guessing that all the tribute—all the money—from the bosses' activities had flowed through Mab to the Circle on the sly. I wondered how much that missing income stream was hurting the group. Probably not much, if they were as rich and powerful as Tucker claimed, but I had no way to know for sure. Only one thing was certain—Mab had only been one head on this monstrous hydra, and I'd have to cut off all the others to finally kill the Circle for good.

I stalked back and forth in front of the board, looking at all the questions in turn, and massaging the cold, aching scars embedded deep in my palms—each one a circle surrounded by eight thin rays. Spider runes, the symbols for patience—something that I was in short supply of these days.

My fingers crept up to the ring on my right hand, which was also embossed with my spider rune, and I twisted it around a few times before grabbing the spider-rune pendant around my neck and sliding it back and forth on its chain. The silverstone ring and pendant both pulsed with my Ice and Stone magic that was stored in the metal, but all my elemental power hadn't helped me solve the riddle of the Circle.

The more I looked at the questions, the more depressed I became. But the fidgeting certainly wasn't helping anything, so I dropped my necklace, stepped forward, and grabbed a dry-erase marker from the shelf that ran along the bottom of the board.

I made a new box on the board and drew a crude hat in it. *Fedora*, I wrote under the box. *Assassin. Acrobatic. Good with guns.*

And . . . and . . . and that was all that I knew about her. Those were the sum total of facts I had about the woman. Once again, I cursed myself for not being faster, stronger, smarter. For not being able to at least capture and question her.

As an assassin, information was key. Who your target was, where he lived, the number of bodyguards he had, his family, friends, pets, habits, even his hobbies. All of that was important and useful in planning a hit on someone. But I didn't have any of that when it came to the Circle.

I didn't have *anything*.

I glared at the stupid hat I'd drawn, more disgusted than ever before. Part of me wanted to swipe my marker across it and the rest of the board, until I'd blotted out Fedora, Tucker, and all my damn questions. But that would have been childish, and I would just have had to erase everything and start all over again.

I still drew devil horns on top of Tucker's head, though. Just because I could. I put them on top of the hat too.

It actually made me feel a little bit better, and I stared at the board, wondering how else I could mark up Tucker's photo—

Creak.

I whipped around to the container door. That sounded like someone had taken hold of the handle and tried to yank the door open but hadn't quite succeeded, given how thick and heavy the metal was.

Creak.

Sure enough, that person tried again, and this time, the door started swinging open.

Someone was outside—and they were coming in.

I dropped the marker, palmed a knife, and darted over to the door, plastering myself up against the metal wall beside it.

A second later, a woman wearing dark clothes and a toboggan slipped into the container, her head moving back and forth as she looked around.

"What in the blue blazes is she up to now—"

I didn't give the woman time to finish her muttered sentence. In an instant, I grabbed her shoulder, spun her around, shoved her up against the wall, and raised my knife to her throat.

Lorelei Parker looked back at me, her pale blue eyes steady on mine. "Is this how you greet all your guests, Gin?" she said.

I hissed out a breath. "Sorry. I thought you were someone else."

"Don't be. I came prepared."

Something jabbed into my side. I looked down. Lorelei had one of her elemental Ice guns pressed up against my stomach. Even though the weapon was only loaded with a single bullet, it would still do plenty of damage, especially in that spot.

"Touché," I murmured.

I dropped my knife from her throat and stepped back. Lorelei slid her Ice gun back into the holster on her belt.

"How did you know that I was in here?"

"I was doing a final check of the yard before leaving for the night, and I noticed that the padlock was open on the container. So I figured that you were probably in here." She jerked her head at the door, which was wide-open now. "You might want to close that. And lock it from the inside next time, if you don't want people sneaking up on you."

I gave her a sour look, but Lorelei merely arched her eyebrows in a chiding response. So I shut the door and slid the metal bar down, locking us in the container.

Lorelei Parker was the smuggler supreme of the Ashland underworld, ready, willing, and able to get anything for anyone at any time. Weapons, cash, gold bars, art, designer fashions, exotic animals, fancy food and wines. If there was a black market for it, then Lorelei knew where to get it and how to best bring it into Ashland on the sly. She was also one of the few allies that I had in the underworld, despite the gun she'd just pulled on me.

Lorelei glanced around, taking in the tables and chairs that dotted the inside of the container. "You've been busy since the last time I was in here."

"Well, I just had to decorate my new fancy digs," I snarked back.

"Assassin chic. I like it." She grinned. "You should come do my office in the warehouse while you're at it."

Given her smuggling interests, Lorelei had coveted the shipping yard for a long, long time. With Dimitri Barkov dead, she'd quickly and quietly taken control of it, paying off what was left of his crew to vacate the premises and bringing in her own people. Since I was the head of the underworld, such a move needed my approval, and I'd been happy to give it. All I'd asked in return was for one shipping container to call my own.

Lorelei was the only one who knew about my container. Not because I didn't trust my other friends, but because Tucker and the Circle could be spying on all of us, and I hadn't set up shop here just for them to realize what I was doing. More than that, I actually wanted to have something concrete to show my friends before I brought any of them here. Especially Bria and Finn, who wanted—needed—answers as badly as I did. Sometimes, I thought that we were like the three blind mice, desperately running around, searching for answers about our dead mothers, and all of us likely to get chopped to pieces by Tucker and the rest of the Circle.

Lorelei wandered over to the board, staring at all my scribblings and fiddling with the end of her black braid, which trailed out from underneath her royal-blue toboggan.

She snorted and pointed at the devil horns on Tucker's photo. "I didn't realize that you were such a talented artist."

"I just wish that I could get my hands on him in person," I muttered. "I'd paint his face all interesting shades of bloody then. Better than Picasso."

Lorelei eyed me, hearing the anger and frustration in my voice. "You'll find Tucker eventually, and the rest of the Circle too. I have faith in you."

"And why is that?"

She shrugged. "Because you, Gin Blanco, are the single most stubborn, determined person I know."

My eyes narrowed. "That sounded suspiciously like a compliment. Why are you being so nice to me all of a sudden?"

"Because we're friends, sort of, and that's what friends do, right?" Her voice was casual, but she didn't look at me as she said the words, and her mouth was set into a tense line, almost as if she was afraid that I would dismiss her soft sentiment outright.

"We *are* friends, sort of," I said in a strong voice. "And do you know what else friends do?"

"What?"

I walked over and picked up the marker that I'd dropped on the floor. I handed it to her, then grabbed another one for myself, along with a bottle of gin and a couple of plastic cups from the metal rack.

"They have a drink and draw really bad caricatures of all their enemies," I said. "What do you say to that, friend?"

Lorelei looked at the gin, the marker in her hand, then at me. Her pretty features creased into a grin. "I say that sounds like a grand old time, friend."

✦ 4 ✦

Lorelei and I spent the next hour doodling on the dry-erase board before she finally put her marker down, saying that she needed to go home and check on Mallory, her grandmother. We said our good-nights, and I turned off the lanterns, locked up the shipping container, and drove home myself.

I took a shower and went to bed, although I spent a good portion of the night glaring at my bedroom ceiling, still cursing myself for letting Fedora get away. Once again, the Circle had been three steps ahead of me the whole time, and I still had no new information about them.

Eventually, I drifted off to sleep, got up the next morning, and went to the Pork Pit, my barbecue restaurant in downtown Ashland. I parked six blocks away from the restaurant and stepped onto the sidewalk, easing into the crowds of commuters scurrying to work on this cold December morning. The sun was shining for a change, but the weak rays gave off no real warmth, and everyone had their chins tucked down into their coats, their breaths billowing out around them in thick clouds of frost.

I hurried along with everyone else, although I kept glancing around and looking at the reflections in all the glass storefront windows, trying to see if anyone was following me. I didn't spot anyone, but that didn't mean anything. Not with a skilled professional like Fedora working for the Circle. I wouldn't even see someone like her coming until she had put three bullets in the back of my head. Still, I kept as good a watch as I could. Just in case.

I made my way to the Pork Pit and did my usual check of the front door and windows, on the off chance that someone had left a rune trap, bomb, or other nasty little holiday gift for me. But the door and windows hadn't been tampered with, so I headed inside and repeated the process. The blue and pink vinyl booths were clean as well, along with the tables and chairs, and no one had been inside since I'd locked up last night. So I put a blue work apron on over my clothes and got started on my morning chores, including making a vat of my mentor Fletcher Lane's secret barbecue sauce.

Getting into my usual routine and breathing in all the cumin, black pepper, and other sweet and spicy fumes from the simmering sauce made me feel a smidge better. So had doing those silly drawings with Lorelei last night. Sure, Fedora might have gotten away, but Phillip and I were okay, and that was the most important thing. Besides, sooner or later the Circle would make a mistake. I just had to be ready to take advantage of it when they did.

At ten o'clock, a soft knock sounded on the front door, and I let Silvio Sanchez inside the restaurant.

"You don't have to knock, you know. I gave you your own key weeks ago. You can come in anytime you want to."

"Knocking is the polite thing to do," the vampire murmured back to me. "And in this case, it's the prudent thing as well. Especially when your boss is an assassin who doesn't take too kindly to people sneaking up on her."

"Point taken."

Silvio shrugged out of his long gray trench coat, revealing his matching gray suit, shirt, and tie underneath. He hung his coat on the rack by the door, then swept off his gray fedora and placed it there as well.

My gaze locked onto his fedora, and just like that, my mellow mood vanished. Silvio realized what I was staring at.

"It's just a hat, Gin," he said in an amused voice. "Not a vessel for the ultimate evil."

I grunted and stepped behind the counter that ran along the back wall of the restaurant. I pulled out a sharp, serrated knife from a butcher block and started slicing tomatoes, lettuce, and onions for the day's sandwiches. Cutting things always made me feel better.

Silvio perched on his usual stool at the counter and fired up his phone and tablet for the morning briefing, as he liked to call it. The vampire ran down everything he'd found out about Fedora overnight, which basically was nothing. He'd been in touch with Bria and Xavier and had gotten a license-plate number for the SUV off a security camera in the neighborhood. Silvio had tracked the vehicle to its rightful owner, who had reported it stolen a few hours before the attack at McAllister's mansion.

No doubt Fedora had abandoned the vehicle by now. Another dead end.

So Silvio moved on to other underworld matters, including a couple of bosses who needed me to mediate yet another petty dispute. I sighed. More often than not, I felt like being the head of the Ashland underworld was like serving as the CEO of the most dangerous company ever. Only I didn't get a cushy payday, a corner office, a private jet, or any other sweet corporate perks. Just more and more people planning, plotting, and biding their time until they decided that they were finally ready to try to kill me.

But I forced myself to listen to Silvio and follow along. Everyone else still thought that I was the big boss, so I had to act like it. At least until I found out more about the Circle, how they fit into the Ashland underworld, and whose strings they were pulling, other than my own. Besides, if the other bosses ever found out about the Circle and realized that I was not the ultimate power in Ashland, that would only make them that much more determined to kill me so they could move up in the underworld food chain.

Silvio suggested that we schedule some meetings with a few of the more important criminals, and I reluctantly agreed.

Then I moved on to the other pressing topic of the day. "What about Jonah McAllister? Is he still holed up in his mansion?"

Silvio nodded. "As of ten minutes ago, according to one of Jade's people. She has them texting me updates, but so far, everything is quiet."

"Fedora wouldn't come back until tonight anyway. That's what I would do. How did Jade take my request?"

"Jade was more than happy to offer her assistance," Silvio said. "She already had several folks working in the area, including a security guard who patrols that particular neighborhood. She's not even going to charge you for it, although she would like to request a small favor in return. Although said favor is unspecified at this point."

"Of course she would."

Jade Jamison was a savvy businesswoman, and she knew that having me owe her one would be worth more in the long run than any money I might pay her for her surveillance services.

Silvio mentioned a few other things that needed my attention before a couple more knocks sounded on the front door, and the rest of the workers started showing up, including Catalina Vasquez, Silvio's niece, and Sophia Deveraux, who was wearing a long black trench coat with a silver sequined skull wearing a red Santa hat stitched across the back. It matched the rest of her Goth clothes, including her black-and-silver, candy-cane-striped sweater. Sophia always showed her holiday spirit in a unique way.

We all started working, and by the time eleven o'clock rolled around, several folks were waiting outside the door, stamping their feet to stay warm, more than ready to come inside and get their barbecue on. It must have been too cold for criminal shenanigans today, because most of my customers were just regular folks, eager to chow down on a hot plate of barbecue, along with baked beans, fries, onion rings, coleslaw, and some mac and cheese that I made special because of the chilly weather.

I had a large dish of the mac and cheese for my own

lunch. Al dente pasta, sharp white cheddar melted into an ooey, gooey sauce, crushed, toasted butter crackers sprinkled on top for a bit of crunch. It was perfect, warm, hearty comfort food, and I could use all the comforting I could get right now.

The lunch rush came and went with no problems, and the restaurant slowly emptied after that, with only a couple of folks to wait on. Most everyone was staying inside today, not wanting to venture out into the cold any more than they absolutely had to. I knew the feeling. Ever since I'd found out about the Circle, I'd just wanted to stay holed up at Fletcher's house, curled in bed, with pillows and blankets tucked in all around me, as if that would somehow change everything that Hugh Tucker had told me—and the threat that he and his mysterious group represented to everyone that I cared about.

I'd just finished off the last of my mac and cheese when my phone beeped with a new text message.

Can you come to the bank? Finally ready to let the genie out of the box. F.

My heart lifted, and new, fresh hope surged through me at the message from Finn. It was about time. I'd been waiting on this for days now, and so had he.

I texted him back. *Be there in 30 min. G.*

I pushed my empty bowl away, got to my feet, and slid my phone into my jeans pocket. Then I turned around and grabbed a large cardboard box from the back counter, along with several take-out containers.

"What was that about?" Silvio asked, watching me scoop mac and cheese into a bowl.

"Oh, just Finn. Apparently, he's trapped in another

crisis-management meeting at the bank and wants me to bring him some food."

"Mmm-hmm. You know, that would almost be a believable lie except for how happy you sound."

I glanced at the vampire. "I can't sound happy when I'm talking about my friends?"

Silvio crossed his arms over his chest and gave me a knowing look. "Not *that* happy."

I finished with the mac and cheese and moved on to a pot of baked beans, putting them in a separate container. "You know, Silvio, you're becoming as paranoid as Finn always says that I am."

He sighed. "I know. And it's all your fault. You've driven me to it."

"And how have I done that?"

"Not telling me where you are and what you're doing. Turning your phone off so I can't track you. Parking your car in odd locations at all hours of the day and night." He ticked the points off on his fingers. "What exactly *were* you doing in Southtown at midnight last night?"

"Maybe I was out for a moonlit drive," I quipped.

"In the ice and cold? I don't think so. You were up to something, just like you're *always* up to something." He shook his head. "Being your assistant is like trying to wrangle a recalcitrant three-year-old."

I arched my eyebrows and moved on to a vat of coleslaw. "Wow, I've grown up quickly. You said more or less the same thing last week, only I was a stubborn two-year-old then."

He huffed, not at all amused by my joke, so I decided to tell him the truth. At least, part of it.

"Well, if it makes you feel any better, I *am* going to the bank, and I *am* taking Finn some food." I held up the container of coleslaw as proof.

"Among other things," Silvio said, not buying it for a second.

"Among other things," I agreed.

I finished packing Finn's food into the cardboard box, then went over to a glass cake stand, grabbed a fresh-baked chocolate chip cookie, and placed it on a napkin.

"Here." I held it out to Silvio as a peace offering. "Cookies make everything better, even grumpy vampire assistants."

"Mmm-hmm."

Silvio's gray eyes narrowed, but I smiled in the face of his glare. Finally, he relented, took the cookie from me, and broke off a piece. He popped it in his mouth and sighed again, this time with pleasure.

"Cookies do make everything better," he muttered, grudgingly agreeing with me. "Even paranoid, secretive assassin bosses."

I laughed and handed him another cookie.

✲ 5 ✲

I asked Sophia and Catalina to watch over the restaurant, grabbed the food for Finn, and drove over to First Trust of Ashland.

First Trust was the city's most exclusive and highfalutin bank, catering to the extremely wealthy, powerful, and dangerous. The seven-story building took up its own block in the heart of downtown, and the gray marble gleamed in the weak winter sun. I left my car in a nearby parking garage, grabbed the box of food, and headed for the main entrance.

A couple of weeks ago, a single giant guard would have been posted outside, casually watching folks hurry by on the sidewalk. But thanks to Deirdre Shaw's recent and almost successful robbery attempt, security had been dramatically increased, and four guards now flanked the double doors, all keeping a sharp lookout, and all with their hands on the guns holstered to their belts.

I'd brought Finn lunch enough times over the past few weeks that the guards knew who I was, but they still eyed me with suspicion as I approached, and they kept watching as I opened one of the doors and stepped inside. Even then, one of them peered in through the glass, tracking my movements.

The doors opened up into an enormous, elegant lobby that had a light, bright, airy feel. Seams of white swirled through the gray marble floor before snaking up the walls and spreading out onto the ceiling, where they curled around several impressive crystal chandeliers. Dark, heavy antique desks and chairs were clustered together in groups throughout the lobby so that folks could have a bit of privacy as they talked about their finances.

Given that this was a weekday, several folks moved through the area. People coming inside to make deposits, others leaving after having handed over their money, bankers carrying papers from one desk to another. Tellers typed away on their keyboards, and the murmur of half a dozen conversations filled the air, along with an occasional high-pitched *beep-beep* from a cell phone.

Once again, my gaze was drawn to the giant guards, all eight of them, stationed in teams of two in the four corners of the lobby, all on high alert, with their hands on their guns, just like the four guards outside had been. Normally, I would have gone over to the receptionist— another newly installed giant guard—sitting at a desk close to the entrance and told her whom I was here to see, but a man standing by the tellers' counter waved at me.

"Gin!" he called out. "Over here!"

His voice wasn't all that loud, but compared to the

other hushed murmurs, it boomed like thunder through the open space, and everyone stopped what they were doing to look at him, then me. I grimaced and tightened my grip on the box of food. Still aware of the guards' gazes on me, I walked over to the counter, which ran along the back wall.

Finnegan Lane, my foster brother, straightened up at my approach. To the casual observer, he looked the same as always—a handsome investment banker poured into a slick Fiona Fine suit. But his walnut-brown hair was more mussed than styled, his white shirt was rumpled, and his navy-blue suit jacket hung loosely on his shoulders, instead of being impeccably tailored. He'd lost weight these past few weeks, despite all my attempts to coax him to eat.

Finn eyed the cardboard box in my hands and sighed. "More food? I still have leftovers from the barbecue chicken that you brought over for lunch a few days ago."

I passed the box over to him. "Well, now you have more."

He nodded his thanks, but his green gaze moved past me and darted around the lobby before focusing on a spot along the left wall—the same spot where he'd first found out that Deirdre Shaw was his mother. Finn's shoulders sagged, making his suit jacket droop even more, and I could tell that he was reliving her betrayal yet again.

Deirdre had claimed that Fletcher had threatened her, forced her to leave Finn behind, and kept her away from her own son for almost Finn's entire life. She'd swooped back into Ashland a few weeks ago, saying that with Fletcher dead, she could come home, get to know her son, and finally be a part of Finn's life.

Damn, dirty lies, all of it.

In reality, all those years ago Deirdre had threatened to freeze a newborn Finn with her Ice magic if Fletcher didn't let her leave town. She hadn't cared about Finn at all—until she needed him to help her rob First Trust in a desperate, last-ditch effort to pay back the millions that she owed to Tucker and the rest of the Circle.

Finn stared at that spot along the wall a second longer before turning away and screwing a smile on his face, as though everything were normal, and he were still the carefree, happy-go-lucky guy he'd been before Deirdre had blown into town. Before she'd ripped his heart to shreds and betrayed him in the worst way possible. Before she'd tortured him with her Ice magic. Before he'd killed his own mother to save me.

"Alrighty. Let's get this show on the road," Finn chirped.

He left the tellers' counter behind and walked over to a metal door set into the back left corner of the lobby. The two giants stationed there eyed me, but Finn showed them his access card, and they opened the door. I followed Finn down a long flight of stairs that led to the basement, where the senior bank officials' offices were located. Finn left me standing in the hallway while he ducked into his office and put the box of food on his desk. Then, together, the two of us walked over to Big Bertha.

Big Bertha was the bank's largest and most secure vault, featuring hundreds of safety-deposit boxes that were a literal treasure trove of cash, precious jewels, stocks, bonds, and other valuables. Since this was a normal business day, the vault's thick outer metal door was wide-open, although the inner door was still shut and locked. That inner door was actually a tight mesh of silverstone, an extremely tough and durable metal that could absorb and store magic. The mesh had three distinct layers now, each separated a few inches from the next, instead of the one layer that Deirdre had so easily blasted through with her Ice magic during the attempted robbery.

To my surprise, a dwarf with wavy silver hair, sharp hazel eyes, and rough, craggy features was standing in front of the vault, waiting for us. Stuart Mosley, the head of First Trust, and Finn's boss.

I looked at Finn, who shrugged at me. "No one goes into the vault now without Mosley's approval. I had to tell him what I wanted in there."

I didn't like anyone knowing what we were up to, especially not Mosley, since I had no idea if we could trust him. But there was no way to avoid the dwarf, so we walked over to him.

"Ms. Blanco," Mosley said in a deep, gravelly voice. "So nice to see you again."

"Mr. Mosley."

We shook hands, as though this were just an innocent business transaction, then Mosley looked at Finn. "You have the key?"

Finn nodded, reached into his pants pocket, and drew out a safety-deposit box key, which he held up for his boss's inspection. Mosley stared at the number—1300— that was engraved in the metal. For a moment, a hint of a smile played across the dwarf's face, deepening the lines at the corners of his eyes and mouth, but it was gone so quickly that I wondered if I'd only imagined the amused emotion. I stared at Mosley, but his face was stone-cold somber again, and I couldn't get a read on what he was thinking.

Mosley turned around and punched in a code on a keypad that was attached to the first silverstone mesh door. The light on the keypad flashed green before winking back to red. He punched in two more codes; the light flashed green twice more before staying that color, and all three of the silverstone mesh doors slowly slid back one after another.

"Well, you know where that box is, Finn," Mosley rumbled. "I'll leave you to it. Be sure and lock the vault again when you're done."

The dwarf nodded at us, then turned and walked down the hallway and around the corner, presumably going back to his office.

"Am I the only one who thought that was odd?" I asked. "It almost seemed like he was about to crack a genuine smile there for a second."

Finn shook his head. "Honestly, I can't tell around here anymore. Up is down, and down is sideways, with all the new security measures and changes. Anyway, let's go see what Dad left us."

We stepped into the vault. The last time I'd been in here, the space had been in ruins, since I'd used my Ice and Stone magic to collapse the ceiling on top of Deirdre and Rodrigo Santos, the professional thief who'd been helping her. But the piles of rocky rubble were long gone, as was all the gray marble dust, shattered lengths of silverstone rebar, and other debris. The area looked pristine, and the rows of safety-deposit boxes gleamed as though they had all just been shined by hand. Maybe they had been, given Mosley's attention to detail.

"This way," Finn said.

He led me to the back left corner of the vault. All the boxes were marked with small black numbers, and Fletcher's box—1300—was the center box in a row of three across and three down. Nine boxes total, set off by themselves from all the others.

Finn held the key out to me. "You found it, so you do the honors."

After Tucker had taunted me with the knowledge that my mother had been part of the Circle, I'd gone to Blue Ridge Cemetery to dig up her grave to see if Fletcher might have left a clue for me there, as he had in Deirdre's empty casket. I'd found the safety-deposit box key buried in the dirt in my mother's grave and had been wondering about it ever since.

But now that we were finally going to open the box, doubt filled me, along with more than a little worry about what we'd find inside. What horrible secrets had Fletcher discovered about my mother? What hard truths about her had he hidden away for all these years? And how much would they hurt me now?

"Gin?" Finn was still holding out the key to me. "Are you okay?"

I blew out a breath. "Yeah. Let's do this."

Before I could think about it any longer, I took the key from him, slid it into the slot on the front of the box, and turned it. The lock clicked open, and I grabbed the handle and slid the safety-deposit box out of the wall. I carried the long, rectangular container to a waist-high table at this end of the vault and set it down there. Finn nodded at me, and I slowly lifted the lid of the box to reveal . . .

A single sheet of paper.

I frowned. Not what I was expecting. Not at all. Given all the photos and broken mementos that Fletcher had packed into the box in Deirdre's casket, I'd assumed that this box would be filled to the brim with information too. But maybe the old man hadn't had time to find out everything about my mother and the Circle. Maybe he'd left behind a list of the members' names. That would be more than enough for me to start tracking down Tucker and all the others, however many of them there were.

Heart pounding, I reached for the paper. My fingers were trembling so badly that it took me three tries before I was finally able to grab hold and lift it out of the box. Finn moved to stand beside me, and I held the paper up where we could both see it to find . . .

A rectangle drawn on the sheet.

That was it. That was all. Just a large, simple rectangle drawn on a plain white sheet of paper.

I turned it over, hoping that something was written on the back. A note, a phone number, an address. But nothing was there. I held it up to the light, thinking that maybe there was a rune, watermark, or some other faint symbol that I hadn't noticed yet. Still nothing. Desperate, I stared at the front again, but it was the same as before.

Nothing—there was nothing here. Fletcher hadn't left me any clues about my mother, Tucker, or the Circle. Not a single one.

Once again, I had zip. Zilch. Zero. Nada. A whole big fat lot of nothing. More damn *nothing* than ever before.

"That's it?" I growled. "That's all there is? You've got to be kidding me!"

Disgusted, I tossed the paper down onto the table. The single sheet zipped across the smooth metal surface, floated through the air, and landed right in front of those rows of safety-deposit boxes. The whole bank of them looked like a doughnut now that Fletcher's box was missing from the center. I glared at the paper, wondering if the old man was somehow mocking me from the great beyond. That's certainly how it felt.

Finn walked over and retrieved the wayward stationery from the floor, setting it back down on the table. He cleared his throat, breaking the tense, angry silence. "I know you're disappointed. I am too. I expected there to be more in the box."

"But?"

He shrugged. "But maybe Dad just didn't have time to put any info in the box. You know how many hidey-holes he had in his office and all over town. Hard to keep track of them all, much less what he put inside each one. Or maybe he just didn't have any information about your mother and the Circle to share. He's gone now, so we'll never know for sure."

Disappointment burned in my heart, charring all my earlier hope to brittle black ash. "No, I guess we never will."

I glared at the paper again, equal parts angry and frustrated. Part of me wanted to snatch up the sheet, rip it to shreds, and throw the whole mess into the closest trash can. Instead, I reached out, carefully folded it up, and slid it inside my jacket pocket. Maybe it was silly, but I was going to keep the sheet, if only for the simple reason that Fletcher had scribbled on it.

Finn cleared his throat again. "I know you're disappointed."

"But?"

"But there's something else I need to talk to you about."

He hesitated, then reached into his suit jacket and drew out a thick wad of papers, which he laid on the table in between us.

"What's all that?"

"It came in the mail a few days ago." He slid the documents across the table to me. "See for yourself."

I picked up the papers, unfolded them, and scanned the first page. I frowned. "This . . . looks like some sort of . . . deed made out to you."

Finn shot his thumb and forefinger at me. "Winner, winner. It's the deed to the Bullet Pointe resort complex, which I now own lock, stock, and barrel."

I blinked at the name. "Bullet Pointe? That cheesy Old West theme park down in Georgia? The one that's all cowboys, all the time?"

Bullet Pointe was moderately famous in Ashland and the surrounding area, sort of like the poor, distant Southern cousin of one of the Disney theme parks. The rides, costumed characters, and live shows made it especially popular with families and schools. If you lived within driving distance, chances were that you'd been to the theme park on at least one family vacation or school field trip.

Finn nodded, a bit of excitement flashing in his eyes. "Yep, that's it. Dad took us there once for vacation. Do you remember, Gin?"

I snorted. "Oh, I remember all right. You and Fletcher spent the whole weekend playing cowboys, while I followed you both around like a third wheel."

"You got sick too. I remember you eating way too much pizza and then puking your guts out the second we got off one of the swing rides." Finn grinned. "Good times."

I rolled my eyes, then asked the obvious question. "And how exactly did you wind up with the deed to this tourist trap?"

He shifted on his feet. "Deirdre left it to me in her will."

My eyebrows shot up into my forehead. "Your lying, ice-queen bitch of a mother actually *left* you something?"

Finn winced, the teasing grin dropping from his face and the excitement snuffing out of his eyes. Too late, I realized how harsh my tone had been and how much he was still hurting from everything that Deirdre had done. But I couldn't put the words back into my mouth so I plowed on ahead.

"I thought that Deirdre was flat-busted broke," I said in a more neutral voice. "That the reason she robbed Briartop and tried to do the same thing here at the bank was to pay back all the millions that she owed to Tucker and the rest of the Circle."

Finn shrugged. "Looks like she was at least able to hold on to the resort. Maybe Tucker didn't realize she owned it. Maybe she hid it from him. But even if he did know about the resort and pressured her to sell it, it's not the kind of thing that you can just take down to the corner pawnshop and hock for cold, hard cash."

Well, hiding assets certainly sounded like something that Deirdre would have done. Even when Tucker had tied her down to a chair and tortured her, she'd still been scheming how she could turn the situation around to her advantage. Mama Dee had always been plotting *something*, so it didn't surprise me that she'd squirreled away some assets for a rainy day. But an Old West theme park? I would have never expected *that* from her. It just didn't fit in with Deirdre's diva personality and addiction to the finer things in life.

"She actually talked to me about the resort a few times," Finn continued. "Before . . . everything that happened."

I waited, but he didn't elaborate, and I realized that I was going to have to pry it out of him. "And what did she say?"

Finn bit his lip and shifted on his feet. He looked past me, staring out the vault entrance and into the hallway, focusing on the spot where Deirdre had tortured him with her magic. His green eyes darkened, and his shoulders tensed, remembering the cold, horrible Ice burns that she'd inflicted on him. His hands curled into fists, and a faint, almost imperceptible shudder rippled through his body before he was able to stop it.

"Finn?" I asked again in a gentler voice, trying to shake him out of his painful memories. "What did Deirdre say about the theme park?"

He blinked, snapping back to the here and now,

although he dropped his head and started drawing a line on the floor with his black wing tip, instead of looking at me. "Deirdre thought that the Old West theme was rather quaint. She told me that she bought the park on a whim decades ago, that it was one of her very first investments. The park itself is all cowboys, all the time, just like you said, but there's also a hotel on the grounds, also named Bullet Pointe. Deirdre said that she'd focused all her efforts on the hotel. It still has the same Old West look and feel as everything else, but she claimed that she'd slowly turned it into a luxury resort. She bragged that folks come from all over the country to stay there and take advantage of the spa, the golf courses, and the lake that rings it and the theme park. Here. See for yourself."

Finn took the sheaf of papers from me and pulled out a slick, glossy brochure, which he passed back over to me. I opened it up and scanned through the pages. He was right. The Bullet Pointe hotel looked like a swanky place with just the sort of insanely expensive, over-the-top luxury that Deirdre had indulged in. Still, I wondered why she had left it to Finn and especially why the deed had shown up now.

Usually, the wheels of estates and inheritances ground much more slowly, especially in Ashland. Most of the time when somebody died, long-lost relatives and second cousins twice removed came out of the woodwork like hordes of termites, with each and every one demanding a piece of the dearly departed's money pie, no matter how large or small it was. But here was Finn, a scant two weeks after Deirdre's death, deed in hand, with this shiny, new significant real estate to his name. It was all a bit convenient and far too quick and easy for my tastes. Something was going on here.

"So what do you plan to do with your new windfall?" I asked.

"Well, that depends on you."

"Why me?"

"Because I know what you're thinking—that this all happened way too fast and way too easily. And I totally agree with you. It's definitely fishy. I didn't even think that it was real, at first."

"But?"

"But the second I got the deed, I started calling around, making sure that it was legit. The lawyer who did Deirdre's will assured me that it was and put me in touch with the resort manager."

"And?"

Finn hesitated. "And fishy or not, I thought that we could go down there this weekend and check it out for ourselves. The resort manager wants to meet me, the new owner, and make sure that I'm happy with how things are being run."

"You mean the manager wants to suck up and kiss your ass so he can keep his cushy job."

"Actually, it's a she, but something like that." Finn flashed me a faint smile, a rare occurrence these days. "But, hey, I'm not one to turn down a little free, enthusiastic ass-kissing."

"Those words sound *so* wrong coming out of your mouth."

"What's the matter, Gin? Don't like double entendres?"

I huffed. "Those are not double entendres, and you certainly are no James Bond."

Finn straightened his tie. "Of course not. I'm much better looking than that limey bloke."

"You certainly have a much bigger ego."

He winked at me. "That's not the only thing that's bigger on me."

I groaned and shook my head. "It always amazes me how the ego of Finnegan Lane cannot be contained by a mere mortal like myself. It just oozes everywhere, infecting everything it touches."

"Infecting it with *awesomeness*," he shot right back at me.

My eyes narrowed, but Finn grinned even wider, crossed his arms over his chest, and leaned back against the table, knowing that he'd won our verbal sparring match. In that moment, he seemed more like his old self than he had in weeks, since everything with Deirdre had gone down. I didn't have the heart to burst his bubble with more suspicions and worries right now, so I looked at the hotel brochure again.

"You really want to drive down there this weekend?" I asked. "Don't you need to stay here and help Mosley? I thought you guys still had some more safety-deposit boxes to sort through and make sure that the contents were returned to their rightful owners."

"We finished up with the last of the boxes a few nights ago." Finn paused. "Mosley's gone through all of them and double-checked everything. Apparently, he has a master list of every single item in every single box, right down to the last uncut diamond and gold coin."

"And how did he manage that? I thought the safety-deposit boxes and their contents were supposed to be completely confidential."

Finn shrugged. "I didn't ask, and frankly, I don't want to know. I'm just glad that everything's back in its proper place. All Mosley is doing now is hiring and vetting new guards and poring over new security procedures and protocols. Believe me, he's briefed me on those quite thoroughly."

Finn muttered the last few words, and his cheery expression vanished. This time, I winced for him. Anyone would have fallen for Deirdre's deceptive charm and gotten ensnared in her elaborate plan to rob First Trust. But like it or not, Finn was the one who'd given Deirdre, Rodrigo Santos, and their crew of thieves access to the bank, even if it had been at gunpoint, and several of the bank's guards had died as a result.

Naturally, Stuart Mosley had come down hard on Finn. Oh, the dwarf didn't yell or scream or threaten him. Mosley didn't even say a single word about firing him. He just made sure that Finn was involved in every single aspect of getting the bank back up and running again, from reviewing the new security procedures, to assuring customers that their valuables were still safe, to attending the funerals of all the guards who'd died.

Finn would have done all of those things anyway, but that last one had been particularly hard on him, since he'd worked at the bank for years and had been friendly with all the people who'd been killed. He didn't say anything to me, but he'd come to the Pork Pit after a few of the funerals, his eyes dark, his face gray with grief, his entire being radiating sick misery. I knew that it tore him up inside that his coworkers were dead and that their families were suffering their devastating losses. Finn blamed himself for all of it, and the guilt was like a lead weight yoked to his shoulders. I knew that he wasn't eating like he should, and Bria had told me that he was barely sleeping as well.

Finn absolutely loved his job, so the robbery and everything that Deirdre had done to him had been punishment enough, but Mosley made him suffer a little more, just because. Something else that had added to Finn's misery the last few weeks, although he hadn't complained about his boss's tactics. Not even once. Finn thought that he deserved to be punished, and nothing that I, Bria, or anyone else said convinced him otherwise.

"Besides," Finn continued, "I think that we could all use a break after everything that's happened the last few weeks, and where better to get your mojo back than at a fancy hotel? A seaweed wrap will do wonders for the skin, and frankly, my dear, you could use some cucumber slices on your eyes. Get rid of those dark circles and worry lines, and turn your perpetual frown upside down."

"Frowning makes me look more intimidating, and the only cucumbers I'm interested in are the ones in the Pork Pit's salads."

He rolled his eyes. "You are *so* wrong about *so* many things in life, I don't even know where to start."

I grinned at him, and he sighed, knowing that I'd won round two. But Finnegan Lane was never down for long.

"Come on, Gin," he wheedled. "You, me, Bria, Owen.

We'll road-trip down there, spend the weekend playing cowboys and getting pampered, and be back in time for you to open up the restaurant on Monday morning. It'll be fun. A vacation from everyone and everything in Ashland."

"Vacation?" I scoffed, and crossed my arms over my chest. "Do you remember what happened the last time we went on vacation?"

He winced, thinking about our time in Blue Marsh.

"A psycho vampire almost sucked out all my magic, along with my blood, and I ended up tromping through a swamp in the middle of the night," I said. "So forgive me if I am not eager to go on another *vacation*. To me, *vacation* just means *extreme danger in a different place*."

Finn waved away my concerns. "That was a onetime bout of bad luck, and you know it. Nothing like that will happen again."

I arched my eyebrows at him.

"Well, *probably* not," he said. "Although I do know for a fact that you won't be tromping through any swamps."

"And why is that?"

"Because they aren't any down there."

He smiled, pleased with his logic, but I kept glowering at him. The smile slipped from his face, and his shoulders sagged again.

"Please, Gin," he said in a much quieter voice. "It would mean a lot to me."

"Why?"

His lips pressed together in a tight line, and it took him a moment to answer. "Deirdre said that she spent a lot of time at the hotel. I'd like to see her room and her things, whatever she might have left behind."

Just like that, everything made sense. Even now, after how horribly she'd betrayed and tortured him, Finn still wanted to know more about Deirdre, the same way that I wanted to know more about my own mother, and if she'd really been a terrible person like Tucker had claimed. Finn needed to know if there had been anything more to Deirdre than her insatiable greed and cold, cold heart. I couldn't blame my brother for his curiosity, since the same questions burned in my own heart about Eira.

"Besides," Finn continued, sensing that I was wavering, "maybe there's some clue in her things about the Circle. She was their money manager, after all. At least, one of them. Surely, she kept records somewhere on their business interests and finances."

He had a point. We hadn't found anything in Deirdre's personal possessions in her rented penthouse suite here in Ashland, but perhaps she had left something behind at the hotel. Something that the Circle hadn't gotten to yet. Something that might help me identify the other members—or at least figure out how my mother had been involved with them.

Maybe Finn was right. Maybe a change of scenery would do us all some good. Clear our heads and hearts, and let us come back to Ashland with fresh eyes and renewed determination. Right now, I was just spinning my wheels when it came to the Circle, and I'd run out of people to question and places to look.

I sighed, and Finn grinned, realizing that he'd won this third and final round and thus the whole shooting match.

"Well, Gin?" Excitement was creeping into his voice again. "What do you say?"

I shook my head and tossed the brochure down onto the table. "The only thing I can say. Cowboy up, y'all. We're going on a road trip."

* 6 *

"Shoot me," Owen Grayson muttered in a low voice that only I could hear. "Just go ahead and shoot me now. Please. Someone, anyone, put me out of my misery."

I looked over at my significant other, who was sprawled across the backseat of the Range Rover. We'd left Ashland early this Friday morning, and now, three hours later, we were finally approaching the Bullet Pointe theme park, which was located on the outskirts of Chattanooga, although it was actually in Georgia instead of Tennessee.

Finn was driving and singing yet another cowboy-themed song, just as he had been ever since we'd left home. His warbling was enthusiastic but gratingly off-key. I didn't know that so many Western songs existed, much less that Finn knew the words to so many of them, but he'd made a special playlist just for our trip. Yee-haw.

Owen sighed and ran his fingers through his black hair as if he were thinking about pulling it out, just as he'd done a dozen times already in the last hour alone. The sunlight streaming in through the windows highlighted the rugged, handsome planes of his face, including his slightly crooked nose and the scar that slashed along his chin. Owen swiveled his neck from side to side, trying to release some of the tension that had gathered there and in his broad, muscled shoulders.

I reached over and grabbed his hand, threading my fingers through his. "Relax," I whispered. "We're almost there."

"You so owe me for this," he murmured back.

"And how would you like to collect?"

His violet eyes flashed with a sudden, intense heat, and a slow, sexy smile pulled up his lips. "Oh, I can think of a few ways."

"Well, then." I grinned back at him. "I'll be more than happy to pay up."

Detective Bria Coolidge was sitting in the front passenger's seat, and she must have heard our whispers because she turned around and looked at me, her blond hair flying out around her shoulders.

"I just saw another sign!" she chirped, her voice more manic than genuinely enthusiastic. "We should be pulling into the hotel any minute now!"

Both of her blue eyes twitched. So did her fingers, and she glanced at Finn, then the volume control on the radio, as if debating which one she wanted to shut up more. Owen wasn't the only one who was tired of my foster brother's three-hour karaoke act.

But Finn kept right on bellowing along to the music, singing about horses and beer and other cowboy things. I was the only one who seemed to notice how strained his smiles were and how forced and fake his over-the-top, giddyap cheer really was. Finn seemed determined to have a good time and forget all about his problems back in Ashland, at least for the weekend.

I admired his determination, if not his singing.

Thankfully, Bria was right, and Finn turned off the main road and into a long, paved driveway that arched up a tree-covered hill. According to the brochure I'd read, the Bullet Pointe hotel was located at the top of the hill, with the Western theme park spread out down in the shallow valley below it.

"And here we are," Finn said, steering out of the trees and into a wide, circular area in front of the hotel.

He pulled up close to the entrance and stopped, and the four of us got out of the car.

The Bullet Pointe resort hotel loomed up before us. The seven-story structure was made out of enormous gray rocks fitted together, along with thick, sturdy beams of old, gray weathered wood. Wide, short windows gleamed like rectangular diamonds in the sunlight, while the black slate roof rose to a sharp point. The front of the hotel was flanked by a stone porch that featured rows of rocking chairs and old-fashioned barrels with checkerboards and other games perched on top.

Christmas had definitely come early here. Large clusters of potted poinsettias were spaced every few feet along the porch, while mistletoe and other greenery wrapped around the stone columns, along with white twinkle lights. Still more white icicle lights dripped down from all the windows and eaves, while ten-foot-wide evergreen wreaths topped with red velvet bows dangled from the sides of the structure. The hotel reminded me of some rustic Western hunting lodge that had been decked out for the holidays and dropped into the middle of the Appalachian Mountains.

"Isn't it cool?" Finn said, his face lighting up with excitement. "This is going to be such a great weekend. Let's get our luggage and go inside."

Although it was just after ten o'clock in the morning, a steady stream of people moved in and out of the hotel, checking in, checking out, hauling suitcases, coolers, and more here and there. A valet dressed like a cowboy took Finn's car keys, while a couple of bellmen, also dressed like cowboys, hustled up and loaded our luggage onto a brass cart. The four of us headed for the main entrance, a stone archway that was lined with deer and elk antlers with white lights wrapped around them.

Finn was busy talking and pointing out things to Bria and Owen, but I looked around, examining everything and everyone around me. The valets and bellmen were hurrying to do their jobs, while the other guests were busy wrangling their kids and their luggage. I also reached out with my Stone magic, but the rocks that made up the hotel only murmured with all the fast-paced hustle and bustle of the thousands of people who stayed here every year, and I didn't detect any loud, obvious notes of malice, mayhem, or murder.

Still, I couldn't help but feel like someone was watching me.

A familiar ominous dread filled the pit of my stomach, and the spider rune scars embedded in my palms started itching and burning, almost in warning. I could have sworn that someone was staring at me. I looked around again, but the busy scene was the same as before, with guests, valets, and bellmen all caught up in their own luggage, tips, and chores. So my gaze wandered higher toward the upper levels of the hotel—

A white curtain twitched in a window on the third floor.

My head snapped up, and my eyes narrowed as I peered at that window, but the curtain had already dropped back into place, and I couldn't see who—if anyone—was standing behind it. Still, I stayed where I was, hoping that the curtain would move again, revealing exactly who was on the other side—

"Come on, Gin!" Finn called out. "Time's a'wasting!"

He waved at me before stepping through the arched entrance. Bria and Owen followed him, but I stayed where I was and looked up at the window again.

The white curtain remained perfectly still, although my uneasy sensation of being watched didn't vanish. If anything, it intensified the longer I looked up at the curtain, as though I were locked in a staring contest with someone I couldn't even see—

"Gin!" Finn called out again, hanging on to the side of the archway. "Come on, already!"

At his second, louder shout, guests and workers alike turned to stare at me, increasing my discomfort, and I had no choice but to duck my head and hurry forward. Still, as I stepped into the hotel, one thought kept running through my mind.

We'd just gotten here, and I already felt like we'd made a dangerous mistake.

I stepped through the archway and caught up with Bria and Owen, who were looking around the lobby while Finn talked to one of the cowboy clerks at the checkout counter.

The Bullet Pointe hotel might have seemed rustic from the outside, but Deirdre Shaw had certainly spared no expense remodeling the inside, which was all rich, luxe comfort. An enormous gray stone fireplace at least fifty feet wide took up one entire wall of the lobby, with padded rocking chairs and overstuffed sofas scattered in front of it. Given the cold outside, several folks were relaxing in front of the crackling flames and sipping tall mugs of hot chocolate and spiced apple cider, while other guests were perched on stools at a bar close to the fireplace, sipping harder brews.

Waiters dressed like cowboys and waitresses in saloon-girl costumes moved from the bar, through the crowd in front of the fireplace, and back again, serving and refilling drinks. Still more costumed waitstaff circulated through the lobby, dropping off plates of appetizers and small snacks, before heading back down a hallway to a nearby kitchen.

More chairs and sofas were clustered in groups throughout the lobby, for those who preferred to relax away from the heat of the fireplace, along with tables that

featured tall lamps made out of deer, elk, and moose antlers. Those same sorts of antlers also wrapped around the
wide wagon-wheel chandeliers that dropped down from
the ceiling.

But the rustic decor couldn't compete with all the
Christmas trees. More than a dozen of them were spread
throughout the lobby, ranging in size from cute three-
foot tabletoppers to the showstopping thirty-foot spruce
in the center of the lobby. No fakes here. These trees were
definitely genuine, given the strong tangy evergreen scent
that perfumed the air.

Each tree had a different theme and decorations to
match. One tree was its own toy box, with rag dolls, miniature trains, and tin soldiers dangling from its branches,
along with popcorn and cranberry strings. Another had
a cowboy theme, naturally, with miniature boots, lassos,
and silver spurs covering it from top to bottom. One was
its own winter wonderland, decked out in crystal snowflakes, glass snowmen, and silver tinsel. On and on they
went, each tree boasting more lights and ornaments than
the last.

I enjoyed holiday decorations, and trimming the tree
was one of my favorite things about Christmas, but it
always made me a little melancholy too, and I always
missed Fletcher a little more during this time of year. The
old man had always embraced the holiday spirit, decorating the Pork Pit with lights, tinsel, and mistletoe, con-
ducting toy and food drives, and buying me, Finn, and
the Deveraux sisters silly little gifts. This year, I felt even
bluer than usual, Fletcher's loss compounded by all these
unanswered questions about my mother.

"Hey, guys," Owen called out. "Come check this out."

I moved away from the Christmas trees and went over to Owen, who was peering at a large wooden display case. Bria walked over to us as well.

To my surprise, several pieces of old-fashioned jewelry lay inside the case, perched on black velvet stands. A square pendant, a wide choker, several rings, earrings, and bracelets, even a couple of antique hair combs. All the pieces were done in silverstone, and all were missing the most important things—the gemstones that went in the settings.

"The Hidden Treasure of Bullet Pointe," Owen rumbled, reading the information placard inside the glass. "This jewelry belonged to Sweet Sally Sue, a wealthy coal baroness who built the Bullet Pointe hotel and theme park back during the Great Depression."

Several photos were also propped up in the case, showing Sweet Sally Sue, a tall, slender woman with blue eyes and long auburn hair curled into fat ringlets. She must have loved her theme park and jewelry because in every single picture she was dressed like an old-fashioned saloon girl and decked out in all her gems.

I leaned closer, peering at the photos. A large, square sapphire went in the empty pendant, while the choker had featured three rows of diamonds. More sapphires and diamonds adorned the rest of the jewelry, along with generous helpings of rubies, emeralds, and other precious stones. Sweet Sally Sue hadn't skimped on her baubles. Even back then, the gemstones would have been worth a fortune.

"Sweet Sally Sue loved puzzles," Owen continued reading. "To celebrate what would have been Sweet Sally Sue's one hundred twenty-fifth birthday this year, her jewels were removed from their settings, placed into a black velvet bag, and hidden in the Bullet Pointe theme park, where they remain to this day. Whoever finds the bag of gemstones will be allowed to keep them, as well as their original settings. They will also receive a free lifetime pass to the theme park and hotel."

Owen stopped and blinked, as if the final sentence on the placard surprised him. He cleared his throat and finished reading. "The contest was the brainchild of the current resort owner, Deirdre Shaw."

I eyed the empty jewelry settings. They reminded me of an engagement ring that Fletcher had once given to Deirdre—one that she'd pried the diamond out of and sold on the sly.

"Hidden treasure? Up for grabs for whoever can find it in the theme park?" Bria huffed. "Sounds like a publicity stunt. A way to get more people to come to the park and spend their money searching for something that's not even there."

"Probably, knowing Deirdre," I said. "That, or she sold the stones to pay for her own creature comforts and upgrades to the hotel and didn't want anyone to realize what she'd done."

"Well, don't tell Finn," Bria warned, "or he'll have us all out scouring every park bench and trash can for those rocks."

"Actually," Finn said, coming up behind her, "that is on my to-do list."

Bria winced and faced him. He arched his eyebrows,

but she shrugged, realizing that it was too late to take back her snarky words.

"Anyway," Finn said, "I've got us all checked in, and the bellmen are taking our luggage up to our suites. The manager's expecting me upstairs in her office. Let's go see what she has to say for herself."

He held his arm out to Bria. "Shall we, my lady?"

She nodded and threaded her arm through his, and the two of them headed for the elevators in the back corner of the lobby.

I stayed by the display case, still staring down at the empty jewelry settings. They were just metal husks now, stripped of the stones that had made them so lovely, but the longer I looked at them, the more heavy worry weighed down my stomach. Even though Sweet Sally Sue was dead, and Deirdre along with her, I could almost feel their ghosts hovering in the air around me, whispering taunts that I couldn't quite make out.

"Gin?" Owen asked. "You ready to go?"

"Yeah," I said, once again trying to banish my nagging feeling that something was seriously wrong here. "As ready as I'll ever be."

❖ 7 ❖

Finn held the elevator for Owen and me, and the four of us rode up to the third floor, where the resort manager's office was.

The elevator opened up into a long hallway with rooms and offices branching off either side. Unlike the lavish lobby, this floor was much more Spartan and businesslike, with no antlers, wagon wheels, or other Western decor anywhere in sight. The only decorations were the photos that lined the walls, showing scenic views of the hotel, the theme park, and the lake that ringed them both, along with several posed, autographed glamour shots of rich and famous people who'd stayed here over the years.

I didn't care about the celebrities, but I would have liked to have lingered and studied the other photos, but Finn was in a rush, and he hurried right on past them to the corner office at the end of the hallway. He knocked on the closed door, then turned the knob and opened it a crack.

"Ms. Wyatt?" he called out. "It's Finnegan Lane. I believe you're expecting me."

"Of course, of course," a bright, cheery voice replied. "Y'all come right on in."

Finn opened the door the rest of the way, and the four of us trooped into the office.

Well, now I knew why the rest of the floor didn't have any Western decorations. Because they were all in *here*.

Every single thing in the office had some sort of Western vibe to it, from a pair of matching lamps shaped like silver spurs, to a chair that had fake rifles for arms, to a cowboy sculpture made out of lassos that had been, well, lassoed together. Silver studs trimmed all the dark green leather sofas and chairs, while bits of turquoise glimmered in the top of a glass coffee table. Paintings of cattle and cowboys covered the walls, and what looked like a genuine bearskin rug stretched across the floor in front of the fireplace in one corner.

The bear wasn't the only dead animal in here. A large buffalo head was mounted on the wall above the fireplace, with several smaller deer, elk, and moose heads flanking it. A stuffed red fox snarled on the wide mantel above the fireplace, while a bobcat glared up at it from the floor. Hooked to each animal was a small white tag that featured a location, along with a date. Somebody liked to hunt—and show off their trophies.

A desk stood in the opposite corner of the office, across from the dead-animal shrine that clustered around the fireplace. A phone, a monitor, a laptop, pens, notepads, papers. The desk was the only normal thing in sight.

Because the woman sitting behind it was anything *but* normal.

She got up and stepped forward, beaming at us. Instead of wearing a typical business suit, the woman was dressed like a cowgirl, from her pink plaid shirt studded with pearl buttons to her tight white jeans to her white boots with silver tips. A saucer-size silver buckle studded with a dazzling array of pink and white rhinestones clung to her white leather belt, along with two white holsters, both of which contained an old-fashioned, pearl-handled revolver. Her long blond hair was done up in two thick braids that trailed down her chest, and her eyes were a light, pretty green. The only thing she was missing was a white Stetson on her head. Oh, wait. There it was, hooked on an antler on another stuffed moose head close to the desk.

"Roxanne Wyatt, at your service, but y'all can call me Roxy," she chirped, her voice dripping with folksy charm. "Everyone round here does."

Finn stepped forward and shook her hand. "Roxy, pleased to meet you. These are my friends Bria Coolidge, Owen Grayson, and Gin Blanco."

Roxy came around the desk and walked down the line of us, nodding and shaking our hands. I was last, and she smiled and reached for my hand.

I felt her Fire magic the second her fingers touched mine.

Her hand was pleasantly warm, but I could sense the hotter, elemental magic that lay just below the surface of her skin. Roxy started to drop my hand, but I wrapped my free hand around both of our joined ones and gave her another long, vigorous shake, trying to determine exactly how much power she had.

I didn't sense an explosive, deadly burn, one that could incinerate you on the spot, not like I had with Mab Monroe and Harley Grimes, two other Fire elementals that I'd battled. Oh, Roxy could still light someone up and toast them alive with her magic, but it would take her a while. Her Fire power was moderate, at best.

Roxy gave me a strange look, and I flashed her a smile and finally dropped her hand.

She stared at me a second longer, then gestured over at a large wooden cabinet adorned with bone handles. "Can I offer y'all a drink? You must be thirsty after driving down from Ashland. Water, tea, coffee, something stronger?"

We all asked for waters, and Roxy passed out the bottles before telling us to make ourselves comfortable on the leather sofas.

Roxy plopped down in her desk chair again, cracked open her own water, and took a long swig before setting it aside and looking at Finn. "I was very sorry to hear about your mother's passing. Please accept my heartfelt condolences on your tragic loss."

I snorted. Roxy gave me a sideways look, but Finn leaned forward on the sofa, blocking her view of me, and cranked up the wattage on his smile.

"Thank you," he said. "How well did you know Deirdre?"

Roxy leaned back in her chair and laced her fingers

together over her sparkly belt buckle. "Well, Ms. Shaw hired me as the new resort manager about two months ago. I only ever actually met her in person a few times, although I emailed with her frequently about resort matters."

Finn nodded. "My mother told me that she owned the hotel and theme park, but I have to say that I was surprised to get the deed in the mail. And so quickly."

"Yes, well, Ms. Shaw called me up about a week before her, um, passing and told me that she was changing her will and leaving you the whole kit and caboodle." Roxy held her hands out wide. "I want to honor her wishes to the fullest, especially in death."

"I appreciate that," Finn murmured.

Roxy gestured at several neat stacks of papers on her desk. "I've prepared some information about the hotel and theme park for you, if you'd like to review it now. Or maybe a quick tour of the hotel first? I've got to go get ready for the high-noon show soon, but I could show you around for a few minutes right now."

"Actually, I'd like to see my mother's room," Finn said in a smooth voice. "Deirdre told me that there was a suite set aside for her personal use. I'd like to go through it and see her personal effects. And, of course, I'll be boxing those up and taking them with me when we leave."

Finn sold it well, and it sounded like a perfectly innocent request from a grieving son, instead of the plan we'd worked out to get access to Deirdre's suite without attracting any unwanted attention. Finn might own the resort, but this was still new, uncharted territory, and we needed to tread lightly until we knew exactly whom we were dealing with.

Roxy blinked, as if she hadn't expected Finn to ask for that right off the bat, and for a split second something almost like satisfaction flashed in her green gaze. My eyes narrowed. Why would she be so interested in our looking at Deirdre's suite?

But the emotion vanished, and she smiled again, her white teeth gleaming almost as big and bright as the rhinestones on her fancy belt buckle. "Sure thing. Just let me text Ira. He has the keys to all of the hotel's private areas, including Deirdre's suite. He should have time to show you where it is before he announces the high-noon show."

She pulled her phone out of her jeans pocket and sent a text.

"Who's Ira?" Bria asked.

Roxy hesitated and wet her lips, as if what she was about to say made her uncomfortable. "Ira Morris was the resort manager before me."

"Before you?" Owen asked. "And he still works here?"

"You might say that Ira is rather . . . attached to the place. He's been here for years and is quite the character. Why, I imagine that one day the old codger will drop dead in the middle of the theme park with his boots on." She let out a laugh, but a harsh, mocking undercurrent rippled through the sound.

"But if this Ira guy cares about the resort so much, then why did Deirdre hire you as the new manager?" Bria asked.

Roxy shrugged. "With the economy the way it's been the past few years, the hotel and theme park haven't been doing so well. People have been cutting back, and vacations are often the first things to go when folks are trying to save money. One of the reasons that Ms. Shaw decided to remodel the hotel and turn it into a luxury resort was to attract higher income folks, people who can still afford to spend money on trips, spa services, gourmet food, and the like."

"I suppose that makes sense," Finn said.

Roxy nodded. "Plus, poor Ira is a bit . . . old-school, shall we say, when it comes to things like marketing and publicity and getting folks to come to Bullet Pointe. He thinks that just putting up billboards along the interstates is advertising enough, but that just doesn't cut it in this day and age." She shook her head. "Ira did the best he could, bless his heart. But Ms. Shaw thought that it was time for some new ideas, new leadership, so that's why she brought me in."

Bless his heart? Well, that was the classic Southern insult and put-down. Roxy's voice practically dripped with sympathy, but I could hear what she wasn't saying. Ira hadn't been making enough money for Deirdre's liking, so she'd demoted him.

"Anyway," Roxy continued, "if y'all will follow me, I'll take you down to the lobby and show you where Ira's office is."

We all got to our feet. Roxy grabbed her white Stetson and plopped it on top of her head, completing her cowgirl outfit. She gave us all another bright smile and stepped out into the hallway. The others followed her, but I trailed behind, glancing around her office again. I realized something—the window beside her desk overlooked the main hotel entrance.

I went over, pulled back the white curtain, and glanced down. Sure enough, it was the same window and twitching curtain that I'd noticed from down on the ground. Hmm. Perhaps I hadn't imagined my earlier watcher after all. It made sense that Roxy would have been up here keeping an eye out for Finn, since he was her new boss and she probably wanted to keep her job. Still, the simple explanation didn't make me feel any better, and that uneasy dread once again bubbled up in my stomach.

"Gin!" Finn called out from the hallway. "Let's go!"

I could do nothing at the moment to ease my worry, so I let the curtain drop back into place and left the office.

My friends and I crowded into the elevator with Roxy and rode down to the lobby. Roxy chattered on the whole time about the hotel, the theme park, and the surrounding lake, spouting out so many facts and figures that my eyes quickly glazed over. Finn paid rapt attention, soaking up every single word she said, but I wasn't so enamored of our hostess. By the time the elevators doors opened less than a minute later, I was seriously considering snatching that white Stetson off her head and shoving the hat into her mouth just to get her to be quiet.

Owen noticed my annoyed expression and grinned and nudged me with his elbow. I rolled my eyes and shrugged at him.

"Of course y'all have seen the lobby already," Roxy said, stepping out of the elevator. "We have a fully stocked bar here, as well as lots of places where folks can sit and enjoy the decorations, along with the view."

She gestured at the floor-to-ceiling windows that lined

the back wall of the lobby. Through the glass, I spotted several paved paths that curved from the hotel down the hill to the theme park below. Neon lights flashed on a variety of rides, including several carousels, a couple of small roller coasters, and the dreaded swing ride that had made me puke my guts out way back when, as Finn had so gleefully reminded me. But the centerpiece of the park was a wide street with wooden storefronts and sidewalks, fashioned to look like something right out of the Old West, although I couldn't make out all the details from this height.

In the distance, off to the far west side of the park, the surface of Bullet Pointe Lake shimmered and rippled under the steady breeze. A large wooden dock stretched out like a finger into the lake, pointing to the dense woods on the opposite shore. Sleek, modern boats lined either side of the dock, along with a few canoes and kayaks. All the vessels bobbed up and down on the choppy waves, but no one was out on the lake, given how cold it was.

"And of course, our world-class spa is also located on this level," Roxy chirped again, pointing to a hallway that branched off the left side of the lobby. She looked at Bria and me. "Ladies, feel free to take advantage of any services and packages you like. I made you both standing reservations, so all you have to do is call down and let the spa folks know that you're coming."

"Oh, Gin definitely needs a seaweed wrap and some cucumber slices," Finn said. "At the very least. Maybe that'll get her to loosen up and relax this weekend."

Bria and Owen both snickered, while Roxy plastered a neutral smile on her face, not getting his joke. I glared at

Finn, but he'd already stuck his hands in his pants pockets and was whistling as he strode away.

Roxy spouted off a few more facts about the hotel's amenities, and eventually we wound up in the center of the lobby, close to the wooden display case that talked about Sweet Sally Sue and her legendary jewels.

"The treasure hunt seems like a great promotional tool," Finn said, eyeing the couple who were staring down into the case and using their phones to snap photos of the empty jewelry settings.

Roxy nodded. "Oh, yeah. Attendance at the park and hotel has gone up by ten percent since the treasure hunt started two months ago. It was a brilliant idea on Ms. Shaw's part."

"Has anyone actually found the gems yet?" Bria asked.

"Actually, about the treasure hunt . . ." Roxy's face scrunched up, and she glanced around, as though she didn't want to be overheard, before focusing on Finn again. "The contest was Ms. Shaw's idea, and she took care of everything, including hiding the jewels. She didn't happen to tell you exactly *where* in the park she might have put them, did she?"

Finn frowned. "No. Why?"

Roxy cast another furtive glance around. "Well, no one else seems to know where they are. And believe me, we've looked for them. We've *all* looked for them." Her voice dropped to a low mutter.

We? Who was *we*? And the way she said that made me think that Roxy had much more than just a casual inter- est in the hidden stones.

I studied her again, even more closely than I had up

in her office, but I saw the same exact thing as before—someone who seemed to enthusiastically embrace the cowboy theme of Bullet Pointe and was desperately trying to please her new boss.

Still, something about her struck me as inherently fake, like all those shiny rhinestones on her belt buckle. Like my friends and I were just another group of tourists and she was wearing her cowgirl costume and persona and putting on a show just for our benefit. I'd been fooled by Hugh Tucker, thinking that he was nothing more than Deirdre's lowly personal assistant. I wasn't going to be fooled again. I'd definitely be keeping an eye on Roxy Wyatt.

"Well, I'm sorry, but Deirdre didn't tell me anything about the treasure hunt or where she might have hidden the jewels." Finn winked at Roxy. "If she had, I would already be down in the park, getting them for myself."

He let out a big belly laugh, which Roxy returned with a giggle of her own, one that was a little too high-pitched and went on far too long to be genuine. Oh, yeah. She was definitely someone to watch.

Roxy glanced at her watch. "Aw, shoot. I'd love to show you guys around some more, but I really do have to get down to the park for the high-noon show. Y'all should come down and check it out. It's the highlight of the day for the guests and everyone who works in the theme park."

"Sure," Finn said. "I was planning on it. We'll be there. Sounds like fun."

She flashed him another smile. "Great. Is there anything else I can do for you in the meantime?"

"I still need the key to Deirdre's suite," he reminded her.

"Of course. If y'all will go down that hallway all the way to the very end, you'll see Ira's office tucked away in the back corner." Roxy pointed to a hallway that curved around the right side of the lobby. "I'll see you down at the show. Y'all take care now, ya hear?"

She tipped her white Stetson at us, hooked her thumbs into her jean pockets, and then turned and sauntered away. Seriously, she *sauntered*, walking with a slow, easy gait as though she were a real cowgirl out for a casual stroll.

"That woman is definitely up to something," I said.

My friends stared at me.

"Why would you say that?" Owen asked.

"Because no one is that naturally cheerful."

"She probably just wants to keep her job," Bria said. "I'd be nice to the new boss too, if I were in her shoes, er, boots."

I looked at Finn, expecting him to agree with the others, but his lips were puckered in thought.

"I'm going to have to go with Gin on this one," he said. "Roxy was nice, but she wasn't tripping all over herself, and she didn't do *nearly* enough ass-kissing if she was truly concerned about keeping her job. Foxy Roxy is not all that she seems."

Bria crossed her arms over her chest. "Foxy Roxy? Really?"

"Well, yeah. Did you not see that cowgirl getup she was wearing? And she was wearing it *really* well."

Bria glowered at him, but Finn plowed on ahead the way he always did.

"You know, while we're here, we should get you an outfit like that," he said in a suave tone.

She smiled sweetly at him. "I am not a cowgirl—I'm the sheriff in this here town. And why don't we get *you* an outfit instead? Why, you could dress up like a saloon girl. I think that would be the *perfect* look for you."

Finn grinned. "Only if you agree to slap me around with the long arm of the law, Sheriff."

"You wish."

"You bet I do." His grin widened, and he batted his eyes at her. "And I would totally dress up like a saloon girl. Anything for you, Sheriff."

Bria huffed and jabbed her elbow into his side, but Finn slung his arm around her shoulder, bent down, and whispered something in her ear that made her blush. Owen blanched and shook his head, as if trying to banish the thought of the two of them playing dress-up. Yeah, me too.

Finn and Bria headed toward the hallway to find Ira Morris, with Owen following them. I started in that direction as well, but a group of people chose that exact moment to cross the lobby, separating me from my friends.

Hugh Tucker was one of them.

* 8 *

I did a double take.

Black hair, black eyes, black goatee, tall, lean frame, expensive suit. It was the vampire all right, looking exactly the same as the last time I'd seen him at the shipping yard the night he'd kidnapped me. Tucker moved past me in an instant, in the middle of the crowd, but I was sure that it was him.

So sure that I palmed a knife, whipped around, charged forward . . . and ran straight into a luggage cart.

Clang.

I hit the brass rails hard and bounced off, landing on my ass. Suitcases tumbled off the cart and went flying in several directions, sliding across the stone floor like oversize shuffleboard disks. I started to scramble to my feet, but the giant bellman who'd been pushing the cart tripped over one of the larger suitcases and fell right on top of me, driving me back down to the floor.

"Oof!"

All the air rushed out of my lungs at the hard, bruising impact, and the bellman accidentally shoved his big, bony elbow right into my ribs, adding injury to injury. But I ignored the aches and pains, shoved the bellman off me, and staggered to my feet, my knife still in my hand. My head whipped left and right, scanning the lobby. Where was Tucker? All I needed was a dark, quiet spot and five minutes alone with him. . . .

I'd taken only three steps forward when I realized that everyone in the lobby was staring at me. The guests relaxing by the fireplace, the folks examining the Christmas trees, the people looking at the treasure-hunt display case, all the costumed clerks, bellmen, and wait-staff. All conversation had abruptly ceased, and the only sound was the Christmas carols playing in the background. *Fa-la-la-la-la* . . .

I stopped short and quickly slid my knife back up my sleeve before anyone noticed it. Then I forced myself to smile and sheepishly shrug my shoulders, silently apologizing for interrupting everyone's holiday fun. Slowly, all the folks in the lobby returned to their drinks, conversations, and chores.

I turned around, leaned down, and helped the fallen bellman to his feet. "Sorry about that. I just didn't, ah, see you standing there."

The bellman looked at me like I was crazy, since it was really, really hard to miss a seven-foot giant dressed like a cowboy and pushing a luggage cart. He sidestepped me and started picking up the suitcases I'd scattered across the lobby.

Owen rushed over to me, along with Finn and Bria.

"Gin!" Owen said. "Are you all right?"

"I'm fine," I muttered, rubbing my sore ribs and looking around the lobby again.

That group of businessmen and women were over by the elevators now, but Tucker wasn't with them. I scanned the rocking chairs in front of the fireplace, the ones around the Christmas trees, and even the stools at the bar, but I didn't spot the vampire anywhere. It was like Tucker had walked past me and then just vanished into thin air. The bastard was quick, but was he really *that* quick?

"What was that about?" Finn asked.

"I thought . . ." I started to tell him that I'd seen Tucker but changed my mind.

No one had spotted the vamp besides me, and he wasn't in the lobby now. Oh, my friends would believe me if I told them about Tucker, but now, I was starting to doubt myself. Given my admittedly suspicious and paranoid nature, not to mention my obsession with the Circle, it wasn't out of the realm of possibility to think that I'd just seen someone who looked like Tucker, instead of the man himself.

"Gin?" Owen asked again, his face creasing with concern.

"Sorry. Clumsy me, not watching where I was going."

I let out a brittle laugh, and Finn's eyes narrowed. He realized that I wasn't telling the truth. So did Owen and Bria. The three of them stared at me, waiting for me to fess up, but I remained silent.

"Well, let's go find this Ira person," Finn finally said.

"Sure," I said. "Lead the way."

He gave me one more suspicious look, then put his arm around Bria's shoulders again and headed back toward the hallway. Owen raised his eyebrows at me, but I shook my head, telling him that I didn't want to talk about it.

He held out his arm. I put mine through his, and together we walked out of the lobby. Still, right before we stepped into the hallway, I couldn't help but look back over my shoulder, wondering where Hugh Tucker was.

Or if he'd even been here to start with.

The hallway wrapped all the way around the perimeter of the hotel, with shops full of designer goods and gourmet restaurants branching off both sides of the wide stone corridor. Though it wasn't even noon yet, dozens of people moved in and out of the shops and restaurants, so it took us the better part of fifteen minutes to navigate the crowds and reach the office in the far back corner.

No one was in this remote part of the hotel, not so much as a janitor going about his daily duties, and everything was still and quiet. Way back here you couldn't even hear the Christmas carols from the lobby sound system. A piece of paper with *Ira Morris, Bullet Pointe resort manager* scrawled across it in thick black ink was taped up to the door, along with a single string of white holiday lights that continuously flickered as though they were going to burn out at any second. A sad testament to just how far Ira Morris had fallen.

"Wow, Deirdre really banished this guy, didn't she?" Bria said. "I don't think you could get any farther from the lobby and still be in the same building."

"Oh, I'm sure if there was a basement, Deirdre would have kicked him all the way down there," I said.

Finn gave us a warning look and knocked on the door.

"Come in," a low, gravelly voice called out.

Finn opened the door, and the four of us stepped inside. Unlike Roxy's lavish office, this was a small, cramped space, barely big enough for the rickety metal desk and two mismatched chairs squatting in front of it. Gray metal filing cabinets lined two of the walls, the drawers on each one partially open, since they couldn't possibly contain all the reams of paper that had been haphazardly stuffed inside them. Still more sheets were stacked on top of all the filing cabinets, curving upward like flimsy spiral staircases. The air even smelled like paper, old, dry, and slightly musty, but it wasn't an unpleasant aroma. It reminded me of Fletcher's office back before I'd started cleaning it out.

Where the furniture and paper mess stopped, the photos began. Color shots, black-and-white portraits, even some old tintypes, covered all the available space on the walls, the frames crammed in next to each other like the pieces of a jigsaw puzzle. All the photos showed some aspect of Bullet Pointe. The sun setting behind the hotel roof. The lights of the carousels and other theme-park rides flashing at night. People eating funnel cakes and playing carnival games.

The photos were far more candid and interesting than the celebrity glamour shots that had been tacked up to the walls outside Roxy's office. I was betting that they'd all been taken by Ira Morris himself, given the old cameras, lenses, and other photography equipment that perched here and there, like metal birds roosting in a paper tree.

"Just a second," a man said.

He seemed to be sitting behind the desk, although I couldn't actually see him, given the massive stacks of papers there, each towering pile wobbling in the faint breeze we'd created just by opening the door and stepping inside the office.

Owen noticed the leaning towers of papers and gently closed the door behind us, cutting off the treacherous breeze.

A pair of rough, weathered hands emerged, grabbing one stack of sheets, then another, and moving them to opposite sides of the desk, revealing the man in the middle of the mess. No wonder I hadn't been able to see him before. He was a dwarf, a little more than five feet tall, with a thick, strong body. His black hair had been cropped close to his skull and was shot through with a generous amount of silver, making the short, stubby strands look like needles poking up out of his scalp. His ebony skin was a shade lighter than his hair, while his eyes were a dark hazel. Given the deep lines that grooved around his eyes and mouth, he was probably more than one hundred years old, although it was always hard to tell a dwarf's true age.

Just like Roxy, he didn't look like your typical resort manager, especially since he was wearing a holiday sweater, bright green with a giant red poinsettia in the center. As I watched, small red lights winked on one by one, ringing his chest and illuminating the tips of the poinsettia before flashing in unison. I didn't think it was possible, but the dwarf's sweater was even more garish than Jonah McAllister's had been. At least the sleazy lawyer's garment hadn't had blinking lights on it.

"Just a sec," he repeated, his voice more sharp, twangy Western than soft, drawling Southern.

The dwarf shuffled some more stacks from one side of his desk to the other, frowning in concentration as he looked at all of them, as though they were of the utmost importance. I didn't see how they were any different from any of the other papers crammed into the office, but this wasn't my work space to judge. Finally, he set the last of the sheets aside, adding them to the teetering stack on his left and looked up at us.

"What do you want?" he growled.

Not exactly a warm welcome, but Finn was undeterred. He plastered a smile on his face, stepped forward, and held out his hand. "I'm Finnegan Lane, the new owner of the resort."

"Ira Morris," the other man snapped. "So you're Deirdre's spawn."

Finn winced a little, but he kept his smile fixed on his face. "Yeah."

"Hmm."

The simple sound had a whole lot of judgment in it. I got the impression that Ira hadn't thought too highly of Deirdre.

Ira ignored Finn's outstretched hand, crossed his arms over his chest, and leaned back in his chair, which let out an ominous creak, as if it were about to collapse. "And who are your friends?"

Finn introduced us. Ira glanced at Owen and me,

dismissing us outright, but he stopped and did a double take when he finally looked at Bria.

The dwarf studied her for several seconds. "Your last name is Coolidge?"

"Yeah," Bria replied warily. "Why?"

Ira stared at her for several more seconds, then his gaze darted around the office, as though he were looking for something. His gaze moved along the wall to his right, although I couldn't tell what stack of papers or photo he might be searching for.

He finally shrugged. "No reason." He leaned forward in his chair, making it creak again. "I'll ask again. What do you want?"

His twangy tone was as brusque as ever. Finn frowned and slowly lowered his hand to his side, looking a bit crestfallen. No ass-kissing here. I hid a smile.

Finn cleared his throat. "Roxy said that you had the key to my mother's suite and could show me where it is. I'd like to go up there after the high-noon show and look through her things, if I could."

Ira snorted. "I reckon you can do anything you want to, since it's your resort now."

The dwarf shoved away from his desk, and his chair slapped back against yet more stacks of paper, rattling them and the photos on the wall above. Ira yanked open a drawer in the middle of his desk and pawed through the junk inside. After the better part of a minute, he came up with an old-fashioned iron skeleton key, which he tossed on top of his desk.

"That's the key to Deirdre's fancy suite. Top floor. You

look like a smart enough guy. I'm sure you can find it all by yourself."

Finn blinked. He'd expected the dwarf to ooze cowboy charisma, charm, and cheer, just like Roxy had. But I kind of liked Ira's surliness. At least he was honest about hating us. After all of Tucker and the Circle's machinations, I appreciated honesty more than ever before.

"But Roxy said—" Finn started.

Ira glared at him. "I don't give a damn about what Roxy said. I have a show to narrate. I don't have time to take his royal highness around."

Finn's mouth opened and closed, but no words came out.

Ira snorted again, then stood up and turned sideways, deftly maneuvering through the narrow corridors created by all the paper towers, some of which were almost as tall as he was. Finn, Bria, and Owen all fell back out of his way, but I held my ground, forcing him to stop and peer up at me.

He started to barrel right on past me, but I crossed my arms over my chest and widened my stance. He realized that I wasn't going to move until I was good and ready, and he stopped and stared at me a little more closely, his hazel eyes narrowing in thought, and causing more lines to crease his craggy, weathered face.

"Blanco, right?" he barked.

"Yeah."

"Hmm."

There was that harsh, judgmental sound again. Usually, it took me at least a few minutes to piss people off.

Then again, I was willing to bet that just about everything pissed off Ira Morris since his demotion.

"Well?" he snapped. "Are you going to move, or are you just going to stand there all day?"

I stared him down a moment, letting him know that I wasn't afraid of him, before finally stepping aside. The dwarf huffed, moved past me, threw open the door, and stormed away. His quick motions made a violent breeze gust through the tiny office, causing sheets of paper to swirl through the air like snowflakes, before slowly settling back down on top of their respective piles again.

I peered out the door and watched the dwarf disappear around the curving hallway. Then I looked back over my shoulder at Finn.

"Wow," I drawled, "I've never seen such enthusiastic ass-kissing in all my life. He just *loved* you."

Bria and Owen both snickered.

"Shut it, Gin," Finn growled, then grabbed the key off the desk and stomped out of the office just like Ira Morris had.

❋ ¶ ❋

Now that we had the key to Deirdre's suite, I wanted to go up there immediately and start searching through her things, but Finn had other ideas. He insisted that we walk through the theme park and stake out a good seat for the high-noon show. So we headed back to the lobby, then meandered along one of the paved paths that wound from the hotel down the hill to the theme park in the valley below.

Bullet Pointe boasted all your usual attractions. Carousels, roller coasters, and other rides. Food carts serving corn dogs, nachos, and my favorite, funnel cakes. Shops selling T-shirts, boots, commemorative shot glasses, and other merchandise and souvenirs, all of which were imprinted with the theme park's rune—a cowboy hat with two old-fashioned revolvers crossed over it.

Everything had some sort of Western theme, and signs shaped like grinning cowboys, prancing horses, and prickly cacti adorned practically everything, including the old-fashioned iron streetlights that lined the walkways.

Unlike the hotel, Deirdre must not have bothered with remodeling or upgrading anything in the park, since all the booths, rides, and signs had the same worn, weathered look as I remembered from that long-ago trip with Finn and Fletcher.

But the centerpiece of the theme park was Main Street. A fifty-foot-tall wooden water tower, with the words *Bullet Pointe Main Street* painted on it in faded, rusty red, marked the entrance. All of the park walkways fed into the long, wide packed-dirt street, which resembled the main drag of an old-timey Western town, complete with wooden sidewalks and storefronts on either side. Every single bit of lettering on the stores was done in a Western font, adding to the illusion that you'd stepped back in time to the Old West.

Alleys ran in between the storefront blocks, leading to other areas with more food carts and souvenir shops, with more walkways that led to the park's rides and other attractions, forming a giant circle. At the far end, Main Street opened up into more of a large square, with several sets of gray, rickety-looking wooden bleachers blocking off the area.

The Main Street shops and restaurants were much larger and nicer than those in the rest of the theme park and naturally featured much higher prices. They all continued the Western theme, from the Feeding Trough (a barbecue restaurant) to the Gumdrop (a candy shop) to the Silver Spur (a clothing, hat, and boot store) to the

Gold Mine (a place where you could pan for gold and gems and then design your own settings for them, as well as buy premade rings, necklaces, and the like).

But the largest storefront belonged to the Good Tyme Saloon, an old-fashioned saloon where you could get sarsaparillas, along with more common sodas, beers, and mixed drinks to wet your whistle, according to the tin sign in the window. The saloon was also one of several establishments that put on a show every hour on the hour. The *plinka-plinka* sounds of a piano that desperately needed tuning drifted outside, and through the storefront window I could see several women dressed as saloon girls swishing their brightly colored skirts and dancing across the floor. Still more people in costume—everyone from cowboys to gamblers to gold miners—strolled up and down the sidewalks, tipping their hats to folks, posing for pictures, and spouting cornball phrases in keeping with their characters.

"Get me some crackers to go with all this cheese," Bria muttered, watching a giant cowboy amble by in a deliberate bowlegged stance.

"Well, I think that it's fun," Owen said. "Cheesy, certainly, but fun too."

I looked at him. "I didn't realize that you were such a cowboy fan."

He grinned. "Are you kidding? What kid doesn't want to be a cowboy? Ride the range on your trusty horse, sing songs around the campfire, sleep outside under the stars, the whole shebang." He looked out over the crowds of people moving up and down the sidewalks. "My parents actually brought Eva and me here on vacation once. She was just a baby, so she doesn't remember it, but I do. It was one of the best trips we ever took. My mom even bought me a real Stetson. I kept it right up until she and my dad died . . ."

Owen's voice trailed off, and the smile slipped from his face. Due to his father's gambling debts, his parents had died in a fire set by Mab Monroe when he was a teenager, leaving him and Eva homeless.

I reached over and squeezed his hand, and he flashed me a grateful grin for pulling him out of those old, painful memories.

"Fun? It's not just fun," Finn said, his green eyes bright with excitement. "It's fantastic! I'm so glad we came down here this weekend. It's the best Christmas vacation ever!"

As if all the cowboy stuff weren't cheesy enough, Main Street was also decked out for the holidays. Glittering strands of red, green, and silver tinsel wrapped around all the streetlights, making them look like giant candy canes. Still more tinsel adorned the iron benches that lined the sidewalks. Most of the storefront windows had been decorated with pinecones, mistletoe, and giant snowflakes that pulsed with bright white light. Even the cowboys and other costumed characters had small nods to the holiday season, like red bandannas patterned with Santa Clauses, reindeer, and snowmen tied around their necks. It was a weird mash-up of cowboy and Christmas, but I found it oddly charming.

"C'mon," Finn said, shooing us forward with his hands. "I want to get a good seat for the show."

We fell in with the stream of people heading toward the bleachers at the far end of Main Street. Space heaters were set up along the sidewalks, with several more clustered all around the bleachers, although they did little to drive back the harsh winter chill. Still, despite the cold, there was a full house for the show. I wanted to go up to the top row of bleachers, so that I had a bird's-eye view of everything, but Finn insisted that we sit in the front row and so he elbowed a couple of people out of the way to make it happen. So that's where we ended up.

The crowd chattered, and several folks raised their phones, snapping photos of all the cowboys and other costumed characters who were cordoning off the street for the upcoming show. I pulled out my phone and snapped some pictures too. Not because I wanted any mementos, but just in case Hugh Tucker was lurking around somewhere. I hadn't spotted the sneaky vampire during our stroll through the theme park, but maybe I'd get lucky, find him in a crowd shot, and reassure myself that I wasn't going crazy and that my rampant paranoia wasn't finally getting the best of me.

"Isn't this great?" Finn asked, bouncing up and down on the bleacher like a kid hopped up on sugar.

"Yeah," Bria said. "Great."

She sighed and stuck her chin down into the collar of her navy peacoat, trying to stay warm and obviously wishing that the show were already over. Owen's lips twitched, as if he was holding back a laugh at Bria's obvious misery. She gave him a dirty look, which only made his lips twitch again.

Finn flagged down a guy selling concessions and bought a bag of caramel-apple popcorn for Bria and himself. Owen got a popcorn too, but I shook my head when he offered me some. Popcorn wasn't my favorite thing. Besides, I was still too busy scanning the crowd to think about food.

I didn't spot Tucker anywhere, and no one seemed to be paying any attention to my friends and me. So I sat back and tried to relax, even though I couldn't shake the feeling that the vampire was here somewhere, watching us.

The earsplitting *screech* of a sound system's being turned on filled the air, making everyone wince, and Ira Morris stepped into view, taking up a position on a small dais off to one side of the bleachers. The dwarf still wore his garish Christmas sweater, which he'd topped off with a red suit jacket and red suspenders that hooked into his black jeans. Black cowboy boots covered his feet, while a black bowler hat with a red ribbon around the brim perched on his head. He looked like he belonged in an old-fashioned barbershop quartet, but the odd outfit suited him.

Ira made a big show of hooking his fingers through his red suspenders, then letting go of them, so that they snapped back into place. He gave the crowd a wide grin, looking far more cheerful than he had in his office, and grabbed a microphone from a passing saloon girl. A hush fell over the crowd, and Ira kept grinning until everyone had quieted down.

"Why, hello there, ladies and gentlemen," the dwarf drawled in his low, gravelly voice that would have been perfectly at home in a hundred old Western movies. "Welcome to our little corner of the world, Bullet Pointe. Or home, as we like to call it."

He let out a hearty chuckle. Bria looked at me and rolled her eyes, as if to say, *Really? There's more of this?* Cheesy theatrics weren't my thing either, but Owen seemed to be enjoying it, and Finn was completely enraptured, his gaze fixed on Ira, not even looking at the popcorn he was stuffing into his mouth. If Finn was focused on the show, then he wasn't thinking about Deirdre and all her betrayals, so I supposed that was some progress. I'd take what I could get, even if I had to suffer through a corny show.

"Now, since y'all are new here, you might not be aware, but we have some outlaws in these parts," Ira continued. "Some of the meanest, nastiest folks you'll ever come across. The infamous Dalton gang."

As soon as he finished saying the word *gang*, loud whoops, shouts, and hollers sounded, and a dozen men on horses erupted out of one of the alleys, riding straight into the middle of Main Street, firing their guns up into the air. The crowd gasped and ducked, even though they knew that it was all just part of the show.

The Dalton gang kept circling their horses around and around, shooting off their weapons. Each of them was dressed like a typical cowboy in boots, chaps, and hats, but one guy was bigger and broader than all the rest, a giant who was well over seven feet tall. He was a handsome man, with wavy, dark brown hair and a heavy five o'clock shadow already on his chin. He was dressed all in black, from his boots, jeans, and shirt to the black-and-white paisley bandanna looped around his neck and the black Stetson on his head. He was also a bit more enthusiastic about firing his gun up into the air than the other gang members. Ah, the villain of the piece.

Finally, the gang members lowered their weapons and marched their horses over to a long wooden rail outside the Feeding Trough barbecue restaurant. They dismounted, tied the animals to the rail, and ambled back over to the wide-open space in front of the bleachers.

"Now, there's a rumor going around that Brody Dalton, the leader of the gang, has a mind to rob the bank when the next shipment of gold comes into town," Ira continued.

The muscled giant in black spun his silver revolver around and around on his finger as he paced back and forth in front of the bleachers.

"I'm tired of living out on the range with nothing but hardtack and stale biscuits to eat," Brody Dalton said in a deep baritone. "I'm aiming to take what I want, and what I want is gold—and lots of it."

He didn't look at the crowd, even though everyone knew that he was talking to us.

He pointed his revolver in the direction of the Gold Mine jewelry store, which apparently also doubled as the town bank in this scenario. The other gang members gathered around, all of them eager to follow his lead.

"But, Brody," one of the other giants called out, "what about Sheriff Roxy?"

On cue, the swinging double doors to the saloon opened, and Roxy Wyatt strode outside. She was still wearing the same cowgirl getup as before, with one notable addition—a bright silver sheriff's star was pinned to her chest. Sheriff Roxy took off her white hat and waved it back and forth in front of her face, as though she were hot, despite its being all of twenty-five degrees outside. But I supposed in this little drama, it was always a hot, sunny day in the Old West.

"I ain't worried about Sheriff Roxy," Brody sneered.

"Why, I've got pet rattlesnakes bigger than she is. Ain't that right, boys?"

The gang members snickered. Sheriff Roxy magically seemed to notice Brody and his crew, and she stalked in their direction, her hands dropping to the pearl handles of the two revolvers strapped to her waist.

Ira cleared his throat, his voice far less enthusiastic than before. "Sheriff Roxy had heard the rumors too, and she decided to give Brody one last warning about what would happen if he tried to rob the bank."

"Brody!" Roxy called out. "This is your last warning. Don't go causing no trouble now. Or I'll have to put you down quicker than a cold sarsaparilla on a hot summer day."

The giant snickered and crossed his arms over his chest. "You talk big, but you couldn't hit the broad side of a barn with those fancy guns of yours."

Roxy glanced over her shoulder. I hadn't noticed it until now, but a couple of guys were busy setting out glass bottles on top of one of the storefront roofs. As soon as they were done, the men skedaddled out of view, leaving the bottles behind, a good hundred feet from where Roxy was standing.

Roxy turned back to Brody and grinned. "That's where you're dead wrong, Brody. I'm the best shot in this here county, and I'll prove it to y'all, right here, right now."

Even though I knew exactly what was coming next, I still jumped with the rest of the crowd when Roxy pulled her revolvers out of their holsters, spun around, and started firing.

Crack!

Crack! Crack!
Crack! Crack! Crack!

One by one, the glass bottles shattered. Not only that, but they actually *exploded*, with flashes of elemental Fire shooting up into the sky. Even across the distance, I could feel the hot blasts of magic rippling through the air. Roxy might have only moderate power, but she'd found a way to make it count.

"Hey," I whispered, "she's using *real* bullets. Coated with *real* elemental magic."

Finn and Owen both shushed me, totally into the show. Bria muttered something about being cold and slouched down a little more. But I stared at Roxy, far more interested in her than before. Sure, she'd probably performed this act and had made those same trick shots dozens of times before, but it was still impressive. She was a sharpshooter in every sense of the word. And I'd never seen anyone use silverstone bullets coated with elemental magic before. Not just trick shots, but deadly ones at that.

Roxy showed off more of her sharpshooting skills, hitting more glass bottles, tin signs, and even shearing several lassos in two. She didn't just aim at things head-on and hit them like a normal shooter. She put her guns behind her back or over her shoulders or even down at her knees, twisting into more and more elaborate and impossible positions, with the targets getting smaller and smaller all the while. She even shot a cigar out of a gambler's mouth using a mirror.

The crowd was appropriately impressed, and Brody and his gang were appropriately slack-jawed, right up until Roxy put her empty guns away and told them to git out of town—or else.

In return, Brody stomped around and made threatening noises that Roxy hadn't seen the last of him and blah, blah-blah, blah-blah. The scene ended with Brody and the other gang members untying their horses from the rail and leading them away under Sheriff Roxy's watchful gaze.

Ira brought his microphone back up to his lips. "Sheriff Roxy was no fool, and she knew that Brody would be back, just as soon as a payroll shipment of gold came into the bank." He paused. "And now, folks, we're going to take a short break, so feel free to grab some more concessions while we set the stage for the final act of our little drama."

Ira disappeared, and the concessions people reappeared, offering another round of popcorn, boiled peanuts, hot chocolate, and the like. This time, Finn bought a candy apple, while Bria gave in and got a wad of cherry cotton candy. Owen sipped a sarsaparilla served in an old-fashioned glass bottle, but I raised up my phone and took some more shots of the crowd, still searching for Hugh Tucker, although I didn't see him anywhere—

Suddenly, a great whooping and hollering rang out, along with the *crack-crack-crack* of gunfire. A few seconds later, a stagecoach erupted out of one of the alleys and careened out into the middle of Main Street, with the members of the Dalton gang hot on its tail on horseback.

The gang quickly overtook the stagecoach and forced it to stop, right in front of the bleachers. Gasps rang out from the audience, especially when the gang members tossed the driver off the stagecoach. But the guy did a beautiful pratfall onto what looked like a suspiciously soft patch of hay-covered dirt. Probably the same spot he'd landed on a hundred times before.

The gang pried open the stagecoach door, and two of the members reached inside, then set a locked strongbox on the ground, which Brody dramatically busted open with the butt of his gun. The giant reached down and pulled out a fistful of fake gold coins, which he let slide through his fingers and trickle back down into the box.

"Whoo-eee, boys! We're set for life!" Brody yelled to the enthusiastic cheers of the gang.

The crowd was completely caught up in the story, and pretty much everyone—even Bria—was perched on the edge of their seat, wondering what was going to happen next.

Just as Brody and his gang were trying to figure out how to load the strongbox of gold onto one of their horses, Sheriff Roxy came running out of the saloon, along with several good-guy cowboys. She sprinted across the sidewalk, leaped up onto one of those long wooden rails, and flew through the air, landing perfectly on top of her waiting horse.

Shock jolted through me. I recognized that smooth, graceful acrobatic style. Those were more or less the same moves that Ms. Fedora had used when she'd jumped the fence outside Jonah McAllister's mansion a few days ago. I'd thought that Roxy might be up to something, but I'd never expected her to be an assassin for the Circle.

"Son of a bitch!" I muttered.

Several people shushed me, and Ira Morris gave me a

particularly dirty look for daring to interrupt the show's grand finale, especially with such bad language. Finn, Owen, and Bria all stared at me, but I shook my head, and they all went back to the show. Me too, with my gaze now firmly fixed on Sheriff Roxy.

Roxy galloped down the street, threw herself off her horse, and whipped out her trusty revolvers. "Surrender, Brody!" she yelled, pointing her guns at the giant outlaw. "Don't make me shoot you!"

"You'll never take me alive, Sheriff!" Brody shouted back, pulling out his own guns.

After that, it was like an epic Western movie shoot-out, as *everyone* pulled out their guns and started firing at *everyone* else. All of them using blanks, this time, of course. Costumed characters poured out of the saloon, the jewelry store, and all the other shops to take part in the big showdown, with Brody Dalton and his gang facing off against Sheriff Roxy and the good folks of Bullet Pointe.

I'll give the performers their props. They went all out in selling the show, with exaggerated facial expressions, bloodcurdling screams, and several impressive swan dives from the second-story balconies and even the storefront roofs onto strategically placed hay bales and other soft surfaces below. A couple of dwarves even dropped down into a couple of conveniently placed water troughs and came up sputtering. I shivered. Even though it was all an act, that water had to be frigid today, no matter how many space heaters were in and around Main Street.

The gang members were quickly overpowered by the townspeople, who loomed over them with shotguns, rifles, and pitchforks, and soon Brody was the only out-law left standing.

"Give it up, Brody!" Roxy shouted, slowly advancing on the giant, her revolvers still pointed at him. "You've got no place to go!"

"Never!" Brody hissed back.

The giant's head whipped left and right, searching for an escape route. Then he did something completely unex-pected—he sprinted directly at the bleachers. The crowd gasped, but Brody ignored their surprise and popped off a few more blank shots at Roxy, who gracefully rolled be-hind a water trough for cover.

"You'll never take me alive, Sheriff!" Brody repeated, still racing toward the crowd.

He skidded to a stop right in front of the bleachers, as if just realizing that people were sitting there. His dark brown gaze locked with mine, and a smile spread across his face.

Before I knew what was happening, Brody Dalton grabbed my arm, hauled me to my feet, and pressed his gun against my temple.

✻ 10 ✻

"You're coming with me!" Brody yelled in my ear.

"I don't think so, sugar."

I didn't even think about what I was doing. I just reacted the way I normally did anytime someone shoved a gun up against my head and tried to take me hostage.

Violently.

I rammed my elbow into the giant's stomach three times in rapid succession. Brody let out a loud *oof!* of pain and surprise and lost his grip on me. Before he could recover, I whipped around, yanked the gun out of his hand, and slammed it right back into his face.

Crunch.

The giant might have been shooting blanks during the battle scene, but his revolver was real and heavy enough to break his nose, especially with the force I put behind it. Brody yelped and staggered back, clutching his hands to his suddenly lumpy, swollen nose. Blood gushed down his face and soaked into the black-and-white paisley bandanna tied around his neck. The giant's blood also spattered all over the revolver, which I was still holding up high, ready to slam it into his face again.

For a moment, there was stunned silence.

Brody stared at me with wide, shocked eyes, as did the rest of the performers and everyone in the audience. Even the horses looked at me sideways. I'd forgotten about everything else when I was taking down Brody, but now dozens of people and animals were eyeing me, the crazy woman who'd just ruined this grand Western show by being, well, *me*.

Ira hustled over and plucked the revolver out of my hand before I could do any more damage with it. "Let's give a round of applause to this little lady who, um, saved the day in Bullet Pointe!"

Polite, scattered applause broke out, but everyone in the audience kept shooting me wary glances, and the cast looked particularly sour. Brody glared at me with hate-filled eyes, even as he ripped off his bandanna to wipe the blood off his face and his still-swelling nose.

"Why don't you give a nice wave to the crowd, little lady," Ira said in a loud, pointed voice, jabbing his elbow into my side much the same way that I'd done to Brody.

Despite his one-hundred-plus years, the dwarf was still strong, and the blow dug into my ribs. I started to retaliate, but Ira gave me a sharp warning glare. So I gritted my teeth, raised my hand, and gave a short, jerky wave. No more applause sounded, though, and I hurried back over to the bleachers and sat down next to Owen, hunching my shoulders and trying to make myself as small and invisible as possible.

Owen looked at me, a grin spreading across his face. "You know," he said, "I think there just might be a new sheriff in this here town."

"I think you're absolutely right," Bria chimed in, enjoying my misery as much as he was.

"Shut it, you two," I groused, crossing my arms over my chest.

Finn leaned forward, staring at me. "You just had to go and ruin the show, didn't you, Gin?"

"I didn't do it on purpose," I groused again. "He had a gun."

"Which was loaded with blanks." Finn snorted. "He had a *toy*."

Still, he grinned and tossed his last few pieces of popcorn at me, letting me know that all was forgiven. Well, at least my friends thought that my embarrassing myself was freaking hilarious, because the Bullet Pointe performers certainly did not. They all gave me another round of sour looks before walking down the street and heading back inside the shops to take up their previous stations. Naturally, Brody was the angriest of all, giving me a *drop-dead-bitch* glare before he stomped off toward one of the alleys.

Ira stared at me, his arms crossed over his chest, his mouth puckered in thought. Then he shook his head, as if dismissing me as just some crazy lady, and started messing with the sound system close to the dais, putting his microphone away and turning everything off until the next show.

Sheriff Roxy was the only one who wasn't upset by my showstopping antics. Even though I'd ruined her big, triumphant moment to play the hero, she seemed genuinely amused by the whole thing, and she even went so far as to grin and tip her white Stetson at me. The move was eerily similar to how she'd saluted me with her gun outside McAllister's mansion, further convincing me that she was the lawyer's would-be assassin.

But instead of charging over and confronting her, I gave her a sheepish grin and shrug in return, pretending that I was still clueless about her real identity—and how dangerous she was.

Roxy nodded back at me, then turned on her bootheel and hurried down the street, heading after Brody. I wanted to know what the two of them might say about me, so I decided to go be a fly on that wall.

"You know," I said, "I really should go apologize to Brody for overreacting like that."

Finn nodded. "That would be a nice gesture." He waggled his eyebrows at me. "And you should totally ask Brody for his autograph. You know, soothe his bruised ego and busted nose a little bit."

He snickered, and Bria and Owen chuckled right along with him.

I rolled my eyes. "Fine, fine. I'll go make nice with the giant. You guys go check out the shops on Main Street, and I'll come find you in a few minutes. Okay?"

We all got to our feet, and Finn, Bria, and Owen fell into the stream of folks leaving the bleachers and wandering back toward the storefronts. I started to head toward the alley that Brody and Roxy had disappeared into, but Ira rounded the dais and blocked my path.

The dwarf crossed his arms over his chest and spread his legs wide, as if bracing for a confrontation. "Who are you?" he demanded. "And what are you and your friends *really* doing here?"

"I told you before. My name is Gin Blanco."

I waited, wondering if Ira might be on the Circle's payroll just like Roxy was, but he didn't show a flicker of recognition at my name. He was either a good actor or he really had never heard of me before.

"And Finn told you why we're here," I continued. "He's Deirdre's son, and he owns the resort now."

Ira huffed. "That city slicker's name might be on the deed, but Bullet Pointe belongs to *me*." He stabbed his finger into his chest, right where his heart was. "Sweet Sally Sue herself took me in and gave me a job when I was just a teenager, and I've been here ever since. I'm the one who's kept this place running all these years, despite Deirdre Shaw's best efforts to the contrary."

My eyes narrowed. "What do you mean? What do you know about Deirdre?"

He huffed again. "That she was a spoiled, selfish brat who didn't give a damn about anything other than herself. She certainly didn't care about the theme park and the people like me who love it, who depend on it to put food on their tables and clothes on their kids' backs. All she did was live the high life in her fancy suite and squeeze as much money as possible out of the hotel and park. And then, when she decided that I wasn't making her enough money anymore, she replaced me with that, that *phony*."

Well, I couldn't argue with his assessment of Roxy. She was a phony, right down to those flashy colored rhinestones on her oversize belt buckle.

"And now you and your friends come here," Ira continued in his rant, "and the first thing you do is ruin the high-noon show. Absolutely *ruin* it. I saw your face during the show. You thought it was silly, stupid even. But the performers train hard for it, and they like showing off their skills and getting cheers and being asked to pose for pictures. Not to mention how much the audience enjoys it, especially the kids. But none of that happened today, thanks to *you*, Ms. Gin Blanco."

I'd never thought about the show that way before, how hard the performers worked to put it on every single day, and how much enjoyment they and the audience got out of it. I shifted on my feet, guilt weighing down my stomach. "I really am sorry about that. I didn't mean to ruin the show."

Ira slapped his hands on his hips. "Sorry? You're *sorry*? No, *I'm* sorry. I'm sorry for hoping for one second that your friend Mr. Lane might actually be different from his mama. That he might actually give a damn about this place and do what's best for it and all the people who work here."

I opened my mouth to say that Finn was different from Deirdre, but Ira snapped up his hand, cutting me off.

"Forget it," he growled. "I have work to do. I don't have time for the likes of you, you . . . *menace.*"

Ira gave me another angry glare, then turned and stomped off, disappearing into the crowd.

I stood by the empty bleachers, digesting his tongue-lashing, which ironically enough was similar to what I'd said to Jonah McAllister a few days ago. And just like mine had been back then, Ira's words were all too true now.

I didn't care about Bullet Pointe and what happened to it, and neither did Finn. We'd come down here to get answers about Deirdre and the Circle. Nothing more, nothing less. This was just a lark for us, just a holiday, just a couple of days' respite from our own lives, problems, and worries back in Ashland.

But to Ira Morris, this resort with all its costumed characters, cheesy decorations, and corny shows was his home, and he was determined to fight for it. Even if he might still secretly be working for Tucker and the Circle, I admired the dwarf's conviction. It was the same way I felt about the Pork Pit and all of Ashland. Once the weekend was over, and my friends and I had our answers, I'd talk to Finn about his plans for Bullet Pointe, about making sure that the resort continued on.

But for right now, Roxy was here, and she was the only lead I had on Hugh Tucker and the Circle. So I squared my shoulders, left the bleachers behind, and set off down Main Street, more than ready to find some answers about what was really going on in these here parts.

I headed for the alley that Brody and Roxy had walked into, which was one of several that ran between the storefront blocks that made up the two sides of Main Street. A few of the performers were leaving the alley and heading back out to the street, and they all gave me the stink-eye as they passed me. It made me feel as though I were still back in Ashland, still back at the Pork Pit, being glared at by the underworld bosses while I served up barbecue. Always popular, yep, that was me. Making enemies wherever I went.

I ducked my head and hurried on. Just before I reached the end of the alley, I glanced back over my shoulder, but no one else was in the corridor, so I sidled up and peered around the corner, staring out into the space beyond.

A large square had been converted into a break and staging area for the performers and shows. A series of open-air wooden pavilions spread out across the square, each one a different station. Racks of cowboy, saloon-girl, gambler, and other costumes were lined up in one pavilion, along with several lit mirrored vanity tables so everyone could put on their beauty marks, scars, and other makeup to get fully into character. Metal footlockers for folks to store their personal possessions and clothes took up most of another pavilion. Still more supplies were housed in the other areas, everything from boots and high heels, to strongboxes full of fake guns and ammunition, to pickaxes, saws, and other tools, to lassos that were curled up like thick rattlesnakes in plastic barrels.

The stagecoach that had been used in the high-noon show was also parked back here, complete with piles of luggage that had been lashed to the top. A dirt path led off to the right and over to a rusty red barn where the horses were kept, and the air smelled like manure, dust, and hay. A ten-foot chain-link fence topped with razor wire cordoned off the back of the square, and through the trees, I could see the dark blue surface of the lake glinting in the distance.

Since the show was over, all the performers were back at their usual stations on Main Street, and the square was empty except for Brody, who sat in front of one of the vanity-table mirrors, peering at his broken nose. Roxy leaned against the side of the mirror, her arms crossed over her chest. Her lips quirked up into a smile as she watched the giant try to push his nose back where it was supposed to be. I slipped my phone out of my jeans pocket, set it to video mode, and pointed it at them.

"That bitch," Brody growled. "I can't believe she broke my nose."

"Well, that's Gin Blanco for you," Roxy said. "From what Tucker told me, she just sledgehammers her way through life. Worse than a bull in the proverbial china shop. In this case, you just happened to be the china."

Roxy chuckled at her own bad joke. Brody gave her a sour look, which she ignored.

He leaned forward and smiled at himself in the mirror. "Well, at least she didn't get any of my teeth. I just had these babies whitened."

So Roxy was working for Tucker, just like I'd thought, and apparently Brody was too. I was glad that I'd busted the giant's nose. My only regret was that I hadn't hit him harder and made him eat his precious teeth like they were peppermint candies.

I thought about palming a knife and confronting the two of them, but we were only a few dozen feet off the main drag. Their screams would be sure to attract unwanted attention. Besides, I wanted to get as much information as I could first. Because I still didn't know what the point of all this was.

It was obvious now that Tucker had arranged for Finn to receive the deed to Bullet Pointe, but why had the vampire lured us down here to the resort? Did he plan to somehow get Finn to sign the property over to him?

Or did he want something else from us? Once I knew the answer to that, I could plan my next move and kill Roxy and Brody to my heart's content. So I stayed quiet and still in the shadows in the corner of the alley, recording them with my phone.

"How much longer do we have to make nice with these people?" Brody growled.

"Until Tucker says otherwise," Roxy said. "You know that."

The giant tossed his ruined, bloody bandanna onto the vanity table. "All I know is that we've been stuck here for the last two months in this stupid theme park, dressing up like stupid cowboys, and putting on stupid shows. And what do we have to show for it? *Nothing*."

Well, at least I wasn't the only one who was frustrated by a lack of progress.

"Ah, come on," Roxy said. "Hanging around here has been fun."

"You're just saying that because of your cowboy fetish." Brody shook his head. "You actually *like* all of this cheesy Western stuff. The cowgirl costume, the aw-shucks attitude, playing sheriff, the whole shtick. You even had all your creepy animal heads shipped up from Blue Marsh so you could decorate your office with them."

Roxy shrugged. "I like souvenirs of my hunts. I've got a guy working on that black bear that I killed last weekend up in Cypress Mountain. It's going in the corner, right next to my bobcat."

So she was a hunter, just like I'd thought when I'd seen all those poor stuffed animals in her office earlier. More than that, she liked to keep trophies of her deadly prowess.

Brody snorted. "No, you just like killing things. And now you think that Gin Blanco is going to be your big-game prize."

Roxy grinned. "Absolutely. That bitch is already dead. She just doesn't know it yet. And I'm going to be the one who finally puts her down for good. I would have done it outside McAllister's mansion, but Tucker wanted her down here instead."

My eyes narrowed. My head stuffed and mounted on a wall? Never going to happen, sugar.

"Yeah, McAllister, the guy you failed to kill," Brody sniped. "I can't believe he fooled you with a silverstone vest."

"Who thought he would be that smart?" Roxy muttered, her sunny disposition slipping just a bit. "Besides, Tucker just wanted him dead to prove a point to Blanco. McAllister doesn't know anything important. Still, I'll go back and finish him off after we get done with Blanco and her friends. Just for not dying when I wanted him to."

Brody crossed his arms over his chest. "And of course getting to show off your little tricks with your revolvers is just the icing on the cake," he snarked, continuing his rant. "This whole job has been like a dream come true for you."

"Well, it was certainly better than sitting in that penthouse in Bigtime, waiting to take that guy out with a sniper rifle." Roxy huffed. "There's no *fun* in that. No thrill of the chase, no outwitting your opponent, no hunting them down and seeing the fear in their eyes before you pull the trigger."

It sounded like the two of them were some sort of

tag-team hit squad for Tucker, traveling around the country and doing whatever dirty jobs he paid them to. I wondered just how many people Tucker had working for him. Maybe he was higher up in the Circle than I'd realized. Maybe he was actually one of the leaders, instead of just Deirdre's minder and an errand boy like I'd thought.

"Besides," Roxy said, "working at the resort was the only way that we could come in and search for the jewels without tipping off everyone as to what we're really doing here."

It took a moment for her words to sink in, but once they did, understanding flashed through me like a lightning bolt.

The jewels. Of course.

So Deirdre had swiped Sweet Sally Sue's gemstones, but apparently, she hadn't hocked them for cold, hard cash or used them to pay for the hotel renovations. She must have stashed them here at Bullet Pointe as her golden parachute, in case things went south with Finn in Ashland. Only Finn had killed Deirdre instead, and she'd never had a chance to come back to the resort and retrieve the diamonds, sapphires, and rubies.

"Tucker knows that Deirdre hid those stones somewhere around here," Roxy said. "And he has made it very clear that we're not leaving until we find them."

"And I say that they're not here," Brody growled. "We've looked *everywhere* for those things. I don't see why Tucker wants them so badly anyway. He's got plenty of money of his own."

Roxy shrugged. "Sure, Tucker's loaded, but Deirdre Shaw owed millions to him and his friends, and he plans to get at least some of that money back by whatever means necessary. It's the principle of the thing. Besides, Tucker's friends aren't the kind of people you want to disappoint. He needs to smooth things over with them, even if it's only by putting a small dent in Deirdre's massive debt."

The giant stuck his lower lip out in a petulant pout. "Well, I still don't see why we just can't kill Blanco, Lane, and the other two and be done with this job already."

"Because Tucker thinks that Blanco might be able to find the gems with her Stone magic," Roxy said in a patient voice, as though she were explaining something to a three-year-old. "Or that Deirdre actually told Finnegan Lane where she hid them."

"But you asked Lane flat out if he knew about the jewels, and he told you no."

Roxy shrugged again. "Maybe he knows something, maybe he doesn't. Maybe Deirdre fed him some clue that he doesn't even realize is a clue. Either way, I'll get it out of him." She paused. "Or Tucker will."

They both blanched a little at that. Apparently, they were well acquainted with how Hugh Tucker got answers from people. The image of Deirdre handcuffed to a chair, with cuts, bruises, burns, and deep, ugly bite marks all over her body flashed through my mind. Deirdre had worked for the vampire, and he hadn't had any qualms about making her suffer, just because she'd disappointed him. I could well imagine how much more enthusiastic he would be in torturing me, Finn, Bria, and Owen if he thought it would get him what he wanted.

"And Blanco?" Brody said, getting to his feet. "What do you want to do about her?"

"Well, you were supposed to grab her so we could get her out of the way before we went after Lane." Roxy tapped her own straight, perfect nose. "Not let her smash your face like it was a piñata."

The giant growled, but Roxy waved her hand, dismissing his anger. "We'll take care of Blanco later. And if she can't find the gems, or if Lane doesn't know anything about them, and the stones really are gone for good, well, at least we'll have a bit of fun with them before we leave."

She grinned, plucked one of the revolvers out of the holster on her belt, and started spinning it around and around, making the silver barrel glimmer in the afternoon sun. Cold rage surged through me at the way she'd so casually talked about torturing and murdering me and my loved ones—and how much she was going to enjoy it.

This bitch was the one who was already dead. She just didn't know it yet. And the Spider was going to be the one to put her down for good.

❈ 11 ❈

I'd heard enough, so I shut off my phone and slid it back into my jeans pocket. I glanced over my shoulder, but the alley was still deserted, although people moved back and forth out on Main Street, heading from one block of shops to the next. Once I was satisfied that no one was paying any attention to me, I palmed a knife and looked at Roxy and Brody again, plotting the best way I could get close enough to kill them both quietly.

My gaze moved from one side of the staging area to the other. If I could get over to that barrel full of lassos without being seen, I could crouch down behind it, then sprint over to that rack of saloon-girl costumes. Once I was in position there, I could step out from behind the clothes and hit Roxy and Brody with a spray of Ice daggers. If I used a big enough blast of magic, I could probably kill them both before they realized what was happening. Even if they survived my initial attack,

I could always finish them off with my knives. They might let out a few screams, but I was willing to take that chance, now that I knew the torture they had in mind for me and my friends.

I tightened my grip on my knife, feeling the spider rune stamped into the hilt press against the larger, matching scar in my palm. The sensation steadied me, the way it always did. I drew in a breath, reached for my Ice magic, and stepped out of the alley—

Something *beep-beep*ed, and Roxy turned in my direction. I swallowed down a curse and slid back into the shadows before she spotted me. She holstered her revolver, stepped forward, and picked up her phone off the vanity table, staring at the message on the screen.

"Jim says that Lane, Coolidge, and Grayson are in the Silver Spur, trying on hats. No sign of Blanco, though."

Brody shook his head. "Forget about Tucker wanting her alive. I'm telling you, Roxy, you need to kill that bitch now. Not play this stupid stalking game with her. She's not some dumb animal that I can flush out of the swamp so you can kill her on your own terms."

"But it's such a *fun* game," Roxy purred. "Especially since the illustrious Spider doesn't even realize that she's my target yet. She's never even going to know what hit her."

She grinned, pulled out one of her revolvers, and started spinning it around and around in her hand again. The giant rolled his eyes. Yeah, me too.

Forget about being quiet. If Sheriff Roxy wanted a piece of me, then I was more than happy to show her what a real outlaw looked like—and just how dead I could make her. I reached for even more of my Ice magic and crept forward—

Laughter sounded at the far end of the alley. I whipped around and realized that two giant cowboys were ambling in my direction. Their heads were down, both of them looking and laughing at something on one of their phones, so they hadn't spotted me yet, but it was just a matter of seconds before they would.

I swallowed down another curse. Witnesses and collateral damage were things that I tried to avoid at all costs, so I did the only thing I could—I tucked my knife back up my sleeve, stepped out of the alley, and walked out into the staging area where my enemies were.

"Oh, there you are!" I called out in a loud voice, waving my hand. "I've been looking everywhere for you two!"

Startled, Roxy and Brody both whipped around in my direction. Brody's hands curled into fists, while Roxy stopped spinning her revolver around, the gun pointing down at the ground.

For now.

They glanced at each other, obviously wondering if I'd overheard their conversation, but I plastered a benign smile on my face and went right over to them. They weren't the only ones who could put on a show.

I stopped in front of the giant and stared at his swollen, crooked nose, which looked like a rotten tomato that had been mashed into his face. I winced and hissed in a breath between my teeth in fake sympathy. "I just wanted to tell you how very *sorry* I am for hitting you. I just don't know *what* came over me. It must be all these self-defense classes I've been taking lately."

I let out a light, pealing laugh, trying to play the whole thing off as a joke, but the giant was anything but amused. Brody's fingers clenched together even tighter, his knuckles cracking under the slow, steady pressure, and his lips twisted with rage. At that moment, the giant wanted nothing more than to lunge forward, wrap his hands around my throat, and strangle me to death for breaking his nose.

Roxy laid a warning hand on his shoulder and gave me an innocent smile in return. "Oh, Brody knows that you didn't mean any harm, Gin."

"Of course not," I chirped back at her. "It was all just part of the show, right?"

"Right."

We stared at each other, both of us smiling wide as though everything were fine, and this were a normal conversation. But Roxy kept her gun out, her finger on the trigger, ready to snap up the weapon and pump me full of Fire-coated bullets, and I had my own elemental power pooling in my palms, ready to whip up my hands and blast her in the face with my Ice magic.

But the two cowboys I'd spotted before stepped into the square, still chuckling over whatever silly video they were watching, and the moment—and our potential showdown—passed.

For now.

The cowboys waved at Roxy and Brody, then went over to a costume rack to hang up their hats for the day and change back into their regular clothes.

"Well, then, I'll leave you to get cleaned up," I said, breaking the tense silence that had gathered around me, the giant, and the Fire elemental. "Again, I really am sorry. If you need an Air elemental to snap your nose back into place, please, feel free to send me the bill."

Brody glowered at me, anger turning his cheeks as red as his nose.

Roxy, however, gave me another innocent smile. "Oh, we have a healer on staff, so that won't be necessary. I was just about to call and get him to come over."

I nodded as though the information pleased me.

"Actually, Gin, I'm glad that you're here," Roxy said. "I know that y'all probably want to explore the park and the hotel for the rest of the day, but I was wondering if you and your friends would like to join Brody and me for an early lunch tomorrow before the high-noon show. It would be a chance for me to speak to Finn about the resort and for all of us to get to know each other better."

I would rather have carved out her heart with a butter knife than break bread with her, but I played along. "Of course. Sounds like fun."

"Great!" Roxy chirped. "Just show up at eleven o'clock tomorrow morning at the Feeding Trough restaurant on Main Street. I'll set everything up."

I nodded at her, then at Brody. "Again, I'm so very sorry, and I hope that you feel better soon. Y'all take care now."

I smiled at them again, turned around, and walked out of the square at a normal pace. My shoulders tensed, and I reached for my Stone magic, ready to send it rushing out through my entire body. I wouldn't put it past Roxy to shoot me in the back, especially if she thought that I'd overheard any of her conversation with Brody. She might want to find the jewels, but she wanted me dead too so she could add another trophy to her wall.

But I didn't hear the distinctive *click* of her thumbing back the hammer on her revolver, and I rounded the corner and stepped back into the alley, out of sight of the staging area.

Not out of the line of fire, though. Not even close.

I left the alley behind and headed back out onto the main drag with its shops, crowds, and costumed characters. More than ever before, I felt like people were watching me and analyzing my every move. Every time one of the cowboys, gold miners, gamblers, or saloon girls sashayed past or smiled at me, I eyed them, wondering if they were going to text Roxy my current location the moment my back was turned. Probably. My shoulders tensed again, still expecting a bullet to blast into my back at any second, but I forced myself to step into the crowds.

I found my friends in the Silver Spur, right where Roxy had said they were. Part of the Silver Spur was an old-timey mercantile shop, with soaps, elixirs, and other goods, while the other half featured designer clothing, including the hats that Finn and Owen were both trying on. Bria leaned against a nearby rack of fringed leather vests, looking bored.

"What took you so long?" she groused. "I've seen about as many cowboy hats as I can stomach."

She jerked her head at Finn, who was staring at himself in a full-length mirror, admiring the white Stetson on his head and trying to talk Owen into buying the same hat in gray. Before I could answer her, Finn strutted over to us. He was also wearing a green-and-white paisley bandanna around his neck and white leather chaps bedazzled with pale green rhinestones over his jeans. He looked like some country-western singer about to go onstage. All he needed was a shiny guitar.

"Hey, Gin!" he called out, turning around in a circle and making the rhinestones shimmer under the lights. "What do you think? Is this me or what?"

I forced myself to smile at him. "It's *totally* you."

He grinned and signaled one of the clerks to ring it all up for him.

Owen walked over and tipped his gray Stetson at me. "Ma'am," he rumbled, "do you like it?"

I reached up and tipped the hat back on his forehead. "Wear it for me tonight, and you'll see just how much I like it, cowboy."

He laughed and went to get in line with Finn to check out.

The Silver Spur was busy, and it took twenty minutes for the clerk to wrap up Finn's new duds, along with Owen's hat, and for us to finally leave the shop. I glanced up and down the sidewalks, but I didn't see anyone obviously watching us. I knew they were there, though. I could feel their gazes on me and my friends. We needed to get out of the theme park and back to the hotel, up in our suites where I could tell the others what was going on, and we could plot our next move.

But once again, Finn had other ideas. "Come on. Let's get some hot chocolate."

He set off down the sidewalk, and Bria, Owen, and I had no choice but to follow him. Finn strolled over to a food cart sitting at the entrance to one of the alleys, where he bought hot chocolates for all four of us, before leading us over to two iron benches that were set close together, facing each other. Finn and Bria took one bench, with Owen and me sitting across from them on the other one.

Finn took a sip of his hot chocolate, then glanced around and leaned forward, staring at me with sharp, knowing eyes. "What's going on, Gin?"

"Why do you think something's going on?"

"Because normally you would have mocked me mercilessly for buying rhinestone-studded, white leather chaps. As well you should have. But you said that they looked great. That's not the snarky, sassy Gin Blanco that I know and love." He paused to take another sip of his hot chocolate. "Plus, there's a cowboy who's been following us from store to store, texting on his phone the whole time. He's behind me now, leaning against a post and trying to look casual."

My gaze slid past Finn, and sure enough, that cowboy was right where he said. I should have realized that Finn would have clocked someone watching him. He might not be a bona fide assassin like me, but Fletcher had trained his son just as well as he had me.

"Plus, you were gone a really long time," Finn added. "Normally, I would have said that you had to stop, kill someone, and hide their body, but there isn't any blood on your clothes." He gave me another stern look. "So spill it, Gin. What kind of trouble did you get into?"

I sighed, realizing that it was confession time. "Well, you're right. I didn't actually kill anyone, although I certainly wanted to. . . ."

While we sipped our hot chocolates, I told my friends everything that Roxy and Brody had said about working for Tucker and the vampire wanting us to find the hidden jewels for him.

When I finished, Owen looked at me. "So that's what was going on in the lobby earlier when you ran into that luggage cart. You thought you saw Tucker and were going to chase after him."

I nodded. "Guilty as charged, but he disappeared before I could get to him. But he's around here somewhere. He has to be."

The four of us fell silent, clutching our empty cups. To the casual observer, it looked like we were just taking a break from the festivities, sitting on the benches, having a warm snack, and people-watching. Oh, we were people-watching all right.

"The cowboy's gone, but there's a giant miner in his place, glancing over at us every minute or so," Owen said.

"The saloon girl working that popcorn cart is checking us out too," Finn added.

"And I see a gambler up on one of the second-story balconies, looking right at us and texting," Bria said.

I nodded. "I don't know how many folks work for Roxy and Brody directly, but we have to assume that any of the resort staff could be on their payroll and a potential threat. Not to mention Tucker lurking around, and any men that he might have hiding in the shadows with him." I looked at my friends. "The way I see it, we have two options. We can hightail it out of here, head back to Ashland, and regroup."

"Or?" Finn asked, even though he knew as well as I did what the second choice was.

"Or we can stay and search for the jewels. According to Roxy, Tucker thinks that Deirdre gave you some clue about where she hid them, or that I can somehow find them with my Stone magic. Maybe he's right about that."

I kept my voice neutral, even though I burned to stay here. I didn't care about the gems and how valuable they were. Not in the slightest. For me, this was all about Hugh Tucker. The vampire had been three steps ahead of me for weeks now, and I wanted to turn the tables and beat him at his own game. I wanted to take away something that he cared about, for a change. But most of all, I wanted to have him at my mercy—or lack thereof—so I could finally carve some answers out of him about my mother and the Circle.

But staying at the resort would be dangerous—maybe even deadly. Nothing that we hadn't faced before, of course, but we'd come down here to relax and take a break from the constant danger in Ashland. Not get ourselves into even more trouble.

Oh, I'd be happy to take on Roxy, Brody, and every other person here if it meant getting closer to discovering the members of the Circle, but this wasn't my choice to make. Not really. Because Tucker had lured *Finn* down here, had sent *him* the resort deed, and had gotten *his* hopes up about learning more about Deirdre. So he should be the one to decide.

I looked at Finn. "So what do you want to do? This is your weekend and your resort, so it's your call. Right, guys?"

Bria and Owen both nodded, and the three of us stared at him.

My foster brother tapped his finger against the side of his cup, staring down into the dregs of his hot chocolate as though they were tea leaves that would somehow reveal the future. After several seconds, his finger stilled, and he raised his head, staring at Bria and Owen, and then finally at me.

So many emotions flashed in Finn's eyes. Worry about the danger we were in, hurt that Tucker had manipulated him again, disappointment that he hadn't learned anything new about Deirdre yet. But all of that melted away, hardening into a stubborn determination that I knew all too well—the same determination that Fletcher had instilled in me, as well as his son. In that moment, Finn seemed more like his old self than he had in weeks.

"Fuck it," Finn said, a grin spreading across his face. "Let's find those rocks and shove them down Tucker's throat."

I grinned back at him. "I was hoping you'd say that."

❊ 12 ❊

We left Main Street behind, walked back to the hotel, and rode the elevator up to the seventh and top floor where our suites were, like everything was normal.

Then again, my friends and I being in mortal danger with enemies all around *was* perfectly normal. Vacation. Heh.

All the while, we kept an eye out, but the theme park and hotel workers just watched us. Roxy and Brody must have told their minions to leave us alone for the time being. At least, until we found the jewels for them.

The elevator opened, revealing a long hallway with only a few doors set into the walls. We stepped forward. The elevator doors closed behind us with a whisper, and the only sound was our soft footsteps on the thick gray carpet.

"This floor is all penthouse suites," Finn said. "Our rooms are over there." He swept his hand out to the left, indicating a couple of doors on that side of the hallway.

"And according to the room number on that key Ira Morris gave me, Deirdre's suite is there." This time, he pointed to the right, where a single door was set into the wall.

Of course there was only one door and one suite on that side. Deirdre wouldn't have wanted to share a single inch of space with anyone.

Finn stared at that closed door for a moment, then turned away, pulled a plastic key card out of his pants pocket, and opened the door to his suite. We all trooped inside, and Finn and Owen put their packages down on a table by the door.

Actually, it was two suites in one, with each area featuring its own spacious living room, bedroom, and bathroom, with connecting double doors in the middle. Our luggage was sitting in the foyer in Finn and Bria's suite, although both living rooms had a table featuring an enormous fruit basket, along with platters of chocolate-dipped strawberries and other gourmet treats.

"Here's to your stay and our great new partnership, Roxy," Bria said, reading the note on the fruit basket in her and Finn's suite.

She tossed the note back onto the table and opened her mouth, but I held my finger up to my lips in warning, and Bria bit back the rest of her snarky words.

"Well, then," I said, "let's get settled and see if Roxy left us any other . . . surprises."

The others nodded, picking up on my real meaning, and we all went to work, discreetly checking our respective suitcases and suites for hidden cameras, listening devices, and rune traps. Just in case Roxy had coated something with her Fire magic to try to kill us in our rooms.

"Anything?" Owen asked about ten minutes later.

I peered a final time into the air vent that was set low in the wall and got to my feet. "Nope. We're good."

We stepped through the open connecting doors back into Finn and Bria's suite. The two of them were sitting on one of the couches in the living room, typing away on their laptops on the coffee table in front of them.

"Any creepy crawly things in here?" I asked.

Finn shook his head. "No cameras or listening devices. The room's clean."

"So is ours," I said. "Roxy knows that the jewels aren't in here, so she didn't bother to bug our rooms. She must have just told her people to watch us when we're out in the hotel and theme park."

Bria hit some more keys on her laptop. "Did you know that the resort has its own webpage devoted to the treasure hunt? There's even a place where people can post about all the places they've looked in the theme park. There are hundreds of comments here and just as many pictures."

Finn shook his head again. "Forget about the theme park. Deirdre wouldn't be caught dead in a place like that. More important, she wouldn't have stashed those jewels anywhere she couldn't get her hands on them in a matter of minutes."

Owen crossed his arms over his chest. "You think they're here in the hotel somewhere?"

Finn nodded, never taking his eyes off his laptop screen. "They have to be."

"Well, if that's the case, wouldn't Deirdre have kept them in her own suite?" Owen said.

"And no doubt that's the first place Roxy and Brody

searched and came up empty," I said. "But we haven't looked there yet. Maybe we'll find something they missed."

"Which is why I'm pulling up the hotel schematics right now," Finn said. "I want to make sure that Deirdre didn't have any false walls added to her suite or anywhere else in the hotel."

This suite had its own printer, and Finn asked Owen to help him hook his laptop up to it. Bria kept surfing, scribbling down all the places that folks had already looked for the jewels, concentrating on the hotel locations.

While the others worked, I pulled my phone out of my pocket and called Silvio. He answered on the second ring. In the background, I could hear him typing away as fast and furiously as ever, even though I had no clue as to what he could be working on since I wasn't even in Ashland right now.

"I thought that you were going to have a nice, relaxing weekend while I was gone."

"And I thought that you were going to do the same. In trouble already?" Silvio countered in a dry, knowing voice.

"Is that any way to talk to your boss?"

"It certainly is when that boss is *you*. What's going on?"

I huffed at his tone, but I told him everything that had happened, including our search for Sweet Sally Sue's jewels.

"So let me get this straight," Silvio said when I finished. "You've only been at the resort for, what, three hours now? And you've already got people trying to kidnap and kill you? I think that's a new record even for you, Gin."

"Roxy and Brody want to torture and murder us *after* we find the gems," I corrected. "It doesn't make any sense for them to kill us before then."

For a moment, Silvio stopped typing, and there was complete silence. "Your optimism never ceases to amaze me."

I didn't think that it was optimism so much as it was fatalism, but I didn't argue with him. In the background, the typing noises started up again, with every rapid-fire keystroke sounding like a tiny gun going off in my ear.

"Hmm," Silvio murmured. "I've pulled up the hotel website. Looks like the four of you have a lot of ground to cover. Do you need me to come down there? It might not hurt for you to have some backup."

He was right. My friends and I were severely outnumbered, and it certainly wouldn't hurt to have Silvio waiting in the wings. Still, I hesitated. I didn't want to endanger another of my friends. And I really *had* wanted the vampire to have a nice, relaxing weekend, free from all the blood, bodies, destruction, and drama that went along with working for me.

"I thought that you had plans," I said, trying to talk him out of coming down here. "You know, finally having coffee with that cute younger gentleman you've been flirting with for the last few weeks at the Pork Pit?"

Silvio huffed. "I'm too old to flirt with anyone. That cute younger gentleman and I just happen to share some of the same interests."

"Uh-huh."

"Besides, he can wait. I can be down there in a few hours. Just give me the word, and I'll load my electronics into the car."

I would load up the car with knives, guns, and other assorted weapons, but then again, I supposed that electronics were Silvio's weapons of choice. So I decided to let him do some damage with them. "Actually, I need you to stay put for the moment. I want everything you can dig up on Roxy Wyatt and Brody Dalton. Criminal histories, credit reports, where they went to elementary school. I want to know every little detail about them. They work for Tucker, but I'm guessing that they haven't been nearly as careful as the vampire."

"You think that they've left a trail behind that you can follow back to Tucker and the Circle," Silvio said, picking up on my train of thought.

"Maybe. At the very least, it sounded like they'd dropped several bodies for Tucker. I want to know who's been on the vampire's hit list. It might give me some clue about him or the other members of the Circle or at least what their business interests are."

"Done. I'll have an update for you tonight, or first thing in the morning at the very latest. And I'll go ahead and load up the car anyway. Just in case."

"You don't have to do that. I can take care of myself, you know. I am an assassin after all. People actually fear me and stuff." I sighed. "Normal, sane people, anyway."

"Uh-huh. Talk to you soon, Gin."

Silvio hung up on me. I thought about calling him back and ordering him to stay put in Ashland, but I knew that he wouldn't answer. Not when he was hot on the trail of Roxy and Brody. Even if he did pick up, I could talk until I was blue in the face and he'd just ignore my protests.

Sometimes I thought that Silvio Sanchez was more the boss of me than the other way around.

Finn finished surveying the hotel schematics, but he didn't find any obvious hiding places where Deirdre might have stashed the jewels. So we decided to check out her suite for ourselves.

The four of us walked down the hallway to Deirdre's door. Finn slowly hefted the skeleton key in his hand, as though it were as heavy as a brick. After a moment, he curled his fingers around it, slid the key into the lock, and turned it.

"Here goes nothing," he said, opening the door and stepping through to the other side.

The suite was massive, even larger than Deirdre's penthouse at the Peach Blossom apartment building back in Ashland. We moved through the foyer and stepped down into a sunken living room that featured white leather couches and chairs, glass-and-chrome tables, and black-and-white Persian rugs. No cowboy or Western decor was in sight, although a ten-foot-tall white Christmas tree stood in the corner, with a couple of open plastic boxes filled with decorations scattered around it. Floor-to-ceiling windows lined the back wall of the suite, showing off a lovely view of the surrounding trees and ridges and Bullet Pointe Lake in the distance.

A large kitchen lay off to one side of the main space, although it was immaculate, and all the white marble countertops and chrome appliances gleamed, as though no one had ever cooked anything in there. Deirdre certainly hadn't. When I'd been spying on her in Ashland, she'd ordered room service for every single meal. I hadn't seen her make so much as a sandwich in all the time I'd watched her.

"I never thought that I would admire Deirdre's decorating style, but I gotta say that I'm glad there are no boots or lassos in here," Bria said.

"It looks exactly like her other apartment." Finn paced from one side of the living room to the other and back again, looking over everything. "There's nothing here. *Nothing.* I don't even see a magazine."

Bria looked at me, and I shrugged back at her. My sister stepped in front of Finn, cutting off his rapid pacing. "You don't know that yet. Let's take a look around. Maybe you know something or will see something that Tucker and the others missed. Okay?"

"Okay," Finn muttered.

So the four of us went through the suite, opening and closing the coffee-table drawers, looking under the couch cushions, and even rifling through the empty pots and pans in the kitchen cabinets. I also kept an eye out for any hidden cameras, listening devices, and rune traps, but there was nothing in the front two rooms, so we walked down a hallway to the master bedroom and bathroom in the back, where things finally got a little more interesting.

Apparently, Deirdre had spent far more time here than she'd led Finn to believe because the bedroom was brimming with her stuff. Pantsuits, cocktail dresses, and ball gowns filled one side of the enormous walk-in closet, all neatly hung on racks and organized according to color, from lightest to darkest. The other side of the closet featured shelves full of hats, purses, and stilettos—more stiletto heels, pumps, and boots than any one woman could possibly wear in a lifetime.

But I was most interested in the closet's back wall, since all the shelves there were lined with white velvet, making that area its own freestanding jewelry box. Deirdre had had a *lot* of jewelry. Necklaces, bracelets, rings, earrings, watches, hairpins, tiaras—dozens and dozens of each of those perched prettily on the white velvet shelves, once again organized according to color, from light to dark stones. Black velvet bags and boxes were also lined up on the shelves, so she could transport her baubles from place to place. It looked as though Deirdre had had a different piece of bling for every single day of the year—and then some.

I moved from one side of the wall to the other and back again, carefully examining each shelf and all the jewelry on it in turn, wondering if perhaps Deirdre had stashed Sweet Sally Sue's jewels in here with her own. I also reached out with my Stone magic, listening to all the gems. Whether it was a diamond, sapphire, or ruby, the more expensive a gemstone was, the louder it would sing about its sparkling beauty.

But no loose stones were lying around, and the gems only murmured softly—if they even murmured at all. Some of the pieces were completely quiet, telling me that they were made of glass instead of precious stones. I snorted. Of course Deirdre's jewelry would be as fake as she was. She had made everyone in Ashland think that she was rolling in dough, even though she was completely broke. This was yet another of her many smoke screens.

Still, even with the few genuine pieces of jewelry that

I spotted, the gemstones didn't sing all that loudly. Oh, they were nice enough bling, but not in the same league as Sweet Sally Sue's jewels. Not even close. All these shelves full of rings and necklaces, and you'd be lucky to get ten grand if you hocked everything.

So I moved on to the bathroom, which contained a variety of expensive soaps, shampoos, lotions, face creams, makeup, and perfumes, along with a whole rack of champagne bottles. Deirdre must have used those to mix her extravagant bubble baths, just like she had back in Ashland.

Looking through all her stuff in the closet and bathroom was interesting, but it was still just *stuff*. There were no computers, phones, tablets, or flash drives lying around that would tell us anything more about Deirdre Shaw than what we already knew.

"Nothing," Finn growled, throwing down another empty beaded clutch. "There's *nothing* here. Not one bloody thing about her, the Circle, or anything else."

He looked around at the mess we'd made pulling Deirdre's clothes, shoes, hats, and purses out of her closet and dumping them in the middle of the bedroom floor. Disgust filled his face, and he whipped around on his heel and stalked back to the living room.

"I'll go after him," Bria said.

She walked out of the bedroom, leaving Owen and me standing in a sea of sparkling sequined dresses and stiletto shoes. Owen glanced over the piles of clothes to check if we'd left anything untouched, while I went back into the closet, knocking softly on the walls, the floor, and even the ceiling, in case we'd missed a hidden panel.

But there was nothing, just like Finn had said. No loose panels, no hidden cubbyholes, no secret wall safes, nothing but clothes and shoes and fake jewelry. Frustration surged through me, along with sadness and disappointment for Finn. He'd come here hoping for answers, and it didn't look like he was going to get a single one.

And neither was I.

"Roxy and Brody really cleaned this place out, didn't they?" Owen called out.

I went back to the bedroom and kicked a black stiletto out of my way. "What do you mean?"

He threw his hands out wide. "Look at all this stuff. There are thousands and thousands of dollars' worth of designer clothes here. Not to mention those ridiculously expensive shoes and purses and all that overpriced champagne in the bathroom."

"So?"

"So this looks like it was Deirdre's home base. There's certainly a lot more of her stuff here than there was in that penthouse in Ashland."

"But . . ."

Owen shook his head. "But there's not a single piece of *paper* anywhere in the suite. I have papers all over my house, even if it's just a receipt from where I bought gas on my way home. But Deirdre? She doesn't even have so much as a room-service slip in here. Roxy and Brody must have taken it all, every last scrap."

I'd been so focused on Deirdre's clothes and jewelry that I hadn't thought about something as simple as receipts, but Owen was right. Everybody had paper. Some people, like Ira Morris, had far too much, but Deirdre seemed to have none at all.

"Anyway," he said, "I'm going to go check on Finn and Bria. You coming?"

"In a minute."

Owen nodded and walked down the hallway, disappearing from sight.

I looked out over the bedroom again with a far more critical eye. It wasn't just paper that was missing. There were no knickknacks, no mementos, no odds and ends of any kind—nothing *personal*. Not so much as a crumpled wrapper in the trash can that would tell me what kind of gum Deirdre had liked to chew.

Oh, I hadn't thought that Deirdre would have a collection of ceramic dolls or a secret love of macramé, but she'd had photos of Fletcher, Finn, and herself. She'd had to have kept those *somewhere* before she came to Ashland. And you would think that there would be more pictures here, even if they were only of herself.

But Owen was right, and Roxy and Brody had taken it all, probably on Tucker's orders, searching for clues about the gems. I had to admire how efficiently and completely they'd sanitized her suite of anything important. Roxy and Brody had stripped this place bare better than a pair of locusts.

Still, the longer I stared at the haphazard heaps of Deirdre's clothes and shoes, the angrier I got. This had been nothing but a gigantic waste of time. Tucker had probably told Roxy and Brody exactly what to leave behind in the suite, just to get our hopes up, just so we would think that we were finally getting somewhere. The vampire kept dangling carrots of information in front of me, and like a stupid fool, I kept trying to get them, even though he snatched them away from me every single time.

Once again, Hugh Tucker was playing a game with me—and I was losing badly.

✦ 13 ✦

Disgusted, I went back out into the main part of the suite where the others were.

Finn was standing by the windows, his arms crossed over his chest, staring out at the view and brooding. Bria and Owen were going through all the drawers and cabinets again, searching for false bottoms and secret panels, just in case we'd missed something. I looked at my sister, who shook her head, telling me that Finn was still upset and to give him some space. Well, he wasn't the only one who was angry, but I decided to channel my frustration into something productive. So I joined Bria and Owen in their renewed search, and the three of us left Finn to his own thoughts.

I ended up at the white Christmas tree in the corner. It was one of those artificial, pre-wired trees, so I plugged it in, just to see if it actually worked. The lights immediately flared to life, going from white to pink to green to blue and back again, and casting out pretty patterns on the glass windows. No ornaments hung on the tree, though. I supposed that Deirdre hadn't had time to decorate it—or order someone at the resort to do it for her—before she'd come to Ashland. So I sat down on the floor and started going through the boxes of ornaments, curious as to what kind of decorations she would have.

Just like with the rest of Deirdre's things, they were designer—elaborate swirls, loops, and towers of silver, gold, crystal, and stained glass, hammered into snow-flakes, wreaths, icicles, and gingerbread men. They were all lovely, if totally impersonal. No *Baby's First Christmas*, no handmade snowmen, no tacky mementos from places Deirdre had visited. All the decorations were jumbled together, telling me that Roxy and Brody had already pawed through them the way they had everything else in the suite. Still, going through the ornaments was a pleasant enough pastime, so I kept pulling them out, examining each one, and then setting them aside.

In the very bottom of one of the boxes, I found a crumpled wad of tissue paper, which I pushed aside to reveal a large snow globe. Unlike everything else, the globe had obviously come from the theme park, since it featured a miniature scene of Main Street, complete with a small sign with sparkling stones that spelled out *Bullet Pointe*. I shook it and watched the tiny silver boot- and spur-shaped glitter swirl around inside before slowly settling back down.

Two more snow globes were also nestled in the bottom of the box. One featured a summer scene of Bullet Pointe Lake made out of dark blue pebbles with fish and sailboat glitter, while the other contained a winter scene of the hotel, covered with ceramic snow, shimmering red and green holiday decorations, and wreath- and tree-shaped glitter.

Bria crouched down beside me. She stared at the Main Street snow globe that I was still holding before glancing at the other two that I'd placed on the floor with all the other decorations. They all looked like unwrapped presents perched under the tree.

"I saw some of those globes down at the Silver Spur earlier today. Cute, if a bit tacky," she said. "They remind me of all those snow globes that Mom had. Remember how you, me, and Annabella put them all on our Christmas tree that last year?"

"Yeah," I rasped. "I remember."

That had been such a normal afternoon, and something that I'd all but forgotten about until now. No, that wasn't true. Ever since I'd found out that my mother had been part of the Circle, I'd been thinking back, trying to remember every single thing I could about her, especially if she'd ever shown any hint or sign that she was involved with such dangerous people.

Or if she was dangerous herself.

But I hadn't been able to remember much. Just hazy images of my mother smiling at me or brushing my hair or laughing as the two of us watched Bria skip around the mansion, playing, singing, and talking nonsense to her dolls. It seemed like the harder I tried to pull those images into focus, the blurrier and more distant they became until they faded away altogether. The pain they brought along with them lingered, though, as sharp and clear as one of my knives in my hand. Because my mother was still dead—would *always* be dead—and I didn't have any clue as to what she'd been involved in that had gotten her and Annabella killed.

Being here at this hotel only made me wonder even more about my mother, the Circle, and everything else. I wondered how often Deirdre had come here. I wondered if she'd ever invited Tucker or any of her other Circle cronies to her resort. I wondered if my mother had ever been here before her death.

I wondered . . . I wondered too many damn things that I had no way of getting the answers to. The more I tried to uncover the past, the more unraveled I felt myself, like a spiderweb that was slowly disintegrating one strand at a time into nothingness.

Disgusted again, I slammed the snow globe down onto the carpet hard enough to make the boot and spur glitter smack against the side of the glass. A few of the stones adorning the Bullet Pointe sign also rattled out of their spots and *plink-plink-plink*ed against the inside of the glass before drifting down to litter the tiny street. Cheap and tacky, just like Bria had said.

I glared at the globe, my fingers itching to grab it and throw it against the closest wall, along with the other two, then stomp on them for good measure, until they were all as empty and broken as my heart.

"Come on," I growled, getting to my feet. "Finn's right. This is pointless. There's nothing here. Let's go."

I leaned down and yanked the cord out of the socket, killing the lights on the Christmas tree. I didn't wait for my friends to follow me as I spun around on my heel, stormed over to the door, and left Deirdre Shaw's suite behind.

We'd spent most of the afternoon in Deirdre's suite, but after coming up empty there, none of us felt like searching the rest of the hotel for the jewels. At least, not tonight. So the four of us ate a good, expensive Italian dinner in one of the hotel restaurants, then had a nightcap of spiced apple cider by the lobby fireplace. Once again, I was aware of the hotel staff watching us, but that's all they did. Like I'd told Silvio earlier, Roxy and Brody probably wouldn't make a move until we'd found the gems—or they decided that the stones were lost for good.

After our nightcap, we went back to our respective suites—Finn and Bria in one, and Owen and I in the other. We all took precautions to make sure that we'd be safe for the night, including barricading the doors with several heavy tables and chairs and making sure that we all had our weapons handy. No one was getting in here tonight without making a whole lot of noise and getting a whole lot of dead in return.

Once that was done, Finn and Bria disappeared into their own room. Owen and I both showered, changed into our pajamas, and got into bed. Owen fell asleep almost immediately, his soft, rumbling snores like a steady chorus beside me. But I lay in bed for a long time, staring at the ceiling, turning things over and over in my mind, thinking about my mother, Tucker, Deirdre, and especially where she might have stashed her treasure.

But the answers didn't magically come to me, so I quit

glaring at the ceiling, rolled over onto my side, and snuggled down even deeper under the covers. Eventually I drifted off to sleep, to the land of dreams and memories. . . .

"You're doing it wrong," a cross voice snapped.

I looked up from the snow globe I was tying to the Christmas tree. "What?"

Annabella, my older sister, scowled and stabbed her finger to the right. "Not you—her."

She glared at Bria, who was sitting on the floor, shaking one globe after another, sometimes two at once, humming to herself, lost in her own little world.

Annabella glared at Bria again. "She's supposed to be helping us put these stupid things on the tree. Not just sitting there. After all, this was her *idea."*

We were trimming our Christmas tree in the upstairs family room, something that I absolutely loved doing. At dinner last night, Mom had asked us how we wanted to decorate it this year, and Bria had piped up and suggested that we tie all of Mom's snow globes to the tree. I'd thought it was a cool idea, but of course Annabella had decided it was totally lame, *just like she did everything that wasn't her idea or didn't involve her hanging out with her friends. Still, Mom had insisted that Annabella help us, especially since Mom had a meeting and couldn't come up here until she'd finished.*

So for the last hour, Annabella, Bria, and I had carefully nestled snow globes in the tree and tied them down to the branches with green wire, making sure that they wouldn't slip off and break on the floor. Well, really, Annabella and I had been doing all the work. Bria had just been sitting by the tree, playing with the globes the way she always did.

Annabella huffed. "If Bria's not going to help, I'm not putting the stupid tree up all by myself."

"But—" I started to protest that I was helping, but it was too late.

"Forget it," Annabella snapped, cutting me off. "I'm calling my friends."

She whirled around, her long blond ponytail flying out behind her, and stomped down the hallway. Several seconds later, I heard the sharp bang of her bedroom door slamming shut. Saying that Annabella was a moody teenager was a total understatement. Just because she was in high school, she thought that she was all grown up, and she never wanted to do anything fun anymore, especially not when it came to playing with Bria and me. That was kid stuff, and she wasn't a kid anymore, as she was so fond of reminding anyone who would listen.

I looked over at Bria, expecting her to be in tears because Annabella had stormed off, but she was still playing with the globes, and she hadn't even noticed that Annabella was gone. I let out a relieved sigh. Good. One sister's temper tantrum was all that I could handle today.

"Stay here, Bria," I said. "I'm going to see if Mom has finished her meeting yet and can come help us."

"Okeydokey, smokey," Bria replied in a distracted, singsong voice.

She'd probably sit there for another hour before she noticed that I was gone, so I put my globe down and slipped away while I could.

I headed downstairs, hugging the walls so I wouldn't be in the way. Mom was hosting her annual holiday party later tonight, and all sorts of people were moving from one room of our mansion to the next. Caterers clutching cases of cham-

pagne, florists carrying evergreen wreaths, even a couple of musicians dragging around harps, getting ready to set up their instruments in the main living room.

The kitchen was on the way to Mom's office, and I stopped and peered inside. The caterers had been the first ones to arrive this afternoon, and they'd already been cooking for hours. Honey-baked hams and deep-fried turkeys rested on wooden boards, waiting to be carved, while the chefs worked on cranberry sauce, mashed potatoes, gravy, and other classic holiday fixings. Everything smelled amazing, and my stomach rumbled in anticipation.

"Sounds like someone's hungry," an amused, masculine voice called out.

I looked to my right to find a middle-aged man staring at me. He wore a blue work apron over his clothes, and his walnut-brown hair peeked out from underneath his tall white chef's hat. His eyes were a bright, merry, Christmas green, and his cheeks were red from the heat of the stoves.

"It's hours until dinner," I said, my stomach rumbling again.

The man looked left and right, but the other chefs were busy, so he reached over and grabbed a chocolate shell shaped like a poinsettia from a tray. Chocolate mousse, one of my favorites, was piled high in the shell, topped with fresh raspberries, making it look like a real poinsettia.

He winked and passed the dessert over to me. "I won't tell if you won't, Genevieve."

I frowned, wondering how he knew my name, but I was too hungry to care. "Thank you," I said, and took a big bite.

It was just as fantastic as it looked. The chocolate mousse was light and fluffy, and the raspberries added a sweet, fruity flavor. The dark chocolate shell crunched under my teeth, *then melted in my mouth, adding even more rich, decadent flavor to the dessert.*

"Good, huh?" the man said in a teasing tone.

"Mmm-hmm." I quickly polished off the rest of the dessert.

He winked at me again, then went back to work, piping more chocolate mousse from a pastry bag into those poinsettia molds.

I left the kitchen and headed to the very back of the house, where my mom's office was, overlooking the gardens. Workers were out there too, stringing up white holiday lights, thick boughs of evergreen mistletoe, and red velvet bows. One of my favorite things about the holidays were all the bright, bold colors, along with the shimmers of the lights and the sparkles of silver and gold—

"I can't do this anymore," a voice said.

"Well, that's too bad, Eira," another, snider voice replied. "You're part of the group, so you're in the thick of things, along with the rest of us, whether you like it or not."

I frowned. He was talking to my mom. But what couldn't she do anymore?

I tiptoed down to the end of the hallway. The office door was cracked open, letting me see my mom sitting at her desk. She was so pretty with her long blond hair and blue eyes. Not for the first time, I wished that I looked like her the way that Bria and Annabella did. But instead, I'd gotten my father's dark brown hair and gray eyes, although I barely remembered him, since he'd died right after Bria had been born.

I eased to one side, staring at the other people in the office. One of them was a beautiful woman with short blond hair that had been styled into loose, elegant waves. She was *wearing a red cocktail dress, and a large heart-shaped pendant glinted around her neck. She must have been bored by the meeting because she was standing in front of some shelves, picking up my mom's snow globes, shaking them, and watching the glitter fly around inside, just like Bria had earlier.*

A man was sitting in the chair off to one side of my mom's desk. A black suit jacket draped over his shoulders. It matched his hair and eyes, as well as the trimmed black goatee that clung to his chin. He smiled at my mom, revealing a set of fangs in his mouth, but his expression didn't seem to be all that friendly.

The vampire propped his elbows up on the chair arms and steepled his fingers together. "Let me make this simple, Eira. You can either continue to carry on your role within the group, or we will find someone else to take your place."

She lifted her chin. "Go ahead, Hugh. Find someone else. That would suit me just fine."

The vampire let out a low, ugly laugh. "You know as well as I do that there is only one way someone leaves the Circle."

My mom crossed her arms over her chest. "Is that a threat? Because I don't take kindly to threats."

The blond woman picked up another snow globe and shook it. "Really, Eira. Do you always have to be such a troublemaker? Why can't you just be a good girl and go along with things?"

"Because, Deirdre," my mom snapped back, "unlike the rest of you, I happen to have a little bit of my conscience left."

Deirdre rolled her eyes, but she put the globe down, turned around, and looked over at the vampire. "Spending all these years away from Ashland made me forget how self-righteous she always is. How do you stand to deal with her, Hugh?"

He shrugged.

My mom's lips pressed together into a tight line. "I never wanted any of this."

"But you are part of the Circle, just as your parents were before you." Hugh paused. "And just as your lovely daughters will be after you."

Anger sparked in my mom's eyes, along with a shimmer of her Ice magic. "Leave my girls out of this. They have nothing to do with you and me and the rest of this rotten business."

He arched his eyebrows. "Funny, but Tristan thought the same thing. And look what happened to him."

I frowned. My dad had died in a car accident. What did that have to do with me, my sisters, or anything else? The two of them were talking in riddles that I didn't understand. But that was the way things had been around here lately. More often than not, Mom stayed holed up in her office for hours on end, talking on the phone or meeting with all sorts of strange people. Normally, before the annual holiday party, she would have been helping us decorate our tree, since that was our family tradition. But instead, she'd been back here all afternoon, meeting with one person after another.

I raised my hand to knock on the door but thought better of it. Mom wouldn't want to be interrupted. Besides, I didn't like the look of the woman or especially the vampire. Sure, he seemed like just another businessman, one of dozens that my mom dealt with, but his black eyes were cold and dead, like Christmas lights that had burned out. Eyes like that . . . they made me shiver.

There had been a lot of people with those sorts of eyes

around here lately. It made me . . . uneasy. Oh, not that I was actually worried *about anything. Not really. My mom was one of the strongest Ice elementals around, and she could easily take care of herself, as well as me and my sisters. But all these meetings and all these strange people . . . it just didn't seem like* her.

Neither did the worry that tightened her face—worry that she just couldn't seem to get rid of no matter how hard she tried. Even when she was hanging out with Annabella, Bria, and me, Mom always seemed distracted and far away, as though the weight of the world was on her shoulders.

"Think over my proposal," Hugh said, getting to his feet and buttoning his black suit jacket. "Maybe that will give you the illusion that you actually have a choice in all of this."

Deirdre snickered, amused by his cryptic words.

More anger flared in my mom's eyes, but she got to her feet and gave him a curt nod. The two of them looked at each other over the top of her desk, each giving the other a flat stare. Finally, Hugh smiled and tipped his head at my mom, as though they were having a pleasant conversation instead of the tense . . . whatever this was. Deirdre walked over to him, and together, arm in arm, they headed for the door.

I scrambled back down the hallway, not wanting them to know that I'd been eavesdropping. But Deirdre and Hugh were too quick for me, and the vampire opened the door before I could vanish around the corner. So I surged forward again, pretending like I had just gotten here, although the knowing look he gave me told me that he realized I'd been listening to them the whole time.

"Hello, little Genevieve," he murmured. "So lovely to see you again."

Again? I'd never seen him before, but for the second time tonight, a strange man knew my name.

Deirdre held her hand out in front of her, studying her long red nails, as if she were debating whether she needed a manicure. She completely ignored me, but Tucker kept staring at me. I shifted on my feet, trying not to shiver under his intense black gaze.

"You're looking very well today. And so much like your father. More and more all the time."

My mom appeared in the office door. "Good-bye, Hugh," she said in a loud, pointed tone.

Hugh winked at me, then strode down the hallway, with Deirdre still on his arm. They disappeared around the corner, but I could hear the echo of their footsteps as they moved through the house, each one banging against the floor seemingly as loud as a drum.

My mom listened to them go, her lips flattening out into a thin, worried line again. "He'll be back," she whispered, almost to herself. "And then things will be worse."

Worse? Worse than what? What had the vampire done to her? And what did she think that he was going to do to her in the future? I looked up at my mom, but she was still staring down the hallway, lost in her troubles, worries, and fears. . . .

My eyes snapped open, and I sucked in a ragged breath. For a moment, I didn't remember where I was, but then a warm body shifted beside me, and Owen rolled over onto his side, so that he was facing me.

"Gin?" His voice was thick with sleep. "Is everything okay? You were mumbling in your sleep."

"Everything's fine," I whispered, trying to calm my racing heart. "Just fine."

But Owen heard the tension in my voice, and he blinked, coming a little more fully awake. "What is it? Did you have another bad dream?"

Owen and I often spent the night together, so he was well acquainted with my nightmares, all the memories of the past that crowded into my mind when I slept. More than once, I'd woken him in the middle of the night as I thrashed around and screamed my fool head off about some long-ago battle.

But I hardly ever dreamed about my mother, save for her murder. That nightmare had haunted me for years until I'd gotten my revenge on Mab Monroe—revenge that had seemed false, hollow, and empty ever since Tucker had told me that the Circle had given Mab the go-ahead to kill my mother. Now, to realize that he and Deirdre had been in her office, in our mansion, threatening her and my sisters . . . it was just another horror show to add to my ever-growing collection. I rubbed my hand across my forehead. I wondered what other terrible things I would remember before this was all said and done.

"What did you dream about this time?" Owen asked.

I turned over onto my side so that I was facing him. "It was Christmas. The last Christmas that my mother and Annabella were alive. We were decorating our tree, and I went to my mother's office to see if she wanted to help us. Tucker was there. So was Deirdre."

Owen frowned. "Are you sure?"

"Yeah. Unfortunately."

I told him all the dirty details, and he lay there, digesting my words. "But you don't know what they were meeting about?"

I shook my head. "No. But I know there's more to the dream than that. There always is. It'll come to me sooner or later. Given what she was involved in, I might wish that it was later, though."

"Nobody's parents are perfect," Owen pointed out. "Mine certainly weren't, especially not my dad with his gambling problems."

"I know." I sighed. "But I always thought that my mom was this good person, this great woman. She always seemed so kind, caring, and strong. So much *better* than me. I know that I don't have any right to judge her, not given all the terrible things that I've done. But now to realize that she was involved with the Circle, that she probably did a lot of bad things, either on their orders or of her own free will . . . I don't know what to think about that. I don't know what to *feel* about that."

Owen pulled me into his arms, so that my head was resting on his shoulder, and pressed a kiss to my temple. "I know," he whispered. "I know."

He held me like that for a long time, both of us lost in our own troubled thoughts about our parents.

But eventually, I grew sick of wondering and worrying about my mother, Tucker, and the Circle. I didn't want to do that anymore. No, for the rest of this night, I wanted to focus on the one thing that I knew was true—my love for Owen and his for me.

I propped myself up on one elbow, staring down at

him. Moonlight slipped in through the crack in the white curtains, casting Owen's face in shadow, except for the glitter of his violet eyes. I reached out and traced my fingers over the sharp planes of his face, dipping into all the shadows that the night created. He grabbed my hand and pressed a kiss to my palm, right in the center of my spider rune scar.

Owen was only wearing black boxers, and he lay back against the pillows as I continued my slow, languid explorations, trailing my fingers down his bare chest, enjoying the feel of his warm, solid muscles. One spot right along his ribs was particularly sensitive, bunching and flexing under every flick of my fingers.

"Why, Mr. Grayson," I murmured, "I do believe that you're a bit ticklish tonight."

"Me? Ticklish? Never."

He cleared his throat and pressed his lips together, as though holding back a laugh. That only made me concentrate on that one spot, lightly running my fingers over it again and again, staring at him the whole time.

Finally, Owen gave in and started laughing, his whole chest shaking with his soft chuckles. I laughed with him, tickling him for another minute, before sliding my hand lower, dipping below the waistband of his boxers, and wrapping my fingers around his thick, hard length.

His laughter vanished, replaced by sharp, ragged gasps as I started stroking him.

"Is this ticklish too?" I teased.

He slid his hand up underneath the soft T-shirt I was wearing and cupped my breast, rolling my nipple in his fingers. "Just as ticklish as this is."

The soft, warm desire that had been simmering in my veins flared hotter, and I rose up and stripped off my T-shirt and panties while he got rid of his boxers. Owen moved forward, flicking his tongue over my nipple before nipping at it with his teeth. I groaned, and he drew me down on top of him, his lips coming up to meet mine. He kissed me, his tongue plunging into my mouth over and over again. I wound my fingers in his hair and drew him closer.

Owen rolled me onto my back, sucking one of my nipples, then the other, even as his hand dipped between my legs. His finger slid inside me, and this time, I gasped.

"Ticklish indeed," he murmured in a low, satisfied voice. "Ticklish indeed."

I dug my nails into his back, wanting him to keep going, but Owen moved even lower on the bed, eased my thighs apart, and put his mouth on me, his tongue darting in and out. His movements were slow at first, as he teased me just the way that I had him, but then his strokes grew quicker, sharper, harder. I arched back on the bed, my fingers twisting into the sheets, feeling the pressure and pleasure mount in equal parts, heat roaring through my entire body.

"Come on, baby," he whispered. "Let go for me."

And I did.

The climax exploded, and I fell back against the pillows, enjoying the languid heat that flooded my veins, making every part of me feel warm, relaxed, and satisfied. Owen kissed his way back up my body and started to gather me in his arms again.

I held out my hand, stopping him. "Oh, no." I gave him a wicked grin. "We're not done yet."

I pushed him flat on his back, then got a condom from his wallet on the nightstand. I took my little white pills, but we always used extra protection. That wasn't the only thing that I grabbed from the nightstand. The gray Stetson that Owen had bought earlier was sitting there, so I plopped it on his forehead.

"I told you that I wanted you to wear this for me."

"That's just fine with me, ma'am," he drawled. "I always aim to please."

"Me too."

Owen laughed and tipped his hat at me before pushing it back from his forehead so he could see me better. I gave him a devilish grin, then went to work, kissing, licking, stroking, and sucking him just as he had me.

"Oh, yeah," he rasped, his entire body twitching as he struggled to hold still and make the pleasure last as long as possible.

But I didn't make him wait long. When he was ready for me, I unrolled the condom over him, then rose up onto my knees and straddled him, sinking down onto his long, hard length in one smooth stroke. This time, we groaned together.

I rode him hard and fast, and Owen put his hands on my hips, urging me on. The pressure and the pleasure started building again, each stroke rougher, quicker, and more satisfying than the last. This time, we both moaned and went over the edge together.

And I lost myself in him for the rest of the night.

* 14 *

I would have liked to sleep in late the next morning, but my phone rang at exactly seven o'clock. I knew who was calling this early and why. I was surprised that he'd waited this long to update me.

Owen grunted, rolled over to the far side of the bed, and pulled the covers up over his head while I fumbled for my phone on the nightstand.

"Don't you ever sleep?" I grumbled when I finally brought the device up to my ear.

"A good assistant never sleeps when there is work to be done." Silvio sounded annoyingly alert and cheerful. "Or when there is information to share. Just think of this as our morning briefing, Gin. Brought to you through the magic of technology."

I managed to swallow down my snarky retort, although I flopped back onto the pillows, not so much holding the phone as wedging it between my ear and shoulder. "I take it that you dug into Roxy and Brody?"

"Of course. You were right. Neither one of them has been very secretive about their movements, so it was easy to track them. Not even a challenge." Silvio sounded disappointed by that. "Both Roxy Wyatt and Brody Dalton grew up in Blue Marsh. Seems their fathers were hunting buddies who ran charters out into the swamps, helping tourists bag deer, bears, gators, and the like. From what I've gathered, Roxy, in particular, took to the family business like a duck to water, leading the charters after her father died. She's also exceptionally good with guns. She's won several trick-shooting competitions all around the country, and she even makes her own bullets."

I thought of how easily she'd shot those bottles off the roof during the high-noon show yesterday and how they had all exploded with her Fire magic. "Of course she makes her own bullets. Because she's not nearly deadly enough on her own."

Silvio ignored my sarcasm. "I don't know exactly how she ended up working at Bullet Pointe, if Deirdre was the one who hired her or if Tucker strong-armed Deirdre into bringing her on board, but Roxy actually has a background in the resort business. She's worked for several carnivals and theme parks over the years, doing everything from running the concession stands, to being the resident sharpshooter, to actually managing some of the businesses." He cleared his throat. "But in all the cities where she's worked, there's been more than one murder and missing person's case reported shortly after she arrived, although nothing's ever pointed back to her."

"Surprise, surprise," I said.

Roxy must have worked at all those places as cover jobs while she was waiting for Tucker to call and tell her whom to kill next for him.

"Brody? What's his story?"

"Your typical giant muscle. He's followed Roxy around the country, working at all the same places that she has. They appear to be friends, but nothing more."

"So he's her hunting buddy," I mused. "Just like their fathers were before them."

"Something like that," Silvio agreed. "I'm still digging into the murders in the areas where they worked. I'll call you again later today with an update. Try not to get into too much trouble in the meantime, okay?"

"Me?" I scoffed. "Get into trouble? *Never.*"

Silence, although I could well imagine the vampire rolling his eyes. Silvio said that he had more people to contact, and the two of us said our good-byes and hung up.

I couldn't go back to sleep, and neither could Owen, so the two of us got up and took a nice, long hot shower together before we got dressed and went next door to Finn and Bria's suite. My foster brother and my sister were sitting on one of the couches, sipping coffee and looking at printouts of the hotel schematics again.

"Finally," Finn said. "I was wondering if the two of you were just going to laze about your room all day."

I arched my eyebrows. "And what were you two doing in your suite last night and this morning?"

Finn grinned, while Bria blushed and focused on sipping her coffee.

"I rest my case." I nodded at the papers covering the

table. "Do you see anything new or different in those this morning?"

Finn sighed and shook his head. "Unfortunately, not. Nothing obvious. But those rocks have to be around here *somewhere*. And someone's going to find them sooner or later, so it might as well be us, right?"

He tried to inject some cheer and optimism into his voice, but his words came out as a low growl, and I could tell that he was still as upset, disgusted, and disheartened as he'd been after we'd come up empty in Deirdre's suite yesterday. Yeah, me too.

But Finn was right. Someone had to find the jewels sooner or later, and I wanted it to be us, instead of Tucker and his minions.

I *needed* it to be us—I needed a win right now, and so did Finn.

We studied the hotel schematics for a few more minutes, then headed down to the lobby, since that was the most logical place for Deirdre to have hidden the gems besides her suite. She wouldn't have risked stashing them in a guest room for a visitor or housekeeper to accidentally stumble across.

So we rode the elevator down to the first floor and split up, each one of us heading to our designated section to start searching. Finn went over to the bar area, while Bria scoped out the massive fireplace and surrounding chairs. Owen disappeared down the left hallway to check out the shops and restaurants there. I headed in the other direction and took the opposite, right hallway to do the same to the shops and restaurants on that side of the hotel.

Splitting up was a risk, but the group of us poking around would look strange and probably tip off Roxy and Brody as to what we were really doing. Besides, this way, they had four people to follow, which would make keeping track of all of us at the same time a little more difficult. Maybe we could at least identify how many people Roxy and Brody had watching us, so we would know exactly who all our enemies were. I'd take whatever small advantages I could get.

It wasn't even nine o'clock yet, but the hotel lobby was already full of people, with more and more guests arriving to take the places of those checking out on this Saturday morning. Still more people moved in and out of the shops and restaurants, while the costumed waitstaff hustled to bring out food and drinks to all the guests. Instrumental carols trilled in the background, and the lights on all the Christmas trees burned bright and steady. It was a lovely scene. Too bad so much darkness lurked beneath the holiday cheer.

I wandered up and down the hallway, going into all the shops and restaurants, and looking at everything. A couple of costumed clerks took an interest in me, pulling out their phones and texting as I roamed around their shops, but no one actually followed me, so I felt safe enough to keep going.

As I moved from one area to the next, I put myself in Deirdre's shoes, trying to figure out where I would hide a sack full of precious stones. But the more I looked, the more frustrated I became. So many people and so many staff members were constantly moving through the lobby, hallways, and shops. Even in the wee hours of the morning, a few folks would still be out and about, cleaning, straightening up, and getting ready for the next business day. I couldn't imagine Deirdre's stashing the jewels without someone realizing what she was doing, much less their staying hidden for so long with no one finding them, especially given the highly publicized treasure hunt and how hard folks had been searching, including Roxy and Brody.

Or maybe Deirdre Shaw was just that much more clever than I was, and I'd never find the stones.

Either way, my frustration had morphed into a mixture of anger, disgust, and depression by the time I reached the end of the hallway where Ira Morris's office was. I peered through the glass door, but the office was dark. No one was home. I seriously doubted that Deirdre had hidden anything in there, given that Ira hated her for demoting him to this hole in the wall, but it was worth a shot. Besides, it was the only place in my section that I hadn't looked yet.

The hallway was deserted, so I reached for my magic, letting it pool in the palm of my hand. A second later, I was clutching two slender Ice picks, which I inserted into the lock. It snicked open less than a minute later, and I slipped through to the other side, making sure to shut and lock the door behind me.

There were no windows, so I was forced to turn on the lights. Besides, the mood I was in, I just didn't care if anyone realized that I'd broken in here. I squinted against the sudden glare, staring out at the mess. Stacks of papers everywhere, framed photos crammed together on the walls, cameras, lenses, and other photography equipment scattered here and there. How could the dwarf possibly find anything in here? But there was nothing for me to do but tiptoe into the trenches.

So I looked at the first towering stack of papers that I came to, then the next, then the next. To my surprise, all of them had to do with the resort business. Supply invoices, shipping notices, pay stubs. I even found a couple of thick ledgers where guests had scrawled their names upon checking into the hotel thirty years ago. Seemed like Ira Morris was a pack rat who never threw anything away, just like Fletcher. Thinking about the old man brought a smile to my face and eased some of my anger.

Still, after about fifteen minutes of searching, I gave up. If Deirdre had hidden the jewels in here, they were buried under so many papers that I'd need a bulldozer to unearth them. I turned around to leave the office, having to sidestep all the stacks of papers I'd passed on the way in. I moved to my left, which put me close to one of the walls. A gleam of glass caught my eye, and I looked up at the picture closest to me.

Deirdre Shaw stared down at me.

I gasped and stopped so suddenly that I almost knocked over a paper tower that was taller than I was. Even then, I had to lunge forward, grab, and steady it. When I was sure that the papers weren't going to come crashing down, I let go and stared up at the photo.

It must have been taken the day Deirdre bought the resort because she looked to be in her early twenties. She was holding a giant pair of scissors and cutting through a big swath of red tape, even as she smiled and stared straight into the camera. Her pale blue eyes seemed to be directly focused on mine, and I shivered, a little creeped out by this particular ghost.

But then a thought occurred to me—if Ira had this photo of Deirdre, then maybe he had others. We hadn't found any pictures in her suite, but maybe some were in here that I could swipe and give to Finn. Oh, the pictures wouldn't answer any of his questions about his mother, but at least our trip down here wouldn't have been a complete bust.

My heart lifting, I looked at the surrounding pictures, but they were just shots of the hotel, the theme park, and all the people who'd visited them over the years. All the photos were quite lovely, especially the scenic shots, but I didn't see Deirdre in any of them—

Click.

I froze, recognizing the distinctive sound of a key turning in a lock and knowing exactly what was going to happen next.

Sure enough, a second later, Ira Morris opened the door and stepped into his office.

The dwarf was wearing more or less the same thing that he had yesterday—black cowboy boots, black jeans, and a Christmas sweater, this one a bright red and patterned with silver snowflakes trimmed with flashing white lights. Even the snowflakes on his red suspenders had tiny lights on them. What was it with people and all these cheesy holiday sweaters?

Ira blinked, surprised to find me in here, but that emotion quickly melted into outright anger that made his hazel eyes glow almost as bright as the lights on his sweater and suspenders. Of course it did. Because that's the way these things always went in my life.

"What are you doing in my office?" he snapped.

I could have lied. I probably *should* have lied. After all, I still didn't know if Ira was working for Tucker too. But after realizing that Tucker had lured us down here to take part in his twisted treasure hunt, and wasting all that time searching Deirdre's suite yesterday, I was a bit angry myself.

So instead of spinning some weak web of lies that the dwarf would see right through anyway, I shrugged. "Looking for Sweet Sally Sue's jewels. What else?"

"And you think that they're in here?" Ira let out a harsh, bitter laugh. "Trust me. If those rocks were in here, I would have found them, hocked them, and left this miserable place a long, long time ago."

I glanced around at all the resort photos on the walls and all the stacks of papers chronicling its history, one receipt, pay stub, and guest signature at a time. "No, I don't think that you would have."

I moved past the papers, ready to leave, but Ira was still blocking the door, forcing me to stop in front of him. The dwarf glared at me for several seconds before finally stepping aside.

"Thanks," I said. "Gotta get back to the lobby and see if my friends have had better luck than me."

He snorted and shook his head. "You're never going to find those jewels because they *aren't here*. Deirdre Shaw took off with them months ago."

"Maybe. Or maybe I'll surprise you and everyone else and actually find them."

He let out another harsh laugh. "I thought that you were off your rocker when you attacked Brody during the show yesterday. But now I *know* that you're crazy."

I grinned. "Sadly, that's the nicest thing anyone's said about me all weekend."

Ira blinked, then gave me a wary look, apparently thinking that I really was crazy. He wasn't the first, and he certainly wouldn't be the last person to believe that. But I slid past him, stepped out into the hallway, and left him and his mess behind.

Too bad I couldn't get rid of the mess of emotions in my head and heart so easily.

* 15 *

I went back to the lobby and headed over to the winter-
wonderland Christmas tree, where I'd agreed to meet the
others once we'd all finished searching. One of the bar-
tenders was watching me, and he pulled out his phone
and texted someone, probably Roxy. But he didn't approach me, so I ignored him and studied the holiday ornaments and decorations. My friends showed up a few
minutes later, and we stepped to a more secluded spot
behind the winter-wonderland tree.

"Anything?" I asked.

Finn, Bria, and Owen all shook their heads.

"I just don't see where Deirdre could have hidden
the jewels," Owen rumbled. "Every place I looked is too
public with too many people constantly coming and
going."

"Yeah," Bria said. "I have to think that if those gems
were here, someone would have found them already."

"I agree." Finn hesitated. "Or there is another possibility."

"What?" I asked.

He looked at me. "Maybe Roxy realized that you were watching her yesterday, and that's why she talked about the jewels. Maybe she's already found them. Maybe she's just pulling our chains, watching us run around, and laughing at us the whole time."

I shook my head. "I don't think so. She and Brody both seemed genuine when they talked about how long and hard they'd been searching. But who knows, with Tucker involved. I wouldn't put anything past him."

Since we'd struck out in our search, we had nothing to do but go back to our suites and get ready for our lunch with Roxy and Brody. I didn't think that the two of them would try to kill us over plates of barbecue, especially since we hadn't found the jewels yet, but it could always be a trap, so I went into the bedroom and unzipped my suitcase. Owen moseyed inside, plopped down on the bed, and watched me pull out all my clothes, then remove a false bottom from the suitcase.

Nestled in the black foam underneath were four knives, three loaded guns, two extra clips of ammo, and several small tins of Jo-Jo's healing ointment. I thought about sliding a gun against the small of my back, but I was already wearing my usual arsenal of knives, so a gun would probably be overkill, literally. Instead, I grabbed two tins of the healing ointment, stuffing them into the pockets of my black fleece jacket.

"A false bottom?" Owen said. "That's a bit James Bond, isn't it?"

I smiled. "This suitcase belonged to Fletcher. He loved all those old spy movies. He used to do marathons of them on the weekends, especially this time of year. Finn hated them, but I loved watching the movies with Fletcher. It was our own little holiday tradition."

Owen nodded, then got up, rummaged through his own suitcase, and retrieved a gun and a couple of clips of ammo that he'd folded up in a pair of blue boxers.

"A gun stuffed into your underwear?" I said. "I see that I'm not the only one who came prepared."

He grinned back at me. "Well, I couldn't exactly fit my blacksmith hammer inside the suitcase. Besides, after what happened the last time we went on vacation in Blue Marsh, I thought that it would be wise to have some extra insurance on hand."

"And that's why I love you."

His grin widened. "I know."

I went over and kissed him, then we headed next door to Finn and Bria's suite. Together, the four of us rode the elevator to the lobby and walked from the hotel down the hill to the theme park.

Even though it was colder today than it had been yesterday, the theme park was absolutely jam-packed. More folks were out today since it was Saturday, along with double the number of costumed characters. Finn, Bria, and Owen wandered around the park, window-shopping and taking in all the sights. I followed along behind them, pretending to do the same, although I was really doing recon, like any good assassin would.

Looking at the rides, kiosks, and carts. Memorizing the layouts of all the paths, walkways, and alleys. Peering through the chain-link fence that separated the theme park from the parking lots to see where the exits were and how many security guards were stationed around them.

Knowing the turf made me feel better. Oh, I didn't know the theme park as well as I did the mean streets of Ashland, but now if something happened, I wouldn't be wandering around in here blind either.

And something *was* going to happen—I was sure of it.

I didn't spot Hugh Tucker anywhere in the crowds, but I still felt his presence as clearly as if he were standing right in front of me. The vampire had engineered this whole thing, and I knew that he was lurking in the shadows. More workers were watching and following us around today too, all of them radiating tension the same way warm air blasted off the space heaters that were scattered throughout the park. Something had to give sooner or later—and I was betting on sooner.

By the time my friends and I had made a complete circuit of the park, it was time to meet Roxy and Brody for lunch at the Feeding Trough. Yee-haw.

The two of them were standing outside the barbecue restaurant, waiting for us, and they were both dressed in their costumes. Roxy's blond hair was once again plaited into two long braids, and she was sporting a red Stetson, along with a red plaid shirt and white jeans and boots. That silver sheriff's star was pinned to her chest again, and her silver belt buckle was embossed with a giant heart made out of dazzling red and white rhinestones. Brody was dressed all in black, still playing the part of the outlaw leader, just like he had during the high-noon show yesterday.

I focused on the silver star winking on Roxy's shirt, right where her rotten heart was. She might as well have been wearing a sign: *Please, Gin, stab me right here.* I was going to be happy to oblige her—very, very soon.

Roxy gave us a cheery wave, but Brody looked far less enthused, crossing his arms over his chest and scowling at me. He must have seen that Air healer after all, because his nose was straight once more, and no signs of my pistol-whipping remained on his handsome face. Too bad.

"Hey, y'all!" Roxy chirped in a bright voice. "Are you ready for some barbecue?"

Even though I wanted to whip out one of my knives and cut her throat, I grinned back at her, still playing the part of the clueless tourist. "I'm always ready for some barbecue."

Roxy chuckled, then opened the door and stepped inside. I followed her, with my friends trooping in behind me. Brody brought up the rear.

Surprise, surprise, the inside of the Feeding Trough had a Western theme, just like the rest of the stores. Worn wooden booths lined two of the walls, with matching tables and chairs filling in the space in between. A long wooden counter with padded barstools lined the back wall, with a couple of swinging saloon doors behind it leading back into the kitchen. Old-fashioned, rusty tin signs decorated with cowboys, cacti, and cattle covered the walls, and several large tumbleweeds were crammed into the corners, along with some actual feeding troughs.

We sat at a corner table that was large enough for the six of us. A waitress dressed like a saloon girl hustled over, deposited menus on the table, and took our drink orders. Since it was just after eleven, the lunch rush was ramping up, and more and more folks streamed into the restaurant, ready to get their barbecue on before the high-noon show.

Once we were all seated, Roxy turned to me. "I hear that you run your own barbecue restaurant up in Ashland, Gin. How fun! You'll have to let me know how our little restaurant stacks up against yours."

"Of course."

I breathed in. The scent of smoked and charred meat permeated the restaurant, but that was all I sensed. No rich spices or seasonings perfumed the air, which meant that there was no real depth of flavor. This barbecue was going to be bland, at best.

Roxy kept right on talking. "Well, I think that we've got the best barbecue for miles around. Everyone says so."

"Yeah, I saw all the signs for it and the rest of the theme park on the interstate on the way down here," Bria muttered. "You couldn't miss this place even if you wanted to."

Roxy brightened, choosing to ignore my sister's sarcastic tone. "That's the idea. Why, we have some folks who come here every single year for their summer and holiday vacations. . . ."

And she was off and running. Roxy chattered on and on about the number of visitors the park had every year, the other restaurants, the amount of work that went into the daily high-noon shows, and every other small, minute detail about the resort. Despite working here for Tucker, Roxy seemed to genuinely enjoy chatting about Bullet Pointe. That, or she just wanted to bore us all to death.

My eyes glazed over, and so did those of everyone else at the table, except for Brody, who just ignored Roxy and started scrolling through screens on his phone.

Finn, Bria, and Owen chimed in when appropriate, but I didn't bother to make conversation. Instead, I scanned the restaurant, examining everyone inside. Tourists, mostly, along with several workers grabbing a quick bite to eat before the high-noon show. For once, none of the workers were watching us, since Roxy and Brody were here to do it in person, but cold unease still trickled down my spine. My friends and I had all realized that this lunch could be a trap, but we'd all agreed that it was highly unlikely that Roxy and Brody would do anything to us in such a public place with so many witnesses around. Still, now that we were here, I couldn't help but feel like we'd made a serious mistake. And wishing that I'd brought more weapons with me.

But nothing suspicious happened, and Roxy talked for ten minutes straight before the waitress finally came back with our drinks, plopping them down on the table hard enough to make some of the liquid slosh out over the top, drip down the sides of the glasses, and ooze across the wooden table.

"Patty," Roxy said in a sharp tone. "Bring us some napkins. Right now."

Patty winced at the cold displeasure in Roxy's voice, and she quickly scurried off, returned with some napkins, and mopped up the puddles of liquid. She finally took our orders and hurried off again.

"Sloppy service," I said in a low voice that only Finn could hear. "Doesn't make me hold out much hope for the quality of the food."

Finn rolled his eyes. "Everybody's a critic."

I sniffed.

He downed his sweet iced tea in three gulps and signaled the waitress for another one, but it was several more minutes before she returned with a fresh glass for him. Bria and Owen slurped down their drinks as well, but I only had a few sips of mine. Whoever had made the tea hadn't bothered to properly dissolve all the sugar in it, so it tasted like lukewarm grit more than anything else. I sniffed again. I would never serve such inferior sweet tea to *my* customers.

I pushed my tea aside and focused on Roxy, who was slurping down a sarsaparilla. Brody was drinking the same thing, throwing entire mugs of liquid back like they were no bigger than shot glasses.

"So, Roxy," I said in a neutral voice, "where did you learn to shoot like that? Your show yesterday was very impressive. All those trick shots were just amazing."

She eyed me over the rim of her mug, wondering whether I was being genuine, but she decided to play along and set her drink aside. "My daddy was a big hunter, and I wanted to be just like him when I was a kid. He's the one who taught me to shoot. He'd set up glass bottles and tin cans in our backyard, then let me go to town on them. Guess I just had a natural talent for it, because I've been doing it ever since."

"Hunting or shooting?" I asked.

Roxy grinned at me. "Both."

She pulled out one of her revolvers and started spinning it around and around, making the pearl handle and silver barrel flash underneath the lights. The weapon was like an extension of her hand, and she didn't even have to look to know exactly what she was doing with it. Instead, Roxy smiled and stared at me the whole time, the gun moving up, down, and back again in her hand.

Suddenly, she stopped, with the gun pointing right at my heart and her finger on the trigger. "Kapow," she said, grinning even wider than before.

Finn, Bria, and Owen all tensed, wondering if she was actually going to pull the trigger and shoot me in the middle of the restaurant. So did Brody. But I ignored the urge to reach for my Stone magic and forced myself to smile back at Roxy, as though this were just a casual conversation.

I raised my hands in mock surrender. "You got me, Sheriff Roxy."

"I sure did, Gin," she drawled. "I always get my man. Or woman, in this case."

Even though I itched to palm a knife, surge across the table, and stab her in the heart, I slowly lowered my hands back down to the tabletop, as though our mock game were over.

But Roxy didn't want it to be over because she kept her gun trained on me, her finger rubbing back and forth on the trigger, as if she were a split second away from shooting me after all—

"Here you go!" a voice called out.

The waitress chose that exact moment to return with our orders and started dumping plates on the table.

Roxy's green gaze locked with my gray one, both of us staring each other down. After a second, she tipped her red Stetson at me and holstered her gun. Once again, our potential showdown was stopped before it ever really got started.

But we'd face each other for real soon enough.

We all focused on our food, which was exactly what I expected from a theme-park restaurant—overpriced and underseasoned with pitifully small portions.

Finn enthusiastically dug into his meal. So did Bria and Owen, but I only picked at my potato soup and grilled-chicken salad. I just didn't have an appetite. Not when I kept expecting Roxy to whip out her gun again and shoot me at any second. But she and Brody concentrated on their food as well, with the giant shoveling French fries into his mouth in between slurps of sarsaparilla.

We all ordered the same thing for dessert—a surprisingly excellent piece of apple coffee cake, topped with a warm caramel sauce and melting vanilla-bean ice cream. It was the only good part of the meal. Then again, it was hard to mess up dessert.

Finally, the bill came, and Roxy insisted on picking up the check. Well, at least my would-be killer was nice enough to spring for lunch.

The six of us pushed away from the table and trooped out of the restaurant. I glanced around, still expecting something to happen, but I didn't see any of our usual watchers loitering on the sidewalks.

Roxy glanced at her silver watch, which had almost as many rhinestones as her belt buckle. "Well, I hate to cut this short, but Brody and I need to get ready for the high-noon show. Don't we, Brody?"

"Yep," the giant said.

"Finn, maybe you and I can meet later to finally go over the resort financials?" Roxy asked.

"Of course," Finn said.

"It's a date then." She gave us all a bright smile. "Y'all enjoy the rest of your day."

She tipped her red Stetson at us, turned, and sauntered down the sidewalk. Brody rolled his eyes and followed her.

And they just walked away. Just like that. Without so much as a backward glance at us. More cold unease trickled down my spine. Something was very, very wrong here.

"That was almost pleasant," Owen said.

"Yeah," I muttered. "Except for the fact that Roxy pulled her gun on me and she and Brody want us dead. Come on. Let's go back to the hotel."

The four of us headed in that direction, and Finn wobbled on his feet, clutching a wooden post for support.

I eyed him. "You okay?"

"Yeah. I just ate too much."

Bria snorted. "You think? You had all your barbecue-chicken sandwich and half of mine too. Not to mention all the sides you ate."

Finn groaned and clutched his stomach. "I know, and I'm going to pay for that now. Walk slow, guys. Like, waddling-along slow."

The four of us eased into the flow of people on the sidewalk, heading back toward the hotel. Once again, I glanced around, expecting to see our usual watchers, but none of them were in sight, and no one seemed to be tracking us at all. I frowned. What was Roxy up to?

We reached the end of Main Street, and I realized that Finn had fallen several steps behind. "Finn? You okay?"

Instead of answering me, he shook his head and staggered into the closest alley, still clutching his stomach, as if he were going to throw up. It would serve him right for being such a glutton at lunch.

Finn stumbled forward several more steps, then turned and looked at me, his green eyes bright and glassy.

"I . . . don't . . . feel . . . so good . . ." he mumbled.

His eyes rolled up into the back of his head, and he crumpled to the ground.

❋ 16 ❋

"Finn!" I yelled. "Finn!"

I rushed over to him, with Bria and Owen moving much slower behind me. By this point, we were halfway down the alley, underneath a large maple tree with bare, skeletal branches, well away from the crowds on Main Street.

I started to crouch down beside Finn, who was unconscious, but Bria stumbled into me, almost knocking me down.

"I don't feel . . . so good . . . either . . ." she mumbled, her blue eyes as glassy as Finn's had been.

She collapsed too, sprawling across the asphalt at my feet, unconscious just like Finn was. Worry clenched my stomach. What was going on here?

"Gin," Owen rasped in a low voice.

My head snapped around in his direction. He too was wobbling on his feet, but he pointed to the alley entrance.

Roxy was standing there, holding one of her revolvers,

spinning the weapon around and around in her hand, just as she had in the restaurant. Brody was right next to her, along with some of the giant outlaws from his gang. But I focused on the man in the dark suit standing in their midst. Black hair, black eyes, black goatee, cold, smug smirk.

Hugh Tucker had finally shown himself.

The vampire gave me a bored look and waved his hand. "Take them," he called out. "Alive."

I thought of that sugary grit in the sweet iced tea—tea that my friends had all drunk, while Roxy and Brody had sipped sarsaparillas instead. Not sugar after all, but some kind of sedative, designed to knock us out, so Tucker could do whatever he wanted to us.

Owen fell to his knees, still staring up at me. "Run, Gin," he whispered. "Run!"

Then he too collapsed to the ground unconscious.

I palmed a knife to step up and fight Tucker, Roxy, Brody, and all the rest of them. But my stomach rumbled, and for a moment my vision went haywire, making me see two of everything. I'd drunk the sweet tea as well, just not as much of it as my friends had.

Finn, Bria, and Owen were down, and I had a whole passel of bad guys advancing on me. I wouldn't be able to kill them all before I lost consciousness too. I'd be lucky if I was able to take down one of them. So I did the only thing I could.

I turned and ran away like the proverbial yellow-bellied coward.

I sprinted toward the far end of the alley as fast as I could, knowing that I had to put some distance between me and my enemies before the sedative—or whatever they'd slipped us—took effect and knocked me out as well.

Even now, I could feel the drug working on me. My legs wobbled, my breath came in short, ragged gasps, and sweat streamed down my face, despite the frigid temperature. My stomach gurgled, the ominous rumble sounding like a freight train hitting top speed.

"Get her!" Tucker hissed somewhere behind me. "Don't let her get away, you idiots!"

"Sure thing, boss," Roxy called out.

I was so focused on just making it to the end of the alley that her words didn't register for a few precious seconds. When they finally did sink into my brain, I realized what she was up to. I cursed and reached for my Stone magic, trying to harden my skin in time—

Crack!

Too little, too late. A bullet punched through my upper left arm, making me scream, stagger forward, and slam into the wall of the closest building. My blood sprayed all over the dark wood, freezing and sticking there like oddly shaped snowflakes. It was a beautiful, skillful shot, a through-and-through designed to slow me down without killing me.

It hurt like a son of a bitch.

Getting shot was bad enough, but the bullet that punched through my arm had the added, evil bonus of being coated with Roxy's Fire magic. She might only have a moderate amount of power, but she must have spent hours, if not days, coating that silverstone bullet and all the others in her guns with her Fire magic. The result felt like I'd just been blasted by a true powerhouse elemental, someone like Mab Monroe or Harley Grimes.

Even as the bullet tore through my arm, Fire exploded in the wound, and the stench of my own burning flesh filled the air. I screamed again and rammed my body up against the building, trying to smother and snuff out the flames, but this was elemental Fire, and it just kept right on burning and burning.

More screams spewed out of my lips, and I clamped my free hand over the wound and blasted it with my Ice magic. That made me scream too, but the cold force of my power finally extinguished the Fire.

It still hurt like a son of a bitch, though.

The Fire had cauterized the holes in my arm, so that I wasn't bleeding, but I could feel the ugly, blistered burns that it had left behind—ones that pulsed and throbbed with red-hot pain with every breath I took. Even the cooling effect of my Ice power wasn't enough to stop the Fire magic from searing all the way through the wound and the layers of surrounding skin. I knew that it would keep right on hurting until I could get the two holes patched up, as well as do something about the charred skin inside and all around the wound.

But first, I had to get out of here. So I swallowed down the rest of my screams and pushed away from the wall.

Crack!

This time, Roxy's bullet thunked lower into the wall, right where my left thigh had been half a second ago. More Fire exploded, licking at my clothes and making me throw my hand up to ward off the flames, but I kept going, lurching around the side of the building and out of her line of fire, so to speak.

An all-too-brief reprieve.

This alley opened up into a walkway that was full of people, along with food and souvenir carts. I plowed into the heart of the crowd, sidestepping clusters of tourists, but the drug in my system made it difficult, and I ended up stumbling into folks more often than not.

All of which made it easy for Roxy and Brody to spot me.

"There she is!" Brody's voice boomed out behind me. "Get her! Get that thief!"

Roxy might be a sharpshooter, but even she couldn't risk firing at me with all these tourists around. So the giant and the rest of his outlaw gang started whooping and hollering, as though their chasing me were just another act for the crowd. People fell for it, stepping back to make room for Brody and his goons to stampede after me. Some of the tourists even started yelling and clapping in return, enjoying the spectacle.

Well, if the crowd wanted a show, I was going to give them a good one.

I started deliberately plowing into people, knocking them aside and trying to create as many obstacles behind me as I could. I also overturned barrels, kiosks, and other displays, including a whole rack of Western wear that had the guy manning it yelling curses at me. Cowboy hats sailed through the air, floating on the winter wind, while silver belt buckles *plink-plink-plink*ed against the asphalt like bullet casings.

I reached another alley at the end of this walkway, staggered into it, and headed back toward Main Street, where the majority of the crowd still was. I couldn't let Roxy, Brody, and the giants catch me. If that happened, Finn, Bria, and Owen were dead, and me along with them. Tortured first, for whatever information Tucker thought we had about the gems, and then murdered, so that we wouldn't be a threat to him and the Circle anymore. Tucker would probably let Roxy use us all for target practice with her Fire-coated bullets, then have Brody and the rest of the giants dump our bodies in the lake.

So I kept plowing ahead, knowing that I couldn't stop, not even for a second. But I was running out of gas—fast. My heart was pounding from all the bobbing, weaving, and shoving through the crowd, making the drug circulate through my body much more quickly than normal. Even though I was flat out sprinting, my legs still felt heavy, numb, and slow, as though I were running underwater. The double vision was getting worse and worse, and my head felt disconnected from the rest of my body, like a balloon that was about to pop off my neck and drift up into the wild blue yonder.

Even worse, Roxy, Brody, and the giants were gaining on me.

I could hear the steady *slap-slap-slap-slap* of their boots on the asphalt, along with the answering *jingle-jangle* chorus from their silver spurs. In minutes they would run me down, or the drug would finally knock me out, or both. So when I reached the end of the alley and sprinted back out onto Main Street, I darted into the first building I came to, hoping that I could lose them that way.

Naturally, it was the Good Tyme Saloon.

I stumbled through the double swinging doors and ran right into a line of saloon girls, who were swishing their skirts and kicking up their heels to some loud, lively piano music. The girls weren't happy about my slamming into them and interrupting their big finish. Then again, ruining shows was rapidly becoming a habit of mine.

"Hey!"

"Watch out!"

"What do you think you're doing!"

Harsh, angry cries rose up all around me, but the tourists sitting at the tables ringing the dance floor thought that it was all just part of the show, and they cheered, whistled, and stomped their feet even harder and louder than before.

One saloon girl shoved me out of her way, straight into another one, who shoved me right back at that first girl. In an instant, I went pinballing down the whole line of them, bouncing off one after another. Eventually, I staggered forward, landing right in the lap of an old guy with crooked yellow teeth who leered at me.

"Here to give me a lap dance, honey?" he cackled.

"Here's your lap dance," I growled back.

I reached over, snatched up the glass mug of sarsaparilla that he was sipping, and smashed it over his head, making the dark brown liquid foam and spew all over his face.

The guy howled with pain and shoved me away, but not before I grabbed another full mug off his table. I staggered to a stop in the middle of the dance floor, sarsaparilla slopping up and out of the glass, soaking into my clothes, and spattering against the wooden floorboards.

At this point, the piano music abruptly stopped, the saloon girls scrambled off the dance floor, and the tourists finally realized that maybe I wasn't part of the show after all. But before I could even think about moving, Brody crashed through the swinging doors.

"There she is!" he yelled.

The giant came at me head-on, his arms stretching out wide. I ducked out of the way of his bone-crushing bear hug, whirled around, and smashed the sarsaparilla mug across the back of his head. The glass shattered, making Brody yelp, lose his cowboy hat, stumble forward, and plow directly into a table full of guys, knocking their plastic baskets of wings and nachos to the floor and making them spill their beers all over themselves.

That last, cardinal sin was what officially started the saloon fight.

Those guys got exceptionally pissed that they were now wearing their beer instead of drinking it, and they jumped to their feet. Two of them advanced on Brody, while the other two came at me.

I was wobbling so badly that I could barely stand, much less fight back, so I grabbed the closest saloon girl, twirled her around like we were doing a do-si-do, and shoved her at the two guys coming at me. She squealed, and all three of them fell to the ground in a heap of arms, legs, black lace, and crinoline.

Click.

Over the chaos, I heard the hammer snap back on a revolver, and I looked up to see Roxy standing just inside the saloon doors, her gun trained on me, evil intent glinting in her pale green eyes. She took a step forward to better her aim and make sure that she wouldn't shoot a tourist by mistake, but more and more people started pushing, shouting, and screaming at each other, blocking her shot. I whirled around and ran straight past the bar, shoved through another set of swinging double doors, and ended up in the back of the saloon.

It reminded me of the back of the Pork Pit, with napkins, straws, mugs, and other supplies stacked up on metal shelves, along with several refrigerators and a couple of freezers humming away up against the walls. For a mad, mad moment, I considered climbing into a freezer to hide, but I'd run out of air long before Roxy and Brody stopped searching for me.

So I stumbled over to the back door, wrenched it open, and staggered outside. I was expecting another alley, but I was in the staging area with its wide wooden pavilions sheltering all the cowboy clothes, hats, boots, and more.

A white horse tied to a nearby hitching post whinnied and shied away as I limped past, obviously realizing that something was seriously wrong with me and wanting no part of it.

"Zip it, Silver," I hissed. "You're going to blow my cover."

Then I realized that I was trying to shush a horse, and I giggled. I never, ever *giggled*, but right now, all I wanted to do was lie down on the ground and just laugh and laugh and laugh. Oh, yeah. I was *this close* to passing out from whatever drug had been in that sweet tea.

I wasn't going to be able to outrun Roxy and Brody, but maybe I could outsmart them. All I had to do was find a place to hole up and hide until the drug was out of my system. Then, when my giggles were gone, I could come back and kill every last one of these bastards, starting with Hugh Tucker. Not the best plan I'd ever come up with, but my brain was too slow and muddled to think of anything else right now.

But where to hide?

The horse wanted nothing to do with me, and I was no cowgirl anyway, so I couldn't mount the animal and ride away. Given that the pavilions were all open, Roxy and Brody would easily spot me hiding behind the barrels, hay bales, and racks of clothing. I didn't have the energy to try to climb up the stairs to the second story of the saloon, much less make it up onto the roof, and the only other things back here were fake cacti, brittle balls of tumbleweed, and the stagecoach that was used in the high-noon show—

The stagecoach.

That might work.

I hobbled over to the stagecoach, which was parked under its own pavilion at the very back of the staging area. From a distance, the coach looked new and shiny, but up close, I could see just how battered, dented, and worn-out it really was, just like everything else in the theme park. Bits of metal glinted like silver ore all along the sides where the bright, glossy red paint had been chipped off, and all four of the wheels looked like they were barely hanging on to their axles. The stagecoach door was standing open, as though it were broken and wouldn't shut properly, and I could see a large strongbox inside—the same one that had been full of fake gold during yesterday's show.

The strongbox looked just big enough for me to cram myself into, but I hesitated. It was such an obvious hiding place, and no doubt Roxy and Brody would look in the stagecoach when they finally shoved their way through the saloon fight and raced out here. As I cursed and started to turn around to find a better hiding place, I spotted a ladder on the back of the stagecoach that led up to the roof. Several steamer trunks had been tied down to the roof to represent fake luggage, but it looked like there was enough room for me to wiggle in between them. Still, I hesitated again. Because my enemies would no doubt check the stagecoach roof too—

"Do you see her?" Brody's voice boomed through the door that I'd left standing wide-open at the back of the saloon. "Where did she go?"

I was out of time and options, so I grabbed the ladder. My muscles felt about as strong as wet spaghetti, but I managed to hoist myself up onto the roof. The effort made me even more light-headed, and everything blurred together as though I were on a merry-go-round. I staggered to the side and almost fell off the stagecoach before my vision cleared, and I slowly righted myself.

Two rows of steamer trunks lined the top of the coach, with a narrow sliver of space in between them. I sucked in my stomach, pulled my shoulders back, and flopped down, squirming my way into that space like a fish trying to wiggle back onto a hook. It was a tight fit, but I managed it, even though my body was as stiff and straight as a board resting between the two rows of luggage.

A small gap ran in between two of the trunks where

they hadn't been set up flush against each other, so I squirmed up a little higher until I could look through the opening and see out into the staging area. The effort made my head spin, and it was several seconds before I could focus again.

I could hear Roxy and Brody shouting at the giants to move their asses, and a few seconds later, all of them came running out of the back of the saloon. They stopped, glancing from one pavilion to the next, and their faces twisted with fury when they didn't spot me.

"Spread out!" Roxy barked. "Find Blanco! Now!"

"You heard her!" Brody yelled. "Search everywhere!"

The giants hurried to follow their bosses' commands, darting into the alleys that led back to Main Street, while Roxy and Brody stayed behind in the staging area. The two of them spread out, guns in hands, searching behind every single barrel, hay bale, and rack of clothes, just as I'd expected. Brody even grabbed a long, sharp pitchfork and poked it down into all the water troughs, just in case I'd suddenly developed gills and could breathe underwater like a fish. The snarky thought made me want to giggle again, but I swallowed down the crazy laughter.

"She has to be around here somewhere," Brody said. "Why didn't you give her more of that sedative?"

"I couldn't *make* her drink that tea," Roxy snapped back. "It's not my fault that the cook didn't dissolve all the powder in it like I told her to, and Blanco didn't like how it tasted. Besides, she still drank almost half a glass. That should be more than enough to knock her out. The other three are all out cold. I've got some of your boys taking them up to the hotel so that Tucker can question them when they wake up."

"I still don't see why he wants them alive," Brody said. "Deirdre probably hocked those jewels long ago. If they were here, we would have found them by now. He should just cut his losses and kill the lot of them instead of making us keep up this stupid charade."

"And I don't pay you to think, Mr. Dalton," a mild voice murmured.

Roxy and Brody both winced and slowly turned around. Hugh Tucker was standing at the back door of the saloon. The vampire must have followed the commotion of my mad dash through the theme park.

He walked over to Brody, and the giant whipped off his black hat in a sign of respect and deference. Roxy also removed her red Stetson and eased a few steps away from her partner. She did not want to be the center of Tucker's attention. Smart.

And neither did Brody, judging from the way the giant shifted on his feet, making his leather boots creak and the attached spurs jangle out a sharp warning.

"I heard that Blanco pistol-whipped you with your own gun during the high-noon show yesterday. Is that true?" Tucker's voice was steady, without a trace of malice, but his eyes were like two black holes in his face, completely devoid of emotion.

Brody swallowed and nodded. "Yes, sir, I'm afraid that it is—"

Before he could finish, Tucker reached down, snatched

Brody's revolver out of his hand, and slammed the weapon right back into the giant's face.

Crack.

The audible sound of the giant's nose breaking rang out like a gunshot through the staging area.

Brody yelped and staggered back, blood spewing out of his rapidly swelling nose. For a second, his face flushed red and purple with surprise and rage, and his hand hovered over the second revolver strapped to his waist, as though he were actually thinking about drawing on Tucker.

But Tucker arched his black eyebrows in a silent challenge, and Brody thought better of things and dropped his hand from his gun. Tucker tossed the first revolver back at the giant, who scrambled to catch it.

I blinked, wondering if I was hallucinating how fast Tucker was, but, for once, my vision remained clear. Drinking other people's blood gave most vampires enhanced strength and senses, but it seemed to make Tucker exceptionally speedy. Or perhaps he had some sort of natural vampiric ability that helped with that. Either way, he'd broken Brody's nose in the blink of an eye. I'd have to find a way to counter Tucker's speed before I killed him.

"I don't pay you to think," Tucker repeated. "I pay you to follow orders and get me the results that I want. And right now, I want Gin Blanco found and trussed up like a Christmas ham. So get out there, do your damn job, and find her. Or next time, I'll break a lot more than just your nose." His dead black eyes focused on Roxy. "On both of you."

"Yes, sir!" Roxy and Brody both snapped out the words in unison, but Tucker had already gone back into the saloon, disappearing from sight.

They waited a few seconds to make sure that he wasn't coming back, then slowly relaxed. Brody yanked off his black-and-white paisley bandanna and pressed it to his nose, trying to stop the stream of blood dripping down his face. Roxy rubbed her thumb over and over the pearl handle of her revolver, a nervous tic.

"You heard what he said," she growled. "Now let's find that bitch before he comes back and makes good on his promise."

Brody gave her a sullen look, but he wiped the last of the blood off his face and helped her search the rest of the staging area. It didn't take long, and finally they both turned to stare at the stagecoach, since it was the only place they hadn't yet looked.

"She's not here," Brody said. "I'm telling you that Blanco is long gone."

"Well, check the stagecoach anyway," Roxy snapped back. "I sent giants to all the park and hotel exits right before we met Blanco and the others at the restaurant. They've all texted back to say that she didn't get past them. So she has to be somewhere in the theme park."

Brody heaved out a long, loud, suffering sigh, but he followed Roxy over to the stagecoach. She peered in the carriage below me, and a faint creak sounded as she opened the strongbox lid, just to make sure that I hadn't crammed myself in there.

"Look up on the roof," she ordered Brody.

More creaks sounded, this time from the springs, and

the entire coach dipped under the giant's weight as he took hold of the ladder on the back.

I silently cursed, but there was nothing I could do. The drug had completely taken over my body, making me feel limp, languid, and slightly disconnected from everything that was happening. Plus, I was wedged in so tightly between the two rows of steamer trunks that I couldn't even palm a knife to try to take the giant by surprise when he finally spotted me.

And he *would* spot me.

All Brody had to do was look over the first row of trunks, and he'd see me lying here. Then he'd either pound me into oblivion or reach down, toss me off the stagecoach, and let Roxy put a few bullets in me. Either way, I was caught—

"What are you two doing?" a low voice growled. "And why is everyone running around like chickens with their heads cut off?"

Brody stopped climbing, although I could just see the top of the giant's black hat at the rear of the stagecoach. I turned my head and looked back out through the gap in the trunks.

Ira Morris stood in the staging area, his arms crossed over his chest, and an angry look on his weathered face. I had never been so glad to see the surly dwarf.

"Well?" he snapped. "What's going on? You two should be getting ready for the high-noon show, not lollygagging around back here. And what is wrong with Brody's nose?"

Roxy flashed Ira a smile. "Actually, we're going to have to postpone the show until later this afternoon."

Ira's eyes narrowed. "And why is that?"

"Brody and the giants were chasing after a pickpocket who made off with a woman's purse," Roxy said in a smooth voice. "The pickpocket busted up Brody's nose in the scuffle, and we were hoping to find him before he got out of the park. Isn't that right, Brody?"

"Yeah," the giant said. "That's right."

Ira huffed, then held his hands out wide. "Well, that pickpocket is obviously not back here. So why don't you get down from there before you break that ladder? It's too rickety to hold a big fella like you, and I don't need anything else to fix around here."

Brody gave the other man a mulish look, but he hopped down off the ladder, making the entire stagecoach rock from side to side at the sudden loss of his weight. "Whatever," he muttered.

Ira stared him down a moment before turning to Roxy. "Now, why don't you two go search somewhere else and let me do my job? I need to take a look at the stagecoach wheels and make sure that everything is ready for the next show. Whenever the two of you get your act together and finally decide to hold it."

Roxy glanced at Brody, who shook his head, telling her that I wasn't hiding on top of the stagecoach. For once, I'd gotten lucky, and Ira had distracted the giant before he could actually look on the roof. A small favor, but I'd take what I could get right now.

"Well?" Ira snapped. "Are you going to get out of my way and let me do my job? Or are you just going to stand there all day?"

Anger sparked in Roxy's eyes, but she wanted to find me more than she wanted to deal with him right now.

"Sure thing, Ira," she said. "C'mon, Brody. Let's see if the others have had better luck finding that pickpocket."

She smiled at the dwarf a final time, then she and Brody left the stagecoach behind, walked through the pavilions, stepped into the back of the saloon, and shut the door behind them.

"Good riddance," Ira muttered.

I breathed a soft sigh of relief. Roxy and Brody were gone, and all I had to do was wait for Ira to look over the stagecoach and leave. Then I could climb down from the roof and find someplace better to hide until my body flushed the sedative out of my system.

I really should have known better than to even think that I was in the clear.

Ira looked over his shoulder, making sure that Roxy and Brody were gone, then scrambled up to the top of the stagecoach ladder, tipped his black bowler hat back on his head, and stared down at me.

"How did you get down in there?" he said. "Determined little thing, aren't you?"

All I could do was stare up at him, my body feeling cold, heavy, and numb, and my mind growing foggier and foggier as the sedative swept through me.

He shook his head. "Now I'm going to have to slice through all the ropes and move all the trunks just to get you out of there. . . ."

The dwarf kept muttering to himself about how much trouble I was causing him, but I could do nothing to stop him, so I tuned him out.

My fingers felt as cold, heavy, and numb as the rest of my body, and I fumbled in my jacket pocket, trying to pull out my cell phone. It took me three tries, but I finally managed it.

I squinted at the screen, trying to see my contacts. For once, I was glad that Silvio had programmed my phone with a special spider rune beside his name. Like the Bat Signal, but in reverse, for when you wanted to summon Alfred instead of Bruce Wayne.

Ira was standing on top of the stagecoach, and he reached into his jeans pocket, drew out a switchblade, and flicked it open.

I hit the screen, determined to make my call before the dwarf cut through the ropes and then used that knife to cut into me. A second later, the call went through. True to form, the person on the other end answered almost immediately.

"What's up, Gin?" Silvio's voice filled my ear. "Do you need something?"

"I—" That one single word came out as a garbled croak.

"Gin?" Silvio's voice immediately sharpened. "What's going on? What's wrong?"

"I—" I tried again, but the sound was as garbled as before.

The balloon of my mind seemed to be drifting farther and farther away from the rest of me, higher and higher and faster and faster all the while. I needed to tell Silvio what had happened. About Finn, Bria, and Owen being captured. About me being drugged. About the man looming over me with a knife.

But only one thought filled my mind, along with those strange, crazy giggles.

"Don't eat the barbecue," I whispered, giggles punctuating each and every word. "Don't eat the barbecue. . . ."

"Gin? Are you drunk? Are you hurt? Where are you? What's happening?" Silvio's voice sharpened with every single word, and I could hear his fingers flying over a keyboard.

I wondered if the vamp was already trying to track my phone. Probably. He was extremely efficient that way. The thought made me giggle again.

Ira leaned down and pried the phone out of my fingers. "I don't think you need to be making any calls right now."

"Gin? Gin! Who is that talking? Are you still there? Gin!" Silvio's voice continued to sound through the phone.

Ira rolled his eyes at Silvio's frantic cries, ended the call, and stuffed my phone into his jeans pocket as though it were his own. I really was out of my mind because, instead of being concerned, I focused my gaze on the white lights flashing on the dwarf's snowflake Christmas sweater. Such pretty, pretty lights . . .

Ira frowned and leaned down again, the switchblade glinting like liquid silver in his hand.

Mercifully, the drug finally pulled me under before I saw or felt him stab me with the blade.

* 17 *

My mom's annual holiday party was in full swing.

I peered through the railing that lined the second-floor balcony, staring down at all the elegantly dressed people filling our large living room below. Men in classic black tuxedos, diamond cuff links winking on their shirtsleeves. Women in colorful ball gowns, sapphires, rubies, and emeralds hanging from their ears, necks, and wrists. Even up here, above the soft, trilling carols of the harpists, I could hear the whispers of all those precious stones, each and every one vainly singing about its own sparkling beauty.

Waiters clad in red and green tuxedo vests moved through the crowd, handing out dainty appetizers and tall glasses of golden, bubbly champagne, and everyone was talking, eating, laughing, drinking, and having a good time. Mistletoe, tinsel, and soft white lights were strung up along the mantel, with potted poinsettias flanking the fireplace with its cheery, crackling flames. Still more greenery, lights, and poinsettias were clustered in the corners of the room, and the air smelled like pine sap mixed with a hint of woodsmoke. The pretty scene reminded me of one of my mom's snow globes. All it needed was some fake flakes and glitter swirling up into the air to make it complete.

Even though it was almost midnight, the party was still going strong, and my mom was right in the thick of things, moving from one group of guests to the next, smiling, laughing, and shaking everyone's hand. After that tense meeting in her office, Mom had come up to the family room to help Bria and me decorate our Christmas tree, although she'd brushed off all my questions about Hugh and Deirdre and what they wanted her to do. Instead, Mom had pretended like everything was fine, just like she was doing right now, by mingling with all her guests.

I was supposed to be in bed, but I couldn't sleep, so I'd slipped out here to watch the action. But that had been twenty minutes ago, and I was getting bored. So I moved away from the balcony and went over to the Christmas tree in the corner of the family room, the one that my sisters and I had decorated earlier today. Well, mostly decorated. Several snow globes and other ornaments were still strewn across the floor, waiting to be hung. But the tree was plenty decorated enough for me.

I lay down underneath the Christmas tree and scooted over to the far corner, lying on my back and peering up through the branches at all the ornaments, lights, and tinsel above. This was one of my favorite things to do every single year. Normally, I would do it on Christmas morning when we were all gathered around the tree and had finished opening our presents, but Annabella had made fun of me last year, saying that only a little kid would crawl behind the tree. So I'd just go ahead and do it now, when she wasn't around to tease me.

I didn't know how long I lay there, staring up at the lights and the soft glimmers of glass, but I must have dozed off because the next thing I knew, the mansion was silent. The talking, the laughing, the carols. All the noise from the party had vanished. Everyone must have gone home while I was sleeping.

I rubbed the sand out of my eyes and sat up. At least, I started to, but then I remembered where I was and ducked back down at the last second. I just managed to avoid up-ending the Christmas tree and knocking the whole thing down. That would have been a disaster*, especially with all my mom's snow globes on it. No doubt I would have broken every single one.*

As I started to crawl out from behind the tree, the creak of the stairs made me stop. That was probably Mom, coming to turn off the holiday lights. So I stayed where I was, hoping that she would just walk down the hallway and not actually open our doors and look inside to make sure that we were in bed.

I hunkered down and peered through the branches, expecting to see her black stilettos. But instead, a pair of black boots appeared at the top of the stairs. I frowned. Why would Mom be wearing boots?

She wouldn't, I realized. For a second, I thought that it must be Annabella, coming home late after sneaking out to meet her friends, but then I noticed that the boots were far too large to belong to her. I froze, then slowly looked up through the branches, my mind finally putting the pieces together.

Someone was in our house.

The boots stepped forward, and a tall man emerged out of the shadows. He was dressed all in black, with black gloves and a black ski mask covering his head and face.

An intruder was in our house.

That horrible thought kept rattling around inside my brain, with questions popping up beside it, like holiday lights blazing to life one after another. What was this man doing here? Was this a . . . robbery?

Several houses in the neighborhood had been robbed in recent weeks, folks coming home from parties and other late nights out to find that someone had broken in while they were gone and had stolen all the presents from beneath their trees, just like the Grinch in that old holiday cartoon.

I held my breath, wondering what the man could possibly steal, since we hadn't put any of our presents out yet. Or maybe he was here for my mom's jewelry, some of the antique knickknacks in the house, or even the stacks of money piled in her office safe. He stepped forward and dropped his hand down to his side.

That's when I saw the gun.

My eyes widened, and my breath caught in my throat. Not here to steal—here to kill.

All around me, the stones of our mansion whispered, but the vain, happy trills of the partygoers' gemstones had been replaced by dark, harsh mutters. Whoever the gunman was, he was dangerous, and his evil intentions were brutal enough to have already left emotional vibrations in the stone.

The man walked over to the tree and stopped, as though he was admiring the decorations. I clapped my hands over my mouth to hold back the scream rising in my throat and shrank back against the wall, desperately wishing that I could melt into it and escape out the other side.

But all I could do was stay as still and quiet as a mouse, hoping that he wouldn't look down at the floor and spot me through the thick branches, silver tinsel, and twinkling lights. The scent of pine sap, which had been so pleasant before, now seemed like poison sliding down my throat, choking me from the inside out.

Finally, the man stepped away from the tree and left the family area behind. He stopped in the middle of the hallway, as if he was unsure where to go. Then he started forward again, and I realized that he was walking toward Annabella's and Bria's bedrooms.

The thought of the gunman hurting my sisters cut through some of my panic, and anger sparked in place of my fear. He wasn't going to hurt them. Not if I could help it. I chewed my lip. But what could I do against a guy with a gun? I didn't know, but I had to do something, even if it was only run away, find my mom, and warn her what was happening. Then again, she could be asleep too, and I could be the only one who realized that the intruder was in the house.

So it was up to me to stop him.

I waited until the gunman had moved deeper into the hallway, then slowly wiggled out from behind the branches. I crouched by the side of the tree and eased forward, looking into the hallway beyond. The man slowed, as if counting the doors that lined the walls and trying to decide which one he wanted to enter.

I glanced over at the stairs, hoping that my mom would

suddenly appear, come running up here, and blast him with her Ice magic, but she didn't. In fact, I didn't hear any movement anywhere in the house.

My mind churned and churned, trying to come up with a plan that would let me save everyone. I could use my Stone magic to harden my skin the way that my mom had been teaching me to. That would keep me safe from the gunman's bullets, but Annabella and Bria hadn't inherited our father's Stone magic so they couldn't protect themselves like I could.

But my Stone magic wouldn't let me actually hurt the man in return, so I looked around again, searching for some sort of weapon that I could use against him. Maybe if I could sneak up and hit him from behind, I could stop him long enough to scream, run off, and sound the alarm. After that, all I had to do was get my mom, and everything would be fine.

I was sure of it.

But the only things around me were the glass ornaments, silver tinsel, and snow globes we hadn't gotten around to putting on the tree. Not exactly great weapons. Still, I picked up the biggest, heaviest globe and crept forward a few more feet, ready to leap up, reach for my magic, start screaming, and storm down the hallway after the intruder.

But he didn't open any of the doors, and he moved past the bedrooms where Annabella and Bria were sleeping. Instead, he turned the corner at the far end of the hallway and vanished. More stairs creaked, and I realized that he was heading down to the ground floor.

I frowned. Why would he go back there? The only thing on that side of the house was my mom's office—

I sucked in a breath. He was here to kill my mom. I knew

it, deep down in my bones, just like I knew that I had to stop him.

I got to my feet and hurried to the end of the hallway. I looked around the corner there, searching for the gunman. Sure enough, he was already downstairs, moving faster now, and stepping into the hallway that would take him to my mom's office. I ran down the stairs after him, my stockinged feet barely making a whisper on the floor.

The intruder was now right outside my mom's office, standing in the same spot where I'd been just a few hours ago, watching Mom talk to that vampire, Hugh, along with that Deirdre woman. I shivered, remembering the vampire's dead, black eyes. I wondered if Tucker was the masked gunman. He certainly seemed like the type who would sneak into a house and murder someone in the middle of the night.

The man reached into his pants pocket, drew out a silencer, and screwed it onto the end of his gun. While he was distracted, I tiptoed forward a few more steps and hunkered down behind a table set up against the wall.

When he finished with his silencer, the man stretched out his free hand and gently tried the office door. The knob turned easily, and he opened the door a crack and stopped, waiting to see if my mom had noticed anything. But she hadn't, and I could hear the steady, continued clickety-clack-clack of her typing as she worked on her computer.

The man drew in a breath as if to steady himself, then threw open the door and burst into the office. Fear and panic rose up in my throat, choking me, but I pushed the feelings aside, got to my feet, and took off in a dead sprint, knowing that I had to get to him before he pulled the trigger.

"What—what are you doing—" Mom sputtered in a shocked voice.

"Greetings from the Circle," the man spat out, although I barely registered his words, much less had time to think about what they meant.

I careened to a stop in the doorway. In front of me, the man snapped up his weapon to fire. Mom pushed back from her desk and shot to her feet, sending her chair rolling across the floor, but she was going to be too slow to get out of the way of the bullets, much less call up her Ice magic to create a shield to protect herself.

That anger filled me again, stronger than before, and I let out a loud yell and charged forward.

The man was so surprised that he turned to one side, his weapon wavering, but I didn't slow down. I drew back my hand and smashed the snow globe into the side of his head as hard as I could.

The globe shattered on impact, spraying fake snow, glitter, and water everywhere, and a sharp, jagged, curved piece of glass cut into my right hand, leaving a deep, ugly mark in the center of my palm. I yelped in pain, and the man stepped forward and slapped his pistol across my face. Pain exploded in my cheek, and I flew across the room, bounced off the wall, and slid to the floor.

"Stupid kid," he growled, aiming his weapon at me. "You should have stayed in your room."

Dazed, I looked up into the black eye of his gun, knowing what was coming next and that there was no way that I could stop it. . . .

"I told you, mister," a low voice growled. "You need

to quit calling this phone. She's not any more awake than she was the last time you called exactly one minute ago."

My eyes snapped open. I knew that twangy, Western voice. That was Ira Morris, and unless I was still dreaming, the dwarf hadn't killed me after all.

So what did he want with me?

It took me a few seconds to clear the rest of the dreamy cobwebs out of my mind. I slowly sat up and realized that I was lying on a soft, comfortable bed in what looked like a rustic cabin. Dark wooden walls, colorful, braided throw rugs on the floor, gray stone fireplace flanked by a set of padded rocking chairs. The cheery space was made even more so by all the photos. They covered every available inch of the walls and showed the Bullet Pointe hotel, the theme park, and the surrounding lake. This was definitely Ira's house.

I vaguely remembered Finn's telling me that the resort manager lived in a cabin on the property. Looked like Ira had at least held on to his home when Deirdre had demoted him, if not his office in the hotel, which Roxy had taken over. Good for him.

I swung my legs over the side of the bed, wincing at the pounding in my head, as well as the dull aches that rippled through my chest, back, and legs. In horse terms, I felt like I'd been rode hard and put up wet. Weird. I hadn't thought that Roxy had hurt me that badly, but just about every part of me felt bruised, beaten, and battered.

But I shoved the pain away and took stock of my situation. My boots were sitting on a rug next to the bed, but

I was still wearing my black jeans. My black fleece jacket had been removed and draped over one of the rocking chairs, and the left sleeve of my red sweater had also been sliced open.

I pushed the flaps of fabric aside. A white bandage was wrapped around my upper left arm, tied off with a neat little knot. I flexed my fist and moved my arm and shoulder. A little stiffness and pain, but nothing that I couldn't handle. I looked around and spotted two empty tins of Jo-Jo's healing ointment sitting on top of the dresser along the wall. Ira must have found them in my jacket pockets, realized what they were, and used them on the Fire burns and bullet holes that Roxy had put in my arm.

Even more important, all five of my silverstone knives were laid out in a row on the dresser. Ira must have removed them, along with my boots and jacket, to make me more comfortable. But I felt naked without my knives, so I got up and slid them back into their usual slots—one against the small of my back, two up my sleeves, and two tucked into my boots.

I opened the bedroom door and stepped out into the main part of the cabin, which was a living room, dining room, and kitchen all rolled into one. A larger fireplace took up most of one wall, flanked by a green couch with colorful blankets folded across the back. Two small tables at either end of the couch featured lamps shaped like cowboy boots, and other Western-themed knickknacks adorned the rest of the space. But the effect was charming, rather than garish, as it had been in Roxy's office, and best of all, no dead animals were anywhere in sight.

Still more pictures adorned the walls in this part of

the cabin, while cameras, lenses, memory cards, and other photography equipment covered the dining-room table, along with several stacks of papers. But the mess was limited to that one table instead of filling up the entire cabin. Ira Morris was a bit neater in his personal space than in his cramped hotel office.

The dwarf was pacing back and forth from the front door of the cabin, through the living room, and all the way to the kitchen in the back. My cell phone was clamped to his ear, and his face was twisted into an annoyed expression.

"Listen, mister," Ira growled again, "I've told you and told you that your friend is fine. It's not my fault that she got shot and drugged and can't talk to you right now."

From the phone, I could hear Silvio's sharp, demanding tone, if not his exact words.

Ira stopped. "You're going to come down here and pull my guts out through my nose? Really?" He snickered. "You and what army, hotshot?"

"Oh, I wouldn't make it a challenge," I said. "Silvio is quite dangerous when you get him riled up."

Ira pivoted on his bootheel to face me. Surprise flashed in his dark hazel eyes, as though he hadn't expected me to be up and about just yet. Then he scowled, stalked forward, and slapped my phone into my hand.

"Here," he said. "*You* deal with that nut. He's called fifty times in the last hour, despite me telling him that you were unconscious."

I grinned. "He's rather persistent that way."

Ira huffed, ambled away, and plopped down in one of the rocking chairs by the fireplace.

I raised the phone to my ear. "Hello, Silvio."

"Gin!" my assistant shouted. "Where are you? I've been worried sick! That imbecile wouldn't let me talk to you, and Finn, Bria, and Owen aren't picking up their phones."

"Shh," I said, rubbing my forehead. "Quiet voice, please. I have a pounding headache."

Whatever sedative Roxy and Brody had slipped into my sweet tea had been a doozy. Finn, Bria, and Owen would no doubt wake up with splitting migraines, since they'd drunk so much more of it than I had.

If they woke up at all.

Worry twisted my stomach, but I forced myself to push the emotion away. Tucker thought that Finn might know where Deirdre had hidden the jewels. He wouldn't kill my friends until he was absolutely certain that they didn't know anything. Torture them, yes. Kill them, no.

Not yet, anyway.

"Why do you have a headache?" Silvio asked in a much lower, calmer voice. "What's going on?"

"Let's just say that our Wild West vacation has gotten a little wilder than any of us expected."

I filled Silvio in on everything that had happened. When I finished, the vampire was silent, and I didn't hear him typing away on his keyboard as usual.

"Do you have any idea where the jewels are hidden?" Silvio said. "I hate to point this out, but those gems are the only bit of leverage you have right now."

"Oh, I know exactly where they are."

Ira's head snapped around, and surprise filled his eyes again. I shrugged back at him. I *did* know where they were hidden. I should have known all along, the first second that I'd set eyes on them, but I'd been too caught up in my memories, melancholy, and heartache about my mother to notice them.

"So what's the plan?" Silvio asked. "What do you want me to do?"

"Load up some supplies. *My* kind of supplies—guns, knives, ammo, healing ointment, the works, and drive down here. I know that Jo-Jo and Sophia are busy showing off the salon on that holiday tour of homes today, but see if you can find someone else to come with you and watch your back."

"Got it. Anything else?"

I looked over at Ira. "Except for Mr. Morris, we have to assume that every single person who works at the hotel and theme park is in on this in some way, and that they know all about us, including who you are and what you look like. They might not work for Tucker, Roxy, and Brody directly, but they're probably too scared of them not to rat you out the second they see you. So you need some sort of disguise. See if Roslyn Phillips can lend you something."

"Roger that," Silvio said. "I'll see if I can borrow someone else's car too. Just in case Tucker and the rest of the Circle have marked our usual vehicles as well."

"Good idea."

"What do you want me to do once I'm down there?"

I thought about it for a few seconds. "Meet me at the Feeding Trough. It's the barbecue restaurant that's part of the theme park."

"But isn't that the place where you were just drugged?" I could hear the frown in Silvio's voice.

"Yep. And it's also the last place they'll expect me to go back to."

"I'll be down there as soon as I can," Silvio promised. "What will you be doing in the meantime?"

I looked over at Ira again. "Grabbing those missing jewels and finally getting some straight answers about what's really going on around here."

❊ 18 ❊

I hung up with Silvio, then glanced at a clock shaped like a buffalo on the wall. It was just after one o'clock, which meant that I'd been unconscious for about an hour. Once again, worry filled my heart for Finn, Bria, and Owen, but I forced it aside. They were probably still out cold, and Tucker couldn't question—torture—them before they woke up, which meant that I still had time to save my friends.

But first, I wanted to know about the man who'd saved me, so I walked over and sat down in the rocking chair beside Ira. "So, you got me off the stagecoach and brought me over here to your place."

He nodded. "I had a time of it too. You'd wedged yourself down between those trunks something good. Then, of course, I had to actually stuff you into one of the trunks and roll you all the way over here from the theme park. But I move things around like that all the time, so nobody paid any attention to me."

"So that's why my body feels like it's been twisted around like a pretzel," I joked.

He nodded again and kept on rocking.

"And why would you do that? Why would you save me? You could have turned me over to Roxy and Brody. They probably would have given you a reward for it."

He snorted. "Those two? They wouldn't give me a reward for saving them from a burning building, much less pointing you out."

"Still, it was a big risk to take."

The dwarf shrugged and stared into the flames that were crackling in the fireplace. After a few seconds, he cleared his throat. "I saw that vampire, Hugh Tucker, lurking around the hotel lobby this morning, and I knew that something was going on. Something bad. It's always bad when he's around."

I frowned. "Tucker's been here before?"

"Several times. At least once a year, he and some of his buddies would come here for a retreat, and Deirdre would roll out the red carpet for them."

My breath caught in my throat, and my heart lifted with a bit of hope. He had to be talking about the other members of the Circle. So they had been here after all. I wanted to pepper him with questions, but I held my tongue, letting him finish his story.

"Although Tucker and Deirdre weren't getting along lately," Ira continued. "This past year, all they did was fight whenever he came here. A couple of months ago, Tucker made her hire Roxy and Brody. Said something about how the resort wasn't making any money because

Deirdre kept spending it all on clothes and jewelry." Ira huffed. "I could have told him that."

"And that's when Deirdre came up with that fake treasure hunt."

Ira scowled. "I was the one who put Sweet Sally Sue's jewels on display years ago as a tribute to her. I liked walking through the lobby every day and seeing her things, along with her photos. It reminded me of all the good years we'd had here together."

"Until Deirdre stole the jewels."

Anger twisted his face. "Deirdre knew that I would never let her have them, so she waited until I was busy with the high-noon show one day, and then she swiped them. By the time I realized what she'd done, Deirdre had already left the resort. I tried to track her down, but she kept moving from one of her fancy apartments to the next. And of course she wouldn't return any of my phone calls. The next thing I know, she's announcing the treasure hunt, and Roxy and Brody are here, kicking me out of my own office and taking control of everything."

Ira's body stilled, and his dark hazel gaze drifted up to a framed photo on the fireplace mantel that showed Sweet Sally Sue wearing a saloon-girl dress, all decked out in her jewelry. I recognized it as the same photo that was in the display case in the hotel lobby.

"I couldn't believe that Deirdre would disrespect Sweet Sally Sue's memory like that, but I should have known better," he said in a bitter voice. "I should have protected her legacy better."

"You loved her, didn't you? That's why you stayed here all these years, even after Roxy and Brody came in and took over."

Ira nodded and started rocking in his chair again. "Sweet Sally Sue took me in when I had nothing. She was like the mother that I never had, and this was my home. It will *always* be my home."

I understood his sentiments all too well, since I felt the exact same way about Fletcher and the Pork Pit. Despite all the bad things that had happened in the restaurant, including Fletcher's murder, it was my home, and it always would be. Even more than that, it was the legacy that the old man had left me, and I would defend it to my dying breath, the same way that Ira had been trying to keep Bullet Pointe going for all these years, despite Deirdre's best efforts to run it into the ground.

Ira quit rocking and looked at me. "I've been following Tucker around all day, wondering what he was up to. I heard him talking to Roxy about you and your friends and all the trouble you've caused for him up in Ashland. Is it true? That you're some kind of assassin who wants him dead?"

"Absolutely."

I told Ira a condensed version of my history with Tucker, including all the things he'd said about my mother being part of the Circle. "Have you ever heard of them? Did Deirdre ever say anything to you about some group called the Circle?"

Ira shook his head. "Sorry, but I've never heard of any Circle. And Tucker didn't always come down here with the same people."

"What about Eira Snow? Have you ever heard of her?" I held my breath, hoping, hoping, hoping. . . .

He shook his head again. "Sorry, but that name doesn't ring a bell." He waved his hand at all the photos on the walls. "A lot of people come through here every year. I can't keep track of them all."

It had been a total long shot, that my mother had been here once upon a time and that Ira would remember her out of all the thousands of visitors, but disappointment washed over me all the same. Another dead end.

Still, it wasn't his fault, so I forced myself to smile at him and gestured at the cabin walls. "I've been wondering about your photos. I noticed them in your office. They're quite stunning, especially the scenic shots of the hotel, park, and lake."

For the first time since I'd met him, a genuine smile lit up the dwarf's face, softening his perpetual scowl. "Sweet Sally Sue gave me a camera the very first Christmas that I was here. I've been taking pictures ever since." He glanced around at the photos, his gaze moving from one frame to the next. "Bullet Pointe might be a business, but I like seeing people so happy in the park and hotel. I like taking shots of their memories. It makes me happy to see them having a good time. It means more to me than the money."

I nodded. I felt the same way about the food I served at the Pork Pit. Seeing the enjoyment that other folks got out of my cooking always put a smile on my face. I liked brightening someone's day, even if it was just in the small way of fixing them a good, hearty meal. Ira and I were more alike than I would have thought possible.

"Thank you for saving me. For sticking your neck out for me. Not many people would have done that."

Ira waved his hand, dismissing my thanks. "What was I supposed to do? Let you lay outside and slowly freeze to death?"

I grinned. "Well, I still appreciate it all the same."

As much as I was enjoying sitting here by the warm flames and talking to the dwarf, I stopped rocking and got to my feet. Because time was ticking away, and I needed to get the jewels and figure out how to save my friends before Tucker tortured and killed them.

"What are you going to do now?" Ira asked.

"Go back up to the hotel. That's where the jewels are."

He shook his head. "You'll never make it. Roxy and Brody have everyone looking for you. And you can't get out of the park or the hotel either. They've got all the exits blocked." He waved his hand again. "And it won't be too long before they get the bright idea to come here and look for you."

"Don't worry. I'm leaving. I'm not going to put you in any more danger. You've done enough for me already."

His weathered face creased into another rare grin. "Darling, I don't care about the danger. Helping you and thumbing my nose at Roxy and Brody is the most fun I've had in months. But I'm not about to send you out there to get yourself shot up again."

"What do you mean?"

"You need a disguise, just like you told your friend on the phone."

Ira got to his feet and disappeared into his bedroom. Some clangs and bangs sounded, as though he was rustling around in his closet. He came out a minute later holding up a wire hanger that featured an old-fashioned saloon-girl dress wrapped in clear plastic. Unlike the cheap costumes the performers wore, I could tell that this was the real deal, made of expensive silk, lace, and crinoline.

"This belonged to Sweet Sally Sue herself." Ira smiled at the dress and the memories it brought back. "She was a spitfire, just like you are, and I think that she'd like you wearing it. Especially if it will help you kick Tucker, Roxy, and Brody out of here for good."

I hesitated. I didn't want to wear the dress for fear of ruining it, and Ira's memories along with it, but he was right. I couldn't go outside as Gin Blanco, the outlaw that everyone was searching for. I needed a disguise, and I wasn't about to look this gift horse in the mouth.

"I'm honored." I took the dress from him.

I held out the garment, and a smile spread across my face as I realized what shade it was.

Bloodred. Always my color.

Ira's cabin might have been relatively tidy, but he had a small shed out back that was just as messy as his hotel office. But instead of stacks of papers, the shed was filled to the brim with all sorts of odds and ends, including shoes, makeup, and even some wigs that the performers had discarded. I grabbed a few things for my disguise, then went back into his bedroom to get ready.

The first thing I had to do was put on a corset.

Seriously, a real, old-fashioned corset complete with whalebones to give it—and me—that classic hourglass shape. The frilly thing was covered with tons of black lace, and it took me a lot of time and a whole lot of effort to shimmy into it. The only saving grace was that the black ribbons laced up the front, instead of the back, but I still cursed whoever had invented such a foul, uncomfortable contraption.

Next up was Sweet Sally Sue's dress. The stiff black crinoline underskirt made the top layers of bloodred silk poof out all around my legs, making me feel like a human bell. On the plus side, the dress had long sleeves that hid the white bandage on my upper left arm, as well as two deep pockets for me to carry my knives. I tucked my other three knives into the garter belt and stockings that went with the dress.

Black shoes with square, chunky heels and ankle straps were next, along with a pair of fingerless, black lace gloves that made the spider rune scars in my palms itch. I also stuffed my spider rune necklace down into my corseted bodice and tied a black velvet ribbon with a red cameo around my throat.

Once my clothes were in place, I donned a blond wig with the long hair done in fat ringlet curls, powdered my face, and painted my lips the same bloodred as the dress. For the final touch, I stuck a small black beauty mark on my left cheek, close to my lips to draw attention away from my eyes, whose gray color I couldn't change.

I looked and felt ridiculous, and I didn't see how the performers endured these costumes day after day during their eight-hour shifts. I'd only had the dress on for ten minutes and I already wanted to tear it off, starting with the corset. It was too bad Finn wasn't here. He would have been cackling with glee at my misery.

The thought of him, Bria, and Owen made my stomach tighten with worry again. Time to get on with things. So I left the bedroom and stepped back out into the main part of the cabin where Ira was sitting in his rocking chair by the fireplace again.

I twirled around for his inspection. "Well? What do you think?"

Ira looked over at me and did a double take. He blinked and blinked, then frowned, studying me carefully.

"What? Did I get lipstick on my teeth or something?"

Ira shook his head. "Nothing like that. You just . . . look like a lady that I remember photographing a long time ago."

"I thought you couldn't remember the names of everyone you photographed."

He shrugged. "Not their names, but I never forget a face."

He got up out of his rocking chair and wandered around the cabin, staring at all the pictures on the walls, searching for the one he wanted. He stopped and shook his head a minute later. "I'm not sure where that photo is. It might be in my office in the hotel."

"Well, maybe I'll duck in there and try to find it," I joked. "If I don't get killed before then."

A distinct possibility since it was just little ole me against Tucker, Roxy, Brody, and all their men.

"You get up to the hotel and get those stones," Ira said. "I'll mosey around the park and see what information I can pick up about Tucker and his plans. Then, when it's time, I'll head over to the main entrance and keep a watch out for that annoying Silvio fella."

I nodded. I'd told Ira that this was my fight, not his, but the dwarf had insisted that this was his home, and if he could help boot Roxy and Brody out of it for good, then he'd do whatever he could to help. So this was the plan we'd come up with. I didn't want Ira around if Tucker and the others did get their hooks in me, and having the dwarf watch out for Silvio would hopefully help my assistant and whomever else he'd managed to round up in Ashland slip into the park unnoticed.

"All right, then." I headed for the front door. "Wish me luck."

Ira gave me a knowing look. "Oh, I think you're the type who makes her own luck."

"Nah." I grinned. "I just make people dead."

✻ 19 ✻

Ira's cabin stood off by itself in a patch of woods that overlooked the lake. He followed me out of the cabin, locking it up behind him, and we went our separate ways. He headed for the main theme-park entrance to see what he could find out from the other workers, while I took a trail that led back out to the staging area, staying hidden behind a screen of trees.

It must have been time for some late-afternoon show because the staging area was full of folks changing into cowboy and gambler costumes, slapping on wigs and makeup, and making sure that their fake weapons were full of blanks. I looked around, but I didn't see Roxy or Brody anywhere, although I did spot several of their outlaw-gang giants, getting ready along with everyone else. But the performers had this down to a science, and the staging area emptied out about five minutes later, as everyone rushed to take their places for the show.

When I was sure that the area was deserted, I slid out from behind a tree and hurried through the wooden pavilions, wanting to get back out to the relative safety of the Main Street crowds as fast as possible. I'd just passed the back door of the Good Tyme Saloon when something unexpected on a nearby bulletin board caught my eye.

A *Wanted* poster with my picture on it.

I stopped and went over for a closer look, wondering if my eyes were playing tricks on me. But they weren't. A grainy black-and-white photo of me that looked like it had been taken from a security camera inside the hotel took up most of the poster, while the word *Wanted* arched across the top in that old-timey Western font that was on everything around here. *Gin Blanco* was also done in the same type, curving under my glamour shot, along with the promise of a thousand-dollar reward for any confirmed sightings of me in the hotel or the theme park. Well, that was a bit insulting. You'd think that I'd be worth at least five grand—dead or alive.

My own poster. I grinned. Just what I'd always wanted.

I couldn't help myself. I carefully took the poster down off the bulletin board, rolled it up, and stuck it into one of my dress pockets.

I left the staging area behind and made it through the alley and back out to Main Street. At the far end of the street, down in front of the visitor bleachers, cowboys, gamblers, saloon girls, and other costumed characters were dancing to some old-timey, upbeat country-western music and putting on what looked like an elaborate square dance. I didn't see Roxy or Brody among the performers, though.

They were probably still combing the park for me or were maybe even stationed up at the hotel, waiting for me to try to rescue my friends.

The music rose to a roaring crescendo for the big finale, with all the performers yelling, whooping, and throwing their hats up into the air. The crowd surged to its feet, cheering and clapping, and all the performers took a bow. The crowd streamed down the bleachers, and all the costumed characters stepped up to meet them, sign autographs, and pose for pictures. Well, that show had certainly gone a lot smoother than the other two that I'd loused up this weekend.

It was now or never, so I drew in a breath and stepped out onto the wooden sidewalk. I smiled at the people I passed, just another worker playing her part, even as every step took me closer and closer to the hotel and the jewels—

"Hey! You there!" a loud voice called out behind me. "You in the red dress!"

I tensed. Well, that was definitely me. Damn. I'd hoped to at least get away from the saloon and closer to the hotel before someone stopped and questioned me. But it would look more suspicious if I ran, so I slowly turned around and plastered a smile on my face.

"Yes?"

Brody Dalton jogged up to me. I slid my hand into my dress pocket, my fingers curling around the silverstone knife inside, ready to whip out the blade, ram it into the giant's throat, pick up my skirts, and run, run, run.

Brody stopped, his cheeks flushed from the cold. He must not have had time to visit that Air healer again because his nose was still a red, broken, lumpy knot in his face from Tucker's beating. Good.

"What do you think you're doing, making me walk all the way over here?" he snapped. "You should have come over to me the second that I yelled at you. Don't you know who I am?"

Even though I wanted to punch him in the face, I ducked my head in apology. "I'm so sorry, sir. I just didn't hear you at first above all the crowd noise."

Brody gave me a suspicious look, like he didn't believe me, but apparently he had other things to worry about. He raised his hand, and I realized that he was holding a thick stack of papers. He peeled a sheet off the top and shoved it into my free hand. It was a copy of my *Wanted* poster.

"Here. Carry this with you at all times," he snapped again. "And if you see this woman, you text Roxy or me immediately with her location. Do you understand?"

"Yes, sir." I ducked my head again, as though I were studying my own picture. "What did she do?"

"She's a shoplifter and a pickpocket, among other things," the giant growled. "Now get out there and mingle like you're supposed to, and keep a sharp eye out for this one."

I bobbed my head at him. "Yes, sir. I'll get right on that."

Brody gave me another suspicious look, probably because of my syrupy-sweet tone, but he huffed, whirled around, and stomped away. I watched him for a few seconds, but all he did was stop every worker he passed, shove one of my *Wanted* posters at them, and demand that they be on the lookout for me.

The giant hadn't realized that he'd had me within arm's reach. He was going to pay for that later. I would make sure of it.

But right now, I had two jobs—get the jewels and find out where Finn, Bria, and Owen were being held. So I rolled up my second *Wanted* poster and slipped it inside my pocket right next to the first one. Then I upped the wattage on my smile, turned around, and melted into the crowd of tourists.

It took me thirty minutes to work my way from Main Street up the hill to the hotel, mostly because people kept stopping me and asking me to pose for pictures. I hated every single second of it, but it was my job as an unofficial Bullet Pointe saloon girl, and I didn't want any of the tourists complaining and drawing unwanted attention to me. So I batted my lashes, swished my skirts, and smiled for all the photos. By the time I reached the hotel, my cheeks were aching from holding on to my fake sunny expression for so long.

I slipped into the lobby and stopped, wondering if I would stand out more here than I had in the theme park, but my saloon-girl dress was close enough to the ones that the hotel waitresses wore for me to pass muster. An empty silver tray was sitting on the corner of the bar, and I casually walked over and swiped it when the bartender's back was turned. People with empty trays always looked like they had places to be, and no one gave me a second glance as I strolled across the lobby, despite the loud *click-click-click-click* of my heels on the stone floor.

I followed a waitress back into the kitchen, not only because I wanted to blend in with the rest of the staff, but also because I wanted to eavesdrop on the workers. One of them had to know where Tucker was holding Finn, Bria, and Owen. So I pushed through the double doors, stepped into the kitchen, and immediately regretted my decision.

Roxy was here.

She was wearing the same cowgirl costume as before, complete with her red hat and sparkling rhinestone belt buckle. Her hands were clasped behind her back, and she was pacing up and down in front of a line of cooks, cow-boy waiters, and saloon-girl waitresses. The waitress in front of me scurried to get in line with everyone else, and I had no choice but to follow her.

Roxy finally stopped pacing and raised her hand, clutching another stack of my *Wanted* posters. How many of those things had they printed up in the last two hours? I hid a grin. I was starting to like this whole wanted-outlaw thing.

"This woman is somewhere on the resort grounds, and we are going to find her," Roxy barked out like a drill sergeant. "From this moment on, you will examine every single guest you serve and compare them to this woman. If you spot her, then you text me immediately with her location. Do you understand me?"

No one said anything, so she increased the volume of her bellow. "Do you understand me?"

"Yes, ma'am!" we all shouted in unison.

She went down the line of us, shoving a *Wanted* poster into every person's hands. Not only that, but she looked over each and every worker in turn, eyeing everything from their hats to their costumes to their boots. I started sweating, and not from the heat of the stoves.

If she recognized me, I was dead.

I couldn't fight my way through all the people in this cramped, crowded space, much less get past Roxy herself before she pumped me full of Fire-coated bullets. The workers would all pile on top of me, drag me down to the floor, and hold me there until Roxy could summon Tucker to deal with me. Then I'd either be trussed up and tortured alongside my friends or be killed outright.

But I couldn't run away. Not now when she was shoving a poster into my hands. Roxy started to turn away, then stopped and peered at me with sharp, critical eyes. My free hand slid into my dress pocket, reaching for my knife again. I'd only have one chance to take her down, and I had to make it count—

Roxy stepped forward, took hold of my dress, and actually yanked it down, showing off more of my cleavage. My spider rune necklace shifted inside the corset, swimming up toward the top, and I immediately quit breathing, not wanting the necklace to pop out and give me away.

"You can afford to show a little more skin," Roxy snapped. "That's what gets you—and me—better tips. Do you understand?"

"Yes, ma'am," I squeaked out in a high voice, still trying not to breathe.

She eyed me as if she thought that I was mocking her, but I lowered my head, as if I were too scared not to give in to her demands. After several long seconds, she finally nodded and moved away from me, barking out more orders to the staff.

I sucked in a breath and discreetly stuffed my necklace back down where it had been before.

Roxy kept bellowing out commands, and all the waitstaff had to line up again, fill our trays with champagne glasses, and circulate them through the lobby to the guests. I was all too happy to step up, put the glasses on my tray, and skedaddle out of the kitchen.

Carrying my tray of drinks, I hurried out of the kitchen as fast as I could without actually running. I thought about setting the tray down on the first table that I passed and just walking away, but I glanced over my shoulder. Sure enough, Roxy was now standing by the bar, her arms crossed over her chest, watching the staff, including me, just to make sure that we were up to her pimpish standards.

So I smiled and sashayed over to a group of guys sitting in the rocking chairs in front of the fireplace. I even leaned over, giving them a good, long look at my cleavage, once again hoping that my spider rune necklace wouldn't pop out and land in one of their laps. The men all grinned, their gazes locked on my chest, even as they reached for the champagne flutes. Out of the corner of my eye, I saw Roxy nod her head in approval, thinking that I was sufficiently cowed, and turn her attention to another waitress.

I handed out all the drinks on my tray, went back into the kitchen, and got another round. By the time I stepped back out into the lobby, Roxy had decided that the staff was up to snuff and was standing off by herself beside some of the decorated Christmas trees.

I glanced around, but I didn't see Brody or any of the other giants. If not for all the tourists, this would be the perfect moment to pull my knife out of my dress pocket, sidle over to Roxy, and stab the bitch in the back. Despite the potential witnesses and collateral damage, I still seriously considered it, wanting to eliminate at least one dangerous enemy, and I even went so far as to take a step in her direction—

A man walked in front of me, making me pull up short to keep from spilling all the drinks on my tray. Even then, the glasses wobbled dangerously, making the champagne inside fizz and froth up.

I opened my mouth to snap at the guy to watch where he was going, but he glanced at me, and I realized that it was Hugh Tucker. So I quickly turned to my side, angling my face away from him, as though I were still trying to get my tray of wobbling drinks under control.

Out of the corner of my eye, I could see Tucker staring at me, but my disguise worked, and the vampire dismissed me as unimportant because he continued over to where Roxy was standing. I waited a few seconds, then moved in their direction, handing drinks out to all the guests that I passed, until I was close enough to eavesdrop on their conversation.

". . . no trace of Blanco yet," Roxy said. "But I've doubled the number of giants posted at all the hotel and theme-park exits. We've got her trapped in here. She can't escape, and we'll find her sooner or later."

Tucker crossed his arms over his chest, staring down at

his henchwoman. "And I can't believe that you were careless enough to let her slip through your fingers in the first place. You told me that the sedative you gave Blanco and her friends was foolproof. Seems like it turned out to be snake oil instead, since Blanco is still out there."

"I'm sorry, sir." Roxy whipped off her hat and ducked her head in apology. "Don't worry. We'll find Blanco. I promise you that."

"And you'd better deliver," he replied in a smooth, silky voice. "I do not like failure. Deirdre Shaw could tell you that, if she were still alive."

"Yes, sir. Of course not, sir."

Tucker eyed Roxy a moment longer, making sure that the quiet threat in his words had fully sunk in, then glanced at his watch. "How much longer will Lane and the others be out?"

My breath caught in my throat, and my hands jerked, shaking the remaining glasses on my tray, but the two of them didn't notice me or my surprise.

"They're all still out cold in Lane's room, but it shouldn't be too much longer before they start coming around," Roxy said.

So Finn, Bria, and Owen were in Finn's suite on the top floor, no doubt under a heavy guard. Smart of Tucker to keep them so close and so isolated, especially when I was still free and could cause plenty of trouble.

"Let me know the second they wake up," Tucker said. "I want to start questioning them immediately about the jewels. And have my usual tools brought up to the suite for the interrogations."

My stomach twisted, and bile rose in my throat. Just as I feared, he was going to torture the answers out of my friends—answers that none of them had.

"But what about Blanco?" Roxy asked. "Don't you want her found first?"

Tucker shrugged. "She doesn't matter in the big picture. Not really. Finding those gems is the most important thing. And if we can't find them, well, I'll content myself with executing Lane and the others."

I couldn't help but suck in a breath at the casual way Tucker talked about murdering my friends. Cold rage flooded my body, and I itched to reach for one of my knives, charge at the vampire, and slit his fucking throat. I seriously, seriously considered it, just as I had with Roxy a few moments before.

But I pushed my rage aside and held my position. Given Tucker's lightning-fast speed, it was fifty-fifty whether I could kill him before he killed me. Add Roxy and her trusty revolvers to the mix, and the odds weren't in my favor. Not to mention all the innocent bystanders who could get shot—or worse—in the potential cross fire. No, as much as I wanted to end Tucker and Roxy, I couldn't take them on. Not here. Not now.

But soon—very, very soon.

Tucker and Roxy kept talking, but a guy sitting in a rocking chair waved me over, eager for a glass of free champagne and a look at my corseted bosom, so I screwed on a smile and headed in his direction, still thinking about my next move.

Silvio was right. The jewels were the only potential

leverage I had and the only thing that would keep my friends alive.

I knew where the jewels were. Now all I had to do was get to them.

Like everything else in my life, that was easier said than done.

✢ 20 ✢

I gave the guy in the rocking chair the peep show he wanted and moved away before he started drooling on me. I still had two glasses of champagne left on my tray, but instead of handing them out, I crossed the lobby and got into one of the elevators. As the car rose, I worked out the details of my hasty plan.

There was really only one—don't get dead.

The elevator stopped at various floors to let people on and off, until I was the last person in the car. I watched the numbers slowly light up, and I rode it all the way up to the top floor, where Finn's suite was.

The elevator doors pinged open, and I drew in a breath, plastered a smile on my face, and strutted out into the hallway.

Just as I expected, three giants dressed like outlaws were standing guard in front of the door leading into Finn's suite, and I was willing to bet that even more guards were stationed inside, as well as in Owen's and my suite next door. Far too many guards for me to fight my way through without getting injured, especially since Finn, Bria, and Owen were still unconscious and couldn't help me. Even if I did manage to kill all the guards, I couldn't have gotten all three of them out of the suite to safety. So as much as I hated to leave my friends at Tucker's mercy—or lack thereof—it was my only option right now.

The three guards outside the door jerked to attention at the sight of me coming toward them, their hands dropping to the guns belted to their waists. I wondered if Roxy had outfitted them all with her charming Fire-coated bullets. I would have, but I was betting that she kept them all to herself. She wouldn't want to let anyone else use her special bullets, much less have the fun of shooting me with them.

But instead of whipping out a knife and charging at the giants, I sashayed right on by, nodding my head politely at them. All three of them leered at my cleavage, but I kept going down the hallway until I reached the door on the opposite side.

The one that led into Deirdre's suite.

I stopped in front of the door and reached for my Ice and Stone magic, using it to make my hand as cold, hard, and strong as possible. Then I knocked politely on the door. "Room service," I called out in a cheery voice.

Knocking on Deirdre's door was a risk, but I was willing to bet that Roxy had told the giants to guard only Finn's door and not the suite across from his. I was also betting that the giants didn't realize that the suite was empty.

I glanced at the guards out of the corner of my eye, but they kept right on leering, and none of them broke away from his buddies to approach me.

So I knocked a second time. "Room service," I called out in a louder voice.

I turned to the side, so that my poofy dress was blocking the giants' view of the door, wrapped my hand around the knob, and blasted it with my Ice magic, driving the cold shards of my power through the keyhole and into the lock. Once I was sure that it was frozen solid, I sent out another blast of Ice magic, cracking all those shards away, even as I used my Stone-hardened hand to wrench the knob. It took some effort, but the lock broke, and the door opened with an audible *screech*.

I plastered a smile on my face and stared straight ahead, as though I were greeting the guest inside.

"Hello, ma'am," I called out for the guards' benefit. "I have that champagne you ordered. Where would you like me to set it up?"

I stepped inside the suite, shut the door behind me, and put the serving tray and glasses on a nearby table. I glanced around, but everything was the same as before. It didn't look like Tucker, Roxy, or Brody had come in here and searched Deirdre's suite again. But there was only one way to know for sure, so I hurried over to the white Christmas tree in the corner, my breath in my throat, my heart pounding, my palms itching with anticipation.

The tree looked just as I remembered it, right down to the three cheesy Bullet Pointe snow globes that I'd lined up on the floor in front of it—snow globes that didn't match the rest of Deirdre's fancy designer ornaments.

I dropped to my knees in front of the tree, grabbed the globe that featured the Main Street scene, and held it up to the light streaming in through the floor-to-ceiling windows. I shook the globe, and a few more clear stones dropped out of the letters in the *Bullet Pointe* sign, sparkling as they sailed through the water.

"Hello, diamonds," I whispered.

I picked up the other two globes, staring at them in turn. Sapphires made up the lake scene in one, while rubies and emeralds glittered as the holiday decorations on the snow-covered hotel in the other one. And still more gemstones gleamed here and there in all three of the globes. I didn't know if all of Sweet Sally Sue's jewels were here, but it looked like Deirdre had stuffed the majority of them into the three globes. Then she'd stashed the globes with the rest of her Christmas decorations, as though they were just bits of glass and glitter, hiding the gems in plain sight all along, one of the oldest and best tricks around.

"Clever," I whispered again. "Very, very clever, Mama Dee."

I thought back to that memory I'd had of Deirdre in my mother's office, shaking all those snow globes while Tucker had threatened Eira. I wondered if that's where Deirdre had gotten the idea for her hiding place. I wondered what other tricks she might have learned from my mother, although I doubted I would ever know. But for right now, it was enough that I'd found the jewels.

I brought the Main Street globe up to my ear and reached out with my Stone magic. The thick glass and water muted the sounds, but I still could make out the gems' proud trills about their own beauty. I should have noticed the murmurs before, the second I'd picked up the globes when we'd first come in here yesterday, but I'd been too lost in my memories of my mother to pay attention to them.

Well, I was here now, and these babies were coming with me.

I fished the two knives out of the pockets of my saloon-girl dress and slid them into my garters with my other three weapons. Then I stuffed all three of the snow globes down into my dress pockets, since I didn't have time to open them and pluck out the gems right now. For once, I was grateful that my silk and crinoline skirts were so poofy, since they helped hide the round bulges of glass.

By this point, I'd been in the suite for almost five minutes, which was pushing it when it came to room service. So I hustled back over and grabbed my silver tray. I started toward the door, then stopped and cursed, realizing that I had to get rid of the two glasses before I stepped out into the hallway, since delivering the champagne was ostensibly my reason for being in here. So I set the glasses down on the table.

I headed toward the door again, but another thought occurred to me, a way that I could be just as clever as Deirdre had been when it came to the jewels.

So I set my tray down on the table, picked up my skirts, and ran into Deirdre's bedroom. I darted around the messy, towering piles of clothes, shoes, and purses that my friends and I had made when we'd been searching in here yesterday and headed into her closest, going straight to the jewelry wall in the very back. My gaze roamed over all the rings, necklaces, and bracelets resting on the shelves, before focusing on the boxes and other items that Deirdre had used to store and transport her jewelry from this lavish suite to all the other ones she stayed in around the country.

There—that would do nicely.

I grabbed a black velvet bag from one of the shelves and shook it to make sure that it was empty. Just what I wanted.

I grabbed another empty bag as well as several more items from the wall. Then I stuffed everything into my dress pockets, left the closet, and sprinted back out into the main part of the suite. I'd been in here almost ten minutes now. Time to leave before the giants outside got any more suspicious than they probably already were.

I reached for the doorknob again, stopped, and cursed, realizing that this time I'd forgotten the stupid serving tray. So I grabbed the empty platter, then drew in a breath and slowly let it out, trying to calm my racing heart, and plastered a benign smile on my face. I pulled on the door-knob, which was still frozen solid from my Ice magic, and backed out into the hallway, as though I were still talking to someone inside the suite.

"No, ma'am, thank you for such a generous tip and such a lovely conversation," I called out for the benefit of the guards. "Please let me know if you need anything else. I'll be happy to assist you in any way that I can."

Was I laying it on thick? Oh, yeah. But I wanted the giants to focus on my words, not my movements. I closed the door and turned to the side, once again using my poofy skirts to block the giants' view. I held on to the knob, reached for my Ice magic again, and forced more cold shards into the keyhole and doorframe all around the knob, hoping that they would be enough to anchor the door in place long enough for me to get out of here. Only one way to find out.

I let go of the knob and stepped back, my breath in my throat, but the door didn't swing open and give away that I'd forced my way into the suite. But I didn't know how long it would hold. Time to get while the getting was good.

So I walked down the hallway to where the giants were stationed outside the door to Finn's suite. Once again, they all snapped to attention at the sight of me and my heaving, corseted bosom. I dropped my tray down to my side, giving them a better view of my chest, even as I gripped the platter tight, ready to snap it up and slam it into the guards' faces if they tried to stop me.

The giants leered at me again, but they didn't step in front of me, and I nodded and smiled politely as I moved past them. Even though I wanted to pick up my skirts and make a mad dash for the elevators, I forced myself to walk at a normal pace, even though I could hear two of the snow globes rattling together in my dress pockets. I winced and kept going, hoping that the giants wouldn't notice the sounds. My gaze locked on the elevators up ahead, and I started counting off the distance in my head.

Ten feet away from safety . . . seven feet . . . five . . . four . . . three . . . two . . . one . . .

"Hey," one of the giants called out, "let me ask you something."

My finger hovered over the elevator call button. I discreetly punched it, then turned to face the giants, raising my eyebrows. "Yes?"

"Did they give you a good tip?" that same giant called out. "Because I certainly would have with you in that dress."

He leered at me again and let out a low wolf whistle. His two buddies joined in with his hearty chuckles.

I put a hand on my hip and struck a pose, giving him another little thrill. A wide, genuine smile spread across my face at the thought of the millions of dollars' worth of jewels stuffed into my pockets.

"Oh," I drawled, "it was a great tip. One of the best I've ever gotten."

* 21 *

The elevator arrived, thankfully putting an end to my forced flirting with the guard, and I stepped inside and rode it back down to the lobby. I glanced around, but I didn't see Tucker, Roxy, or Brody anywhere, although several giants were stationed along the walls, studying everyone who came and went, and comparing them to my *Wanted* posters in their hands.

Still carrying my empty serving tray, I left the lobby behind, went back into the kitchen, and put the platter down on the first table I came to. One of the cooks gave me an odd look, but I walked right on by him and jerked my thumb over my shoulder.

"Taking my break now."

He nodded and went back to slicing tomatoes for the pasta dish he was whipping up.

I slipped out the back door of the kitchen, which opened onto a small stone patio. A couple of saloon-girl waitresses were standing outside, huddled together against the cold, and smoking cigarettes, despite the large red *No Smoking* sign hanging on the wall. Their eyes narrowed in suspicion, wondering who I was and if I would rat them out to Roxy, but I simply nodded at them, stepped onto a path, and headed away from the hotel, back down the hill to the theme park.

Since it was Saturday afternoon, the park was more crowded than ever before, with throngs of tourists meandering along the paths, getting junk food from the concession carts, and standing in lines for the rides. I also passed several costumed characters, all of whom seemed to be holding a copy of my *Wanted* poster and scanning the crowd for little ole me. Add that to the gems weighing down my pockets, and I felt like every single eye was firmly fixed on me. My spider rune scars itched and burned, and I had to force myself to walk at a regular pace, even though all I wanted to do was run, run, run away from all the people searching for me.

Actually, I couldn't have run away from anyone right now, given how the old-fashioned high heels were pinching my toes. More torture devices, along with the stupid corset. I plastered a bland smile on my face and clomped on through the park.

People stopped me and asked me to pose for pictures, just as they had on my way up to the hotel, and I obliged them because too many other workers were around for me not to. I didn't want to do anything suspicious to attract anyone's attention, much less have one of the performers text Roxy or Brody and complain about the saloon girl who was giving the guests the cold shoulder.

Finally, I slipped off Main Street and made it back to the staging area behind the saloon. A few folks were milling around under the pavilions, talking, laughing, and texting, but they were all just regular workers, instead of being part of Brody's giant outlaw gang, and I didn't see anyone holding a copy of my *Wanted* poster. Once again, I smiled and nodded at everyone I passed. They all gave me cursory smiles and nods in return, then went back to their conversations, although the costumed cowboys went the extra step of tipping their hats at me. How gentlemanly.

I wandered through the pavilions, looking at all the costumes, fake weapons, tools, barrels full of lassos, and other supplies. As I roamed around, I made a mental inventory of things that might be useful to me later on tonight, and I also picked up the one item that I needed right now—a pair of sturdy-looking tweezers. Not exactly the precision tool I wanted, but it would have to do.

When I'd finished with my examination, I left the staging area and went back onto Main Street. I wandered along the wooden sidewalks, peering into the storefronts, and searching for a shop that was crowded enough that the workers would be focused on the customers, but not so busy that I couldn't roam around freely inside. The Silver Spur, the clothing shop, fit the bill, and I went inside.

Yet again, I smiled and nodded at everyone I passed, but the tourists in here were too busy shopping to want me to pose for pictures. Lucky for me, the restrooms were in the very back of the store, well past the dressing rooms, where the majority of the foot traffic was. I headed into the women's restroom, which was empty, slipped into one of the stalls, and locked the door behind me. I closed the toilet lid, sat down on it, and let out a deep breath.

Then, finally, at last, I was able to pull the snow globes out of my dress pockets and examine them.

Up close, they were cheap, flimsy things, not the expensive, heavy ones like my mother had had all those years ago. And Deirdre hadn't done a good job of securing the gems inside either, since more and more of them started coming loose as I turned the Main Street globe upside down in my hands.

The globe was like a mason jar, with the wooden base screwing down into the glass. I quickly took off the base, set it aside, and got down on my knees on the bathroom floor. A drain was embedded in the tile between my stall and the next one, so I held my palm up like a sieve, carefully tipped the globe over, and poured all the water out of the glass, letting it trickle out of my hand and fall away into the drain below.

I went slowly, only pouring out a little of the water at a time, and making sure not to lose any of the precious stones. Once all the water was gone, and the gems were drying on a wad of toilet paper, I picked up the wooden base, which had the Main Street scene screwed into it, and used my stolen tweezers to gently pry the rest of the jewels out of the *Bullet Pointe* sign and other places where Deirdre had glued them down.

Five minutes later, I had an impressive pile of diamonds, along with several other stones. I dropped them all into one of my black velvet bags, then repeated the process on the other two globes.

When I was finished, I hefted the velvet bag in my hands. Without the glass and the water around them, I could clearly hear the gemstones' murmurs, which were loud, vain, and proud enough to let me estimate their value. At least ten million dollars, if not more. Nice. While that was only a drop in the bucket compared to the tens of millions that Deirdre had owed the Circle, every little bit helped.

Even more important, now I had something that Tucker wanted, and he was going to give me my friends in return.

Oh, I wasn't stupid enough to think that the vampire would honor any trade agreement we might make. I fully expected him to double-cross me at the least and kill me at the worst. But I would be ready for Tucker, Roxy, Brody, and all the others. I might be stuck in their theme park, but this Spider could spin her own traps and webs.

I had more work to do, so I put the bag of gemstones aside, drew out some of the other things I'd swiped from Deirdre's jewelry wall, and went to work with the tweezers again. Once I was finished with that second project, I got to my feet, opened the stall door, and threw the empty snow globes into the trash. Then I went over to one of the sinks to wash all the glitter off my hands.

I'd just finished drying my hands when my phone beeped. I pulled it out of my dress pocket and checked the message. It was from Silvio, naturally. He'd made good time driving down here, since it wasn't quite five o'clock yet.

At the restaurant. Wearing a gray hat.

Well, that was interesting. Looked like my assistant

had taken my suggestion to disguise himself to heart. I texted him back.

On my way.

I grabbed the black velvet bag off the sink, making sure that the strings on the top were drawn tight so that I wouldn't lose any of the jewels inside, then stuffed the whole thing down into my corset, right next to my spider rune necklace.

It was a tight fit, and it certainly didn't make the corset any more comfortable, but it was the most secure place I had right now. Once I was sure that everything was going to stay put, I opened the door and left the restroom.

The Silver Spur clothing store wasn't all that far from the Feeding Trough barbecue restaurant, but it still took me twenty minutes to get over there, mostly because I had to stop, smile, and simper for more stupid pictures. Was I the only saloon girl in the entire theme park that people wanted to pose with? Maybe it was the bloodred dress, making me stand out in a sea of pale pinks, greens, and blues. I was sick of smiling for the camera, so I ducked into the restaurant before anyone else could waylay me.

Since it was late afternoon, the dinner crowd hadn't ramped up yet, and only a few folks were inside. Even better, most of them were in costume, with the cowboys, gamblers, and gold miners chowing down on barbecue sandwiches, cheeseburgers, onion rings, and fries before going back to their stations.

The only costumed folks out of place were the three truckers.

They all had on brown work boots, dark jeans, and puffy red vests over red plaid shirts. Gray trucker hats with the words *Cypress Mountain Shipping* stitched across the tops in red were pulled down low on their foreheads, and all three of them had their noses buried in their menus. Despite their disguises, I still recognized them.

I sashayed over to their table. "Y'all care if a poor, simple, hardworking saloon girl joins you?" I simpered in the same syrupy-sweet drawl I'd used on Brody earlier.

"Get lost, toots," one of the truckers growled. "We're waiting on someone."

"Why, Silvio," I chided, "is that any way to talk to your boss?"

The trucker who'd spoken looked up. My assistant had gone all out with his disguise. In addition to his trucker outfit, he was also wearing a shaggy gray wig, and an equally shaggy gray mustache covered his upper lip. It looked like a woolly worm had crawled up there and died.

Silvio squinted. "Is that you—"

A waitress was walking by on her way to another table, so I pulled out a chair and sat down next to Silvio. "It sure is, sweetheart. Sassy Scarlet at your service."

I batted my lashes at him, then turned and looked at the two other people sitting at the table—Lorelei Parker, also sporting a trucker's hat, and Phillip Kincaid, with a hat and a bad fake dirty-blond mustache.

Phillip's blue gaze swept over my blond wig, the black beauty mark, and the bloodred saloon-girl dress. He pulled out his phone, held it up, and pointed it at me. "Say *cheese*, Scarlet."

It would have looked suspicious if I didn't, so I leaned

in next to Silvio, put my arm around his shoulders, and smiled. "You know, I was going to graciously thank you all for coming, for wanting to help, for risking your lives for our friends. The whole nine yards. I had a speech prepared and everything. It was beautiful."

"And now?" Phillip murmured, angling his phone for a better shot.

"And now, I want to stab you with my fork," I said through gritted teeth.

He snickered and took two more pictures.

"Send me those," Lorelei said.

Phillip nodded and hit some buttons on his phone. "Done."

I glared at Lorelei too, but she gave me a sweet smile in return.

"And just think, those suckers are in the cloud now, Gin," Phillip said in a gleeful tone. "Where they will stay and be seen *forever*."

I rolled my eyes, then glanced around the restaurant. "Where's Ira?" I asked in a low voice.

"Mr. Morris was waiting for us at the main park entrance," Silvio said. "He took care of getting our supplies into the park and told all the guards that we were friends of his. They looked Lorelei up and down pretty good, thinking that she might be you, but they finally let us in. Mr. Morris was going to come here with us, but he got a text from Roxy, saying that she was at his cabin, searching for you. So he went to deal with her, while we came here as planned."

I nodded. Ira had said that Roxy would get around to

checking his cabin sooner or later. I was glad that it was later, and I wasn't there to cause him any more problems.

"So what's the latest?" Silvio asked.

I started to answer him, but a waitress chose that moment to come over and take our order. The others requested sweet iced teas, along with bacon cheeseburgers with all the fixings, while I opted for a strawberry lemonade, barbecue-chicken sandwich, coleslaw, baked beans, fries, and onion rings.

"Hungry?" Phillip asked after the waitress had scribbled down my order and walked away.

I shrugged. "Just building up my strength for tonight. Besides, it's not like I had a very satisfying lunch."

While we waited for our food, I told Silvio, Phillip, and Lorelei everything that had happened while I'd been skulking around.

"So Hugh Tucker set this whole thing up and lured you all down here to do his dirty work for him," Phillip mused. "He went to a lot of trouble for some pretty rocks."

Even though they were stuffed down into my corset, I could still hear the gemstones proudly singing about their own beauty. "Not just some pretty rocks," I said. "Millions of sparkling carats' worth."

The waitress returned with our food, and we all dug in. The grub was much better than it had been the last time I'd eaten here a few hours ago. The fries and onion rings were golden and crispy, while the coleslaw had a nice vinegary bite to it. The barbecue-chicken sandwich and the baked beans were disappointing, though, since the sauce on both of them didn't have the spicy cumin and black pepper kick that Fletcher's secret sauce did back at the Pork Pit. And best of all, my lemonade wasn't laced with sedatives.

While we ate, I kept an eye on the windows, watching the ebb and flow of people out on the sidewalks. Every few minutes, a couple of giants would walk by, clutching my *Wanted* posters in their hands and scanning the crowds for me. They even stopped and looked through the windows several times, peering into the barbecue restaurant. But I was just another lowly saloon girl, chowing down on my dinner before I went back to work. Yep, hiding in plain sight was still one of the best tricks around. Thanks for the reminder, Mama Dee.

My friends noticed the giants as well, and they acted casual and concentrated on their food, just like I did, until the guards moved away from the restaurant windows.

Silvio eyed me a moment, then sighed, crumpled up his napkin, and pushed his plate away. "Uh-oh. I know that look."

"What look?"

He stabbed his finger at me. "*That* look. The one that says that you've already thought of some plan to save Finn, Bria, and Owen, at considerable danger to yourself."

I frowned. "Is there any other kind of plan? I'm certainly not going to put you guys in danger." I paused. "Well, no more danger than I absolutely have to."

Silvio sighed again. "And that's exactly what that look means."

"What do you have in mind?" Lorelei asked.

I waited until the waitress had refilled our drinks a

final time, left the check, and moved on to the next table. "It's simple, really. I'm going to give Hugh Tucker exactly what he wants."

Phillip tilted his head. "And what would that be?"

I grinned. "A grand ole time in the Wild, Wild West, Spider-style."

⚜22⚜

I didn't want to get into the specifics of my plan here, so Silvio paid the bill, and the four of us left the restaurant.

"I want to check on Ira," I told the others. "Get our supplies, and make sure that he's okay and that Roxy didn't cause him any problems. His cabin is that way."

Silvio, Phillip, and Lorelei ambled along the wooden sidewalks, pretending to window-shop like all the other tourists, while I strolled along behind them, keeping them in sight, even as I smiled and posed for yet more stupid photos. Slowly, the four of us made our way from Main Street, down one of the alleys, and over to the curving, wooded path that led to Ira's cabin.

Once we'd left the crowds behind, we moved much quicker, although I made my friends step off the path and creep through the trees when we got close to the cabin. I sidled up to a large maple and peered around the thick trunk.

In the clearing beyond, Ira sat in a rocking chair on the front porch of his cabin, the lights on his snowflake sweater flashing and making the shotgun laid across his lap gleam. I carefully examined the area around the cabin and the woods beyond, but I didn't see Roxy, Brody, or any giants lurking around. They must have come and gone already, when they realized that I wasn't here. I breathed a sigh of relief. I'd been worried about Ira.

Still, I gestured for my friends to stay back as I stepped out of the trees and slowly approached the dwarf, still looking around for any sign that he wasn't alone. Ira stopped rocking and got to his feet at my approach, his shotgun dangling from his hand.

"Don't worry," he said, patting the barrel of his weapon. "They're gone. And they won't be back. I told Roxy and Brody that if I ever spotted them on my land again, that I would put a load of buckshot in both of their hides."

I laughed. "You should do that anyway."

He thought about it a second, then grinned back at me. "You're right. I should."

I waved my friends over, and we stepped into the cabin. Ira locked the door behind us, while Phillip moved over to one of the windows, keeping watch on the off chance that Roxy and Brody decided to come back after all.

Ira jerked his thumb at a large black steamer trunk that sat in front of the fireplace. "It wasn't easy, but I managed to bring in those supplies that your friends brought along with them. Lots of guns for just the four of you."

"Believe me," I said, "we'll need them."

Ira opened the trunk, and Silvio started sorting through all the items inside, complaining that the dwarf had just thrown everything into the trunk and had ruined Silvio's careful organization. Ira slapped his hands on his hips, ready to snark right back at the vampire, and Lorelei went over to mediate between them.

That left me to get the ball rolling with Tucker, so I pulled out my phone and dialed the main number for the hotel.

"Hello, this is the Bullet Pointe resort hotel. How may I assist you today?" a cheery feminine voice chirped in my ear.

"This is Gin Blanco. Tell Roxy Wyatt that I want to speak to Hugh Tucker. Don't worry, I'll hold."

"Um, okay. Just a second. Let me see if I can find her."

"Oh, I'm sure that she'll come running once she realizes that I'm on the line."

"Um, okay," the clerk said again, obviously having no idea who I was or what was going on.

She put me on hold, and I leaned against the fireplace, listening to the same sort of *plinka-plinka* piano music that they played incessantly in the Good Tyme Saloon.

Five minutes and endless off keys later, my phone clicked. I put it on speaker and waved at my friends, who all fell silent. A few seconds later, someone picked up on the other end of the line. He didn't say anything, though, so I decided to start the conversation.

"Why, hello there, Tuck," I drawled. "Bet you can't guess who this is."

"Blanco," the vampire's voice filled my ear. "How disappointing. I was holding out a faint hope that you'd crawled up into a hole somewhere and died."

"We both know that you could never be that lucky."

"No, I suppose not." His voice was calm and emotionless. "What do you want?"

"I want my friends back. And I'm going to get them back. How much bloodshed there is in the meantime depends on you."

Tucker let out a low, sinister laugh. "As if I care about bloodshed. Besides, why would I give your friends back when I went to all the trouble to get them down here in the first place?"

"Oh, I don't know. Maybe several million dollars' worth of shiny gemstones? Surely, that's worth a life or three, even to a coldhearted son of a bitch like you."

Silence, although I could almost hear the gears grinding in Tucker's mind as he debated whether I was telling the truth.

"You're bluffing. My people have been searching for weeks now and haven't seen any trace of the jewels. There's no way you've found them in a single afternoon."

"Oh, sugar. I never bluff."

He snorted.

"Besides, the very reason that you lured me and my friends down here was so we could find those shiny stones for you. And now you're saying that I haven't delivered?" I clucked my tongue. "You can't have it both ways, Tuck."

"I still don't believe you."

"Well, I could take a picture and send that to you, but you probably wouldn't believe that either. You'd just claim that I had a handful of fakes. So why don't you go ask the giants you have guarding my friends about the dashing saloon girl in the bloodred dress who moseyed into Deirdre's suite a little while ago."

"What—"

"Don't worry," I said, cutting him off. "I'm in a generous mood, so I'll give you some time to confirm everything. I'll call the main hotel line again in ten minutes. If I were you, I'd tell the clerk to put me right on through. Better get a move on now, ya hear?"

"Wait—"

I hung up on him.

"You enjoyed that," Lorelei said.

I grinned. "It's the small things that make life truly worth living."

By this point, she and Silvio had cleared the papers and photography equipment off Ira's dining-room table, pulled all the supplies out of the steamer trunk, and had laid the gear on the surface. Guns, ammo, knives, tins of Jo-Jo's healing ointment. All the usual suspects.

Silvio had also gotten a map of the theme park, which he spread out on top of the weapons, and he went into full-fledged assistant mode, comparing the paper map to some aerial photos he called up on his tablet.

"This place is like a maze," he said. "Look at all those paths circling around and around and going nowhere."

I nodded. "I know. And that's what's going to give me the advantage."

Silvio looked at me out of the corner of his eye, clearly wondering what kind of advantage I was talking about.

The ten minutes went by quickly, although I waited five more, just to make Tucker sweat a little bit. He'd gone to a lot of trouble to set this whole thing up, and I knew that he would do whatever it took to get those gems back, even wait on my call. I wondered just how much pressure the other members of his precious Circle had put on him to recoup at least some of their money that Deirdre had squandered. It must have been a considerable amount, since it seemed like he was more afraid of them than he was of me.

Tucker was a fool that way.

Finally, I dialed the main number for the hotel again. As soon as I told the clerk my name, she sputtered and put me on hold. Tucker picked up less than thirty seconds later.

"What do you want?" he growled.

"So you believe me now. Excellent," I purred. "And I want what I've always wanted—the safe return of my friends. Them for the jewels. A simple swap. Even you can do that math, Tuck. Of course, I want to talk to them first. Make sure that they're still alive. So why don't you get this call transferred up to Finn's suite. Don't worry. I'll wait."

"You don't give the orders around here, Blanco—"

I cut him off. "Or I could always mosey on down to the lake, get into a boat, and drop this lovely bag of sparkling stones in the middle of the water. Your choice, Tuck."

"Fine," the vampire growled again. "Hold on."

Phillip was still standing by the windows, keeping watch, but he glanced at me, respect shining in his eyes. "Making him run around and do your bidding? That's got to be driving Tucker crazy."

I grinned again. "That's the point."

While we waited for Tucker to come back on the line,

Silvio pulled a red highlighter out of the pocket of his red plaid shirt and started marking all the park entrances.

"I don't like this," he said, shaking his head. "I don't like this at all."

"I don't like it either," I replied. "But it is what it is. We have to make the best of it—for Finn, Bria, and Owen's sake."

Silvio nodded, but his face pinched tight with worry.

Finally, my phone clicked, and a faint buzz sounded, telling me that someone was on the line. I waited, my fingers curling tight around the phone, and my breath caught in my throat.

"Gin?" Finn's voice finally sounded.

My entire body sagged, and I held the phone away from my face so that no one on the other end would hear my sigh of relief. Then I brought the device back up to my lips again. "How are you?"

"A little groggy." His words slurred a bit. "You found the jewels?"

"I found them, and I'm going to get you guys out of there. Just hold on. Okay?"

"Okay." Finn paused. "And watch out for the June bugs. They're everywhere this time of year. I can see them now, flying around in here. . . ."

His voice drifted off, and he let out a little giggle, as though he were still under the influence of that sedative. But *June bugs* was a code phrase that Fletcher had coined for us long ago, and I recognized the words as the warning they were. Finn was telling me that whatever meeting Tucker set would be a trap and that the vampire had lots of men with him. I already knew all of that, but my heart still lifted at the fact that Finn was in good enough shape to try to help me.

"Are you satisfied now?" Tucker snapped, coming back on the line. "All your precious little friends are still alive. But they won't stay that way for long unless you give me those jewels."

"And if you hurt any of them, you'll never get the stones. So I'd say that we have ourselves a good old-fashioned standoff."

Silence. Tucker cleared his throat. "Well, then, if you'll just bring the jewels up to the hotel, we can resolve this whole messy situation—"

I laughed, cutting him off again. "So you can have Roxy, Brody, and all those giants surround and kill me? Forget it. You'll meet me in the theme park, outside the saloon, right in the middle of Main Street. Midnight. Just you and my friends. Nobody else."

"Or?"

"Or I'll forget about the lake and flush every single one of these rocks down the first toilet I come to. Believe me when I tell you that there's one close by."

"You wouldn't do that. Not while I still have your friends."

I laughed again. "Oh, yes, I would. Just for spite. Especially if you hurt them in any way. But let's be honest. That's not a chance you're going to take."

"Fine," Tucker said. "I'll meet you in the middle of Main Street with your friends in tow. And Blanco—don't even think that you can double-cross me and escape. I've got this place surrounded. No one goes in or out—including your friends—until I have those jewels."

"That's—"

I was going to hurl another insult at him, but the bastard beat me to the punch and hung up.

With the exchange set, my friends and I started getting ready for tonight.

The first thing I did was go into the bedroom and get rid of my torturous disguise. I shimmied out of the saloon-girl dress with no problem, although I had to get Lorelei to help me unlace the corset. She snickered the whole time. I also stripped off the old-fashioned heels, blond wig, and beauty mark that I'd stuck on my face.

Thankfully, Silvio had brought me some extra clothes, so I was able to put on my usual assassin attire—black boots, socks, jeans, turtleneck, and a vest lined with silverstone, which would stop any bullets coming my way. I fingered the edge of the vest and thought of how easily Roxy had shot me in the arm earlier today and how much her Fire-coated bullets had hurt. I'd have to invest in a silverstone jacket when I got back to Ashland.

If I got back to Ashland.

I still had all five of my knives, which I slid into their usual spots. I also stuffed an extra knife into one of the pockets on my vest, along with a couple of tins of Jo-Jo's healing ointment. As a final touch, I borrowed a black leather belt from Ira and slid two guns outfitted with silencers into the attached holsters. Guns ran out of ammo far too quickly for my liking, but I'd need all the firepower I could get tonight.

I put one final thing into my vest pocket—a black velvet bag full of jewels. Couldn't forget that.

Once I was ready, I smoothed the wrinkles out of Sweet Sally Sue's dress as best I could and hung it back up on the hanger. I stared at the dress a moment, thinking, then picked up an item from my spread of supplies on the bed and slipped it into one of the dress pockets. Satisfied, I smiled, grabbed the hanger, and took the dress back out to the main room where the others were.

"Here you go." I handed the dress over to Ira. "I didn't get any blood on it, which, let me tell you, is something of a miracle for me. But you should still check it later. Make sure that there aren't any rips or tears or especially holes in the pockets."

He gave me a strange look, wondering why I would care so much about the dress, but he nodded and hung the garment on a knob on the wall to help the rest of the wrinkles fall out of it.

Once that was done, Ira went over to the dining-room table, where Silvio, Phillip, and Lorelei were still looking at the park map, memorizing the locations of everything from the concession stands and food carts to the water fountains and restrooms. I joined them, studying the map as well, just as I'd studied the park when I'd been exploring with Finn, Bria, and Owen earlier today. You never knew what might be important when you were fighting for your life, and tonight I would need every advantage I could get.

"So are you finally going to fill us in on your plan?" Phillip asked.

I pointed at the theme-park map. "That—that's my plan."

Lorelei frowned. "What do you mean?"

Silvio realized what I was up to, and he started shaking his head. "I knew it," he said. "I *knew* you were going to do something like this."

"Something like what?" Ira asked.

I tapped my finger on the map. "Tucker thinks that he has me trapped in the theme park. No matter what he told me on the phone, he won't come and face me himself, and he certainly won't wait around until midnight to get his hands on those gems. Once the park closes for the night, and all the workers and tourists are gone, he'll send in Roxy, Brody, and their giants, hoping that they can find and kill me and bring him the jewels."

That's what I would do in his situation, and I knew that Roxy would be eager to confront me. After all, she was a hunter, and Gin Blanco was big game, baby.

"Tucker wants those stones more than anything else," I continued. "So he'll probably send the majority of his giants into the theme park after me. Hopefully, he'll only leave a few men behind to guard Finn, Bria, and Owen at the hotel. Either way, I doubt that Tucker's realized that I've called for backup. So while I'm running around the theme park being the distraction, the three of you can keep an eye on the hotel. Tucker will have to bring Finn, Bria, and Owen out of that suite and down to the lobby at some point, if only to take them over to Main Street for our meeting. No matter what happens to me, I want you guys to grab the three of them the second you have the chance."

Silvio sighed, still not liking my plan, but he realized that there was no talking me out of it, and he nodded. So did Phillip and Lorelei.

Ira cleared his throat. "Four. There will be four of us." He crossed his arms over his chest, daring me to argue.

I knew when I was beat, and I gave him a grateful smile. "Four of you then."

He nodded back at me.

We hashed out a few more things, but after that, there was nothing to do but wait for the theme park to close. I ended up sitting on the couch, my head resting back against a large, fluffy pillow, and my feet stretched out on a small ottoman. Maybe it was the pleasant heat from the fire or the last dregs of the sedative in my system, but my eyes slowly slid shut, and I started to dream. . . .

The gunman loomed over me, his finger curling back on the trigger, and I knew that I was going to die, right here in my own home.

I'd always felt so safe, so secure here. I'd always thought that nothing bad could ever happen as long as I was within these walls, where the stones softly sang me to sleep every night.

It made me sick to my stomach to realize how wrong I'd been.

The man stepped forward and adjusted his aim. I put my hands down, but I'd landed on a thick Persian rug, instead of the slick stone floor, and I wasn't going to be able to lurch out of the way before he shot me point-blank in the head—

A blue-white ball of magic blasted through the air, slamming straight into the guy's gun. He screamed and staggered back, trying to drop the weapon.

Only he couldn't, since his entire hand was now encased in a thick block of elemental Ice, along with his gun. The man screamed again, reached around with his free hand,

and pulled another gun out from against the small of his back, but his movements were slow and awkward, and I knew what was going to happen next.

Sure enough, another blue-white flash of magic filled the office, cold enough to make my breath frost in the air. Only this time, the light separated into a deadly spray of Ice daggers, all of which punched into the gunman's chest. Blood sprayed out in all directions from the jagged puncture wounds, the warm drops stinging my face like bees. His second gun fell from his hand, and he screamed and clutched at his chest, as though he could pull out all those long, glittering shards of Ice.

But it was too late for that.

The man staggered back, hitting the wall across from me, and his legs slid out from under him. A second later, he was down on the floor, facing me. My gaze locked with his. Even though the ski mask still covered his face, I could tell that he looked surprised, as if he'd never thought that he might end up shish-kebabed like the appetizers at the holiday party earlier.

He opened his mouth to say something, but only a thin trickle of blood came out through the wool, although more and more of it oozed down his chest, soaking into his black clothes. His dark gaze locked with mine again, but his body went slack, and I could tell that he wasn't seeing me. Not anymore.

Still staring at the dead man, I shuddered and wrapped my arms around myself—

A shadow fell over me, and I slowly looked up. My mom towered above me, the blue-white flames of her Ice magic still crackling on her hand. She stared at the man, making sure

*that he was dead, then dropped to her knees in front of me.
She was still holding on to her magic, and the cold chill of it
sank into my body, just as the Ice daggers had punched into
the intruder's chest. I shrank away from her, trying to press
myself up against the wall, into the wall, through the wall,
and out the other side to some place far, far away. Where
there were no gunmen creeping around. Where it was safe.
Where I was safe.*

*Anywhere but here, where I had just seen my mom kill
a man.*

*"Genevieve! Are you okay?" Mom's voice was as loud as
thunder in the absolute quiet of her office.*

*All I could do was just stare at her. I felt cold and numb,
inside and out, as though she'd frozen me with her Ice magic,
instead of the gunman.*

*Mom released her hold on her Ice magic and leaned for-
ward, as if she were going to run her hands over my body and
make sure that I was okay, but I shrank back from her again.
For a second, confusion filled her blue eyes, along with more
than a little hurt. But that hurt quickly melted into grim
understanding.*

*She slowly dropped her hands to her sides and rocked back
on her knees, putting a little distance between us. She stayed
like that for the better part of a minute, just letting me stare
at her, even as my mind churned and churned, trying to
understand everything that had just happened.*

*"You're bleeding," Mom finally said, pointing to the ugly
wound in my palm. "Mind if I take a look at that?"*

*I glanced down and realized that I was cradling my in-
jured hand up against my chest, smearing blood all over my
blue snowflake pajamas. I'd forgotten all about the snow-*

globe glass cutting into my palm, but now that I was looking at it, I could feel the deep, throbbing wound.

"Genevieve?" Mom's voice was almost a whisper. "Can I look at your hand? Please?"

That soft please finally penetrated my shock, horror, and disbelief. Because my mom always said please and thank you, and she'd drilled those words into me and my sisters as well. It made her seem like, well, Mom again, and not the powerful Ice elemental who'd just killed a man.

I nodded and held out my hand to her.

Mom leaned forward again, her fingers cool against my skin as they gently probed the wound. I tried not to think about the Ice magic lurking just beneath the surface of her own skin. I'd always known that she was a strong elemental, but to actually watch her unleash that power against another person . . . to actually feel all her cold strength . . . to actually see how easily she'd killed the gunman with her magic . . .

I didn't know what to think about that—or her—right now.

"It doesn't look too deep," Mom said, trying to inject some false lightness into her voice. "We'll get you cleaned right up. I'll put some Air elemental healing ointment on it, and you'll be as good as new in the morning."

"And how are you going to clean that up?" I whispered, pointing a shaking finger at the dead man.

She didn't look at him, but her mouth flattened into a tight, thin line. "Don't worry about him, Genevieve. He broke into our home and threatened you. He got exactly what he deserved."

The cold venom in her voice shocked me, and I stared at this strange person that I'd never seen before. "But you always say that we shouldn't use our powers to hurt other people. That that isn't what our elemental magic is for."

Mom leaned forward again and gently cupped my face in her hand. Perhaps it was my imagination, but her fingers seemed colder than before, and I almost thought that I could see the Ice magic running through the blue vein at her temple. I pressed my lips together and held back a shudder.

"That's right. We don't use our magic to hurt others, unless it's absolutely necessary to defend ourselves and the people we love. Just like it was for me tonight. Do you understand?"

I nodded, pretending to understand and trying to ignore how scared and horrified I still was deep down inside. Right now, all I could think about was the black eye of that gun, lining up with my forehead, and how much I didn't want to die. I held back another shudder.

"Can you tell me what happened?" Mom's blue eyes were still on my gray ones. "How did you know that man was in the house?"

My gaze darted past her to the dead man and all the blood still oozing down his chest, but I forced myself to focus on her again. "I fell asleep under the Christmas tree during the party. I'd just woken up when I heard someone coming up the stairs. I thought that it was you coming to check on us, but then I saw his boots. So I stayed quiet until he went past me. I thought that he might go into one of the bedrooms and hurt Bria or Annabella, but he came here instead. So I crept out from behind the tree and followed him."

Mom's face hardened into a blank, remote mask. "The man came straight back here to my office? Instead of searching the house?"

I nodded.

She glanced over her shoulder at him. "So Tucker sent him as a warning, then," she murmured, talking more to herself than to me. "Probably just to scare me. Maybe rough me up a little. I bet Tucker didn't think that I'd actually kill him instead."

Every word she said made more and more worry ball up in the pit of my stomach. "A warning?" I whispered. "A warning about what?"

"About what will happen to you and your sisters if I don't do something for him and his friends," she replied, still distracted by her thoughts.

"What? What do you have to do?"

Instead of answering me, Mom kept staring at the gunman, her expression getting angrier and angrier by the second, until her eyes were glowing an arctic blue with her Ice magic. She snapped up her hand, and another blast of power rolled off her and shot across the room. I winced and looked away from the bright flash of magic. After several seconds, she dropped her hand and released her grip on her power, although the air was still bitterly cold. I looked over at the gunman and gasped.

She'd frozen him solid.

The man was now encased in elemental Ice from head to toe, looking more like a Popsicle than an actual person. And still my mom eyed him, like she wanted to blast him over and over with her power, even though he was already dead. I'd never seen her so angry before, not even the time a couple of months ago when she'd caught Annabella sneaking into the house after her ten o'clock curfew.

"Don't worry, Genevieve." Mom turned back to me. "Everything's fine now."

I opened my mouth to argue, to scream and shout and yell that everything was most certainly not fine. *That there was a dead man in her office that had almost killed both of us.*

She gave me a stern look. "You will not say anything about this to Annabella or especially Bria. Not one word. Do you understand me?"

"But—"

"Do you understand me?" she snapped, cutting me off.

Anger spurted through me, that she was ordering me around like this. That she was telling me to keep quiet. That she was lying right to my face and saying that everything was okay when it was so obviously not *okay. But then I looked at her again, and I noticed her tight lips, trembling fingers, and the faint shudder that shook her entire body before she could hide it.*

And I realized that she was afraid.

I thought of the man in her office earlier. Hugh, the vampire. And somehow, I knew that he was behind everything that had happened tonight.

"Do you understand me?" Mom's voice came out softer this time, more of a desperate plea than a direct order.

"I understand," I whispered, even though I didn't.

But I would have done anything in that moment to take away her fear.

She smiled at me, but it was a wobbly expression. "Good. That's good. Don't worry, Genevieve. I'll take care of this. Everything will be the same as it's always been. You'll see. No one will ever come in here and hurt you again, not as long as I have breath and magic left in my body."

I just nodded, not sure what she expected me to say. Not sure what I could say that wouldn't be an outright lie.

Mom stared at me, then her shoulders shook again, and a choked sob escaped her lips before she was able to swallow it. She reached over and pulled me into her lap, her arms going tight around me, hugging me close and rocking me back and forth, back and forth. Trying to comfort me—and herself.

"Everything's going to be all right," she whispered. "You'll see."

Mom kept repeating those two phrases over and over, as if she was trying to convince herself, even more than me. . . .

"Gin?" a soft voice asked. "Gin, are you awake?"

For a moment, I could still feel my mother's arms around me, still feel her warm breath in my hair, still feel her Ice magic coiled in her body, ready to strike out with it at anyone who dared to hurt me. In an instant, the feelings faded, and she was gone, lost to the dark corners of my mind. Although fresh pain, loss, and longing kept knifing through my heart.

"Gin?" that same voice asked again.

I opened my eyes to find Silvio standing beside me. "Yeah," I said, my voice thick with heartache, sleep, and memories. "What's up?"

"Ira says that the park is closing in thirty minutes. It's time."

❄ 23 ❄

We all checked and made sure that we had our weapons and other supplies at the ready. Then we all gathered in front of the fireplace, me in my black clothes, my friends still in their trucker garb, and Ira in his Christmas sweater, although he'd turned off the lights on it.

"No matter what happens to me, get Finn, Bria, and Owen to safety," I said.

Silvio, Phillip, and Lorelei nodded back at me. Ira patted his shotgun.

"Be careful," Silvio said, worry filling his gray eyes.

I flashed the vampire a confident smile and winked at him. "Always."

I opened the door and left the cabin. My friends did the same, although they stepped onto the path heading up to the hotel, while I took the one that wound past the lake and back over to the theme park.

According to Ira, Bullet Pointe closed at eight o'clock

sharp, and it was just after seven thirty now. Darkness had already cloaked the landscape, blacker than coal in some places, but since it was the holiday season, strands of small white lights had been wrapped around many of the trees, lighting my way. Still, I kept to the shadows as much as possible, walking just inside the tree line instead of out on the path itself.

I reached the staging area and slid behind the stage-coach, crouching down and peering out from behind one of the back wheels. The area was deserted, but I knew that would soon change.

"Attention, y'all," a voice boomed through the park's loudspeaker system. "The theme park will be closing in fifteen minutes. Attention, the park will be closing in fifteen minutes. Please gather your belongings and head for the nearest exit or the hotel. Thank you."

Over the next fifteen minutes, more than two hundred folks streamed into the staging area, everyone from the costumed characters to the people who manned the food carts to the ticket takers at the front gates. The workers moved through the pavilions, opening their footlockers and exchanging their cowboy boots, chaps, and hats for regular old sneakers, jeans, and toboggans to ward off the winter chill. They all looked like snakes shedding their skins for something far more comfortable.

I looked out over the crowd, but I didn't see Roxy, Brody, or any of their giants. They'd be here soon enough, though.

And I'd be ready for them.

I held my position behind the stagecoach and waited for the workers to clear out. It didn't take long. Ten minutes later, everyone was bundled up, their phones in one hand and their car keys in the other, ready to go home to their families after a long day of dealing with everyone else's. They left the pavilions, headed down the alleys, stepped out onto Main Street, and vanished. Five minutes later, I was all alone, and I didn't even hear the faint murmurs of their conversations anymore.

Good.

I got to my feet, stepped out from behind the stagecoach, and moved through the pavilion, gathering up the supplies I'd scoped out earlier and stuffing them into the empty black duffel bag that I'd brought along for this purpose. I wasn't supposed to meet Tucker until midnight, but the vamp would send Roxy, Brody, and their giants into the park after me as soon as the last of the tourists and workers cleared out. I had maybe half an hour, tops, to prepare for them.

So I slung my duffel bag of supplies over my shoulder, walked down the alley, and stepped out onto Main Street. As in the rest of the park, white lights were wrapped around practically everything, from the iron benches to the hitching posts to the signs overhead. On a normal night, I was guessing that the lights would have been turned off by now, but Tucker wouldn't want his men stumbling around in the dark after me. But I didn't mind the lights because they would give my enemies false confidence—and there were still plenty of shadows to hide in.

I glanced up and down the street, surveying all the shops and storefronts, thinking about the items that each one sold, and how I could potentially use them to my advantage. Some of the shops had absolutely nothing that would help me, like the Silver Spur, with its fancy designer clothes and oversize belt buckles, or the Gold Mine, with its display cases full of jewelry. My gaze went past those two shops down the rest of the street to the barbecue restaurant, the candy store, the saloon . . .

The saloon.

I focused on the Good Tyme Saloon, a grin spreading across my face. Now *that* could be interesting. So I walked over to it. The swinging doors were shut, and two normal doors were closed and locked behind them. But I'd grabbed a gold miner's pickax from the pavilions earlier, and a couple of swings from that were more than enough to break the locks on the doors.

I pushed through the busted doors and stepped into the saloon. More white lights glimmered in here, casting plenty of illumination. I stuffed my pickax back into my duffel bag and dropped the whole thing on the floor before going around behind the bar and staring at the old-fashioned bottles of liquor on the mirrored glass shelves. I picked out a couple, pulled out the stoppers, and sniffed the contents inside. Every time, the caustic whiff of alcohol wafted up to me. Not just for show then. Excellent.

I spread several bottles around the saloon, slapping them down on the tables in the corners like they were centerpieces. I also lined up four bottles on the bar itself, then reached into my duffel bag and came up with a crisp white cowboy shirt that I'd grabbed from one of the clothing racks. A couple of passes with my knife reduced the shirt to long strips, which I stuffed into the tops of those bottles. I also plucked a stolen cigarette lighter out of my bag and put it on the bar next to the bottles.

Once that was done, I grabbed my duffel bag and left the saloon. My next stop was the water tower at the entrance to Main Street. I peered up at the tower, which was also decked out with holiday lights. The sturdy structure sat on four legs of thick, solid wood—at least until I gave the two legs facing the street a couple of swipes with a battery-powered electric saw from my supplies. I didn't cut all the way through the wood, and the tower remained standing, but I'd weakened those two supports enough for my purposes. I also grabbed a nearby water hose and opened the nozzle wide, letting water cascade out all over the walkway in front of the tower.

I checked my phone. Twenty minutes had passed since the park had closed. I probably had ten more minutes before it was open season on Gin Blanco, so I headed into the alley across from the water tower. This time, I pulled several long lassos out of my duffel bag and uncoiled them one by one. I was no cowboy, but I could tie a decent enough knot, and I'd made plenty of traps over the years. Once I had the lassos arranged, it was time for me to get into position.

I hid my duffel bag behind one of the water troughs, then jogged down the path that would take me to the main theme-park entrance, since that was the most logical place for my enemies to gather. Right before I reached the entrance, I stepped off the path and into the woods, slipping from one pool of shadows to the next, until I was within spitting distance of the main gate. It was locked up tight for the night, just like I expected, but I didn't care.

I didn't want to get out.

I wanted people to come in.

I moved through the woods until I found a tall tree—one that was not wrapped in white lights or close to any others that were illuminated. I climbed up it twenty feet until I found a sturdy branch that I could sit on without being easily seen from below. I didn't want to be down on the ground when Roxy, Brody, and the giants first entered the park, and my perch would let me see them coming. Besides, they would assume that I was hiding somewhere deeper in the park, not right here at the entrance.

My roost also let me look out beyond the gate, which opened up into a concessions area, with a series of empty parking lots beyond that. All the workers had gone home, and the tourists had done the same or trudged up the hill to the hotel if that's where they were staying. Even the giants who'd been guarding the entrance to keep me from sneaking out had vanished, now that Tucker knew that I wasn't leaving without my friends. So I was all alone.

But it didn't stay that way for long.

I'd only been in position for about five minutes when several giants rounded the corner of the concessions stands and approached the main gate. That area was lit up with holiday lights, just like the rest of the park, so I could see Brody leading the pack of them. He was dressed in his usual cowboy outfit, all in black, just like me.

There was no sign of Roxy, though. She must be staying behind with Tucker to guard my friends. Or maybe she was waiting for Brody to flush me out for her, like he'd done on their previous hunts. Either way, she wasn't here, so she wasn't important right now.

Brody didn't waste any time going over to the main

gate and pulling out a key, which he slid into the pad-lock.

The Dalton gang had come for me.

Brody got the padlock open easily enough, but the chains wrapped around the gate slid through the metal bars and crashed to the ground, creating a series of loud *clank-clank-clank*s. The giant winced and let out a mut-tered curse at the noise. If he'd wanted to slip into the park quietly, he was doing a lousy job of it. I would have heard those chains all the way over at the saloon on Main Street. But I held my position and watched Brody bend down and drag the chains out of the way. I checked my phone. Just after eight thirty. Right on schedule. Tucker hadn't wasted any time in sending his men into the park after me.

I texted Silvio. *Party time here at the main gate.*

He hit me back a few seconds later. *In the lobby with the others. No sign of our friends or Tucker yet.*

I'd expected as much, but disappointment still filled me. I wanted—needed—to know that Finn, Bria, and Owen were safe. Nothing else mattered.

Not even whether I lived or died here tonight.

Brody got the last of the chains out of the way and threw the gates open so that his men could stream inside. All of them were giants, and they were all still dressed in their cowboy costumes, complete with boots, chaps, jeans, and even hats in some cases. Several of them, in-cluding Brody, were also wearing large silver belt buckles, and a few had silver tips on their boots. I shook my head. Idiots. They should have been dressed all in black like me.

All that shiny metal just made them that much easier to spot in the glows from the holiday lights.

Easy to see, easy to kill.

Brody waited until all the men were inside before shutting and locking the gate behind them. I did a quick head count. Thirteen giants in all, including Brody, for a baker's dozen. As I watched, the giants all pulled out their guns, checking to make sure that they were ready to rock 'n' roll. No fakes here tonight. Once again, I wondered if any of them had Roxy's Fire-coated bullets loaded in their guns, but there was no way to know until they started shooting at me. But I had weapons and tricks of my own, and I was ready to unleash them.

Brody turned to his men. "Remember, this Blanco bitch is sneaky. So I want you to stay together in teams of three and be in constant contact on earbuds at all times. If you find Blanco, you can wound her, but don't kill her. Tucker still needs to question her first. Understand?"

Brody didn't mention the jewels. Probably because he realized that his men would kill me, take the gems off my body, and skedaddle instead of handing them over to him like they were supposed to.

The giants all murmured their agreement, then started making sure that their earbuds were working, as well as splitting up into four teams of three, except for Brody's team, which had him as the fourth and extra man. Four hit squads of giants just to kill little ole me. Tucker wasn't messing around. I was flattered.

I sent Silvio another text, letting him know exactly how many men Brody was bringing into the park. He texted me back a few seconds later, saying that he, Phillip,

Lorelei, and Ira were still in the lobby, holding their positions until they spotted Tucker or our friends.

I slid my phone back into my jeans pocket and focused again on the men below, studying them more carefully than before. I didn't sense any elemental magic emanating off any of them, but they didn't need it. Not with all those guns, not to mention their own inherent strength and toughness. I would have to be quiet about how I killed them, at least at first, until I'd thinned the herd out a bit. Otherwise, they'd gang up and take me down. Then the party would be over before it even got started.

"Spread out," Brody said, checking his guns. "And watch your backs. This isn't a regular person we're dealing with. This bitch is an assassin, and one of the best. Got it?"

Well, at least he was giving me my props. And he was right. I was one of the best.

And I was going to kill every single son of a bitch here tonight.

The men nodded back to Brody, and the four teams spread out, slowly heading down the walkway that led from the main gate into the park. I studied the men again, concentrating on how they moved, and who seemed like the biggest threat. That was obviously Brody, and the three guys with him looked just as tough and strong as him. But there were three giants who had teamed up at the back of the pack who were a bit shorter and leaner than all the others, so I decided to go after them first.

I waited until all the men had moved down the walkway, well away from my position, then climbed down the tree and followed them, still staying in the woods and off the path.

The four teams of giants reached the first big fork in the theme park and split up, with each team heading in a different direction. I palmed a knife and headed after the three men that I'd picked out to kill first.

The giants moved down the walkway, dutifully searching behind every food cart, barrel, and hay bale. But they were so busy looking at what was in front of them that it never even occurred to them that I could be trailing along in their wake. Oh, every once in a while, they would glance over their shoulders, but they mostly focused on what was up ahead, and not the Spider silently creeping along behind them.

The three giants reached the end of this walkway and stopped to regroup. I crouched down in the shadows behind a couple of prop tumbleweeds and watched them.

"Maybe she's not in here," one of them suggested. "Maybe she got out of the park with the tourists earlier."

A second giant shook his head. "No way. We reviewed all the security footage and checked every single person who left all afternoon long. Blanco wasn't one of them. She's in here somewhere. We just need to find her. Let's keep looking."

The final man nodded, and the three of them started forward again, heading down a new path. My knife still in my hand, I got to my feet and followed them.

With a lot of ground to cover, even along this one walkway, the giants did the inevitable thing that was going to get them killed—they split up.

Two of the giants headed over to check behind some food carts that were clustered together, while the other stepped into a short alley, peering behind every single barrel and water trough that lined the walls. I waited until the lone man was deep into the alley, then darted over to the entrance and stopped, hiding behind a tall cardboard sign of a cowboy playing a banjo.

Then I waited—just waited for him to come back this way.

The alley was a dead end, and it didn't take the giant long to search it. A minute later, he headed back toward my position. The other two men were still checking the food carts and completely ignoring their friend.

My knife in my hand, I readied myself, slowly breathing in and out, drawing air deep down into my lungs for the explosive burst of energy that I would need to take down all three giants.

The lone giant moved past the sign that I was hiding behind, not bothering to search behind it again. His second—and last—mistake. In a hunt like this one, you always had to check places coming and going, because you never knew who might be sneaking up on you.

The giant stopped at the end of the alley and raised his hand to his ear. I held my position and waited, knowing that he was going to check in with Brody.

"Rattlesnake Alley is clean," the giant said. "Heading over to help Ellis and Clyde check some food carts."

He waited a second for Brody's reply, which I couldn't hear, then nodded. "Roger that. We'll keep searching."

I slithered out from behind the sign. Despite all the holiday lights, the giant never noticed my shadow creeping up alongside his, and I was able to get right up behind him. He stopped to look around, and that's when I struck. I reached up, dug my fingers into his hair, yanked his head back and down, and cut his throat.

He was dead before he hit the ground.

But I was already moving, jumping over his body and sprinting across the walkway toward the food carts, plastering myself up against the side of one just as the other two giants came around the far end. Those men were still looking for me, so it took them a few seconds to spot their buddy's body lying at the alley entrance.

"What the—" one of them sputtered.

I stepped around the cart and threw my knife at him. The blade zipped through the air and sank into his throat, cutting off the rest of his words. He staggered back against one of the carts, his legs sliding out from under him, already closer to dead than alive.

The third and final giant whipped around in my direction, raising his gun, but I darted forward, snapped up my hand, and sent a spray of Ice daggers shooting right into his face and throat. The man's gun slipped from his hand and clattered on the ground as he coughed and coughed, trying to dislodge all the sharp, jagged pieces of Ice from his throat. I closed the distance between us, palmed another knife, and sliced the blade across his stomach, right above his ghastly dinner plate of a belt buckle.

He couldn't even scream as he flopped to the ground, trying to shove his guts back in where they were supposed to be. I ended his struggles by driving my knife through his heart, then ripping it back out again.

I whirled around, staring at each giant in turn, but they were all dead, so I looked past them at the walkways beyond. But everything was quiet, and no one had heard me eliminate this first team of men.

So I went over, pried my thrown knife out of the giant's throat, wiped it clean on his plaid shirt, and slid it back up my sleeve. Still holding my other knife in my hand, I stepped over their bodies and headed deeper into the theme park.

Three down, ten to go.

24

It didn't take me long to find the second team of giants. They were only two walkways over, checking the shadows around a series of food carts, just like the first team of men had done. But they were far more cautious than the others, staying together, with one man constantly looking behind them, watching their backs. I wouldn't be able to sneak up on them like I had the first set.

So I glanced around, thinking about where we were in the park in relation to the traps that I'd set. The lassos were the closest. Those would work. I slid my knife up my sleeve and grabbed one of the silenced guns out of its holster on my belt. I made sure the weapon was ready to fire, then got to my feet and sprinted from the shadows, across the walkway and over to one of the alleys, all in plain sight of the giant serving as the rear guard.

"Hey!" he yelled. "There she is! Heading into that alley! Come on!"

The three men abandoned their search and raced after me. I risked a glance over my shoulder, wondering if one of them might rush past his buddies in his eagerness to get me, but they stayed together in their tight pack formation. I grinned. Perfect.

I veered into the alley. Halfway down the corridor, I stopped running and crouched down behind a barrel that had been pushed up against the wall. The gun was in my right hand, and I reached down with my left and snatched up three long, thick, heavy lassos that I'd attached to a hook in the opposite wall and snaked across the ground to this side of the alley. I used my Stone magic to protect my palm from the rough ropes, braced myself up against the barrel, and peered around the side, waiting for the men to get close enough.

A second later, the three of them sprinted into the alley, running as fast as they could.

"Hurry up!" one of the giants yelled. "Don't lose her—"

Zip!

I yanked the lassos tight, and all three of them sprang up off the alley floor, creating a trip-wire right at ankle height.

The three giants stumbled over the lassos, landing in a heap in the middle of the alley. Their heavy weight yanked the ropes out of my hand and pulled me off balance, but I recovered before they did. Even as they yelled and scrambled around, trying to get back up, I got to my feet and emptied my gun into them.

Pfft!

Pfft! Pfft!

Pfft! Pfft! Pfft!

When that first gun clicked empty, I pulled out the second one from the holster on my belt and fired it as well.

Pfft!

Pfft! Pfft!

Pfft! Pfft! Pfft!

The giants' screams dissolved into wheezing rasps and gurgles. Then, even those noises stopped.

Six down, seven to go. Not quite halfway done.

Since my guns were equipped with silencers, the shots were fairly quiet, but, of course, the giants' panicked cries rang out, echoing through the theme park like claps of thunder, and I knew that it wouldn't be long before the other two teams came running. So I tossed my two empty guns away, darted forward, and scooped up two new ones from the dead giants. All the while, I kept glancing around, realizing how exposed I was. But maybe my luck would hold, and I could slip back into the shadows before the other two teams of giants converged on my position—

Crack! Crack! Crack!

Bullets slammed into the wall beside me, making wood chips fly in all directions. I really needed to quit jinxing myself like that.

I snapped my head around to see three more giants sprinting down the alley toward me.

"There she is!" one of the giants yelled. "Get her!"

Crack! Crack! Crack!

More and more bullets zinged through the air toward me, but none of them exploded with Roxy's elemental Fire. Looked like she'd kept all those burning babies for herself. But bullets were still bullets, so I reached for my Stone magic, using it to harden my skin, even as I snapped up my own stolen guns and started firing back.

Crack! Crack! Crack!

My shots made the giants hunker down behind a couple of water troughs for cover, but I wasn't as good a shot as Finn was, and I was too far away to take them all down the way that he would have. Still, I kept firing as I backpedaled away from the giants, just trying to buy myself a few seconds' head start. But all too soon my guns *click-click-click*ed empty, so I threw them away just like I had the others.

The giants peered around the water troughs and surged to their feet, realizing that I was out of ammo, but I had already turned and started running away.

Well, I wasn't running away from the giants so much as I was running toward something—the water tower.

Crack!

Crack! Crack!

Crack!

Bullets chased me down the alley, tearing holes through barrels, pinging off metal signs, and blasting apart balls of tumbleweed. The giants had recovered quicker and were moving faster than I'd anticipated. Good thing I'd already done my prep work.

I skidded around the corner and stopped, since this was where I'd left that water hose running. The steady gush of water had already coated this part of the walkway, making it gleam like polished jet underneath the soft white glows from the holiday lights. I crouched down, slapped my hand against the wet asphalt, and blasted it with my magic, turning all of that water into a solid sheet of elemental Ice. The second that was done, I ran over to the water tower, the one with two wobbly legs, thanks to yours truly.

I wrapped both my hands around the first sawn-through post and let loose with another blast of my Ice magic, driving the shards of my power deep down into the cut I'd already made. The wood creaked and groaned at the sudden blast of cold, but it didn't snap. And it wouldn't—not until I wanted it to.

Once I finished with the first post, I went over and repeated the process on the second. Then I backed up far enough so that I could see both posts at the same time and waited for the giants to get in range.

Sure enough, the three men who'd been shooting at me raced around the corner, never even stopping to think that I might have set a trap for them. Cowboy boots might look cool, but they don't have great traction. The second the giants stepped onto the Iced-over asphalt, their boots slipped, propelling them forward, and they all shouted and threw their hands up into the air, like three skaters stepping out onto a rink for the very first time. One after another, they all fell on their asses in the middle of the walkway, right in the shadow of the water tower. Perfect.

I tuned out their surprised yelps and reached for my Ice magic again, gathering up more and more of my power until I had two silvery balls of magic pulsing in the palms of my hands. Then I threw both hands forward at the same time, aiming at the two posts that I'd already cut into and frozen over.

My Ice magic slammed into the two posts, and the already weakened wood snapped like a couple of matchsticks.

Crack! Crack!

Without those two posts for support, the tower couldn't stay upright. With a loud, ominous *creak*, the wooden container tipped forward and toppled to the ground, splintering into a thousand pieces and spewing water over everything in its path—including the three giants who were still sitting in the middle of the walkway on my sheet of elemental Ice.

The giants yelled and tried to scramble to their feet, but it was too late. Water gushed out like a geyser from the broken container, drowning out their panicked cries. Even as the water cascaded over them, I stepped forward, raised my hands, and sent out blast after blast of Ice magic, right into the center of all that rushing liquid. The water was already cold from sitting in the tank in the December chill, which made it easier for me to freeze—and the giants right along with it.

The water hit the ground, then blasted up in sheets of elemental Ice, frozen solid by my magic. I thought that the giants shouted for help or maybe even screamed curses at me, but I was too busy sending out wave after wave of magic to care. My mother had been right. These men had come into the park to murder me, so they were getting exactly what they deserved.

A minute later, all the water was gone, but a field of elemental Ice had risen up to take its place, the odd dips, waves, and curls reminding me of the tumbleweeds that were scattered throughout the park.

And the giants were frozen solid, right in the middle of it all.

They were still sitting down, although their hands were raised up over their heads, as they'd instinctively tried to ward off the water crashing down on them. They looked like three cowboy statues that had been erected in the center of the walkway.

I studied the giants, but they were all encased in solid sheets of elemental Ice. If they weren't already dead from being flash frozen, they would suffocate soon enough. No way was any air getting in through all those cold, thick layers.

Nine down, four to go—

Crack! Crack! Crack!

Once again, bullets sprayed all around me, cracking my elemental Ice sculptures and spraying sharp shards everywhere. I ducked down behind a water trough and peered around the side. The three remaining giants were at the far end of the street, beyond my Ice field, with Brody standing at the head of them.

"Shoot her! Shoot her, you idiots!" he screamed, waving his gun at me.

The giants raised their guns to fire at me again, but I whipped around and sprinted down the walkway, heading even deeper into the theme park.

❋ 25 ❋

The sounds of gunfire continued behind me, but they quickly stopped once the giants realized that I was out of range. I kept running, though, determined to make the most of my head start. I had a straight shot to where I was going, and the giants would either have to pick their way across the elemental Ice field or spend precious time going around.

But they wouldn't come charging blindly at me anymore. They'd be far more cautious this time, and they'd stay together in a group. I would need all my skills to end them. Good thing I had one more trick up my sleeve.

So I headed for the centerpiece of Main Street—the Good Tyme Saloon.

I pushed through the broken doors and hurried over to the bar, where I'd lined up those four bottles of liquor, complete with white rags peeking out the tops of them.

I grabbed the bottles along with the cigarette lighter, and sprinted up the stairs to the second floor.

Brody and the giants would expect me to hole up behind the bar, since it was made out of thick, heavy wood that would offer the most cover and protection from their bullets. But Fletcher had often said that the key to surviving was to do something entirely unexpected, and that was my plan right now. So I lined up three of the bottles on the second-floor railing, close to the support beam that I ducked behind. The fourth bottle was in one of my hands, and I had the lighter in the other.

Once I was in position, I started counting off the seconds in my head.

Five . . . ten . . . fifteen . . . thirty . . . sixty . . .

Five minutes passed before I heard a telltale creak on the wooden sidewalk in front of the saloon. The giants must have spotted the broken doors and realized that I'd come in here. Good.

"Give it up, Blanco!" Brody called out. "I've got this place surrounded! You can't escape! Not this time!"

I grinned. Surrounded? Please. He had three men left. That wasn't enough to surround an armadillo. Besides, I didn't want to escape. Not until I'd killed every last one of them.

"Blanco!" Brody yelled again. "This is your last chance!"

I still didn't respond, although I could hear the other three giants muttering to each other out on the street.

"Do you really think that she's in there?"

"Maybe this is another trap."

"Maybe she's already long gone."

"She's not leaving without her friends," Brody snapped,

cutting into the chorus of doubt. "Trust me on that. And the doors are busted wide-open. She's in there, all right. Now, are we going to go in and get that bitch, or are we just going to stand here and argue about it all night? Because I don't want to be the one to go back to Tucker and tell him that the four of us couldn't capture one woman, do you?"

The other three giants muttered their agreement, apparently more afraid of Tucker than they were of me. I shook my head. Fools. You should always be most afraid of the person who could kill you most immediately. In this case, me.

The giants kept debating and arguing among themselves. I rolled my eyes, wanting them to get on with things already and quit wasting my time. Because once they were dead, I could check in with Silvio and see if he'd set eyes on Finn, Bria, and Owen yet.

Finally, Brody and the other three giants realized that I wasn't going to come out, and they decided to come in after me. I held my position behind the support beam, the bottle and cigarette lighter still in my hands, with the three other bottles all in a neat row on the railing in front of me.

The broken doors creaked open, and a lone black hat appeared. I tensed, but then I realized that it was only a hat on a stick that someone, probably Brody, was waving around.

Someone around here had watched a few too many Western movies.

Still, I'd give the giants credit for trying to get me to make the first move and give myself away. But I'd been doing this for a long, long time, and a hat on a stick wasn't going to fool me, so I held my position and waited for them to come inside.

A minute passed, then two, then three, and still the giants stayed outside. Finally, though, one of them let out a frustrated snarl and threw the hat and stick out into the middle of the saloon. The stick clattered to the floor, while the hat spun around and around before finally settling down.

I stayed in place, the same as before. I'd seen more than a few Westerns myself, thanks to Sophia, who loved them, and there was a reason why people always said not to shoot until you saw the whites of your enemies' eyes.

That meant that they were finally close enough for you to kill them.

Slowly, the doors swung open, and all four of the giants crept inside, guns up and ready to fire. I thought that Brody might be leading them, but he was the last to enter the saloon. Smart. Very smart. I wondered if his men realized that he'd set them up to walk into my trap and die first. Probably not.

The four giants tiptoed forward, and they looked right and left, examining the saloon. But they only saw empty chairs, and they didn't pay any attention to the liquor bottles that I'd positioned like centerpieces on some of the tables when I'd first broken in here. I could have cracked open some of the bottles and doused everything in alcohol, but the giants might have smelled that, and I didn't want them to realize exactly what they were walking into until it was too late.

Brody stepped forward and stabbed his finger at the bar, thinking that I was hiding back there. He held up his gun and waved it at the other men in a clear signal. They all nodded, then raised their own weapons, took aim at the bar, and started firing.

Crack!

Crack! Crack!

Crack! Crack! Crack!

Brody and his men shot up the bar, putting hole after hole into the thick, heavy wood. Splinters flew through the air, and the mirrored shelves and bottles of liquor behind the counter shattered, spewing glass everywhere. Someone couldn't hit the broad side of the bar.

One by one, the giants emptied their guns, although they all quickly reloaded their weapons. For a moment, everything was eerily quiet. The stench of gunpowder filled the air, along with the harsh, caustic scent of all the spilled booze.

Finally, Brody pointed his gun at the bar again. "Check it!" he hissed at the lead giant.

The other man swallowed, reached up, and adjusted his hat, tipping it back a little on his forehead. He also checked his gun, making sure that it was fully loaded again, and raised the weapon up into a firing position. Then he drew in a breath and eased forward, surprisingly quiet for such a large man. He moved closer to the bar . . . and closer . . . and closer still. . . .

Behind him, the other two giants spread out, with Brody taking up a position closest to the double doors. All three men aimed their guns at the bar, expecting me to pop up from behind the long slab of wood at any moment. But I didn't do that, and every second that passed only ratcheted up the tension. The lights might be on, but the heat wasn't, and the December chill had already sunk into the building, making the giants' breath steam in the air.

The lead giant came at the bar from an angle, and he finally got close enough to stand up on his tiptoes and peer over the side. He frowned, his eyebrows creasing together, and blinked a few times, as if the empty space behind the bar confused him. After a few seconds, he surged forward, put one hand on the wood, and leaned over it, his head snapping left and right as he looked for me.

He whipped back around to Brody. "She's not back there!"

Brody frowned. "What do you mean she's not back there?"

The giant flung his hand out. "I mean, she isn't hiding behind the bar—"

He never got the chance to finish his sentence.

I clicked on the cigarette lighter, ignited the white cloth in the end of the bottle of gin that I was still holding, and tossed the whole thing down below right into the middle of the saloon.

Whoosh!

My makeshift Molotov cocktail exploded with a roar and a bright ball of orange-red flame.

The giants yelled and scrambled out of the way, but I was already lighting the next bottle of gin and tossing it down on top of them. This time, my aim was better, and I hit the giant by the bar square in the chest. The bottle shattered on impact, splashing gin all over him, and the alcohol ignited instantly. The giant screamed and screamed, slapping at the flames that danced all over his body, searing his skin, but it was no use. He crashed into a table, which splintered under his weight, and did a nosedive onto the floor. All around him, the pieces of wood began to smoke as they too started to catch fire.

Brody and the other two giants finally realized that I was on the balcony and raised their guns to fire at me. I lit my third and fourth Molotov cocktails and tossed them down in quick succession, this time aiming for two separate tables, each one with a bottle of liquor sitting in the center of it.

Bull's-eye.

Both bottles landed exactly where I wanted them to, and that entire area exploded with flames, catching another of the giants by surprise. Once again, liquor splashed everywhere, and he too lit up like a Christmas tree. This giant did the smart thing and stopped, dropped, and rolled around on the floor, just like you were supposed to. But what he didn't realize was that he was rolling around in the growing fire that was spreading around the first giant that I'd hit. So instead of putting out the flames, all the second man did was spread them around the rest of the saloon. Red-hot sparks and embers flew everywhere, and small fires sprang up among all the old, weathered wood.

Through the smoke and flames, Brody and the fourth giant raised their guns again and finally started firing at me, but I took hold of the railing, swung my legs up and over it, and leaped off the balcony. On the way down, I grabbed hold of my Stone magic, turning my body into a hard, impenetrable—and heavy—shell.

Crash!

I did the perfect swan dive right on top of the two of them, sending all three of us crashing to the floor. Brody cursed and quickly scrambled up and back out of my reach, but the other man's head snapped against the floor, stunning him, and I took advantage, palming a knife and cutting his throat. He died with a bloody gurgle.

"You bitch!" Brody snarled.

He raised his gun and started firing at me again, even as he backed toward the doors. I kept my grip on my Stone magic, and the bullets harmlessly *ping-ping-ping*ed off my body and rattled into the walls, wrecking even more of the saloon. I tightened my grip on my knife, got to my feet, and started forward, but Brody decided not to stick around to meet the same fate as his buddies. He fired off a few more shots, then ran out the double doors.

This time, I chased him.

At least, I tried to.

I headed for the saloon doors, but a blast of fire made me stop short. The saloon was more of a tinderbox than I'd thought, and the flames from my Molotov cocktails had already spread throughout the first floor. Thick black smoke boiled up into the air, making it hard to breathe, and the heat licked at my skin, eager to burn right through all my Stone magic. I had to get out of here, or the smoke and flames would quickly overcome me.

Coughing all the while, I headed toward the saloon doors again, but another explosion ripped through that area, and the flames started burning there even brighter and hotter than before. Since I couldn't get out through the double doors now, and the flames had already blocked the rear ones behind me, I went for the only other exit. I used my Stone magic to make my skin even harder and dove headfirst through the plate-glass window that lined the front of the saloon.

Crash!

I flew through the glass, which busted with a roar, and hit the wooden sidewalk outside. My momentum propelled me forward, and I rolled off the sidewalk, hit one of the water troughs, bounced off it, and ended up sprawled at an awkward angle in the dirt street. To add insult to injury, I hit the trough hard enough to rock the water inside, making a wave of it spill out over the top and cascade all over me, soaking me to the bone. In an instant, I was bitterly cold, despite the growing heat from the saloon fire. The shocking chill also made me lose my grip on my Stone magic. Sputtering, I staggered up and onto my feet, my knife still in my hand, swiping the wet, loose strands of hair back from my face. Brody was still out here, and I wouldn't put it past him to double back and attack me if he thought that he finally had the advantage—

The giant's fist cracked into the side of my face.

The blow sent me stumbling back, and I ended up sitting ass-down in the water trough, just like all the cowboys so comically had during the park's high-noon show yesterday.

"Fuck taking you alive," Brody growled, raising his gun.

Before he could pull the trigger, I whipped up my hand and sent a spray of Ice daggers shooting out at him. The giant growled and turned to the side, ducking most of the blast. For such a big guy, he was quick, much quicker than me, especially when I was so waterlogged.

I tried to climb out of the trough so that I could stab him with my knife, but Brody finally wised up and quit trying to shoot me. He dropped his gun and surged forward, wrapping his hands around my throat. Given his bigger frame and far heavier weight, he easily shoved me back down into the trough, well under the water. My wrist banged against the side of the wood, and my knife slipped from my fingers and disappeared into the water. Without a weapon in my hand, all he had to do was hold me under long enough for me to pass out. Then he could either fish me out and take me to Tucker or drown me like he really wanted to.

I was betting on that second option.

I kicked and bucked and thrashed and heaved, but I was no match for Brody's superior strength, and I was too far down in the water to fight back. The only part of him that I could even reach were his hands and arms, and I couldn't do enough damage to any of those to kill him before he suffocated me.

So I quit thrashing, since all that was doing was wasting precious air and energy, and thought about how I could escape from the giant. Or at least get out of the water long enough to take a breath.

My Stone magic might save me from bullets, but it wouldn't do me any good in this situation, so I focused on my Ice power. I'd used up most of it freezing the giants in the street earlier, but I still had the reserves stored in my spider rune ring and matching necklace. But just freezing the water in the trough wouldn't do me any good, since I would still suffocate without any air, so I focused on the only other thing I could do with my Ice magic.

Break the wood around me.

No wood meant no trough and no container to hold all the frigid water. So I dropped my hands from Brody's, no longer trying to pry his fingers off my neck. Instead, I held my hands out wide so that I was touching both sides of the trough at once, my spider rune scars mashed up against the cold, slimy wood. Then I let loose with my Ice magic.

Even with the magic stored in my ring and pendant, it was still hard, especially since more and more white, gray, and black spots began to swim in front of my eyes. But I focused and managed to blast the wood on either side of me. The second I thought that it was frozen enough, I sent out another blast of Ice magic, cracking away all those cold crystals.

Come on, I thought. *Break, damn you, break!*

But the wood was old, tough, and weathered, and it didn't want to bend, much less break outright. But I kept blasting it with my Ice magic over and over, and I finally forced a few cracks into the boards. At least, I thought I did. I couldn't see what I was doing since Brody was still holding me underwater, choking the life out of me. But I reached and clawed and scraped up all the Ice magic in my spider rune ring and pendant, blasting it outward through my hands, forcing it into the wood over and over—

Whoosh!

The wood finally broke apart, the trough split into pieces, and water gushed everywhere. I barely managed to suck down a breath before Brody slipped and fell down on top of me, driving the air right back out of my lungs again with his heavy weight.

He came up sputtering, but he didn't loosen his grip on my throat, not even for an instant. "You bitch!" he yelled. "Why won't you just die already!"

I didn't bother wasting precious breath to answer him.

My Ice magic was gone, and I couldn't get to my knives, given the way that his body was pinning me in place. But I could reach one other weapon—the spare gun holstered to Brody's belt.

So I shoved my hand down in between us, trying to get to the gun, but Brody was wearing one of those over-size belt buckles that Roxy was so fond of, and it kept getting in the way of my cold, numb grasping fingers.

"What are you doing now?" he sneered. "Trying to cop a feel?"

I ignored his taunt, shoved my hand past the belt buckle, curled my fingers around the gun, and yanked on it as hard as I could.

Brody frowned, realizing that I was, in fact, not trying to cop a feel. "What the—"

The gun slid free of the holster. I snapped up the weapon, pressed it against the side of his head, and pulled the trigger.

CRACK!

The sound seemed as loud as a stick of dynamite exploding in my ear, and blood sprayed all over my face, stinging my skin with its shocking warmth. For a moment, Brody's eyes widened, then everything inside him just—stopped. Without a sound, his hands fell away from my throat, and he pitched forward on top of me. I waited several seconds, but he didn't so much as twitch, and I felt more and more of his blood dripping down my face and neck. The giant was dead.

I heaved and grunted and finally managed to shove him off me before slowly getting to my feet. I dropped his gun in the mud, bent down, and put my hands on my knees, just trying to get my breath back. Brody was lying on his side, his fingers stretched out in my direction, his sightless eyes fixed on me in a silent accusation that I knew all too well.

I held my hand up, as though I were tipping the brim of an imaginary cowboy hat at him. "The outlaw Gin Blanco wins again."

✳ 26 ✳

Something exploded inside the saloon, causing more flames to shoot out the busted storefront window and driving me away from Brody's body. The fire also reminded me that I still had work to do tonight. Now that Brody and the giants were dead, I needed to get to the hotel to help Silvio and the others save the rest of our friends.

I held up my hand, squinting against the glare, and looked out over the muddy mess around the water trough, searching for the knife that I'd lost in my fight with Brody. There it was, lying in a puddle, the hilt just visible through the thick, sloppy mud. I started to bend down and reach for it—

Crack!

A shot rang out, and I screamed as a bullet blasted through my left arm, close to where I'd already been shot earlier today. Once again, elemental Fire erupted in and around the wound, burning hotter than the flames still shooting out of the saloon. Roxy hadn't come into the park with Brody and the giants, but she was here now, and the bitch had shot me again with one of her Fire-coated bullets.

I pitched forward, right into the middle of the large puddle, with mud splashing all over me. But the thick, gloppy mud actually doused the Fire, although the magic continued to burn and burn in the wound itself. Curses and snarls spewed out of my lips, and I fought to get the pain under control. Even as I slopped around, I kept expecting another bullet to tear through my body at any second—

"Well," a familiar, snide voice called out, "that was certainly dramatic."

I raised my head to find Roxy and Hugh Tucker standing in the middle of Main Street.

And they weren't alone.

Finn, Bria, and Owen were behind them, standing off to the far side of the street. Their hands were bound tightly in front of them with thick lassos, while black bandannas had been stuffed into their mouths to keep them quiet. My friends all looked tense and angry, but no visible cuts or bruises dotted their faces. It didn't seem as though they'd been tortured, and they all nodded at me, silently telling me that they were more or less okay. Relief flooded me. Good. That was good.

What wasn't good was the half a dozen giant guards that flanked my friends. Tucker might have sent Brody and his outlaw gang into the theme park after me, but the vampire had realized that he would need more men, and he'd planned accordingly. Still, I'd put a bigger dent in their numbers than I'd expected, and the odds were far more even now than they had been before.

Especially since the rest of the Blanco gang was lurking around here somewhere.

I didn't glance around, but I knew that Silvio, Phillip, Lorelei, and Ira had to be nearby. They would have seen Tucker leaving the hotel with our friends, and they would have followed him down here.

Unless the four of them were already dead—killed trying to rescue our friends at the hotel. . . .

Dread filled me, washing away my relief, but I pushed the emotion aside. I wasn't going to let myself think like that. I couldn't. Not if I wanted to rescue Finn, Bria, and Owen. Silvio and the others were waiting for the right time to strike, just as I'd asked them to. I had to believe that, just like I had to believe that we were all going to get out of this cursed theme park alive—and that I wasn't going to die in the next minute or two.

Roxy stepped forward, her revolver pointed at my head. Her gaze flicked to Brody's body, and rage flashed in her pale green eyes. "Get up," she growled, focusing on me again. "Slowly. Any sudden moves, and I'll put another bullet through you."

I slowly raised my hands up out of the mud and staggered to my feet. I risked a glance down and realized that my knife was still sticking up out of the puddle. I stepped in front of it so that they wouldn't see it lying on the ground.

Tucker looked at me, then at Brody lying dead in the street, and finally at the still-burning saloon. "Well, you've certainly made a mess of things here."

I grinned. "What can I say? I just can't help myself."

"She killed Brody," Roxy snapped. "So cut the cute chitchat and let me shoot the bitch again already."

Tucker gave her a cold glare. "Not until I get what I came here for."

The vampire snapped his fingers, and the men guarding Finn, Bria, and Owen raised their weapons, shoving their guns up against my friends' sides.

"Give me the jewels or my men will kill your precious little friends right in front of you," Tucker hissed.

I knew that he meant it, so I didn't hesitate. "Okay, okay. Just take it easy. I'll give you what you want. They're in one of my vest pockets. So tell Annie Oakley there to hold off her sharpshooting."

Roxy growled, but I gave her a sweet smile in return. Tucker jerked his head at Roxy, who lowered her gun to her side, although she kept her finger curled around the trigger, ready to snap the weapon up and shoot me the second I did anything suspicious.

I held my hands out to my sides, then slowly brought them in to my chest. Then, just as slowly, I unzipped one of the pockets on my wet, muddy, bloody silverstone vest, drew out a black velvet bag, and held it up where Tucker and Roxy could see it.

"Here are your pretty little rocks. Every single one of them."

"Go get them," Tucker snapped at Roxy.

She pressed her lips together, clearly pissed at being ordered around like a simple servant, but she walked down the street toward me, her gun still in her hand, clearly itching to shoot me again. I tensed, thinking about reaching for my Stone magic to harden my skin, but I'd exhausted almost all the reserves in my spider rune ring and necklace. I'd only be able to protect myself one more time from her bullets, and I didn't want to waste the few scraps of magic that I had left. Not yet.

So I stood there and waited, wondering if Roxy was going to be stupid enough to get within arm's reach of me.

But she was too smart for that, and she stopped about ten feet away. "Throw the bag over here. No tricks, or your friends die."

"No tricks from me."

I gently tossed the bag about five feet in front of me, so that it landed in between us in the middle of the street. Roxy kept her gaze on me and her gun at the ready as she sidled forward, bent down, and scooped up the bag, but I didn't make a move. I wouldn't risk my friends' lives like that.

While Roxy straightened up, I looked past her. Finn and Bria both had tense, worried looks on their faces, and they kept glancing at the men guarding them, hoping for an opportunity to try to take them down.

Finally, I stared at Owen. He looked back at me, his violet eyes steady on my gray ones, not the least bit afraid, completely confident that I would get him and the others out of this. When he was sure that no one but me was looking at him, he winked, then turned his bound hands so that his fingers were pointing off to my left. I didn't look in that direction, but I knew what he was trying to tell me—that Silvio, Phillip, Lorelei, and Ira were in position and ready to help. Owen must have spotted them at the hotel.

My heart lifted. We still had a chance to get out of this. As much as I wanted to wink back at him, I kept my face blank, not wanting to give Tucker, Roxy, or the guards any inkling as to what was going on.

Roxy stepped back and tossed the black velvet bag over to Tucker, who easily caught it. The vampire hefted the bag in his hand, opened the drawstrings, and tipped the contents into his palm. Diamonds, sapphires, and rubies flashed under the lights and the flames from the saloon fire, and I could hear the stones softly singing about their beauty.

Satisfied, Tucker nodded, dropped the jewels back into the bag, and closed it up tight before slipping it into the pocket of his black suit jacket. "Why, Gin, you surprised me. You actually gave me what I wanted. Just like that."

I shrugged. "You didn't give me much of a choice."

"No, I didn't," Tucker murmured. "And I believe that this concludes our business for the evening." He grinned, and I knew what was coming next. "Actually, this concludes our business forever. Kill her."

He gestured with his hand. He hadn't even finished the motion before Roxy grinned, whipped around, and shot me.

I'd realized that this little scenario only ended one way—with Roxy shooting me—and I could have reached for my Stone magic to protect myself. But I chose not to. Because Roxy was pissed that I'd killed Brody, and I was betting that she'd want to make me suffer before she finally ended me.

And I was right.

This bullet just grazed my right arm, but I still screamed, especially as the elemental Fire exploded again, searing my skin with its hot intensity. I staggered back and slapped at my arm, using my mud-covered fingers to snuff out the Fire as best I could. My friends surged forward, trying to shout through the bandannas stuffed in their mouths, but the guards held them in place. Tucker crossed his arms over his chest, amused by the whole spectacle.

"I could use you for target practice," Roxy said, spinning her revolver around and around in her hand. "But that wouldn't be very sporting of me. We're in the Old West, so let's settle things the old-fashioned way. How about a showdown, Gin? Just you and me and our guns in the middle of Main Street. Winner take all."

She didn't wait for me to answer. Instead, she gestured at Brody's gun, which was still sitting in the middle of the mud where I'd dropped it before. "Pick it up."

I hesitated, wondering how I could twist this to my advantage—

Crack!

This time, the bullet grazed my outer left thigh. More elemental Fire seared my skin, and the stench of my burned flesh filled my nose, making my stomach roil. I gritted my teeth, slapped out the Fire as best I could, and pushed the pain away, locking it down tight. I could handle a little pain, a little Fire, a little charred skin. As long as I got to dish out a whole lot of death in return.

"I said pick it up," Roxy snarled. "Right fucking now."

"Okay, okay," I said. "You want your high-noon showdown, Sheriff Roxy? Fine by me."

Keeping one eye on Roxy, I limped over to where the

gun was and slowly bent down, trying to pick it up without collapsing to the ground. I stretched out my fingers toward the gun—

Crack!

A bullet hit the butt of the gun, making the weapon skitter out of my reach and elemental Fire explode under my fingertips. I snarled and slapped my hand against my thigh, once again snuffing out the flames, although not the continued searing burn they left behind.

Laughter rang out, sounding almost as loud as the gunshots, as Roxy, Tucker, and the guards yukked it up at my expense. I looked up. Roxy grinned, a cruel light flashing in her eyes, and gestured for me to try again.

So I sighed and limped forward, realizing that I had no choice but to play her sick game. The only good thing about it was that everyone was focused on me now, including the giants guarding Finn, Bria, and Owen, who'd lowered their weapons from my friends' sides. I hoped my suffering would give Silvio and the others a chance to finally make their move.

But right now, I had another round of torture to endure, so I gritted my teeth and stretched my hand out toward Brody's gun again, knowing what was coming next—

Crack!

More Fire, more burns on my skin, more laughter from Roxy, Tucker, and all the guards.

I smothered the latest round of Fire, slowly straightened up, and glared at her. "No wonder you have all those stuffed animal heads in your office. You are one sadistic bitch."

Roxy crooked an eyebrow at me. "Well, Gin, if you don't want to play along, I guess I'll just have to use you for target practice after all."

Before I could snipe back at her, the bitch snapped up her gun and shot me again.

Crack!

This bullet punched into the meaty part of my left thigh. More of that damn elemental Fire exploded and seared my skin, adding to the agony of the wound. Roxy hadn't grazed me this time, but she wasn't done playing with me either, since the bullet hadn't hit anything vital. A painful, through-and-through wound, but not debilitating.

Still, I screamed louder than I had before, staggered forward, and crumpled in a heap in the middle of the mud, as if I were done for. I thought it was pretty convincing, as far as pratfalls went.

"Mmm! Mmm!" My friends' muffled shouts filled the air, but they could do nothing to help me.

Roxy grinned and strutted over to me, spinning her gun around and around in her hand, making the pearl handle and silver barrel flash, and doing all sorts of fancy trick moves with the weapon. I did my own trick move, digging my hand down into the mud, and curling my fingers around the hilt of my knife that was still buried there. I also reached for the last remaining scraps of my Stone magic, getting ready to pour the power out to harden my skin one final time. I'd only get one shot at this, and I had to make it count.

This time, Roxy kept coming until she was within arm's reach, looming over me. "You know, I don't have a human head in my office, but I think that I'll make an exception for you, Gin." Her eyes gleamed with sly satisfaction.

"Never going to happen, sugar—"

Before I could finish, she snapped up her gun and shot me in the face.

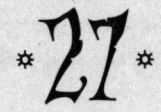

* 27 *

At least, Roxy tried to shoot me in the face.

At the last second, I lunged out of the way, slithering forward through the mud. But the bullet from the close-range shot still punched into my left shoulder. I grunted at the hard, bruising impact and flash of Fire, but my Stone magic kept the bullet from actually tearing through my body. Roxy snarled and started to pull the trigger again, but I didn't give her the chance.

I gritted my teeth, raised my knife up out of the mud, and stabbed her booted foot. This time, Roxy was the one who screamed.

Such a sweet, sweet sound.

She tried to shoot me again, but I ripped my knife out of her foot and swiped it across her wrist, making her drop her trusty revolver. She staggered back, trying to get away from me and desperately reaching for the second revolver on her belt, but I threw myself forward, tackled her around the knees, and knocked her ass down in the mud. She tried to kick me away, but I grabbed hold of her shiny rhinestone belt buckle and used it to pull myself up on top of her.

Then I raised up my knife again and slammed it into her chest, right next to that shiny silver sheriff's star pinned over her heart.

And I didn't stop.

I stabbed her once, twice, three times, each wound as deep, brutal, and deadly as I could make it. Her blood spattered against my face and hand, but I didn't mind the warm sensation. Not at all.

Roxy screamed and screamed, clawing for her gun all the while. She managed to get her fingertips on the pearl handle, so I raised up my knife a final time and snapped it down, driving it all the way through her hand and into the squishy mud below.

"Never bring a gun to a knife fight," I hissed.

Roxy gurgled once, as if agreeing with me, then her body went slack and still under mine.

As much as I would have liked to slump down in the mud next to her, Tucker and the guards were still here, still alive, so I yanked my knife out of her hand, rolled off her body, and staggered to my feet.

Tucker was already stabbing his finger at me. "Kill her, right fucking now—"

Crack!

Crack! Crack!

Crack!

More shots rang out, but this time, the Blanco gang were the ones firing.

With all the guards' attention on me, Silvio, Phillip, Lorelei, and Ira had finally decided to strike. Somehow, Silvio and Ira had managed to sneak up onto the second-floor balcony of one of the storefronts and were firing down at the giants, while Phillip and Lorelei were doing the same thing from their position behind a food cart down here on street level.

Finn, Bria, and Owen immediately threw themselves to the ground, out of the line of fire.

Crack!

Crack! Crack!

Crack!

One giant fell, then another one. Bria scrambled over and pulled a dead giant's gun out of his hand. She tossed it over to Finn, then fumbled to get the giant's second weapon out of the holster on his belt. Owen was also grabbing the weapon from the dead giant closest to him.

My friends battling the giants meant that only one man was left. I scanned the street for Tucker.

But the bastard wasn't here.

My head snapped left and right, searching for him. I hadn't gone through all this just to let him get away now. So where was he? Where was that sneaky rat bastard—

I spotted a flash of movement out of the corner of my eye, and I turned my head just in time to see Tucker leave the street behind and sprint into an alley. I started to head in that direction but stopped and glanced over at my friends.

Finn had seen the vampire too, and he ripped the bandanna out of his mouth and waved his still-tied hands at me. "We're fine!" he yelled. "Go! Get Tucker!"

I flashed him a grateful smile and did as he commanded, hurrying down the street after my enemy.

I was hampered by all the holes and burns in and on my body, especially the ones in my thigh, but I ignored the pain of my many injuries and limped along as quickly as I could. But Tucker was exceptionally fast, and he easily put some distance between us. He was at the far side of the staging area before I'd even stepped out of the alley. But instead of taking the path that led back to the hotel, he headed toward a different one. I frowned, wondering where he was going, but then I realized exactly where that path led—the boat dock down at the lake.

No doubt Tucker had his escape route already mapped out. Take a boat across the lake where he would most likely have a car waiting, then vanish into the night, along with the jewels.

I wasn't about to let him get away that easily.

So I gritted my teeth and forced myself to move faster. I was good at plowing through things, so that's exactly what I did, knocking over barrels, hay bales, tumbleweeds, and everything else that stood in my way. The good thing about running was that it got rid of the chill that had sunk into my bones from being dunked in the water trough. The bad thing was that it made my entire body scream with the pain of my burns and bullet wounds. But I ignored the agony as best I could and kept running.

I left the staging area behind and stepped onto the path that led down to the lake. With no obstacles here, I picked up my pace.

But I was still too damn late.

In the distance, I heard a boat engine rumble to life. I snarled out a curse and kept going.

I left the woods behind and sprinted down a hill, straight toward the wooden dock that stretched out like an arrow into the water. Holiday lights had been wrapped around the dock too, letting me clearly see Tucker standing in a boat at the far end, casting off a rope, and gunning the engine. I put on an extra burst of speed, doing my best to catch up with him.

But it was no use.

By the time I reached the end of the dock, Tucker was already thirty feet out into the water, with the engine idling. With no guns and no magic left, the bastard knew that I couldn't kill him now, and he'd stayed behind just to taunt me.

Tucker shook his head. "You just don't know when to quit, do you, Gin?"

"Only losers quit. You? You're just going to die."

He smiled, his teeth flashing like opals in his face. "Not tonight."

"No," I muttered. "Not tonight."

"Tell me one thing, though," he called out.

"What?"

He reached into his jacket pocket and pulled out the black velvet bag, letting it swing from his hand like a clock pendulum, mocking me with it. "Where did Deirdre hide the jewels? My men and I searched everywhere for them."

"They were in her suite. Hidden in a couple of snow globes like they were just worthless stones."

Tucker shook his head again. "That bitch. Deirdre was clever, but I'd never thought that she'd be *that* clever."

"Oh, I imagine that she got the idea the day the two of you paid my mother a visit in her office, right before her annual holiday party."

Tucker froze, the smug smile dropping from his face. "You remember that?"

"Yeah. I remember it. I especially remember the man you sent to hurt my mother that night."

He eyed me a moment, then shrugged. "It was just business. Surely, you of all people can understand that."

"Oh, I do understand it. And I'm going to make it my business to end you and the rest of the Circle."

The vampire smiled, his black eyes glittering in his face. "Careful what you wish for, little Genevieve. That's one can of worms you might not want to open."

"I—"

Tucker gave me a mock salute and gunned the engine, drowning me out. The vampire waggled the black velvet bag at me again, mocking me a final time, before steering the boat around, pushing the throttle, and gliding across the lake.

Tucker was right. He wasn't going to die tonight.

But soon—very soon.

I'd make sure of that.

✶28✶

"Gin! Where are you? Gin!" My friends' voices drifted through the air to me in a loud, worried chorus.

"Over here!" I called out. "Down at the boat dock!"

A minute later, Finn, Bria, and Owen appeared, running down to the dock. I hobbled back in their direction, the pain of my injuries flooding my body with every single step. My friends skidded to a stop, guns in their hands, looking left and right.

"Where's Tucker?" Finn growled. "Where is he?"

I jerked my thumb over my shoulder. "He's gone. Got into a boat, zoomed away, and left me standing here like an idiot. That son of a bitch must be part cat, as many lives as he seems to have."

Bria gave me a sympathetic look. "I'm sorry, Gin."

I shrugged. "It's okay. You guys are safe, and that's the most important thing. Besides, Tucker will show himself again sooner or later. And I'll get him when he does."

Owen stepped forward and cupped my face in his hand, his gaze steady on mine. "*We'll* get him when he does."

I smiled back at him. "You're damn right we will."

Owen had insisted on scooping me up into his arms and carrying me over to Ira's house so I could get cleaned up, as well as use some of Jo-Jo's healing ointment to patch up all the burns and bullet holes that Roxy had inflicted on me. The ointment didn't completely heal me, but it stopped the constant, searing pain of the Fire burns and took the edge off the worst of my wounds. I'd be okay until we returned home to Ashland tomorrow and Jo-Jo could heal me herself.

Finn and Bria went back to the theme park to help Silvio, Phillip, Lorelei, and Ira deal with all the blood, bodies, and other destruction that we'd left behind. Well, that *I* had left behind.

Ira ended up calling the fire department to come put out the saloon fire, and they extinguished it before it damaged any more of Main Street. As for all the bodies in and around the saloon, Ira claimed that security footage showed the giants breaking into the theme park, and he told the authorities that they must have been searching for the hidden jewels. Naturally, the giants had turned on each other, started the fire, and gunned each other down when they hadn't found the precious stones. I don't know if anyone actually bought Ira's flimsy cover story, but Roxy, Brody, and the giants were all dead, so they couldn't say anything different, and my friends and I certainly weren't going to blab. Besides, the theme park was Finn's private property, so there wasn't much the cops could do once Ira told them that the owner wasn't going to pursue the matter, since the perpetrators were all deceased. It didn't seem like anything was going to lead back to us.

We all crashed at the dwarf's cabin, just in case Tucker decided to double back and take another run at us, but the rest of the night passed quietly, and we all slept in late.

Just before noon the next day, I was standing in Ira's kitchen, flipping buttermilk pancakes on a griddle and frying loads of bacon, eggs, and potatoes in a couple of cast-iron skillets.

"Breakfast is served," I called out, then looked over at Ira, who was sitting at the dining-room table. "Please tell me there's a triangle around here somewhere that I can ring."

He chuckled. "I'm afraid not."

"Ah, well."

It was a tight fit, but everyone squeezed in around the table while I dished up the food. Golden, light-as-air pancakes, crispy bacon, fluffy scrambled eggs, and crunchy fried potatoes. It was the perfect hearty, stick-to-your-ribs breakfast, and we all dug into our feast.

Finally, after having three heaping plates of food, Ira pushed back from the table, sighed with contentment, and looked at me. "I should hire you to work at the Feeding Trough. None of my folks can cook like this."

I laughed. "Sorry, but I already have a barbecue restaurant to run."

He grinned back at me.

Finn huffed. "Well, I don't know how the two of you

can be so cheery this morning, considering the fact that my saloon in my theme park just burned down."

Ira arched his eyebrows. "Your theme park?"

My brother shrugged. "My name is the one that's on the deed."

"Good," Ira said, not missing a beat. "Then you can pay for all the repairs."

Finn blinked, then realizing that he'd been one-upped, gave the dwarf a sour look. Ira chuckled, and we all joined in with his light, teasing laughter. Finn sighed and slurped down some more coffee, which perked him right back up again.

"As much as I hate to admit it, Finn is partially right," Silvio chimed in. "After all, Tucker did escape."

Bria nodded. "And he got away with the gems too."

"Some guys have all the luck," Finn muttered.

Ira, Owen, Phillip, and Lorelei all nodded their agreement, but I laughed again, making them all look at me in surprise.

Lorelei's eyes narrowed. "What did you do, Gin?"

I got to my feet, walked across the cabin, and grabbed Sweet Sally Sue's dress from where it was hanging on the wall. I brought the dress over to the dining-room table and held it out to Ira. "Why don't you do the honors?"

He frowned, wondering what I was getting at, but then his face cleared, and I knew that he remembered what I'd told him yesterday. The dwarf took the dress from me, laid it out across his lap, and slipped his hand into first one pocket, then the other. He found it in the second one. Ira blinked in surprise and slowly drew out a black velvet bag.

Everyone gasped, got to their feet, and gathered around his chair.

With shaking hands, the dwarf slowly opened the drawstrings on the bag and carefully tipped the contents out onto the table.

Sweet Sally Sue's jewels glimmered under the lights.

For a moment, there was stunned silence.

Then Finn piped up first, the way he always did. "Those . . . those are the *real* jewels, right?"

I nodded. "Yep, those are the ones I found hidden in those snow globes in Deirdre's suite. Every last one that she'd tucked away in them."

Silvio frowned. "Then what was in that bag you gave Tucker? Because he opened it on Main Street last night, and I saw him pour the stones out into his hand."

"Oh, those were gems too, just mostly fake ones."

This time, Owen frowned. "But where did you get fake jewels on such short notice?"

I grinned. "Straight from Mama Dee herself."

We all sat back down in our chairs, and I told my friends how I'd grabbed a bunch of rings, necklaces, and bracelets, along with an extra black velvet bag, from that wall of jewelry in Deirdre's closet.

"Most of it was just costume jewelry," I said. "Very nice costume jewelry, but still fake. There were a few real gems in the mix, but they were small, poor-quality stones. So I pried them out of their settings and put them in a black velvet bag like they were the real thing. It was good enough to fool Tucker."

The vampire might be clever, but he wasn't a Stone elemental like I was, so he hadn't been able to hear the

stones' soft, muted murmurs last night, and he hadn't realized that I'd been giving him a bag full of fakes. That's
what I'd been counting on, and it had worked like a proverbial charm. Tucker might have escaped, but at least I'd
kept him from getting his hands on the jewels. It was a
small victory, but I'd take what I could get.

"I just wish that I could be there to see the look on
Tucker's face when he realizes that you duped him and
that all he has is a pile of pretty glass," Phillip said.

"Me too." I grinned. "Me too."

Everyone fell silent, sipping their coffee and orange
juice. Ira was still staring down at all the colorful, sparkling stones spread across the table. After several seconds,
he scooped them all up, poured them back into the bag,
and held the whole thing over the table for Finn.

"Here," Ira said in a rough voice. "These belong to you
now. After all, your name is on the deed, just like you
said."

Finn grinned and started to reach across the table for
the jewels, but I cleared my throat and raised my eyebrows. He looked at me, his face creasing into a pleading
wince. But I kept staring at him, and he finally rolled his
eyes.

"You know how much I hate being noble," he whined.
"It makes me break out in hives."

"Finn . . ." I warned.

"All right, all right," he said, dropping his hand and
sitting back in his chair. "Actually, Ira, I think that you
should keep the jewels. After all, you were the one who
loved Sweet Sally Sue."

Another thought occurred to Finn, and he brightened.

"Besides, this is your home. I bet a couple of those diamonds would go a long way toward repairing the saloon and getting the theme park back up and running again."

Lorelei snorted. "And get you off the hook for actually having to pay for anything yourself. Nice logic, Lane."

Finn grinned and shot his thumb and forefinger at her. "Bingo."

We all groaned.

Ira set the bag down on the table and cleared his throat. "Actually, I have something for you too, Gin, Bria."

He got to his feet and disappeared into his bedroom. I looked at my sister, who shrugged back at me. She didn't know what he was up to any more than I did. Ira appeared a few seconds later carrying two framed photos. He handed the first one to Bria, and we all leaned over the table to look at it.

It was a picture of our mother.

The photo had been taken in the hotel lobby during the holidays, and Eira was standing in front of a Christmas tree, examining one of the snow globes nestled in the branches. She looked young in the photo, probably in her early twenties, and she was smiling with childish delight, her whole face shining even brighter than the lights on the tree. The lovely shot of her was much nicer than the photos I had that showed her with Deirdre Shaw and Mab Monroe. My chest tightened.

Ira nodded at Bria. "When I first saw you, I thought that you looked like somebody that I'd photographed at the resort, but I couldn't put my finger on exactly who it was or where her picture might be. Then, when I saw Gin wearing that blond wig, I realized that she looked like that same woman too."

Shock jolted through me. Bria was the spitting image of our mother, but I'd never considered that I might look anything like her. But Ira thought that I did. That pleased me. That I still carried part of her with me, even if I hadn't realized it until right now.

"You never forget a face," I rasped, my voice thick with emotion.

"No, I don't." Ira nodded at me. "You have her nose and cheekbones. Put that blond wig back on, and both you and Bria could be her twins."

"Thank you," I rasped again.

Ira nodded and handed me the second photo. "And I thought you might want to see this one too."

Once again, everyone leaned across the table to see the picture—of Hugh Tucker.

The vampire was sitting in the hotel lobby, also during the holidays, given the mistletoe strung up on the fireplace mantel behind him. Tucker was leaning forward, his elbows on his knees, talking to someone sitting in a high-backed chair that I couldn't see. I brought the picture up close to my face, examining every single detail, but there was nothing else to it. Tucker looked young in the photo too, in his twenties, although he had one of those ageless faces that made it hard to pinpoint how old he had been back then.

"I did a quick scan through all my photos here, and I'm afraid that's the only shot I have of Tucker," Ira said. "I'm sorry, Gin."

"The vampire's not important. Not today, anyway." I set the photo aside and looked at my friends, old and new. "Right now, I'm just happy to be here with all of you." I paused. "And that we all survived another so-called *vacation*."

Finn lifted his coffee mug. "I'll drink to that. Cheers, everyone!"

We all lifted our mugs back to him. "Cheers!"

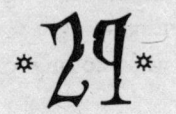

After finishing our late breakfast, we went to the hotel, grabbed our things, and met back down in the lobby, where Ira had another surprise, this time for Finn—that photo of Deirdre's ribbon cutting that I'd spotted in the dwarf's office yesterday.

"Thank you for this, but I don't really need it anymore," Finn said. "For better or worse, I've made my peace with Deirdre. She didn't care about me, so I'm not going to bother to think about her anymore. At least, I'm going to try not to think about her so much anymore."

"Take it," Ira said in a gruff voice. "She was still your mother. You might want it . . . later."

Finn hesitated, but he finally nodded and slipped the photo into his bag.

We said our good-byes to Ira, who promised to keep in touch and let us know how the theme-park renovations were coming along, and left the Bullet Pointe resort complex. Finn, Bria, Owen, and I got into Finn's Range Rover for the drive home, with Silvio, Phillip, and Lorelei following behind in another car.

"So," Finn chirped in a bright voice as we all buckled our seat belts, "who wants to sing some cowboy songs on the way home?"

Bria stabbed her finger at him. "If I hear so much as a single *yippee-ki-yay*, I will shoot you. No more cowboy songs. Ever."

Finn pouted for a minute, then brightened and started rooting around in the center console.

"Uh-oh," Owen muttered.

"Well, then," Finn said, coming up with a green CD case that he waggled at the three of us, "it's a good thing that I brought along my Christmas playlist as backup."

Bria pinched the bridge of her nose, while Owen sighed and slumped back against his seat.

I just laughed.

"Deck the halls," I said. "Deck the halls."

Three hours and several dozen off-key Christmas carols later, we made it back to Ashland. Our first stop was Jo-Jo's salon so the dwarf could fully heal the burns and bullet holes still decorating my body. She took care of my wounds, then fussed over me for an hour, including making me a mug of hot chocolate. So much better than cucumber slices and being pampered at a fancy spa.

After that, my friends and I went our separate ways, each of us getting back into the groove of our regular lives.

The next morning, I got up, took a shower, and went to the Pork Pit an hour early. Sophia and Catalina had done a great job in my absence, and everything was ready to rock 'n' roll, but I still whipped up a vat of Fletcher's secret barbecue sauce, enjoying the way it spiced up the air. The warm, comforting scent always made the restaurant feel like home.

By the time Silvio came in and took his usual stool at the counter, I'd moved on to one of my projects for the day. The vampire watched me use a hammer and a nail to carefully tack up a single sheet of paper on the wall close to the cash register, right next to a photo of Fletcher and his old friend Warren T. Fox that was already hanging there, along with a framed, bloody copy of *Where the Red Fern Grows*.

I stepped back, admiring my handiwork. "Well, what do you think?"

Silvio snorted. "Only you would be proud of a *Wanted* poster."

My grainy image stared back at me from the wall, along with my name and the info about the reward that Roxy and Brody had offered for me. Silvio was right. Maybe it was egotistical, but I loved being the star of my own *Wanted* poster.

I grinned. "I stuffed my suitcase full of posters before we left Bullet Pointe. I have enough of them to paper the entire restaurant if I want to."

He rolled his eyes. "That sounds like something Finn would do. Along with getting *Wanted* posters made up with all our pictures on them for Christmas presents."

"Why, Silvio," I drawled, "I think that's an *excellent* idea. I was going to get you a tie. Or maybe a really bad Christmas sweater. But personalized *Wanted* posters? That is pure *genius*."

His lips curled in disgust, and he actually shuddered.

I snapped my fingers. "Wait a second. I know. Why not combine the two? I'll get you a holiday sweater that looks like a *Wanted* poster, complete with *your* photo on it. What could be more heartwarming than that?"

He just groaned.

The rest of the day passed by without incident, and I closed down the restaurant and went home, happy to be back in my familiar routine.

Late that night, I was in Fletcher's house, relaxing on the couch in the den, with my stockinged feet propped up on the coffee table in front of me, and an old James Bond movie on the TV. Even though it was almost midnight, I'd just taken some chocolate cranberry-apricot cookies out of the oven, and the house smelled rich and decadent. And the cookies themselves? A divine mix of warm, melting chocolate and sweet pops of fruity flavor from the dried cranberries and apricots. The perfect treat for the final bit of work I had to do on this cold winter's night.

Because I still had one more puzzle to solve—the paper from Fletcher's safety-deposit box.

I polished off my second cookie, took my feet off the coffee table, and leaned forward. I'd spread the sheet on the table when I'd first come in here, but it looked the same as it had that day in the bank when Finn and I had first found it. A large rectangle drawn on a single sheet of white paper.

I still didn't have a clue as to what it meant.

No, that wasn't quite true. I knew that it was a message from Fletcher, some cryptic way of telling me something important. The old man wouldn't have left the paper in the box otherwise. And the irony of the situation didn't escape me either. Fletcher had purposefully set up this little treasure hunt, one that was eerily similar to my search for Sweet Sally Sue's jewels.

The information in Deirdre's casket had led me to dig up my own mother's grave, which had led me to the key to that safety-deposit box at First Trust bank. Which had yielded a piece of paper that was going to lead me . . . somewhere else? But where? And to what?

More than that, I wondered why Fletcher had arranged things like this. Why make me jump through so many hoops for a plain piece of paper? There had to be something more to all of this. Or maybe Fletcher hadn't wanted me to find any information on the Circle. Maybe he'd never wanted me to know about my mother's connection to the evil group.

Or maybe he'd been trying to protect me from an even more horrific truth, whatever it might be.

I didn't know. I just didn't know. Even worse, I had this nagging feeling that I was missing something obvious, that this was an instance of Fletcher's hiding something in plain sight, just like Deirdre had put the gems in those snow globes as though they were ordinary rocks. But try as I might, I couldn't see the forest for the trees. Or the trees for the forest. Or however that stupid metaphor went.

I picked up the safety-deposit box key from the table and examined it from all angles, but it too was the same as before—just a key with a number on it. No runes, no marks, no symbols of any sort adorned the metal. Gin Blanco strikes out again.

That familiar frustration surged through me, but I couldn't be too melancholy. Not with freshly baked cookies spreading their chocolate perfume throughout the house. Even if I couldn't figure out Fletcher's riddle tonight, then I could at least have one more cookie—or three—before I went to bed.

I tossed the key onto the table, but it flipped end over end and skittered across the wood, landing right in the center of the rectangle on the sheet of paper. I started to get to my feet to go get more cookies, but something about the key's lying there made me stop, lean forward, and look at it again.

It reminded me of . . . something . . . something that I'd seen recently. Some . . . shape. But what?

I sat there and thought about it for a few minutes, but the answer wouldn't come to me, so I got up, went into the kitchen, and came back with three more cookies on a paper napkin. I set the cookies down on the table next to the sheet of paper and arranged them in a neat row. . . .

That's when I remembered the exact shape that the key in the center of the rectangle represented and, more important, where I'd seen it before. I stared at the key, the rectangle around it, and the cookies lined up on the table. My heart started pounding with excitement. I was right. I was sure of it. But even more than that, I felt a growing sense of anticipation, knowing that Fletcher had left something for me to find after all.

"Fletcher," I said, grinning, "you sly son of a bitch."

❈ 30 ❈

"This is a bad idea," Finn muttered. "A very bad idea. You know how thin the ice is for me around here these days."

We were back at First Trust bank, down on the basement level, standing in front of a closed office door. I'd called Finn first thing this morning and told him what I'd realized about the clue that Fletcher had left behind. Finn had been a little doubtful, but he'd agreed to help me see this thing through.

"Don't worry," I said. "It'll be fine. You'll see. Now knock on the man's door."

He shot me a disbelieving look. Finn stared at the brass nameplate and winced, obviously not wanting to do this, but he raised his hand and knocked on the office door anyway.

"Come in!" a voice barked.

Finn sighed and twisted the knob, and we stepped into Stuart Mosley's office. Although he ran Ashland's most exclusive and influential bank, Mosley's office was simply furnished, with a large wooden desk, two chairs in front of it, and several metal filing cabinets lining the walls. A few large rugs were scattered across the marble floor, and the only painting on the wall featured a lovely scene of a waterfall on Bone Mountain. My eyes narrowed. I'd been to that same waterfall with Fletcher many times. Once again, I wondered just how well Fletcher had known Mosley, but that wasn't what I was here for today.

Mosley was sitting behind his desk, poring over a stack of papers, and he didn't even look up when we stepped inside. "Yes?"

Finn shifted on his feet. I elbowed him in the side, encouraging him to get on with things, and he stepped forward and cleared his throat. "Mr. Mosley, I'm sure that you remember my sister, Gin Blanco. She wanted to speak to you about something."

The dwarf still didn't look up. "And what would that be?"

"A safety-deposit box," I said. "Nine of them, actually."

That finally got his attention. Mosley paused a moment, then set aside the papers he'd been looking at and slowly lifted his head. His black reading glasses made his hazel eyes seem larger than they really were, and I noticed the sudden, sharp interest in his gaze. "And what box would that be?"

I held up the safety-deposit box key where Mosley could see it.

He arched his bushy eyebrows. "Yes? I believe you already looked in that box several days ago, Ms. Blanco."

"Yep. I did look in that box. At first, I was very disappointed with the contents, since the only thing inside was this single sheet of paper, as I'm sure you already know."

I pulled out the paper from my jacket pocket and unfolded it before laying it down on Mosley's desk and placing the key in the center of the rectangle just like it had been on my coffee table last night. At first, I'd thought that the paper was a dead end, but it was anything but. Instead, it had been a message about where the *real* information was—in the safety-deposit boxes all around that first one, forming a rectangle around Fletcher's original box. Or a circle, depending on your point of view and appreciation for irony.

I drew my finger around the rectangle, tracing the shape all the way around. "And now I want to open the rest of Fletcher's boxes. All the ones that form a ring around that first center box. Nine boxes total, counting the one that I already opened."

Mosley took off his glasses and set them aside, then leaned back in his chair and steepled his hands together, studying me. I stared right back at him. Beside me, Finn kept shifting his weight from foot to foot, still uncomfortable about my confronting his boss.

"And why would you think that Fletcher had another box here?" Mosley finally asked. "Especially so many of them?"

"How interesting that you would call him *Fletcher*, instead of *Mr. Lane*. Are you that familiar with all your clients?"

Mosley shrugged, not really answering my question.

"I know that Fletcher had more boxes here because he drew this treasure map to them. He just didn't say *X* marks the spot. He was too smart for that, and he trusted me to figure it out on my own. In fact, I'm guessing that he set things up precisely this way because he realized that I was the only one who'd have the stubbornness and determination to figure out what his clue really meant."

Agreement flashed in Mosley's eyes, along with what looked like respect.

I tapped my finger on the paper. "When Finn took me into the vault a few days ago, I noticed that Fletcher's box was in the middle of this bank of nine boxes that were set off by themselves in the back corner of the vault. I'll admit that it took me a while to figure out what this rectangle meant, that the old man was telling me that I'd only opened the first box, and that all the other ones around it belonged to him too. But Fletcher was paranoid, and he wanted to make sure that no one else found out about those boxes but Finn and me. That makes me real curious as to what's in them. But you already know, don't you, Mr. Mosley?"

He studied me over the tops of his fingers. "And what makes you think that I know what might be in those boxes?"

"Because you're the secrets keeper around here. You know who every single box in your vault belongs to and what is in every single one of them. So you know that all those boxes belong to Fletcher."

Mosley kept staring at me, and I looked right back at him. Finn kept shifting on his feet, glancing at both of us in turn, and the only sound was the faint scuff of his shoes on the floor.

Finally, Mosley barked out a laugh. "Fletcher always told me that you were clever. I didn't think that you'd figure it out myself."

I gave him a thin smile. "Good thing Fletcher didn't share your doubts. Although I wondered why he trusted you with his boxes."

"That's between Fletcher and me." Mosley's smile was as sharp and razor thin as mine was. "Let's just say that the two of us did each other certain . . . favors from time to time."

I opened my mouth to ask exactly what those favors had been, but Finn touched my arm in warning and gave me a stern, pointed look. He knew Mosley better than I did and was telling me that I'd pushed his boss far enough today. So I clamped my mouth shut. Besides, Finn and I still needed to get in those safety-deposit boxes, and I was betting that Mosley was the only one who could open them. That's how Fletcher would have set it up, and it seemed like he and Mosley had been close enough—or at least done each other enough *favors*—for Mosley to honor the old man's wishes.

Finn cleared his throat. "Gin and I would really appreciate it if we could go look in the boxes now."

The dwarf stared back at Finn, and his eyes and face softened, just a bit. For a moment, Mosley's gaze seemed distant, as though he was thinking of something else, or rather someone else—Fletcher. I saw so much of the old man in Finn, and it seemed like Mosley did too.

The dwarf pushed back from his desk and gave me

another cool look. "Well, then, now that Ms. Blanco has decided to be civil about things, I will be happy to let you into Fletcher's boxes."

Mosley made Finn and me step outside his office, then closed and locked the door, not wanting us to see what he was up to. I tilted my head to the side and pressed my ear up against the door, but I couldn't hear a whisper of sound from the other room.

"Don't bother," Finn said. "His office is soundproof."

"What do you think he's doing in there?"

Finn shrugged. "Probably getting the box keys. Rumor has it that Mosley has a secret safe hidden somewhere in his office. That seems like exactly the sort of place that Dad would leave those keys."

Sure enough, a minute later, the office door opened, and Mosley appeared, carrying a small silver key ring in his hand. Finn and I followed him down the hallway to Big Bertha.

Mosley nodded at the two giant guards standing there. Another new security measure. "Jimmy, Tommy, take a break."

At the stern order, the two men nodded and moved off without a word. Mosley punched in the codes on the keypad, and the three silverstone mesh doors slid back one after another. I thought that Mosley might step into the vault with us, but he flipped through the keys on the ring before selecting one and holding it up where Finn and I could see it.

"Per Fletcher's instructions, he wanted you to open this box first," Mosley said.

I took the key from him and looked at the number stamped into the metal—1301. Starting at the beginning, in more ways than one. "Thank you."

"I hope you find what you're looking for, Ms. Blanco. You too, Finn. Bring me the keys back when you're done." Mosley nodded at both of us and left, heading back to his office.

I waited until he was out of sight and the echo of his footsteps had faded away before turning to Finn. "You ready for this?"

He blew out a breath. "I guess I have to be."

We stepped into the vault and went to the back corner where Fletcher's safety-deposit boxes were. They were exactly the same as before, three boxes across and three down, for nine boxes total. I hadn't noticed before, but the boxes were slightly out of order, with 1300 in the center, and 1301 in the upper left-hand corner. Another small clue that I'd initially overlooked.

So I slid the key into the lock, turned it, and pulled the box out of its slot in the wall. Anticipation surged through me, and I hurried over and set the box down on the table at this end of the vault. For once, I didn't have the patience to wait, and I yanked open the top of the box to find . . .

Photos—dozens of photos stacked inside the box.

They were all of the Bullet Pointe resort.

I stared down at the photos, dumbfounded.

Finn groaned. "Are you kidding me? I never want to see that place again."

But I shook off my surprise and started going through the photos, looking at and then handing them off to Finn one by one.

Most of the shots were the same sort that Ira had taken—pretty pictures of the hotel, theme park, and lake. My heart started to sink. Maybe I'd been wrong. Maybe there wasn't any information about the Circle in here at all. Maybe Fletcher hadn't known anything about the mysterious group. After all, the old man had kept tabs on Deirdre to make sure that she wasn't headed back to Ashland to threaten Finn. Maybe that's what he'd been doing down at Bullet Pointe. Following her and seeing what she was up to.

Finally, I came to the last picture, a large rectangular print that had been stuck in the very bottom of the box, as though it were of no importance at all. I glanced at it, expecting to see another shot of the hotel lobby. That's exactly what it was, but I recognized someone in this picture.

My mother.

I sucked in a breath. Finn realized that I'd finally found something, and he put down the photo he was looking at to peer at the one in my hand.

"Son of a bitch," he said. "That's your mom."

"Not just her," I whispered. "Not just her."

The picture showed a group of people sitting at a table in the middle of the hotel lobby sometime during the holidays, given the mistletoe, bows, and other decorations in the background. And my mother wasn't the only person that I recognized. Deirdre Shaw was in the photo too, along with Mab Monroe. Several other people were also gathered around the table, their faces clearly visible, although I didn't know any of them.

The group seemed to be celebrating something, given

the champagne glasses on the table and the pleased grins on everyone's faces—except for my mother's. Her mouth was a hard slash in her face, and her hand was wrapped around her champagne flute, her arm drawn back slightly, as though she were thinking about hurling the glass at the two people sitting across the table from her.

Finn tapped his finger on one of those people. "There's Tucker."

I nodded. "And I'm willing to bet that this is the rest of the Circle."

"Deirdre, Tucker, Mab, your mother. You might be right. But who are the rest of these folks?"

I studied the faces a little more closely, but I still didn't recognize anyone. "No idea." I pointed to the photo again. "But this guy—he's the leader."

The man was sitting next to Tucker and seemed to be the person that my mother was glaring at. He was the only person whose face you couldn't see, since his back was turned to the camera. All I could tell about him was that he had dark hair and looked to be a big, tall, strong guy.

Finn frowned and leaned forward, staring at the photo again. "Why do you think that he's the leader?"

"Because Tucker is sitting next to him, and look at the vampire's posture. He's leaning in and ducking his head. You know Tucker. He wouldn't show that sort of deference to anyone . . ."

"Except his boss."

"Exactly. Besides, my mother is sitting as far away from this man as she can possibly get, clear on the opposite side of the table. He's the leader. I know it."

I did know it—deep down in my bones.

"But why doesn't Dad have a shot of this guy's face?" Finn asked. "He has a clear view of everyone else. Surely it wouldn't have been that hard to discreetly move around the table and snap a picture of the leader. So why didn't he?"

I shook my head. "I don't know. Maybe Fletcher could only get this one shot of the whole group of them. These people are paranoid about their secrecy. They wouldn't have wanted anyone taking pictures of them."

Finn nodded, accepting my explanation, but my mind kept churning and churning. He was right. Fletcher *should* have included a picture of the leader's face, but he hadn't, and I couldn't help but think that it was a deliberate omission. But why? What was so interesting or horrible or shocking about this man that Fletcher had excluded him?

And how was it going to impact me, Finn, and everyone else?

Finn pointed at the photo. "Hey, look at that. What does that look like to you?"

I squinted at the picture. I hadn't paid any attention to it before, but the table boasted an elaborate metal centerpiece, the sort of thing you might put candles in, although this piece had none. "That looks like . . . a group of swords, all bound together and pointing outward."

"Not just a group of swords, but a group of swords in a *circle*." Finn looked at me, excitement flashing in his eyes. "Ladies and gentlemen, I think that we just found the official rune for the Circle." He paused. "Well, the official, probably top-secret, and no-one-knows-about-it-but-them rune. But still."

"I think you're right."

We looked at each other, both of us grinning like fools, realizing that we were finally—*finally*—on track to getting the answers we wanted.

* 31 *

We went through the rest of the safety-deposit boxes, opening them one by one, and examining all the items inside.

They were all filled with photos, just like the first one, and all the pictures were various shots of the people that had been gathered around that table. I hoped that there might be more. Perhaps some diaries or logs of who the people were and all their movements, but nothing like that was in the boxes. Perhaps Fletcher hadn't been able to get all that much information about the members of the Circle. I'd probably never know for sure, but the uncertainty didn't bother me the way it had before. The old man had given me a place to start. That was all that I needed.

The only person Fletcher didn't seem to have photographed was the man with his back to the camera in that first photo, the leader of the Circle. I still wondered why

Fletcher hadn't identified him as well, but I wasn't overly worried about it. I'd find his friends first, and they would eventually lead me to him.

The photos in the last box made tears well up in my eyes. They were all shots of my mother. And not just of her, but me, Bria, and Annabella as well. I didn't know how long Fletcher had been watching us, but he'd snapped dozens of shots of us around our mansion, playing in the backyard, window-shopping, and walking the streets of Ashland. There was even a picture of the four of us sitting in a booth at the Pork Pit, looking over our menus.

Instead of being angry that Fletcher had never shown these to me, I found myself comforted instead. The old man hadn't left these here as a reminder that my mother had been mixed up in the Circle, but because he knew that I would want the photos as mementos of her and Annabella. Of my family. Of happier times.

Simpler times.

I stared at a photo of my mother holding me close to her side and smiling down at me. I'd been thinking a lot about what had happened before the holiday party and then later on that night in her office. I still didn't know exactly how she'd been involved with the Circle, or the horrible things she might have done for them, but the unanswered questions didn't eat away at me the way they had before. Because my mother hadn't worked for Tucker of her own free will, and she'd tried to protect our family as best she could. Those were the things that mattered, and those were the things that told me the kind of person she'd been—a mother who'd loved her daughters.

I traced my fingers over her smiling face, then set that

photo aside and looked through the others. When we finished with the last box, Finn looked out over the table where all the boxes were lined up, their tops open, revealing the pictures inside.

"What do you want to do with all of this?" His voice was rough with emotion. "Take it to Dad's house?"

I shook my head. "No. There's too big a risk of Tucker breaking in there, seeing it, and realizing that we're finally onto the rest of the Circle. Let's leave it all here. It was safe in the vault all these years, and I want it to stay that way. We'll make copies, and leave all the originals here."

"But aren't you worried about Tucker finding the copies too?"

I grinned. "Oh, I know just where to hide those."

I told Finn where I planned to store the information. He snorted out a laugh, and we both got to work, pulling out our phones and taking photos of everything. Once we were finished with that, we slid the original photos into the appropriate containers, put the boxes back into their slots in the wall, and locked them up tight again. After that, we went to Finn's office, where he printed out copies of all the photos, since he had a fancy color printer, among other things.

Two hours later, I left the bank carrying that cardboard box that I'd used to hold Finn's food the other day. Empty cartons were stacked in the box now, and a thick folder of photos was nestled in the very bottom. I kept that folder hidden inside the box while I worked my usual shift at the Pork Pit, closed down the restaurant, and went home to Fletcher's. Then, late that night, after I'd changed into my usual black assassin clothes, I grabbed the folder out of the box, left Fletcher's house, and headed to my new home away from home.

My shipping container.

I drove into the city and cruised around the downtown streets for almost an hour, just to make sure that I wasn't being followed. Then I parked my car three miles away from the shipping yard, just for a little bit of extra insurance. Now that I finally had some information about the Circle, I wasn't going to be foolish enough to let Tucker stumble across it and realize how close I was to identifying his friends. I had the advantage now, and I was determined to keep it.

I approached the shipping yard cautiously and quietly, doing a complete circuit around the perimeter, but except for a single giant guard, the area was deserted, and even Lorelei wasn't here tonight. Still, I kept scanning the landscape and was extra careful as I crept toward my container. Just like the last time that I'd been here, I bent down and listened to the rocks that I'd strategically placed around the metal container, but they were in the same positions as before, and no one had been near them in days. Good.

I opened the padlock, slipped inside, and shut and locked the door behind me. Then I turned on the lanterns and went over to the dry-erase board that I'd set up along one of the walls. All those blank boxes and question marks didn't haunt me nearly as much as they had before. Not now.

I wiped everything off the board, leaving only a few of the silly doodles that Lorelei and I had drawn in the corners. Then I opened up my folder of information and grabbed the group shot of those people sitting in the lobby of the Bullet Pointe hotel. I put that in the top center of the board, since it was my starting point, the first strand that I would use to build my web of death. I traced my fingers over my mother's angry face, then went through all the copies of the photos that had been in Fletcher's safety-deposit boxes, matching up photos of individual people with the ones in the group shot.

It took me a couple of hours, but by the time I finished, I had several sections of photos tacked up to my dry-erase board. I still didn't know their names, but I thought that I now had a pretty good idea of who the members of the Circle were. Big-time movers and shakers in Ashland and beyond, just like Tucker had claimed.

Only one big piece was still missing—the man in the middle of it all. Tucker's boss and the leader of the Circle. The only shot I had of him was of his back, so I still had no real clues as to his identity. But I'd find him eventually. And once I did, I'd ask him exactly why he'd given Mab Monroe the green light to murder my mother, what trouble Eira had been making that had resulted in her death.

Then I would kill him for taking her and Annabella away from Bria and me.

It was late, and I should have gone home to get some sleep. I still had the Pork Pit to open up in the morning. But for the first time since this whole thing had started, for the first time since I'd learned about my mother and the Circle and everything else, I wasn't tired. Wasn't weary or heartbroken or just sick to my stomach.

Now—now I was determined to find the man in the

middle and tear apart the Circle. One person and one body at a time until nothing was left.

I had faces now. The names wouldn't be too hard to get. And once I put the two together, I could finally get even. I'd find the weak link in the Circle and use that person to unravel the rest of their dark, poisonous web.

So I poured myself a glass of gin, pulled a chair up in front of the dry-erase board, and started looking at all the photos again.

The Spider had new targets.

Turn the page for a sneak peek at the
next book in the Elemental Assassin series

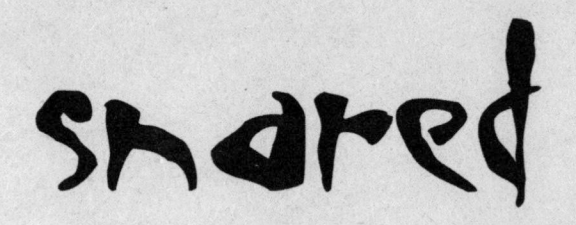

snared

By Jennifer Estep

Coming soon from Pocket Books

❋ 1 ❋

Being an assassin meant knowing when to kill—and when not to kill.

Unfortunately.

I stood in a pool of midnight shadows, my boots, jeans, turtleneck, and fleece jacket as black as the night around me. My dark brown hair was stuffed up underneath a black toboggan that matched the rest of my clothes, and I'd swiped a bit of black greasepaint under my eyes to break up the paleness of my face. The only bit of color on my body was the silverstone knife that glinted in my right hand. I even inhaled and exhaled through my nose, so that my breath wouldn't frost in the chilly January air and give away my position.

Not that anyone was actually looking for me.

Oh, a dwarf on guard duty was patrolling the back side of the mansion. Supposedly, he was here to keep an eye out and make sure that no one snuck out of the woods, sprinted across the lawn, and broke into the house. But he was doing a piss-poor job of it, since I'd been watching him amble around for more than three minutes now, making an exceptionally slow circuit of this part of the enormous landscaped grounds.

Every once in a while, the guard would raise his head and look around, scanning the twisting shadows cast out by the trees and ornamental bushes that dotted the rolling lawn. But most of the time, he was more interested in playing a game on his cell phone, judging from the beeps and chimes that continually rang out from it. He didn't even have the sound muted—or his gun drawn. I shook my head. It was so hard to find good help these days.

Still, I tensed as the guard wandered closer and closer to my position. I was standing at the corner of a gray stone house, set back several hundred feet from the main mansion. Trees clustered all around the house, their branches arching over the black slate roof and making the shadows here particularly dark, giving me a perfect hiding spot to watch and wait out the guard.

I was sure that the man who lived in the mansion charitably referred to this house as a caretaker's cottage, or something else equally dismissive, even though the house was almost large enough to be its own separate mansion. Even Finnegan Lane, my foster brother, would have been impressed by the spacious rooms and expensive furniture that I'd glimpsed through the windows when I'd been getting into position—

"So are you actually going to go into the mansion or are we just going to stand around out here all night in the dark?" a low, snide voice murmured in my ear.

Speak of the devil, and he will annoy you.

I looked to my right. Fifty feet away, a tall, man-shaped shadow hovered at the edge of the tree line. Finn was dressed all in black the same way that I was, although I could just make out the glimmer of his eyes, like a cat's in the darkness.

"I'm waiting for the guard to turn around and go back in the other direction," I hissed. "As you can bloody well see for yourself."

The transmitter in my ear crackled from the force of Finn's snort. "Mr. Cell Phone Video Game?" He snorted again. "Please. You could do cartwheels naked across the lawn right in front of him, and he still wouldn't notice."

Finn was probably right, but the guard was only about thirty feet from me now, so I couldn't risk responding. Instead, I slid back a little deeper into the shadows, pressing myself up against the side of the cottage. As my body touched the wall, I automatically reached out with my elemental magic, listening to the gray stone that made up the structure.

Dark, malicious whispers echoed back to me, punctuated by high, shrill screaming notes of agony as the stone continually muttered about all the blood and violence that it had witnessed over the years—and all the people who had died inside the cottage. The mutters didn't surprise me, given where I was, but their deep, harsh intensity made me frown. I wouldn't have thought that the care-taker's cottage would have been this affected by the man in the mansion, given its distance from the main structure.

Then again, anything was possible when dealing with the Circle.

I shut the stone's mutters out of my mind and focused on the guard, who'd finally reached the cottage. Like most dwarves, he was short and stocky, with bulging biceps that threatened to pop right through the sleeves of his suit jacket. Your typical muscle, except for the thin, scraggly wisps of black hair that lined his upper lip. Someone was trying to grow a mustache with very little success.

The guard stopped about ten feet away from me, raised his head, and glanced at the front of the house, making sure that the door and the windows were shut. He even tilted his head to the side, listening to the whistle of the winter wind as it made the tree branches scrape together like dry, brittle bones.

I tightened my grip on my knife, feeling the rune stamped into the hilt pressing into the larger, matching scar embedded in my palm, both of them a circle surrounded by eight thin rays—a spider rune, the symbol for patience.

Something that the guard had little of, since five seconds later he turned his attention back to his phone and started his slow, ambling walk again, one that took him right by my hiding spot. I could have reached out of the shadows, sunk my hand into the dwarf's hair, yanked his head back, and cut his throat. He would have been dead before he'd even realized what was happening. But I couldn't kill him—or anyone else here—tonight.

Unfortunately.

Once I started dropping bodies, the members of the Circle, a secret society responsible for much of the crime and corruption in Ashland, would realize that I was onto them. Then they would close ranks, increase their security, and come after me—or worse, my friends. Something that I wasn't ready for.

Not yet.

So as easy as it would have been for me to kill the guard, I let him wander away, never knowing how close he'd come to playing his last video game.

Once the guard had moved far enough away, I relaxed and looked over at Finn, who flashed me a thumbs-up, then raised the gun in his other hand and saluted me with it.

His voice crackled in my ear again. "I'll be here waiting, but with guns drawn instead of bells on. Just in case you need the cavalry to ride to your rescue."

I rolled my eyes. "Please. I'm Gin Blanco, fearsome assassin and underworld queen, remember? The only thing I need rescuing from is you and your bad puns."

Finn grinned, his white teeth flashing in the darkness. "You know you love me and my bad puns."

"Oh, yeah. Like a toothache I can't get rid of."

"That's me, baby. Finnegan Lane, rotten as they come."

He saluted me with his gun again, proud that he'd gotten the last word in. I rolled my eyes, but I was smiling as I turned away from him, left the shadows behind, and hurried toward the mansion.

Since it was January, the holidays were officially over, but someone was being a little slow about putting away the decorations. White twinkle lights were still wrapped around the thick columns that supported various parts of the sprawling, two-story, gray stone mansion, along with strands of illuminated snowflakes that glowed a pale blue. Still more lights and snowflakes curved over the archways and outlined all the windows, along with the white velvet bows hanging in them.

But this was a new year, with new targets for the Spider.

I made it across the lawn and hunkered down behind a couple of lounge chairs set up on the patio that ringed the heated pool, as far away from the cheery glow of the holiday lights as I could get. Then I peered around the chairs and over at the mansion.

Despite its creeping up on eight o'clock, lights burned in practically every room on the first floor, and I spotted several servants moving back and forth, tidying up and doing their final chores for the night. In the windows closest to me, two women were plucking red and green glass balls off a massive Christmas tree that seemed to take up most of the room.

I watched the women for a few seconds longer, as well as all the other servants that I could see, but no one moved toward the windows and peered outside. No one had seen me approach the mansion, so I raised my gaze to a particular window on the second floor. Lights burned in that room as well, but I didn't spot anyone moving around inside. Excellent.

I glanced over my shoulder, but the guard was at the very back of the lawn now, several hundred feet from me, and still playing his game, judging by the faint beeps and trills that whispered into the night. I wouldn't get a better chance than this, so I slid my knife up my sleeve so that I would have both hands free. Then I surged to my feet, took a running start, leaped up, and grabbed hold of a trellis attached to this part of the mansion.

The wood groaned under my weight, more used to holding up pretty roses than a deadly assassin, but the slats didn't crack, and I felt safe enough to keep climbing. Even if the wood had broken and made me fall, I could easily have used my Stone magic to harden my body and protect myself from the rough landing.

It took me only a few seconds to scale the trellis, hook my leg onto the first-story roof, and pull myself up and onto that part of the mansion. I lay flat on my stomach for several seconds, listening, but no surprised shouts or alarms sounded. I also glanced at the guard again, but he was a murky, indistinct shape in the night. No one had seen my quick, spidery climb.

Even though lying on the cold roof chilled my body from head to toe, I held my position, once again reaching out with my magic and listening to the stones around me. Just like the ones at the cottage, the stones of the mansion whispered of dark, malicious intent, along with blood, violence, and death. The mutters were much fainter here, more sloppy slurs than clear, distinct notes, as though the stones had been soaked in all the alcohol that their owner so famously imbibed. Still, I could pick out the emotional vibrations from all the evil deeds that had been committed here over the years. Exactly what I would expect from the home of a member of the Circle.

Even so, the stones' mutters weren't as disturbing as those of some of the other places I'd been, and the noise certainly wasn't going to stop me from completing my mission tonight. So I got to my feet and hurried over to the window that I wanted, the same one I'd looked at earlier. After a quick glance in through the glass to make sure the room was still empty, I pushed aside the twinkle lights and tried the window, which easily slid up. I waited a few seconds, but no alarms blared.

I shook my head again. You'd think that someone who was part of a decades-old criminal conspiracy would have enough common sense to lock the windows on the second story of his fancy mansion—or at least order his staff to do it for him. But the mansion's owner thought that he was well protected, anonymous, and untouchable, just like the rest of the Circle did.

Well, they weren't. Not anymore. Not from me.

I pushed aside the white velvet bow, ducked down, and shimmied in through the open window, making sure to close it behind me. Then I turned and looked over the room in front of me.

The office was the inner sanctum of Damian Rivera, the mansion's owner and the first member of the Circle who was on my hit list. Several generations ago, the ancestors of Maria Rivera, Damian's mother, had made a fortune in coal before selling off their mines and branching out into other areas. Maria herself had been big into real estate, buying and selling property all over Ashland, as well as renovating crumbling old homes that she decked out with all the antique furniture and heirlooms she got for a song at various estate sales.

Damian had definitely inherited his mother's flair for decorating and dramatic spaces. The office was enormous, taking up a good chunk of this corner of the mansion. The decidedly masculine area was full of dark brown leather chairs and couches nestled alongside wide, heavy tables covered with all sorts of expensive knickknacks.

Porcelain vases, crystal figurines, wooden carvings, stone statues. All perfectly in place and all perfectly highlighted by the three gold-plated chandeliers dangling from the ceiling.

But the centerpiece of the office was the freestanding bar that took up one entire wall, complete with several padded barstools lined up in front of it. A wide variety of liquor bottles perched prettily on the wooden shelves behind the bar, along with rows of glassware. I eyed the bottles, recognizing them all as being well out of my price range, but they fit right in with the rest of the luxe furnishings. The air reeked of expensive cologne and even more expensive cigar smoke, adding to the gentlemen's club feel of Damian's lair, and I had to wrinkle my nose to hold back a sneeze.

But I wasn't here to sightsee or gawk at the expensive furnishings, so I moved over to the large desk that stood in the back of the room near the window that I'd just slithered through. To my disappointment, the golden wood was spotless, as though it had never been touched, much less actually used, and not so much as a pen or paper clip littered the gleaming surface. Then again, I shouldn't have been surprised. Damian Rivera didn't have to do something as common as *work*. From what I knew of him, his favorite hobbies were drinking, smoking, shopping for antiques, and flitting from one mistress to the next. Not necessarily in that order.

Still, I'd come here to search for information about the Circle, so I opened all the drawers and tapped all around the desk, searching for hidden compartments. But the drawers were empty, except for some stacks of cocktail napkins and paper coasters, and no secret hidey-holes were carved into the wood.

Strike one.

Since nothing was in the desk, I moved over to the bar, searching the shelves underneath it, as well as the glass ones behind it. But all I found were more napkins and coasters, along with several sterling-silver martini shakers and other old-fashioned, drink-making accoutrements.

Strike two.

Frustration surged through me, but I forced myself to stay calm and search the rest of the office. I ran my hands over all the furniture, looking for any secret compartments. Examined all the vases, carvings, and statues for false bottoms. Tapped on the walls, searching for hidden panels. I even rolled back the thick rugs and used my magic to listen to the flagstones, just in case a safe was hidden in the floor.

But there was nothing. No secret compartments, no hidden panels, no floor safes.

Strike three, and I was out.

More frustration surged through me, mixed with even more disappointment, both of which burned through my veins like acid. A couple of weeks ago, I'd found several safety-deposit boxes full of information on the Circle that my mentor, Fletcher Lane, had compiled. Fletcher had only photos of the group's members, but it had been easy enough for me to get their names, since many of them were such wealthy, prominent citizens.

I'd scouted several of the Circle members, and Damian Rivera had been the easiest target with the least amount of security. So I'd broken in here tonight in hopes of learning more about the group, especially the identity of the mystery man who headed the organization, the bastard who'd ordered my mother's murder. But maybe there was a reason that Rivera's security was so lax. Maybe he wasn't as important or as involved with the Circle as I'd thought.

Still frustrated, I turned to the fireplace that took up most of the wall across from the bar. I'd already searched that area for loose stones and secret compartments and had come up empty. So this time I pulled out my phone and carefully snapped shots of all the framed photos propped up on the mantel, hoping that one of them might hold some small clue.

Not only did Damian Rivera love the finer things in life but he also loved himself, since most of the photos were softly lit glamour shots showing off his wavy black hair, bronze skin, dark brown eyes, and startlingly white teeth. Rivera was in his prime in his early thirties, and he was an exceptionally handsome man—and a thoroughly disgusting individual, even by Ashland's admittedly low, low standards.

Not only was Rivera a trust-fund baby, living off his family's wealth, who'd never worked a day in his life, but he'd also never faced any consequences for any of the despicable things he'd done.

And he had done plenty of despicable things.

Silvio Sanchez, my personal assistant, had only been looking into Rivera for a few days, but he'd already found several arrests, mostly for DUIs, stretching all the way back to when Rivera was a teenager. Damian also had some serious anger-management issues, and he'd beaten more than one girlfriend over the years, servants too, and had even put a couple of them in the hospital with broken bones and other serious injuries.

But all of that was nothing compared to the woman he'd killed.

One night during his college years, Rivera had gotten into his fancy SUV and decided to see how fast he could drunkenly steer around Ashland's mountain roads. He'd come around one curve, crossed the center lane, and plowed head-on into a sedan being driven by a single mother of two. She'd died instantly, but Rivera had walked away from the crash with minor injuries. He'd never been charged in the woman's death, thanks to his mother, who'd pulled all the right strings and paid off all the right people to cover the whole thing up.

But Rivera hadn't learned his lesson. He hadn't learned *anything*, since he'd been arrested for another DUI on New Year's Eve. But he wouldn't face any consequences for that one either. His mama was long dead, but Damian still had someone to clean up his messes—Bruce Porter, a dwarf who'd been the Rivera family's head of security for years.

I stopped in front of a photo that showed Maria Rivera, a beautiful woman with long, wavy, golden hair, dark eyes, and red lips. In the photo, she was smiling and standing in between Damian and his father, Richard Rivera, with a dour-looking Bruce Porter hovering behind them in the distance. I raised my phone and snapped a shot of the picture—

"You've been in there a while now," Finn's voice crackled in my ear. "Does that mean you've found something good?"

"No," I muttered. "Just a lot of liquor, antiques, and photos."

"What kind of liquor?" Finn chirped with obvious interest. "Anything I would drink?"

I slid my phone into my pocket, then turned and eyed the rows of gleaming bottles behind the bar. "Oh, I think that you would drink it all, especially since Damian's tastes are even more expensive than yours. Why, you would cackle with glee if you could see all the spirits he has in here."

"Well, why don't you bring me a bottle or two so I can cackle in person?" Finn chirped again. "I might as well get *something* from standing out here in the cold all night long."

Even though he was in the woods outside and couldn't see me, I still rolled my eyes. "I came here for information on the Circle. Not to pilfer Daddy's booze like some teenager."

"You say potato, I say *opportunity*."

I rolled my eyes again and started to respond when a faint creak sounded in the hallway outside, as though someone had stepped on a floorboard. I froze. The creak came again, louder and closer this time, and it was followed by something far, far worse—the distinctive snick of a key sliding in a lock.

"Let's have a drink," a faint, muffled voice said.

Someone was outside the office—and he was about to come in.